Bad Behavior

Jennifer Lane

OMNIFIC PUBLISHING

DALLAS

Omnific Publishing
P.O. Box 793871, Dallas, TX 75379
www.omnificpublishing.com

First Omnific eBook edition, March 2011
First Omnific trade paperback edition, March 2011

Library of Congress Cataloguing-in-Publication Data

Lane, Jennifer.
    Bad Behavior / Jennifer Lane – 1st ed.
    ISBN 978-1-936305-65-0
    1. Young Women —Fiction. 2. Romance —Fiction.
    3. Crime —Fiction. 4. Chicago—Fiction. I. Title

10 9 8 7 6 5 4 3 2 1

Cover Design and Interior Book Design by Coreen Montagna

Printed in the United States of America

For survivors of abuse:
May you find strength and redemption.

1. Concession

He was trembling like a loose-footed sail in a sudden sea squall.

Grant sat in the psychologist's waiting room fighting the urge to jiggle his thigh, tap his fingers on his knee, and nervously clear his throat. Perched next to him, Sophie pretended not to notice his anxiety. She too had been apprehensive when she'd sat in this very waiting room before *her* first appointment.

Though it had been a lighthearted jab yesterday—questioning why her boyfriend hadn't also been mandated to attend therapy—Sophie rued opening her big mouth to their parole officer. Jerry Stone had consequently ordered Grant into counseling as a condition of his parole, then decided they might as well make it couples counseling. Now Sophie wondered what she'd gotten them in to—and if they'd survive. She didn't need her keen psychological insight to discern that therapy was a frightening prospect for the tall, handsome man next to her.

A soft sling secured her left arm uselessly at her side, but she reached out to place her right hand on Grant's thigh. "I'm nervous too,' she admitted, looking into his gorgeous light-blue eyes and finding a flash of embarrassment there.

"Why are *you* nervous?" he asked. "You used to do this stuff for a living."

She offered him a wistful smile. "It's easier to be on the other side of the couch." Gently squeezing his knee, she added, "I'm also worried because Hunter might not agree to see us as a couple. He's never met you before. *I* know what a great guy you are, but Hunter may take…" she glanced down at her shoulder sling "…some convincing."

Grant grimaced. It was his fault Sophie had been shot by his cousin Carlo, and he'd never forgive himself. The sling over her left shoulder was a constant reminder of his family's destructive power.

"Sophie?"

A confident male voice interrupted Grant's self-recrimination. He glanced up to see a solidly built blond man striding into the waiting room, his generous smile quickly fading once he caught sight of Sophie's arm sling.

Grant gallantly guided Sophie to a standing position. As the three stood facing each other, Grant realized Hunter was about the same height as his girlfriend — five foot nine — providing Grant a four-inch advantage over them both.

"What on earth happened?" Hunter asked Sophie, his inquisitive eyes inevitably turning toward the strange man at her side. Grant hovered over her like a protective clansman.

Sophie gave a nervous laugh. "We have a lot to catch up on, I'm afraid. Um, Hunter, may I introduce you to Grant Madsen?" Her eyes darted to her boyfriend's stiff expression. "Grant, this is Dr. Hunter Hayes."

The two men shook hands, appearing to size each other up. Hunter found himself momentarily entranced by the crystal eyes studying him, and the fit of the man's long fingers in his strong handshake further enthralled him.

Grant took in the psychologist's stylish, self-assured bearing and felt a twinge of jealousy. Sophie had been meeting privately with this man for almost two months? He wasn't sure how he felt about that, even though Sophie had assured him Hunter was gay.

An awkward silence descended over them as Hunter seemed a bit mesmerized and Grant a bit wary.

"Should we head back to your office?" Sophie asked.

"Please, yes." Hunter nodded, snapping out of his daze. He gestured for the couple to walk ahead of him — Sophie knew the way — and he felt himself blushing. He'd never experienced such an instant attraction to a client before.

Grant led Sophie to the sofa, Hunter grabbed her chart off his desk, and the three sat down. Grant could not take his eyes off of the beautiful aquarium set into the wall.

Observing his stare, Sophie said, "The aquarium's just as awesome as I said it was, huh?"

Grant nodded. "Very impressive."

Hunter smiled. "So, Sophie, your phone message said you were bringing Grant with you to today's session. Do you want to tell me why? And about how you hurt your arm?"

"Those stories are kind of related, actually," she responded, wincing. Glancing at Grant, she took a deep breath. "Jerry ordered us to get couples counseling as a condition of our parole. We'd like to start today."

Noticing that the male half of the couple remained silent, Hunter aimed a quizzical look at Sophie. "You want to change your individual therapy to couples therapy?"

"Yes." Sophie bit her lip.

"Hmm. The potential problem, Sophie, is that I've already seen you individually for five sessions. I know you fairly well, but I don't know Grant at all. It'll put him at a disadvantage when I have to pick on one of you, as sometimes happens in couples work. It'll be harder for me to take Grant's side."

Sophie nodded, having known Hunter might make this argument. However, she also knew how freaked out Grant was about the counseling thing, and it would be even harder to start with a new psychologist.

Grant interjected, "That's okay — I'm used to it, sir."

Hunter felt instantly uncomfortable being referred to as "sir" but Sophie had mentioned that Grant was once in the Navy. And a therapy session was about the client's needs, not the psychologist's, so Hunter simply accepted the respectful address. He tilted his head to one side, peering at Grant. "You're accustomed to people not taking your side?"

Grant nodded. "Sophie's dad pretty much hates me." *My own father hates me too.*

Feeling the self-loathing roll off the parolee, Hunter studied him sadly. "But you deserve to have people on your side," he said.

Grant dutifully responded, "Yes, sir."

Sophie stepped in. "Hunter, would you be willing to hear what's happened in the past week before deciding whether to take us on as a couple? Maybe then you'll understand, um, how important Grant is to me."

Sophie's face reddened with that admission. Hunter watched Grant squeeze her hand.

"One thing you undoubtedly want to catch me up on is the murder of Logan Barberi," Hunter said. "I saw that on the news."

As expected, Sophie's brown eyes widened at the mention of the mobster who'd put her in prison, but Hunter was surprised to see Grant's face fall. He squinted at Grant, wondering why he seemed upset about a Mafia capo dying.

"Yes," Sophie rasped, attempting to steady her voice. "That was the beginning of everything going wrong. Well, actually our descent into hell began when Logan showed up at Grant's apartment."

Hunter turned to Grant, eyebrows raised. "Logan came to your apartment? Why?"

Grant let go of Sophie's hand and tightly laced his fingers together in his lap, slowly raising his eyes to level his gaze with Hunter's. "He's my brother."

Hunter's eyes bugged out. "Logan Barberi's your *brother?*"

"Yes, sir."

Turning back to Sophie, Hunter stammered, "Did—did you know about that?"

She smiled wryly. "Not until Logan came a-knocking that night."

"*We* didn't know," Grant blurted defensively. "We had no idea about our connection. The pact—"

"The dumbass pact you made not to discuss your pasts," Hunter supplied knowingly.

"That's the one." Sophie chuckled, and Hunter took it as a good sign that she wasn't having a nervous breakdown. "So, naturally I was kind of upset when I found out Grant was related to Logan." She swallowed hard. "I ran out of there and—" she looked apologetically toward Grant "—I said some awful things."

"I deserved them." Grant hung his head low.

"How, um, how are you his brother?" Hunter asked. "You have different last names?"

"My mom died when I was a kid, and her brother—my uncle, Joe Madsen—he adopted me," Grant said. A look of anguish crossed his strong features. "Because my father was serving a life sentence at Gurnee."

So both parolees had lost their mothers? Hunter recalled Sophie sharing how her mother had died of a heart attack while she was in prison. He also remembered Sophie's story about a therapy session she'd had with Logan in which he disclosed how his father had mercilessly beat him and his brother.

Hunter sat up with a start, blinking at Grant. "Your father abused you?"

Grant's olive skin paled, and he reeled back on the sofa as if he'd been hit. Then he whirled to face Sophie, his voice accusing. "You told him?"

"I—I—"

"She told me about your father beating Logan," Hunter gently explained. "I figured you got hit too."

Grant's face was on fire with shame. He swiftly stood, looking like he was going to bolt from the room, but instead he strode to the corner and began pacing while he alternated wringing his hands with jamming them in his jean pockets.

"I'm sorry," Sophie choked out.

Hunter observed them with a studied gaze. Grant reminded him of a caged animal, and he didn't seem like one to share his family's secrets. It would likely be some time before he'd be comfortable enough to disclose what had happened between him and his father.

"Grant," Hunter calmly began, "I apologize for rushing things—that was my bad. We'll go at your pace here; you don't have to talk about anything you don't want to, okay? Would you be willing to take a seat? I promise to be more careful."

Grant halted his pacing and reluctantly returned to the sofa, emitting a long sigh.

"What are you thinking?" Sophie softly asked him. She hoped he wasn't angry with her.

"I'm thinking…I'm thinking both of you know more about Logan than I do." He exhaled loudly. "I never got to know my brother—he wouldn't allow it. And now he's gone."

"Oh, Grant," she cried, taking his hand in hers and stroking it softly. His grief made her heart ache.

Hunter mulled over what Grant had said. Was it possible Sophie knew Logan on a deeper level than his own brother? Did Grant realize the full extent of Sophie's knowledge? Like, for example, that she knew Logan in the biblical sense?

Wanting some answers, he asked, "So, when did Logan come to your apartment?" Logan had obviously been alive then—his visit must have occurred before Thursday.

"Last Wednesday. Sophie cooked me a delicious dinner that night."

"And then what happened?"

"Logan and I—"

"I walked around—"

The pair both spoke at once, then chuckled, and the tension in the room dissipated slightly.

"Ladies first," Grant offered.

"Thank you. After I found out they were brothers, I thought Grant was working some kind of con on me, just like Logan," said Sophie. "I was…devastated. I walked around the city for hours and finally landed on my father's doorstep."

Hunter quirked one eyebrow. He'd been encouraging Sophie to contact her father from day one. "And how did he react?"

"It's a good thing I followed your advice," Sophie replied, allowing Hunter to relax. "My dad took me in, and we talked through a lot of stuff. He doesn't blame me for Mom dying after all. He just couldn't see me because I remind him too much of her."

Grant stared at Sophie, evidently hearing this information for the first time.

"But it's still not great between us. I'm not sure about having my dad back in my life because he's been a total jerk to Grant."

The look of resignation on Grant's face continued to communicate his low self-worth.

"And what happened to *you* after Logan's surprise visit?" Hunter prompted.

Grant appeared uncomfortable. "I, well, I kept asking Lo how he knew Sophie, and he finally admitted she was his psychologist. The judge forced him into counseling after the Great Lakes thing."

"Great Lakes?" Sophie repeated curiously.

"The robbery—" Grant stopped, realizing Sophie had no idea Logan had coerced him to rob the Navy bar near the base. As they attempted to tell their stories to Dr. Hayes, it suddenly felt like they hardly knew each other.

"I'll tell you about that later," Grant promised. "Anyway, I was *so* mad at Logan for ruining Sophie's life, but the kicker was he didn't even know what he did. He didn't have a clue she went to prison because of him."

Sophie's lips parted. "He didn't?"

Grant felt even more anxious with both psychologists' piercing gazes on him. Clearing his throat, he replied, "Logan went into hiding, and he had no idea about the fallout from stashing the guns and the money in your office. He didn't even know you'd lost your license."

Sophie's mouth hung open as she absorbed this information. She'd been furious with Logan for abandoning her, leaving her to deal alone with his mess, but she'd never considered that his betrayal might not have been entirely premeditated.

Grant continued, "Uh, like I said, I was really mad at Logan, and we sort of got into a fight after Sophie left."

Hunter nodded. That explained the yellowish tinge on Grant's cheek — the remnants of a bruise.

Grant glanced at Sophie and then looked down. "I wanted to hurt him just like he hurt you."

"What happened next, Grant?" Hunter prompted.

"I told Lo to l-l-leave…" Grant's voice faded and his stomach clenched with guilt. *I told him I wished he was dead.*

Hunter observed his shamefaced expression. "Did he leave?"

Grant tightened his fists and took a shuddering breath, attempting to stuff down his guilt. "Yes, sir. Um, the next morning I went to see Officer Stone — our PO. I'd been up all night, and I didn't know what else to do. I guess I needed to talk to somebody who knew the whole story. The day before, Officer Stone saw pictures of me at the Barberi compound for my nephew Ben's birthday party, and he told me I should tell Sophie who I really was."

Grant paused and shook his head. It was some kind of miracle that Sophie now knew the truth and was still by his side.

"Grant tried to tell me that night," Sophie quickly added. "He tried to tell me his family was Mafia. But I wanted to be honest with him first, so I explained how I got arrested."

Hunter took in this information, wondering if Grant really would have come clean if not for Logan showing up unannounced.

Sophie resumed the story. "The next morning I went to Roger's ship to resign, and I, um, I ran into Grant." They exchanged a painful glance, recalling her fear at the sight of him.

"This was Thursday, right?" Hunter asked, receiving nods in return. "The day Logan was murdered?" More nods. "Have they found his killer?"

"We'll get to that," Sophie promised wryly. "Neither of us knew Logan was dead until Friday, when Marilyn — Detective Fox — interviewed us about it. We were both suspects."

Opening his eyes wider, Hunter questioned, "They thought one of you killed him?"

"Yes, sir," Grant confirmed. "Particularly me, since they found his, um…they found Logan at Great Lakes, where I was formerly stationed. My cousin Carlo tried to pin the murder on me."

Sophie inhaled sharply. "That bastard!"

"Who's Carlo?" Hunter looked confused.

"We'll get to that too," Sophie responded. She couldn't believe so much had happened since the last time she'd seen her psychologist. "Right after I discovered Logan and Grant were related, I decided I didn't want to see Grant ever again," Sophie said. "But then I found out Logan died, and I was really worried about how Grant would take it. I snuck out of my dad's house to attend the funeral on Sunday."

"Thank you," Grant said softly.

She nodded. "I'm glad I went—not only for you, but for me too. I figured it would be a way to try to get some closure after what Logan did to me."

Hunter felt her staring at him, looking for confirmation from her therapist, and he supplied a small nod. He was too blown away by their story to act very therapeutically at the moment.

"After the funeral, my cousin Carlo, uh, Carlo Barberi, came to my apartment." Grant glanced at Sophie with a look of shame. "He told me I had to join the family or he'd kill Sophie."

The weight of his words hung heavily in the air between them.

Grant resumed, "Carlo took Sophie's note from the fridge—the one with Kirsten's address on it."

"*That's* how he found us!" Sophie exclaimed. "I was so stupid to write down my address."

"*I* was so stupid to post it in plain sight," Grant countered.

Typical post-trauma behavior, Hunter noted. So easy to second-guess after the fact. "Carlo came to Kirsten's?" he prompted.

Sophie nodded. "He held a gun on Kirsten and me, demanding the money I'd turned over to the police. He wanted me to go to my dad to get it."

Hunter had the sense they were nearing the part of the story that explained Sophie's sling.

Grant seemed too tense to speak, so Sophie continued. "Grant showed up, and Carlo was yelling at him to get on his knees, but he wouldn't do it, and then suddenly I knew."

"You knew what?" Hunter was captivated.

"I knew Carlo was Logan's killer."

"He *was?*"

Grant suddenly found his voice. "He was. He tried to deny it, but I could see it on his face." His clear blue eyes darkened. "I wanted to rip him apart, and I started toward him when he…" Grant gulped "…he shot Sophie."

Hunter sat back in his chair, trying to absorb this incredible story.

Sophie watched his reaction carefully. "I'll be okay, though," she offered. "I get out of the sling in a couple of weeks, before classes start at DePaul. I should be okay to teach."

Wanting to ask what in the world it felt like to be shot, Hunter was stymied when Grant jumped in to carry on the story.

"After Carlo shot Sophie, he, uh, got me down on the floor." *I was just waiting for him to kill me.* "Kirsten made a diversion, and I, um, I tackled Carlo. We wrestled for the gun…and…and it went off. I shot him." His voice lowered to barely above a whisper. "I killed him."

Recognizing the far-off look of dissociation, Hunter was pretty sure the man on the sofa was experiencing an acute stress reaction, possibly post-traumatic stress disorder. Grant surely needed his help.

"He saved my life," Sophie said, patting her boyfriend's long leg. Her touch appeared to bring Grant back to the present, and he gave her a mournful look. "They arrested him," she added grimly, "but it was obviously self-defense so they settled on an additional year of parole."

"An additional year of counseling, looks like," Grant said, not looking forward to the prospect in the least.

Hunter sighed loudly and tried to make sense of the multitude of thoughts careening in his brain. "How do you know your family won't pursue you again?"

"Uncle Joe talked to Uncle Angelo, and he promised not to come after me."

"Do you really trust the word of *Angelo Barberi?*" The media footage of a triumphant Angelo exiting the courthouse, cleared of extortion charges by his high-priced attorneys, flashed through Hunter's mind.

"I don't know Uncle Angelo all that well," Grant admitted. "But he's my father's brother, and my father supposedly always keeps his word. That's how he rose to Don."

There was a silence in the room before Hunter muttered, "Hmm, I don't know about this."

Sophie and Grant warily watched Hunter struggle with the decision—their time was almost up.

"One thing I told Grant," Sophie said, taking his hand in hers once again, "is the reason I didn't figure out that he and Logan were brothers. Although they looked alike, there's *no* similarity in what kind of men they were on the inside."

Sophie paused, thinking about what Grant had revealed: Logan hadn't known that hiding guns and money in her office had led to such trouble for her. Maybe Logan wasn't the evil character she'd made him out to be.

Shaking these thoughts out of her head, Sophie returned to her argument. "Grant's a good man, Hunter, and I know you'll discover that too if you see us for couples counseling."

Thinking of Sophie's history with inappropriate partners—bad boys and older men—Hunter gazed suspiciously at Grant. *Was* he running a con on her? She was obviously infatuated with the dark-haired Italian next to her, despite what she risked simply by being with him. Hunter decided then and there to take them on as a couple. It would be the only way to keep an eye on potential evildoings of the Barberi clan—the only way to keep Sophie safe. What was the saying? *Keep your friends close and your enemies closer.* Hunter felt a tendril of unease crawl up his spine. This Mafia family was already infiltrating his thoughts.

"I'll give it a try," Hunter pledged. "But if I believe my objectivity's compromised in any way, I'll have to refer you to another psychologist."

"That's fair." Sophie nodded gratefully. "See you next week?"

"See you then," Hunter said as they all stood.

"Thank you, Dr. Hayes."

Shaking Grant's hand, Hunter dared to look into those arresting eyes, which appeared just as compelling as they had at first glance. The psychologist was in for quite a ride with these two. He could feel it already.

2. Conditions

A sense of calm settled over Grant once he caught a glimpse of the gleaming ship swaying gently near the docks of the Chicago River. Therapy, emotions, secrets, family—he had no idea how to deal with all of that, but ships…well, ships he could handle. The architectural cruise was his livelihood, his home.

Swinging his lanky body onto the deck, Grant surveyed the bar area amidships, grinning as he remembered Sophie serving drinks there all summer long. Now he missed her, but he had no one to blame but himself. He'd been the one to help her secure a teaching job in DePaul University's psychology department, and he couldn't deny how incredibly delighted she'd been upon taking the position. That look of joy was all he needed. He'd do anything to have that glowing excitement cross her features again. His singular focus now was performing kind, caring acts for the woman he loved. Her smile had replaced the need for screaming Navy superiors or grumpy bosses to compel him into action.

And where *was* his grumpy boss? By this time of the morning, Roger was typically cracking the whip over Grant's nephew, Ben, the newest employee of Eaton Architectural Cruises. But the two were nowhere to be found. Shrugging, Grant decided to clean his work station. He leaped up the stairs to the bridge and then froze, shocked by the scene in front of him.

Roger was eating the biggest piece of deep-dish pizza known to humankind. The short, fat, foul-mouthed captain—supposedly on a diet after his heart attack earlier that summer—shoveled in the thick, greasy mass hungrily, swiftly, furtively. His jaws moved like a jackhammer, tearing into the cheese and crust like a lion snapping off a gazelle's leg.

"Step. Away. From. The Pizza," Grant ordered in a deep voice.

Roger halted mid-chew and stared up at his employee with a look of sheer mortification. "Mahdschten," he mumbled guiltily, trying to swallow a massive wad of cheese.

"Rog!" Grant chided. "What the hell are you doing, sir? You're ruining your diet! You can't eat that stuff!"

Eyeing the open pizza box and dismayed to find the pieces already half-gone, Grant waited for his boss to gulp down his most recent bite.

Finally Roger could speak, and Grant tried to ignore the small piece of tomato wedged between his boss's two front teeth. "Don't tell Joe?"

The surly man's meek plea and flushed cheeks surprised his employee.

"Joe?" Grant was confused. "I can't tell him—he's probably out to sea by now." His uncle had returned to Norfolk to resume his duties on the USS Mahan. "Why do you care if Joe knows you're eating pizza?"

"He was so stoked about my weight loss. He was really impressed. I just want him, you know, to be…proud of me. It's stupid."

Grant felt a stab of sympathy for his boss. He knew all too well the desire to make Joe Madsen proud. Ignoring the sinking feeling in his stomach as he remembered how thoroughly *he'd* disappointed his uncle, Grant asked, "What happened? You were doing so well eating vegetables."

"Fucking carrots," Roger muttered.

Grant stifled a grin. "You don't love Ms. Broccoli anymore?"

"Ms. Broccoli is a bitch."

Grant's grin widened. Taking a sly step toward the calorie-laden pizza pie, he suggested, "How 'bout I remove the temptation?"

Roger instantly huddled over the box like a hyena protecting its meal, eyeing Grant suspiciously.

"I know one starving teenager who could finish it off for you," Grant added.

At this Roger sat up. "Where is that fucking kid? I haven't seen him all morning."

Grant frowned. His therapy appointment had made him later than usual, and Ben should've been there by now. "I'll go look for him." Biting his lip, he gestured toward the pizza box. "May I?"

Sighing, Roger waved his hand dismissively. "Take it," he grumbled, clutching his stomach. "My gut's about to explode now anyway. How the hell did I eat this shit every day?"

Grasping the box, Grant stealthily moved away. Remembering what it had been like to work side by side with Rog during those early summer days when pizza was a major staple of his diet, Grant grimly predicted that the bridge would smell quite fragrant later today. And it wouldn't be aromatic river scents either.

After a thorough search of the ship, Grant was concerned enough to head to the office to call Ben's mother, Ashley, when he stopped short on the docks. He detected a sweet smell — one that made him think immediately of Logan. He was flooded by the memory of his brother's brawny arms clutching him tight, and suddenly he was back at their mother's funeral. He'd been twelve years old, and Logan's jacket had smelled of sweet smoke, the exact scent greeting Grant's nose now. Shaking his head a few times to clear it, Grant walked toward the corner of the building to investigate.

He rounded the corner and pursed his lips disapprovingly. As expected, he found the source of the smell: some teenager smoking a joint. The boy exhaled a puff of smoke, and when the haze cleared, Grant gaped.

"Ben!" he snapped.

The teenager's unfocused eyes widened once he noticed his uncle glaring at him. He swiftly dropped the joint and tried to appear angelic.

"Yo, Uncle Grant," he rasped, stomping on the tossed-aside roach. Grant stared at him, slack-jawed. "Don't, um, don't tell Mom or Joe, 'kay?"

This was the second person in five minutes to beg him not to rat out their misbehavior to his uncle.

"What does Joe have to do with this?" Grant asked, again.

"He didn't tell you?"

"Tell me what?"

Ben was taken aback. Great Uncle Joe had turned out to be pretty cool after all. He'd kept quiet about catching Ben with marijuana once before. "Nothin'."

A crease formed on Grant's forehead. "You — you can't smoke pot on the job, Ben! Mr. Eaton will fire you if he catches you."

"So?" Ben challenged, defiantly jutting out his jaw. "This job sucks balls anyway."

Grant felt his face flush with sudden anger. How dare this sixteen-year-old give him punk attitude? Joe had taken a risk by securing him job, just like he had with Grant, and Ben showed total disrespect. Trying to keep his voice even, Grant asked, "You *want* to get fired, then?"

Ben folded his arms across his chest. "I don't care."

Grant studied his nephew. Despite his feigned nonchalance, the boy's voice warbled with emotion, and it seemed like he *did* care. Calling his bluff, Grant extended his arm, beckoning him with a curl of his fingers. "C'mon, then. Let's go tell our boss you quit."

Ben's eyes flashed worry. "Um, maybe not right this second? Maybe I'll quit later."

"Ben, what's going on? Do you want this job or not? Because *if* you want it, you're not doing a good job of showing it."

Hearing his uncle's disappointment, the boy felt a tightening in his stomach. *I don't care, damn it!* He'd hoped that, of all people, his uncle would understand him, but Grant was all up in his grill just like the other adults. Nobody understood him; he was entirely alone. His bottom lip trembled though he remained silent.

Grant observed emotions swirling like wispy clouds in the teenager's sky blue eyes, and he wished he could help him. Sighing, he crossed in front of Ben and leaned his back against the brick wall, standing quietly beside the boy.

"You know what I thought of when I smelled pot from around the corner?"

Ben's sullen expression showed a hint of intrigue. "What?"

Grant looked down. "Your dad."

The younger Barberi's breath hitched; the stinging loss of his father was still quite raw.

Grant continued. "He used to smoke a lot when he was your age." His lips pressed together. "Uncle Joe was really mad at Uncle Angelo for not stopping Logan—for not getting him some help. And then Logan got busted for selling drugs, and he went to juvie. He was just a little older than you are now."

The warning in his words wasn't lost on Ben, and he cautiously asked, "What's juvie like?"

Rubbing his jaw thoughtfully, Grant ventured, "Probably not much better than adult prison, Ben." He sighed. "I think…well, I think juvie made your dad kind of…hard. He changed. He…" A slight tremor entered his voice. "I miss the old Logan, you know? I don't want that to happen to you."

Ben's eyes filled with tears that he furiously blinked away. He felt a throbbing ache any time there was mention of his father, and he hated that internal weakness. With thoughts of funerals, juvie, and prison floating in his mind, he asked, "Uncle Grant? Um, Carlo said…Carlo said that you, um, you went crazy in prison?"

Grant clenched his jaw, furious to hear the name of Logan's killer, then averted his eyes. He hadn't talked about his shameful descent into madness with anyone, and he rued his nephew's directness. After studying his hands for a few moments, he quietly admitted, "Yeah. I did." Feeling the palpable heaviness between them, Grant gave a long sigh.

"So I have a whack-job uncle?"

A slight grin tugged at the corner of Grant's mouth. "Something like that."

Spurred on by his uncle's confession, Ben's expression turned serious. "Uncle Grant? Um, actually I can't quit this job."

"You can't quit?"

Ben sniffed. "Mom and Joe told me I have to work on the boat and stay away from weed, or I gotta go to rehab."

"Joe caught you smoking?"

"Yeah."

Considering their deal, Grant asked, "So then I guess you need to go to rehab now?"

"No! I won't go. Don't tell Mom or Joe—I won't smoke again, I promise."

"Ben—" Grant's voice rose with reproach.

"Please, Uncle Grant? Please don't tell. There's no way I'll turn out like my dad—*I'm* not gonna get caught."

Grant grimaced. "Nobody *plans* on getting caught, Ben. I certainly didn't plan on getting busted, and your dad didn't plan on going to juvie or running into Carlo…" His voice trailed off, and neither of them wanted him to finish the statement. Grant felt a pang of guilt for badmouthing his deceased brother.

"Listen, Ben, I don't want you using drugs or going to prison or getting involved with the family. But I *do* want you to be tough, strong, and smart. I do want you to…to try to take care of others." His voice softened. "Like your dad."

Ben blinked quickly, surprised by his uncle's words. "I didn't think you and Dad got along."

"We didn't. He screwed things up for me," Grant rasped. "But it's not that simple, you know? Sometimes I'm still really mad at him, but sometimes…"

He was quiet for a moment, pensive, feeling a small spark of hope. Although he'd forever lost the opportunity to know his brother, perhaps he still had a chance to know and love his brother's son.

"Are you gonna tell about the weed?" Ben prompted.

Deliberating for a moment, Grant aimed a stern look in his direction. "I need to think about it. It depends on how well you do at work these next few weeks. No slacking, Ben. I mean it."

Grant was surprised when Ben squared his shoulders and nodded. "Okay."

Grant gestured to the river. "We better get back to the ship."

He followed his nephew to the deck, where they ran into Roger emerging from the bathroom. Glaring at Ben, Roger shouted, "You're late! Where the hell have you been?"

Taking a step back, Ben stammered, "I—I—"

"We're sorry we're late, sir," Grant said, rescuing the red-faced teen.

"The passengers will start arriving in twenty fucking minutes!" Roger raged. "And the bathrooms look like shit!"

Ben's eyes widened, and Grant offered, "I'll help Ben clean them, okay, sir?"

The boss eyed the two suspiciously and grumbled, "Get to it, then."

"Yes, sir." Grant hustled to the supply closet, and since Ben didn't want to be left alone with his enraged, roly-poly boss, he scampered after him.

While Ben was mopping the women's head, he asked, "Why do you call Rog 'sir'?"

Grant paused his wiping down the sinks, sponge suspended in midair. "Because he's the boss."

"Does he make you call him that?"

"No."

"Then why?"

Grant sighed and nodded to the mop. Ben took the hint and resumed his duty while Grant explained.

"I guess it goes back to Uncle Joe," he said. "He's in the Navy, you know, and I grew up on a military base. Some Navy dads make their kids address all adults as 'sir' or 'ma'am' but Joe was never like that. He said I should only address superiors as 'sir' if I respected them. It's a sign of respect. Once I joined the Navy, it just sort of became natural to address everyone that way."

Grant rinsed the sponge and continued cleaning. "Maybe I call him 'sir' out of habit now, though I do respect Mr. Eaton. I know he can be grumpy, but he's a good guy. He helped me a lot after I got out of prison."

Wringing out the mop, Ben said, "He was kinda mad. Is he gonna fire me?"

"Nah," Grant assured him. "He'll calm down. Give him a few minutes. He's just cranky because he's on a diet."

They cleaned for a bit longer and then Ben commented, "Man, I'm starved. When's our lunch break?"

A faint smile lit up Grant's face. "Oh, I forgot to tell you—I got some pizza for us later."

"Score! Did you call Gino's?"

"No, I'm not supposed to use the office phone for personal calls."

Ben stared at him curiously. "That's what cell phones are for, dude."

Grant shrugged. "I don't have a cell phone."

"What?" Ben was flabbergasted. "You don't have a cell?" He shook his head disdainfully. "We gotta hook you up, Uncle Grant."

Sophie smiled as she put the finishing touches on her teaching syllabus and then heard the satisfying sound of the printer rolling out the completed document. Typing one-handed with the hunt-and-peck method was rather cumbersome, but she'd finally finished her plans for the *Theories of Personality* class she'd taken over from Dr. Anita Green. Sophie's advisor was overseas on a consulting project, leaving the former-student-turned-parolee to fill in as visiting instructor. Sophie had borrowed liberally from Anita's old syllabus, but she'd inserted a few creative changes of her own. She hoped her students would enjoy the additions.

Leaning back in her chair, she surveyed Anita's office, feeling a sense of peace. Stacks of journal articles, rows of textbooks, carefully arranged teacups—she'd spent many an afternoon in this cluttered yet homey office as a graduate student, discussing research projects or helping Anita grade the undergraduates' tests and papers. Though not quite as familiar as the therapy setting, the academic environment was wholly comforting.

A knock on the door made Sophie sit upright, and she tentatively called, "Come in?"

Once Sophie recognized the long brown hair and blue eyes of her former roommate, she popped out of the chair with an excited grin. "Kirsten!"

Kirsten's smile was tempered only by a sad glance toward Sophie's arm sling—a reminder of the trauma they'd endured at Carlo's hand—and she gently hugged her friend.

"What are you doing here, Kir?" Sophie gestured for her to sit across the desk.

"I've got some problems making the deadline for the paper, Dr. Taylor," she joked.

With a feigned scowl, Sophie informed her, "No extensions, you slacker. Ten points off for each day late."

They smirked at each other, and Kirsten revealed her real reason for visiting the Psychology Department: "I just had a meeting with David."

Humiliation overtook Sophie, but she feigned excitement. "Awesome! Did you set a date for your defense?"

"Yep." Kirsten grinned proudly, "August twenty-fifth."

"That's in less than two weeks!"

Kirsten suddenly looked anxious. "Don't remind me. I'm already freaking out."

Sophie's eyes filled with sympathy. Her roommate had finally finished writing her dissertation, and all that remained was an oral exam: a face-off with five faculty members who would fire tough questions. Sophie had adeptly endured her own dissertation defense three years ago, but she'd benefitted from Anita's undying support. Kirsten's relationship with her advisor, David Alton, was not as encouraging or productive, and Sophie hoped she wasn't to blame for David's lack of mentoring.

"Have you, um, run into David yet?" Kirsten asked.

Sophie blushed. "Not yet, luckily."

"You're going to have to see him sometime, you know."

"I'm trying to delay it as long as possible."

Kirsten watched her friend squirm. David was a Richard Gere loo-kalike whose graying hair made him even more desirable and debonair as he aged, just like the actor. The year he'd taught *Psychological Assessment* to their graduate class, Sophie had fallen hard for him, despite Kirsten's warnings. Kirsten had been appalled that Sophie obsessed over a married man, but Sophie had insisted his marriage seemed unhappy, based on a few comments he'd sprinkled here and there.

It was precisely the type of inappropriate romantic relationship her psychologist was now trying to help her avoid. Hunter and Sophie had been processing the years of painful disapproval from her own father — pain that likely led her to seek solace in the arms of bad boys and older men. Sophie's infatuation with her professor had ended badly when he'd firmly told her she'd misconstrued any possibility of a relationship between them. She'd never felt so embarrassed — until her prison sentencing, that is.

Shaking off shameful memories, Sophie assured Kirsten, "You're gonna do great, you know."

"This damn dissertation has been hanging over my head for so long. If I fail — "

"You *won't* fail. I've read your manuscript and it's awesome, Kir." Noticing the seed of doubt still blooming on her friend's face, Sophie added, "Did I ever tell you what Anita said about the dissertation defense?"

Kirsten shook her head.

"She said we shouldn't call it a defense. That makes us think of a tense standoff or something. Your committee's not against you. They *want* you to succeed." Sophie giggled. "They want you to finally graduate and get the hell out of here!"

Kirsten narrowed her eyes.

"It's not a dissertation defense," Sophie continued, "but rather a dissertation *revelation*."

Taking in her roommate's words, Kirsten nodded slowly. "I like that. My revelation is coming soon then, I guess."

"Damn straight. Hey, are you ready to go? I was just about to head to Grant's apartment."

"It's your apartment too," Kirsten reminded her.

"I know." Sophie packed up her tote bag. "But it's so new. It's hard to think of as mine too. Are you, um, still staying with your parents in the 'burbs?"

Kirsten's apartment was currently cordoned off as a crime scene. "Yeah, and they're driving me *nuts*."

The friends emerged onto the hallway of the academic building, chuckling, then froze at the sight of a self-possessed gray-haired man crossing their path. David's eyes crinkled at the corners when he smiled. Sophie's heart hammered in her chest.

"Hello, um, Dr. Alton," Sophie stammered, her face on fire.

"Please call me David, Sophie. I hear we're to be colleagues now."

To her surprise, she felt not one spark when he took her hand in his and shook it. Surely a man who'd been her crush for over a year would elicit at least some sort of physical reaction?

"What happened to your arm?" David asked, nodding at her sling.

Sophie was suddenly grateful that her meddling father had managed to use his influence to keep her involvement in the shooting out of the newspapers. Of course David knew about her ethical breach and stint in prison, but she didn't exactly want to broadcast her latest Mafia misadventure.

Noticing her friend's silence, Kirsten turned to her advisor. "Um, David? She had an accident, but she'd rather not disclose the details. She'll be out of the sling in a couple of weeks."

He hesitated, puzzled by the evasive response, but his suave demeanor soon returned. "Just in time for your defense then," he nodded, aiming a polished smile at Kirsten.

Seeming to regain her composure, Sophie quietly corrected, "Her revelation."

Shooting her a confused look, David studied Sophie for a moment before seeming to arrive at a conclusion. "Well, then, I must be off. My son's got a baseball game later." His smile now seemed plastic. "Nice to see you both."

Once he was out of earshot, Sophie practically melted into the wall behind her, murmuring, "Oh my God."

"*That* should be interesting—working with him all semester."

Sophie gave a beleaguered half-chuckle. "No kidding. I'm in total hell right now." She gave a dramatic sigh, but Sophie had to admit the interaction hadn't been quite as humiliating as she'd expected. She was pleased to find herself not attracted to him one bit this time around. That ship had sailed…and now she had McSailor. A warm smile crossed her lips as she thought of her gorgeous, gentle, seafaring hero.

She sensed a buzzing in her bag, which was accompanied by dismay as she reached in to find her phone. "Please tell me my father hasn't figured out how to send text messages."

Her dismay switched immediately to delight as she read the message:

How's my beautiful Bonnie today?

"Grant has a cell phone!" she said with a laugh.

3. Conjoined

As Hunter followed the attractive couple down the hallway to their second therapy session, his conversation with a colleague a few days ago floated through his mind.

"It's wise of you to consult about this," Michelle Mendota told him.

Embarrassed, Hunter glanced up at the psychologist across the table in the coffee shop.

"It's difficult for any of us when we're attracted to a client," she continued, brushing an unruly strand of long, wavy black hair over her shoulder. "But as you know, consultation's the best way to handle an ethical dilemma."

He could sense her intelligent brown eyes boring into him, and his cheeks still felt warm after confessing he felt a physical attraction to Grant Madsen. However, Hunter already knew consultation was indeed the optimal route, so he faced the mortification of confiding in his best friend. "I don't want to fall into the same trap my female client did," he said with a shaky sigh.

"Yeah, her story's rather horrendous," Michelle agreed, shuddering. "But the guy — he's heterosexual, right? So he won't be returning your affection?"

"I think so. At least my gaydar isn't picking up much activity there."

Michelle returned Hunter's smirk before she asked, "And you don't think it's a good idea to refer them to another therapist?"

"That's a tough one." Hunter sighed. "It was my first inclination — to make a referral — but my female client practically begged me to stay on." He ran one hand through his neat blond hair. "And I've done some good work with her; she's come a long way. She's convinced her boyfriend is a good guy, but who's to say he's not just like his brother? I want to help her safely figure it out, and that'll be easier if I can observe their dynamics, so I agreed to take them in the end. I guess I feel…protective of her or something."

Michelle smiled. "Sounds like you're drawn to both the man *and* the woman in this couple."

Hunter chuckled. "Yeah, if she were a man, I'd probably have the hots for her too."

"Oh, Hunter, you'll be fine. I trust you to do the right thing. You're the one who helped me through that awful case, right?" Michelle's records had once been subpoenaed for a nasty divorce trial, and she'd struggled mightily with the ethics of breaching her client's confidentiality. "But there's one thing you could do to make it *impossible* for you to get involved with the client."

Hunter's eyebrows scrunched together. "What's that?"

"You could tell Bradley."

His eyes got huge as he almost choked on his coffee. "Tell Bradley? What the hell for?"

Michelle stifled a grin. "That'd make it totally above board," she explained. "No secrets. It's normal to feel attracted to clients now and then, and Bradley would understand."

"If you haven't noticed, Michelle, he's kind of the jealous type."

"Well, you're not going to *act* on your feelings. And telling Bradley would just about guarantee that. You've been together ten years — Bradley can handle it…"

As he followed Grant and Sophie into his office, Hunter felt slightly ill. He hadn't drummed up the courage to tell his partner about Grant, and he didn't know if he ever would. Bradley was a brilliant plastic surgeon, but sometimes he didn't behave very logically upon experiencing intense emotions. And Hunter even glancing at another man tended to arouse such emotions.

"So," Hunter smiled at Sophie, ignoring Grant for the moment. "How's your week been?"

"Pretty good. I can't wait to start teaching." She returned his smile and seemed to wait expectantly for Grant to add his two cents.

Grant uncomfortably cleared his throat. "It was, uh, fine, sir."

Hunter stole a glance at the clownfish in the aquarium rather than meeting the stunning crystal-blue eyes of his client, then broke the silence. "One thing I typically ask clients to do in the first session is set goals for therapy. We had some, uh, *catching up* to do in our first meeting, though, and ran out of time."

Sophie managed a sly grin.

"What would you like to accomplish in here?" Hunter continued. "What would you like to improve or change? Grant, how about you go first."

Grant looked startled. Tapping his fingers nervously on his thigh, he eventually said, "My one and only goal is to stay out of prison."

Hunter was dismayed. "Meaning that if you don't come to counseling, your PO will put you back in prison? You're only here because you're mandated to be?"

Grant nodded.

"That goal sucks, Grant."

Both Sophie's and Grant's eyebrows shot up, and Hunter decided to explain further.

"What I meant," he said, trying again, "was that I understand you're mandated to be here. But you could really get something out of this, Grant. You could work on improving your relationship with Sophie, which I know means a lot to you. You could process your grief over your cousin murdering your brother. You could explore some life goals for yourself, now that you're trying to make a fresh start. The sky's the limit. For you to just sit here and tell me you're fine—well, that's a total waste of time for you and for me."

Grant had been inching up straighter and taller with each word out of Hunter's mouth, and by the time the psychologist finished with the diatribe, he sat rigidly erect on the sofa. His eyes attentive and his mood sober, he replied, "Yes, sir."

"So I'll ask you again, what are your goals for therapy?"

Stealing a helpless glance at his girlfriend, Grant began sweating. He felt like he was back in college ROTC again, enduring a quiz about Navy history from a superior.

Sophie watched him squirm, and she offered, "Do you want to deal with your nightmares?"

Grant whipped his head toward her, disconcerted by her question. "Uh—um—"

"You're having nightmares?" Hunter interjected.

"Not really," Grant lied.

Sophie frowned. Although they'd only spent the night together perhaps four times, on two of those occasions Grant's sleep had been interrupted by what appeared to be intensely distressing nightmares.

"You said something about improving our relationship, sir?" Grant quickly added, redirecting the conversation. "That would be one of my goals."

"Okay, and what would you like to improve about the relationship?"

We need to stop lying to each other, Sophie supplied silently on Grant's behalf.

Then Grant turned to her and shrugged. "I don't really know *how* we could improve our relationship. It's perfect already."

Hunter watched Sophie practically swoon over Grant's comment, and he chuckled softly. "Well, my work is done here. Your relationship's already perfect."

Noticing Hunter's grin, Sophie said, "Our relationship *is* awesome. Grant's right about that." She clasped his hand. "But I do have an idea for something we could work on." Sophie took a deep breath. "Um, I think we need to be more open with each other."

Hunter nodded. "I agree. There's quite a bit you two seem not to know about each other."

And a lot I don't want Sophie to know, Grant thought.

"So that's one of Sophie's goals: to be more open in your communication with each other. Grant, how about you?"

Grant met the psychologist's inquisitive glance and chewed on his lower lip.

"Hunter, Grant's never been in therapy before," said Sophie. "Maybe we could explain what it's like?"

Hunter sat back in his chair and peered at her thoughtfully. "Perhaps that's a good idea."

Feeling the psychologist studying her, Sophie turned to face Grant. "So, in therapy, you talk about what's going on in your life — the good stuff and the bad stuff. And the therapist helps you make sense of it all by asking you questions so you'll see things in a different light, notice patterns —"

Continuing to sense the heat of Hunter's stare, Sophie turned to him and abruptly asked, "What?"

"Speaking of patterns," Hunter said, "I'm noticing one right now. Did you notice that was the second time you swooped in and 'rescued' Grant?"

She appeared indignant. "What do you mean?"

"He was uncomfortable—anxious—and you jumped in to answer the question for him. Twice."

"I did not."

The corner of Hunter's mouth twitched.

Grant slowly began nodding. "Yeah, you did. I was trying to think of an answer to Dr. Hayes' question—"

"Not that you minded her interference," Hunter broke in, earning a rueful grin from Grant. Turning to Sophie, Hunter inquired, "Why won't you let him answer my question?"

With an affronted look, Sophie mulled over what had just transpired. "Well, I know he hates therapy, and I didn't want him to feel anxious."

"I see," Hunter replied. "And do you have any control over whether or not Grant feels anxious?"

Sophie squirmed while Grant watched with fascination. "No," she admitted in a low voice.

"Exactly. I'm sure Grant has some difficult parts of his past—I can only imagine what it's like to be the son of Enzo Barberi. He's had experiences that undoubtedly create a lot of anxiety for him now. And perhaps he'll share some of that with us when he's ready. But his history happened long before he met you, Sophie, and you simply can't stop him from feeling anxiety, or any emotion for that matter."

Sophie groaned.

"Are you all right?" Grant asked, looking anxious yet again.

She exhaled loudly. "I'm doing that enmeshed thing again."

Grant appeared puzzled. "Enmeshed?" He looked to Hunter for help.

"I'll get to your question, but first I want to know what your college major was, Grant."

Startled, he tentatively answered, "MT, um, military technologies."

"Oh, right. You were in ROTC?"

"Yes, sir."

"He went to Notre Dame," Sophie proudly butted in before emitting a small gasp and clamping her hand over her mouth, glancing guiltily at Hunter.

"That's okay, Sophie, you weren't rescuing him this time," said Hunter with a grin. "You were merely bragging about your boyfriend."

She returned his smile and Hunter continued, glancing at Grant. "I was thinking you might be a visual learner with a major like that. Let me draw what Sophie and I were discussing—this idea of an enmeshed relationship."

He extracted a pad of paper from the end table and began drawing a series of circles. "I want to talk about three kinds of relationships. If you envision a circle as representing a person in a relationship, here's the first type: distant."

He drew two circles rather far apart. "In a distant relationship, there's not much caring or time spent together—it's like two people simply coexisting. The two might disagree, but this doesn't cause much conflict because they don't really show much caring toward each other."

Next Hunter carefully drew one circle right on top of another, and Grant was amused that the psychologist's tongue stuck out the corner of his mouth as he concentrated deeply.

"This is an enmeshed relationship," Hunter explained, "like the one between Sophie and her mother."

Sophie rolled her eyes.

"In enmeshment, the two people are very close. They spend a lot of time together. When one person feels a certain way, the other person often feels that way too, and they tend to take responsibility for each other's feelings. You don't hear about disagreement in enmeshed relationships, because disagreement and conflict tend to go underground.

"Common language used in an enmeshed relationship might be 'You're not mad, right?' or 'Don't confront her—I'll take care of it' or even 'You complete me.'" Hunter made a gagging motion and Sophie giggled. "When Sophie tried to rescue you from feeling anxious, Grant, I called her out because that's exactly what she used to do for her mother. She took care of her mother's emotional well-being while ignoring her own needs.

"Sometimes this enmeshed pattern can happen in families with addiction or abuse. Let's say the father's an alcoholic, and the entire family tiptoes around him, trying not to provoke him. Their needs are subverted to his needs. That's enmeshment, or codependence."

"Is that like enabling too?" Sophie asked.

"Hmm, could be. What do you think?" Hunter and Sophie's curious voices faded as Grant felt pulled back in time.

The pounding noise of water gushing from the faucet flooded his senses, and he could feel his mother's gentle touch on his ribcage, delicately brushing her fingers over the angry bruise. She'd just removed his T-shirt in preparation for a bath. He was five years old.

"Oh, honey," she cried.

He shied away from her hand and turned his face to the wall, feeling color rise in his cheeks. He'd been a bad boy, and his father had thrown him against the wall.

"I'm sorry, Grant," Karita choked out, her voice barely audible over the rush of water. "He didn't mean it."

The little boy closed his enormous blue eyes and nodded solemnly.

"You have to be more careful the next time," she added. "No soccer balls in the house."

He nodded again. Then he drew his small hand toward her face, cautiously lifting a veil of blond hair from her temple, revealing a purple contusion blooming above her high cheekbone. "You hafta be more careful too, Mommy."

Her shiny, crystal-blue eyes welled up in tears.

"Grant?" He heard his name and tried to get his bearings. "Grant?" the male voice prompted again.

He found himself staring into Hunter's concerned hazel eyes, and he swallowed hard, surreptitiously glancing next to him at Sophie, who appeared equally alarmed.

"Looks like you're deep in thought," Hunter observed, wondering what traumatic memory his client might have been re-experiencing.

"Yes, sir," Grant responded in a trembling voice. He clamped his teeth together. They were both still staring at him, and he felt panicked as the heaviness of shame weighed down on his chest. "I was, uh, just thinking—" he nodded toward the drawing of stacked circles "—that, um, enmeshment doesn't sound all that bad in a romantic relationship. Two people on top of each other, I mean."

Grant's nervous chuckle was met by dead silence and a palpable awkwardness in the room. Evidently his lame attempt to divert attention away from his sadness wasn't fooling the two psychologists studying him suspiciously. He stole a glance at Sophie and found her looking back at him with such concentrated sympathy that he felt a catch in his throat, a wellspring of emotion threatening to erupt.

Instinctively Sophie sidled up next to him on the sofa and wrapped her arm around his waist, her hand resting exactly where he'd been bruised as a five-year-old. She looked him directly in the eye and confessed, "I love you."

Her comfort felt like a gift, and he lifted his arm to drape it across her shoulders, mindful of her injury.

Sophie didn't care if she was rescuing him again. It felt right to be there for him in this moment, and she nestled the back of her head into his shoulder.

As the tension drained from Grant's body, Hunter watched the two with a degree of wistfulness. Their harmony was a welcome relief from the heated arguments that sometimes occurred between partners in his office, yet he knew it wouldn't be all sunshine and peace ahead for them as they delved into deeper topics.

Clearing his throat, Hunter said, "So, let's discuss the third type of relationship, okay?" He drew two overlapping circles. "The *interdependent* relationship looks like a Venn diagram. It's when you have independent parts of yourself, but also this overlapping area which represents shared interests, caring, time spent together. Each partner has responsibility for his or her own feelings. Conflict is normal, and the partners may resolve their conflicts with language like 'I'm concerned when you don't call' or 'I feel angry when you leave your dirty clothes on the chair.'"

"Hey, you said something like that to me once!" Grant pointed out, squeezing her shoulder.

"I did?" Sophie looked up at him.

"Yeah, on the ship—do you remember? You said, 'I'm angry that you're acting aloof.'"

Sophie sat up a little more, though she remained glued to her boyfriend's side. "No, I said I was *hurt* that you were acting aloof."

"Oh, right," Grant agreed amicably.

"Great job, Sophie!" Hunter cheered. "You practiced the assertive communication we discussed."

Blushing, she murmured, "It wasn't that big of a deal."

"Yes, it was," Hunter said. "It's really hard to break old habits. How did you react when she said that to you, Grant?"

He shrugged. "I, um, I realized I'd been acting like a jerk. We talked, and I...kissed her."

"Sounds like it worked out pretty well." Hunter smirked, watching them both blush.

Sophie laughed. "Yeah, and then we got caught kissing by our PO!" She felt Grant's chuckle rumble deep in his chest.

When their laughter died down, Hunter asked, "What do you think of these different types of relationships?"

"Is the enmeshed one, is that, um, bad?" Grant asked.

"Well, I don't know if it's *bad,* but it doesn't tend to work as effectively as the interdependent relationship, at least in our Western culture. Perhaps in more collectivist societies, enmeshment would work okay." Hunter gave them an inquisitive look. "So, which of these three best represent your family relationships?"

Sophie and Grant scrutinized the different circles. Surprised to find himself interested in what Hunter had talked about, Grant silently concluded that he was distant from his father and enmeshed with his mother. The same way Sophie seemed to be with her parents. But Grant wondered if he'd also been enmeshed with his father at times. He deeply wished Enzo's approval—or disapproval, actually—didn't matter so much to him. With a pang of guilt, he realized his relationship with Logan had likely been distant as well. Was his entire family doomed?

"Oh!" Grant blurted. "I, um, I think my relationship with Uncle Joe is interdependent."

"Go on," Hunter encouraged.

"Well, he's always been there for me, but he doesn't pressure me. It's like he trusts me."

Sophie smiled, pleased that Grant was immersing himself in their psychological discussion. He'd shared the nautical environment with her on Roger's ship, and now she was sharing her world with him.

"Joe's support must mean a lot to you," Hunter said. "Do you have any other interdependent relationships in your life, Grant?"

"Um, not really. Is it possible to get interdependence if you don't have it now?"

"Perhaps. Who do you want an interdependent relationship with?"

Grant blushed slightly. "Sophie. Well, maybe we already have one—I'll let you shrinks figure it out."

Sophie and Hunter exchanged amused looks.

"And Ben, my nephew. He's really struggling right now, and I want to be there for him the way Joe was there for me.'"

"He must be really grieving, huh?" Sophie asked softly.

Grant nodded. "I caught him smoking pot last week."

She inhaled sharply. "Pot? Isn't he only like fourteen?"

Shaking his head, Grant smiled. "He looks young, but he's actually sixteen. Sixteen going on thirty."

"So you're trying to figure out how to be a good parent figure to Ben?" Hunter asked.

"Yes, sir."

Tapping on his drawing of an interdependent relationship, Hunter said, "Actually, this Venn diagram can relate to good parenting too. If you look at this circle as warmth, or caring, and the other circle as firmness, or discipline, you want to achieve the intersection of these two circles for the best parenting: a combination of warmth and firmness. If you only have warmth, then you're too permissive, and if you only have firmness, you're too authoritarian. So try to combine caring and discipline, and you should do a good job with Ben."

"Yes, sir."

Hunter didn't enjoy feeling like he was lecturing. While he wracked his brain for a way to encourage Grant to think for himself instead of robotically following his advice, Sophie interjected, "Grant, what kind of parenting did Carlo get?"

Grant looked taken aback. After several moments, he said, "I don't think Uncle Angelo ever punished him. He got away with a lot."

"I thought so," Sophie replied. Turning to Hunter, she asked, "Isn't it true that children of permissive parents are at risk for antisocial behavior as adults? Just like children of authoritarian parents are more likely to be anxious as adults?"

"Yes, and yes, and I'm kind of surprised at how easily you can talk about him."

"Who, Carlo?" Sophie replied. "The total fucking bastard who's writhing in the depths of hell right now?"

Hunter stifled a grin. "That's more like it."

Sophie smiled, but Grant appeared uneasy, still feeling guilty about killing a man. He was the one who'd shot that "total fucking bastard."

Hunter glanced at his watch. "We're out of time. Good job today. We'll keep working on that interdependent relationship between you two. See you next week."

As they exited through the waiting room, Grant gently clasped Sophie's right wrist, stopping her. A mischievous light danced in his eyes. "Screw interdependence. Wanna go get enmeshed?"

"I thought you'd never ask, McSailor." She aimed a devilish grin his way and they walked out, arm in arm.

4. Confound

Grant jumped slightly when he felt his pocket vibrate. He waited until Officer Stone looked down to rifle through some papers before he stealthily withdrew his mobile from the pocket of his jacket. Peeking at the phone, he read the awaiting text message:

Ms. Broccoli loves you

A bright grin erupted as he stole a coy glance at Sophie, finding her mischievous brown eyes alight with mirth. She'd cast aside her arm sling just yesterday and was apparently capitalizing on having both hands free to type.

"I still haven't received verification from your doctor—"

Jerry halted his statement midstream to look back and forth between the parolees sitting across the desk from him. They were both trying to suppress laughter, and he was immediately pissed off that their little private joke prevented them from focusing on the matter at hand. "What the hell's going on between you two?"

Grant cleared his throat and casually removed his hand from his pocket. "Nothing, sir."

Narrowing his eyes, Jerry glared at the shiny black Chicago White Sox jacket and growled, "You got some balls wearing that jacket in here, Madsen."

Satisfied when Grant appeared duly admonished, he turned to Sophie. "As I was saying, Taylor, I haven't heard from that doctor at the hospital verifying the narcotics prescription. You did test positive for opiates on August tenth, and I need that documentation from your doctor to clear you."

Sophie nodded solemnly as Grant's right hand surreptitiously slipped back into his pocket. "I'll call Northwestern again, Jerry. I already reminded them twice, but you know how hospitals work, right?"

Jerry sighed. This young woman was so endearing to him, even though she seemed up to something at the moment. Gruffly he said, "I want that documentation by the time we meet next week, got it?"

"Yes, sir," she responded, feeling a twinge of anger toward Grant for egging Jerry on to make her take the drug test in the first place. Her anger quickly morphed to anticipation, however, when she felt a vibration in the pocket of her jeans.

"Now, Madsen, I know the architectural cruises stop running in September, so what're you doing about securing employment?"

As Jerry focused his attention on Grant, Sophie carefully glanced down at her cell phone.

Ms. Broccoli and I both agree: the Cubs suck! ☺

She then stared dutifully at Jerry while one corner of her mouth twitched.

There was a knock on the door, further irritating their PO.

"Enter!" he hollered.

Detective Marilyn Fox of the Great Lakes Police Department poked her head inside the office. "Hey, Jerry, I was just in town—" Her mouth dropped open as she recognized the two parolees craning their necks to see who was at the door.

"Ms. Taylor! Mr. Madsen!" Marilyn cried, stepping into the office.

Jerry popped out of his chair and made his way over to Marilyn, and Grant stood as well.

"Ma'am," Grant acknowledged with a shy grin. He felt immensely grateful to Marilyn for believing him and fighting for him after the incident with Carlo.

"Good to s-s-see you, Detective," Jerry stammered, awkwardly stuffing his hands into his pockets as he sidled up to the petite, red-haired woman.

Studying her parole officer's nervous body language, Sophie slowly rose out of her chair and nodded to the detective. "How've you been, Marilyn?"

Marilyn's green eyes sparkled. "I've been great. I see you're out of the sling?"

"Since yesterday." Sophie smiled. Though occasionally there was still lingering pain from her gunshot wound, the most potent reminder of the trauma was a raised circular scar of destroyed flesh above her left elbow. She'd only been able to look at the wound once, and the vivid mark of Carlo's evil had been so upsetting that she'd vowed immediately never to look at it again.

Jerry lowered his voice, and Sophie could barely hear him tell Marilyn, "I didn't know you'd be back in town so soon."

Sophie's eyes widened with realization, and she looked to see if Grant had also caught on, but he appeared quite detached at the moment. His eyes were vacant and his expression despondent. He seemed to enter this trance any time her injury was mentioned. He was once again mired in guilt.

Instead of whispering to him, Sophie drew out her iPhone and began typing a message. Given Jerry's befuddled state, she could get away with practically anything at the moment.

Once again flinching when his phone vibrated—he frequently felt on edge these days—Grant reached into his pocket while turning to Sophie. The look in his eyes slowly transformed as she drew his focus to the present. He was returning to her from wherever he'd just been. Grant read her text message:

Jer has the hots for Mar

He looked up, startled. "Really?" he whispered, and she nodded conspiratorially.

Grant saw the two officers in a new light. Detective Fox *did* seem to be blushing a bit as she spoke to Officer Stone. As he analyzed her expression, she suddenly turned her intense gaze toward him and inquired, "Mr. Madsen, have you heard anything from Mr. Barberi?"

At first Sophie was quite confused, wondering how Logan, who was dead, could possibly contact his brother. Then she realized Marilyn was asking about Grant's Uncle Angelo.

"No, ma'am."

"Nothing? No threats against your life if you don't commit a crime?"

"Thankfully no, ma'am."

"I'd hope you learned your lesson the first time," she said severely.

Grant nodded guiltily. He knew she'd never understand why he hadn't gone to the police when Logan and Carlo had threatened Joe's life more than two years ago.

Sophie appeared puzzled. "What do you mean 'the first time'?"

Marilyn shot Grant a look. "You haven't told her about the circumstances of your arrest?"

Grant squirmed a bit. "No, ma'am. It's not—it's not something I like to discuss. It's in the past." He didn't voice his additional hesitations, such as the fact that both men who'd threatened him were now dead, and he had no proof that the threat had occurred in the first place. When he'd told Detective Fox and Uncle Joe he'd been forced to commit the crime, he'd been surprised by their immediate acceptance of his story. Why would anyone believe a man born into the Barberi family?

Jerry knew he had only a few minutes before his next parolee arrived, and he wanted to spend at least one of those minutes privately with Marilyn, so he broke the silence to move things along. "Madsen's brother and cousin threatened his uncle's life unless he helped them steal some cash," he told Sophie.

Watching her struggle to absorb that information, Grant added, "Logan gambled away some money to a Navy officer, and they needed my help to break into a bar near the base and get it back. He told me…" Grant looked down. "Logan told me he and Carlo would kill Joe unless I did it."

He remembered the resignation in his brother's deep blue eyes as he'd forced the gun into his hand and sent him off into that bar. *Anything bad goes down in there, you don't know who I am, got it?* Logan's words echoed in Grant's head, and indeed, he hadn't known Logan at that moment. What had happened to the benevolent older brother who protected him and their mother from their abusive father?

Sophie was dumbfounded. "That's—that's how you got arrested for aggravated robbery? You were trying to protect Joe?"

Grant exhaled loudly. "Yeah, but I screwed up and got caught." He gave a fake smile, one which conveyed sadness more than anything. "And now—" he gestured to the parole office "—here I am."

Sophie slowly leaned against the wall, stunned and absolutely hating that his family had taken him down like that. Grant Madsen hadn't belonged in prison at all. Grasping that Logan had put both of them behind bars, she felt more connected to Grant than ever.

Sophie tentatively stepped forward, not caring at all that they had an audience. "I'm so sorry," she murmured, her eyes locking on his before she gently wrapped her arms around his waist and rested her cheek on his chest. Tears sprang to her eyes. She'd just learned of one *more* occasion

Grant could have been killed by his destructive family, and she felt pure gratitude that he was still alive.

Grant felt her nestle into him, smelled her clean lavender scent, and automatically enveloped her into his arms. They clung to each other tightly while Marilyn and Jerry looked away, suddenly fascinated by the details of the dingy room.

"It's okay," Grant rasped in her ear, so quietly only she could hear. "I found you."

He felt her body shake with sobs and held her even tighter.

After a few moments, Jerry's wistful expression hardened as he cleared his throat. "Christ, Taylor, are you crying again?"

Sophie released Grant and backed away, keeping her head down and sniffing. As Jerry reached over to get her some tissues, she asked, "What is it about your office that always makes me cry?"

"It's because Jerry's such a teddy bear," Marilyn supplied with a smirk.

Jerry gave her a lighthearted scowl in return.

Grant took notice of that exchange. They really did seem to be lovebirds.

As Sophie wiped her eyes she felt her phone vibrate once more in her pocket. When had Grant managed to type this message? But when she looked at the phone, her face fell.

"Great," she said. "My dad's calling again. I *must* have encountered mortal danger in the hour since his last call, so he needs to check up on me."

"Just don't tell him you're anywhere near me, and he'll be fine," Grant said.

Marilyn was thinking the same thing. Will Taylor hadn't been too pleased with her for helping Grant avoid a return to prison.

Jerry glanced at his watch and began to herd the two toward the door. "Time's up," he growled. "See you next week."

"He sounds like Hunter," Sophie said as they stepped into the hallway. "Like we're leaving a therapy session."

"Nope." Grant shook his head. "We don't have therapy again for six days." He looked at his watch, adding, "Six days, twelve minutes, and fifteen seconds to be precise."

She laughed. "You're *really* looking forward to our next session, aren't you?"

Having just relived one painful scene from his past in the parole office, Grant was hardly eager for more of the same with Dr. Hayes. He sighed, draping his arm across Sophie's neck and giving her shoulder a squeeze. "Can't wait, Bonnie."

❧

"He's gonna be in a fucking cage," Angelo Barberi snarled at the corrections officer who was frisking him a bit too eagerly and thoroughly. "You think I can fit a weapon through a five-centimeter hole in the grating?"

The officer finished patting him down and gave a tight smile. "I wouldn't put anything past you greasy wops." He gave Angelo a shove into the visitation room. "You got fifteen minutes."

Angelo angrily adjusted his shirt and tried to suppress the urge to turn around and beat the shit out of that fucking zit-faced co, who looked all of twenty years old but acted like he owned the goddamned place. He *hated* visiting Gurnee, especially since his acquittal on extortion and racketeering charges five years ago. The trial had been quite public, and law enforcement was still seeking payback for Angelo's *Get Out of Jail Free* card. He hated coming here, but he knew he *had* to be here.

He strolled past the open tables where cons were reuniting with loved ones and headed to a caged area off to the side, reserved for the most violent offenders. A child-killer like his brother certainly fit that description. Truth be told, Angelo was relieved that Enzo would be enclosed in a cage. The metal barrier definitely worked in Angelo's favor, given what they needed to discuss. He'd witnessed his older brother's insatiable rage on multiple occasions, and he preferred to make it out of Gurnee alive today.

He took a seat outside the cage and awaited the arrival of the prisoner. Feeling rather tense, he sucked in some deep breaths, which led to a coughing fit.

Angelo was still coughing when two COs led Enzo Barberi into the cage, the chains of his Y-cuff rattling as he shuffled forward. In contrast to the small patches of gray coloring Angelo's temples, Enzo's hair had gone completely gray. But they were still the same height—a little over six feet—with matching black eyes. Those two pairs of eyes now stared each other down.

After plopping their chained prisoner on the wooden bench, the COs backed out of the cage. "Have a nice visit, Barberi," one of them scoffed.

Angelo was shocked when he did not hear an immediate "Fuck you" come out of his brother's mouth. Instead, Enzo ignored the comment and studied his brother. Something had definitely changed.

"You look like shit" were the prisoner's first words.

"I was just about to say the same to you," Angelo responded, noticing that the gray of his brother's hair seemed to have leached into his ashen complexion. "How long you been out of the hole?"

"Just got out this morning," Enzo bitterly replied. "Fucking warden. Figures the CO I punched was the warden's motherfucking private pet. Twenty-two years. I've been on the inside for twenty-two years, and that's the first time I've been in the hole. It better be the fucking last time too."

Angelo winced. He'd heard that Enzo struck a guard upon learning his son Logan had been murdered, and if he'd just been released from solitary, he probably hadn't learned the identity of the killer yet.

"You should up the ante with the guards," Enzo commanded. "I'm not getting the same preferential treatment I'm used to."

"Uh, Enzo, business ain't so great lately. I'm not sure if we can swing it. We're already forking over five hundred a month to each of those assholes."

Enzo narrowed his eyes and Angelo coughed a few times. "What do you mean 'business ain't so great'?"

Clearing his throat, Angelo admitted, "We're having a few, uh, *personnel* problems."

Enzo clenched his fists, and his brother could see he was trying to control his reaction. Leaning forward, Enzo fumed, "You find Logan's killer, Ange. Find him and…" His teeth clenched. "Find him, cut off his dick, and shove it down his fucking throat."

Having no idea how to respond to this order, Angelo sat frozen, so his brother continued speaking, his voice low and tight. "Do you know how fucking miserable it is to be locked up in this shit-dump while my son's murderer goes free? To be stuck in here while some cocky son of a bitch struts around town, thinking he can pull one over on *me?*"

Angelo slowly raised his eyes to meet the belligerent gaze of his brother. "Logan's murderer did not go free," he said quietly.

Enzo lunged forward, then sprung back, recoiling as his chains restrained him. "You caught him? You got Logan's killer?"

Angelo had no choice but to avert his eyes, sickened to be the one to deliver the news. With palpable waves of fury and anticipation coming through the metal grating, Angelo could wait no longer. "It was Carlo."

A stunned silence blanketed the cage. Enzo had endured some horrendous incidents in his lifetime, but even he succumbed to shocked stupor upon hearing Angelo's confession. Was he telling the truth? He wouldn't lie about this, would he? When Enzo could finally speak again, his voice was controlled. "Your son…killed my son? Carlo killed my boy?"

Angelo nodded, still not meeting Enzo's eyes.

"Look at me, you fuck."

Angelo obeyed his older brother, finding Enzo seething now, the control in his voice long gone.

"Your son Carlo—the reason I've been locked up in this shithole for twenty-two years—he m-m-murdered my son."

Gulping, Angelo confirmed, "Yes."

"*Why?*"

The one-word question was so vehement, so forceful, that Angelo found himself flinching, despite the protective cage.

"I—I'm not sure. He was always jealous of Logan—you know that." Angelo sighed loudly, defeated. "There was something wrong with Carlo from the start. I…" his voice dropped off "…I didn't raise him so good."

Enzo shook his head disgustedly. "You think just because I saved Carlo once, I won't retaliate this time? This is my son's *life* we're talking about, Ange. You better fucking hope you can protect that little sniveling bastard—"

"He's already dead," Angelo interrupted.

"Carlo's dead?" Enzo asked, his eyes narrowing. "Did you kill him?"

Angelo's eyes widened. He could never kill his own son! His flesh and blood! His cheeks colored, remembering how he'd detested the reminders of Carlo's screw-ups, how many times he'd wished his son was gone. Now Carlo *was* gone, and Angelo felt no reprieve. All that was left was remorse.

Finally Angelo answered. "It wasn't me who killed him. It was… Grant."

Enzo's jaw went slack, and his face whitened. He remembered Grant on his first day at Gurnee: dressed in prison blues, his defiant bravado completely failing to hide his fear at facing his father.

Then he flashed back to those big, sky-blue eyes framed by a chubby little face, looking up at him through glassy tears. Half-drunk, Enzo had towered unsteadily over the boy with a folded belt in his hand. Grant pleaded in a small, strained voice, *Please, Dad. Please, no more. I'll be good. I promise.*

Enzo shuddered.

"Do the cops know?"

Angelo nodded.

"Why isn't Grant back inside then?"

"It was self-defense. Carlo came after a couple of girls, and Grant intervened. They, uh, apparently wrestled for the gun, and it went off. Carlo got shot in the chest."

This didn't sound like his younger son at all. This didn't sound like behavior the fucking pansy Joe Madsen would approve of. "Did Grant—did he know Carlo killed Logan?"

Angelo nodded guiltily. Despite himself, Enzo felt pride blooming in his chest. His son, formerly an utter waste, had exacted revenge for Logan's death. Grant had taken care of business more expertly than Enzo's own men, swiftly seeking justice while neatly keeping himself out of prison. Enzo was impressed.

"You give Grant a message from me," Enzo ordered, and Angelo listened intently. "You tell him I want to see him. I need to talk to him. And if you so much as *touch* him for what he did to Carlo…"

"I already told Joe Madsen I wouldn't retaliate."

Enzo's face flushed a crimson red. "Who the fuck cares about Joe Madsen? You promise *me* you won't touch my son, and that's all that matters."

"It's done," Angelo replied succinctly, suddenly overwhelmed by sadness. "Carlo deserved what he got."

As the announcement blared that visitation was over, the two COs unlocked the cage and hauled Enzo to his feet. "Tell Grant I want to see him," Enzo reiterated as he was led away.

Angelo tiredly shuffled to the parking lot, Enzo's parting words ringing in his ears. There'd be no way in hell Grant would willingly visit his father.

As he eased into his car, Angelo glanced at his reflection in the rearview mirror. Enzo was right. He *did* look like shit.

❧

"Is that wind?" Sophie inquired over the phone. "Are you outside?"

"I'm at a construction site," Will Taylor lied. Glancing around him at the neat rows of headstones, he continued trudging toward his destination.

"At least it's a warm wind," she said.

"Yes, the Windy City's much more tolerable in the summer," he agreed. "Listen, honey, I know you have to get back to work, but I just wanted to check on you."

"Dad, I'm fine."

He bit his lip, and his grip tightened on his cell phone. Unable to control himself, he blurted, "You're not spending too much time with Grant, are you?"

She sighed wearily. "I just saw him at our PO's. You do realize we're living together, right?"

"You know you're always welcome in my house. You'd have much more room."

"We've been through this before." Sophie felt her throat tighten. She didn't want to end this conversation with yelling once again. "I have to go," she said coldly.

"Okay," he reluctantly agreed as he arrived at Laura's plot. They exchanged hasty goodbyes, and he folded his phone. He squatted next to his wife's grave and tapped the phone to his forehead with one hand. A sense of dread consumed him. "Please, God," he whispered, bowing his head. "Please keep Sophie safe."

All he heard was the faint howl of a breeze rustling through the ash trees lining the graveyard. Glancing at her headstone, he spoke quietly. "I'm sorry, Laura. It's my fault. I'm so sorry."

He remained huddled near her grave for several minutes before the shrill ring of the phone interrupted his reverie. When he saw the caller ID, he stopped breathing.

Reluctantly flipping open his phone, he listened for a moment, then nodded grimly. "You'll have your money," he pledged. "I've learned my lesson. I'll never forget again."

5. Confession

"Wow, that was fast!" Sophie's hand shot into her purse as she heard the soft bell indicating she had a text message. "I didn't even notice you typing."

Grant smiled proudly. "Ben's working with me during breaks on the ship. That kid's texting skills are amazing."

"How *is* your nephew?"

Grant sighed. "He's your typical teenager: rude, lazy, and exasperating."

Sophie frowned for a moment, then giggled as she read his message, remembering the day they'd traded hotdog puns at the baseball game.

Are your buns warm?

Grinning, she leaned in to him and murmured "McSailor's got mad skills too" before planting a soft kiss on his temple. Grant cupped her chin in his hand and brought her lips to his own. Then, out of the corner of his eye, he noticed a blond man step into the room.

Grant straightened up in his chair and nodded to Hunter, who smirked and shook his head.

"I've *never* seen so much PDA from a couple in counseling," their therapist said.

The couple in question rose from their chairs, a soft blush forming on Sophie's high cheekbones, and accompanied Hunter down the hall.

"But I bet you've never seen a couple mandated for therapy as a condition of their parole either," said Sophie.

"That's true." Hunter opened his office door and the three took their seats. "It's actually nice to see some loving affection, as opposed to partners screaming at each other all the time." An added bonus was that every time he witnessed Grant caressing or kissing Sophie, Hunter's attraction dissipated slightly. Grant was undoubtedly heterosexual, which comforted him.

"So we're doing okay, then?" Sophie asked, turning her gaze to Hunter.

"I'd say your relationship is doing more than okay," he said, "especially given all of the traumas you've gone through."

Grant felt a rush of relief course through him. He didn't know why the psychologist's opinion mattered so much—Grant was still a bit suspicious of this therapy thing—but his relationship with Sophie meant the world to him, and it was quite reassuring to receive the shrink's stamp of approval.

Nodding toward Sophie's left arm, Hunter gave her a warm smile. "It's great to see the sling gone." He glanced at Grant, who also seemed happy the reminder of the gunshot wound had vanished. "So, how's it been going?" Hunter inquired. "Have you two been practicing an interdependent relationship?"

A pink color spread on Grant's olive skin and Sophie emitted a tiny giggle.

"I think you might've made a better case for an enmeshed relationship," said Sophie with a laugh. "At least by Grant's definition of enmeshed—the partners lying one on top of the other."

"Sophie!" Grant looked mortified, his cheeks now crimson.

She laughed again. "It's okay, Grant. It's okay to talk about sex in therapy." She looked to Hunter for confirmation. "Right, Hunter?"

"Absolutely." He nodded, trying to ignore the stirring below his belt as Grant blushed adorably like a schoolboy. He was so damn cute! "Sex is an important part of any relationship."

Hearing those words out loud, his thoughts drifted to Bradley and the steamy session they'd enjoyed last evening. Suddenly Hunter felt better about his arousal. "Sex inevitably comes up in couples counseling."

"We have to talk about sex in *here?*" Grant asked, horrified. "With *you?*"

"Surely you've talked about sex with other guys before," Hunter reasoned. "You were in the Navy, for heaven's sake."

"Well…um, yeah," Grant stuttered unconvincingly. "But they weren't…" He squirmed in his seat. "No offense, sir, but they weren't gay."

Hunter was taken aback. He desperately hoped Grant hadn't picked up on his attraction. Flustered, his gaze darted about the room before landing on Sophie.

"I'm sorry, Hunter," she said in a tight voice. When both men looked at her with puzzled expressions, she continued. "I'm sorry for Grant's homophobic comment."

"I'm not homophobic!" Grant insisted. "I just don't want to discuss my sex life with my damn shrink, okay?"

Hunter was reeling. There were about one hundred potential directions to take this conversation, and he hoped the one he started with would be therapeutic. Still muddled by the very personal nature of his feelings toward Grant, he decided to address Sophie first.

"Hold on, Sophie. You're apologizing to me for Grant's comment?"

"Yes, I thought it was very *disrespectful.*" Her last word was directed at her boyfriend, who now appeared rather nervous about her obvious disappointment in him.

"I see. So you're responsible for the words coming out of his mouth, then?" Hunter asked.

"But—I—he—" She halted, looking flummoxed, then let out her breath in a loud sigh. "Shit. I'm caretaking again, aren't I?"

Hunter's grin eased the tension in the room. Grant glanced back and forth between them, trying to keep up. Eventually he spoke. "I apologize if I've insulted you, sir."

"No offense taken, Grant," Hunter assured him. "You've never known a gay man before?"

Grant looked at the floor. "I don't think so, sir."

"How's that possible?" Sophie interjected. Gay men were everywhere.

"It seems *Don't Ask, Don't Tell* is a rather effective policy," Hunter responded. "Plus, many kids get the message from their religion or their family that homosexuality is wrong—a sin. I'm guessing a Catholic Mafia family would launch a full-out attack on anyone who appeared remotely gay?"

Fucking faggot. Grant didn't remember when or why his father had spit out those vitriolic words, but they immediately popped into his head. He nodded guiltily.

Sophie thought for a moment before admitting, "I guess my dad's hardly the champion of gay rights either."

Hunter tilted his head and scrutinized his clients.

Grant turned away until Hunter began speaking to him.

"The good news is that one of the best ways to reduce prejudice is to get to know a diversity of people, which can break through stereotypes. Obviously we can't be friends since we've entered into a therapeutic relationship, but perhaps this'll be an opportunity to learn a bit about homosexuality, if you like. I'll certainly do my best to answer any questions you have."

"How are you so non-defensive about this?" Sophie demanded. "Doesn't it hurt your feelings that some people refuse to accept your sexual orientation?"

Stroking his chin pensively, Hunter said, "I used to get really riled up about it, and sometimes I still do. But I've also learned, after fifteen years of counseling, that people have reasons for what they do. I may not like it when a client has a different way of looking at the world than I do, but fortunately I get a glimpse of understanding. Surely when you were doing therapy you had the opportunity to appreciate what motivated your clients to behave in seemingly bizarre ways?"

She twirled a strand of strawberry-blond hair, contemplating what he said. She'd certainly grasped why Logan was so reticent and mistrustful. His father had simply beaten the trust out of him. "I guess so," she softly agreed.

"Let's try to understand each other more, then," Hunter suggested. "Now that your ridiculous pact is a thing of the past, how about you two ask each other some questions to get to know each other better? Find out what makes the other tick."

Sophie found herself bursting with questions, and she had no problem being the first to take Hunter up on his suggestion. She turned to Grant, picking up on a comment he made earlier. "So, you didn't talk about sex much with your buddies?"

He shrugged. "There wasn't much to discuss."

"What do you mean? I'm sure you were the big stud. You must have lots of stories."

Grant's face colored as he realized the conversation was taking an undesirable turn. He'd be embarrassed as hell if she learned about his lack of sexual prowess. Trying to throw out something, anything to satisfy her, he mumbled, "I, um, I had some girlfriends when I lived on the base, but I didn't exactly want to deflower the daughters of Navy officers—not if I wanted to live."

Hunter grinned and Sophie asked, "What about in college?"

Damn. Apparently she was going to ask more questions. "Uh, I dated one girl in ROTC."

"What was her name?"

That question seemed safe enough. "Pamela."

Sophie easily slipped into interrogation mode. "Did you have sex with her?"

Grant's eyes pleaded with Hunter to rescue him, but the psychologist stayed quiet, sporting a neutral facial expression. He wanted to hear this as well.

Finally Grant responded. "Yes, but we broke up our senior year."

Sophie considered his answer. "You were both in ROTC — were you ordered to go to different assignments?"

"No, this was before we were deployed. She…" He looked down, nervously clenching his hands together. "She wanted to meet my family. I couldn't let that happen."

"Oh." Sophie bit her lip, not knowing what to say. She looked to Hunter, who nodded at her, seeming to encourage her to continue. He liked it when couples talked to each other instead of through him, as long as the communication was constructive. And considering their ongoing trust issues, Hunter believed they needed to put it all out on the table.

"So, what happened to Pamela?" Sophie asked tentatively. "Should I be worried about her?" she added lightly.

Grant didn't smile. "She's married. I read about it in the Notre Dame alumni magazine." *I'd be married too,* he thought, *if only I came from a different family.*

"Phew," Sophie responded, exaggeratedly wiping her brow.

This did bring a slight grin to Grant's face, though it faded quickly upon hearing her next question:

"How about after college? I bet you had tons of girlfriends."

Once again he blushed furiously. Unable to speak, he simply shook his head.

Sophie's lips parted with disbelief. "Grant Madsen, are you lying to me? You're telling me you've only had sex with one woman?"

"Thanks for rubbing it in," Grant commented ruefully before narrowing his eyes at Hunter. "This therapy thing is *great.*"

"No, I'm not trying to make fun of you!" Sophie protested, suddenly feeling a little nervous about her own more-extensive sexual history. She gazed at him endearingly. "I simply adore that you have no idea how damn hot you are."

Hunter agreed. He adored Grant's modesty too. *Bradley, Bradley, Bradley*, he silently repeated, attempting to focus.

She caressed Grant's strong jaw, eagerly leaning in to him. Facing her on the sofa, he drew her even closer for a loving kiss.

"I also find your lack of experience hard to believe," she added, her face inches from his, "since you're so magnificent in bed." They smiled through their next kiss.

Bradley, Bradley, Bradley…

"And how do *you* know I'm skilled in bed?" Grant retorted, pulling back from the kiss and shooting her an expectant look.

Now Sophie turned to Hunter, hoping for assistance, but he just smiled. "Turnabout is fair play, Sophie."

She scowled. Grant derived great pleasure from the story of her first boyfriend, Derek Bowden, her father's former employee who'd failed a drug test at the construction company. "So I'm not the only boyfriend your father's disapproved of?"

"Oh-ho-ho," Sophie replied, shaking her head and chuckling. "You're certainly not alone in that. My father's disapproved of every single boyfriend I've ever had — except the almost-boyfriend he didn't know about."

"And who would that be?" Grant inquired.

Sophie realized she'd spoken before thinking. She had no desire to share the tale of falling for her married grad-school professor with Grant, though he'd answered all of *her* probing questions.

She glanced up, finding a hint of amusement in his shining blue eyes. "Well, it wasn't really a relationship," she began. "More like a schoolgirl crush on my professor that was very one-sided, as I embarrassingly discovered after confessing my love for him. God, I was such an idiot!"

Grant watched her berate herself, and he wondered how on earth a man could have turned her down.

"He was married," she finally admitted, examining Grant's expression for disapproval, but finding only surprise.

Now Grant wondered why such a beautiful, fascinating woman would need to throw herself at a married man.

"He *is* married," she amended, looking at Hunter. "Did I tell you I have the *pleasure* of working with him now?"

Hunter quirked his eyebrows. "Your professor is still at DePaul?"

Grant felt his stomach twist. Sophie's former crush was working with her every day? Why hadn't he heard about this before?

"Yeah," she confirmed. "David Alton's still there. He's Kirsten's advisor, of all things. And her dissertation defense is coming up, so I'll be seeing a lot of him, I'm afraid. At least I don't have to be on Kirsten's committee."

Grant's voice was not as steady as he'd hoped. "Your professor — Dr. Alton, is it?" When Sophie nodded, he continued, "Why did you like him?"

She bit her lip. "I don't know, Grant… It was over five years ago! David just had this suave, older-man thing going on —"

"How old is he?"

"Almost fifty, I think."

Grant's jaw dropped. He didn't want to ask his next question but knew he must. "Do you still like him?"

"No!" She watched his expression carefully. "What are you thinking? Do you think I'm an awful person?"

"No." His response was just as emphatic. "I'm just trying to wrap my mind around how a woman as beautiful as you would be attracted to these losers."

His compliment made tears prickle at the back of her eyes, and she didn't trust herself to speak.

Hunter jumped in. "That's exactly *my* question, Grant. Do you want to share the insights you've learned about your dating life, Sophie?"

She nodded and took a deep breath. "Hunter and I talked about the *losers* I've dated —" she aimed a small smile at Grant "— well, except for you, of course, and we figured out that I chose bad boys and older men to try to get back at my father. He's never approved of me, and I wanted to show him I didn't need *his* approval by deliberately picking partners he would hate. It's sick, really." She shrugged her shoulders in defeat.

"Hmm," Hunter broke in. "Seems like both of your families have had a negative influence on your dating lives. Grant didn't allow women to get close for fear they'd reject him because of his family, and Sophie intentionally chose partners so she could *keep* getting rejected by her family."

"Whoa." Grant sat still, absorbing Hunter's words. He gazed into Sophie's luminous brown eyes and found a deeper connection than before, if that was possible. Maybe this therapy thing wasn't so bad.

After a few moments of silence, Grant pressed on. "So, um, if nothing happened with Dr. Alton, what about after him? Were you with other men?"

Sophie suddenly seized up with fear. She'd been dreading this conversation for quite some time, and she had no idea how to begin answering his question. Her face felt hot, and she couldn't look at Grant.

"Hey," he said gently, taking her hand in his and stroking her forearm soothingly. "What's wrong, Sophie?"

"Please," she choked out, still gazing down. "Please don't make me tell you about Logan."

Grant abruptly dropped her hand and flinched away from her. "Logan?" he rasped. *Damn it!* How had he forgotten Sophie kissed his brother? He shook his head, trying to get that image out of his mind.

Sophie was shaking her head too, and tears threatened to erupt. "I can't see what good can come of this," she murmured, glancing at Hunter and stealing a peek at Grant. "I can't see what good can come from telling you I slept with your brother."

Grant gasped. "You had sex with Logan?"

Her head snapped up. "I thought you knew!" Her eyes widened as his face went pale. "I told you I behaved inappropriately with a client, remember?"

"You said you *kissed* him!" Grant roared, scooting farther away from her on the sofa.

Hunter felt his chest tighten as he watched the horrible scene unfold.

"I said I kissed him, and I…I did some other things too," she admitted, stinging tears now cascading down her face. She didn't want to hurt Grant—God, she didn't want to hurt him any more! His family had hurt him far enough.

"I was so ashamed," she cried. "I couldn't tell you what we'd done, but I thought you'd figured it out."

Grant took his head in his hands, anguished. Unable to contain himself, he popped off the sofa and began pacing around the room, feeling restless energy and a building pressure in his head that threatened to overwhelm him. He'd buried Logan! And now his brother felt very much alive again; his brother was still here to ruin his life. Logan's palpable presence in the room was immensely disturbing.

Finally, standing by the aquarium set into the wall, his back turned to both psychologists, Grant whispered, "How?"

Sophie wrung her slender hands. "How?" she repeated.

He spun around, and she was immediately frightened by the cold glint in his eyes. "How did it get to the point that you *fucked* my brother?"

Sophie inhaled sharply and drew her hand to her mouth, sobbing in earnest now. Sensing the waves of fury rolling off of Grant, Hunter carefully instructed, "Grant, take some deep breaths. You two will get through this."

The muscles lining Grant's jaw rippled with hostility, but he did struggle to slow his accelerated breathing. Lightning-hot anger coursed through his veins, making his skin tingle.

"You're frightening Sophie," Hunter said evenly, and Grant looked at him with surprise, seeming to shake himself out of a dissociated state. "I'd like you to take a seat."

Grant glanced at his girlfriend, who was almost hiccupping from crying so hard. "Yes, sir."

"Sophie, when you're ready, try to answer Grant's question, okay?"

She nodded and scooped up some tissues from the box he offered her.

There was another silence as both parolees looked down at their laps, lost in their own worlds of suffering. Now they didn't seem so different from most of the other couples Hunter saw. He hoped they could bridge the huge chasm that had developed between them.

Eventually Sophie had steadied herself enough to speak, though her voice still trembled. "I made so many mistakes, Grant," she began. "I told Logan too much about myself. I was initially attracted to him, and I should've referred him, but I didn't."

Hunter squirmed a bit in his chair as Sophie continued.

"Then he told me an awful story from his childhood, and I tried to comfort him. That's when I really screwed up. He…he kissed me, and I let him." She sniffed. "And that eventually led to…other things."

Grant clenched his fists. No wonder Logan had lied about where he met Sophie. If his brother had felt one-tenth the shame and anger Grant was currently experiencing in therapy, he wouldn't admit it to anyone. Grant was furious to still feel that ache inside him, thinking of his brother. He ached to be loved by Logan, a longing that would never be fulfilled.

"What story did he tell you?" Grant growled.

Sophie's eyes got big. "You don't want to hear it," she said, desperate not to hurt him further. "Let sleeping dogs lie."

"*What story?*" he yelled.

Sophie flinched.

Knowing precisely what Logan had told Sophie before he kissed her, Hunter hesitantly nodded at her, preparing for the onslaught.

Sophie pursed her lips and sniffed, glassy tears sliding down her pale skin. "He told me about a time when he was nine, and his, um, his younger brother was four. Please, Grant! I didn't know it was you! I hadn't even met you then!"

Grant clenched his teeth and looked off to the side, watching the fish swim in lazy circles. He couldn't look at her.

Taking a shuddering breath, she resumed, "Your dad had just beat up your mom, and he was striking you both with a belt. In the closet." Grant stopped breathing. "Logan said he tried to cover you so you wouldn't get hit, but your dad dragged him away to his room. And your dad, he…he left you in the closet all night."

Grant's face had gone white.

"The next morning…" Sophie could barely get the words out, she was sobbing so hard. "The next morning, your dad—he got y-y-you out of the closet, and when he saw that you, that you—" She was almost hyperventilating. "That you peed your pants, he…he b-b-beat you again."

So it was true then. It had really happened. Apparently he had truly pissed in his pants, just like a baby—just like his dad said he was. Grant felt numb, and he was swept away on a river of the past, waking up in a sterile white room with a kindly older gentleman explaining that he'd gone catatonic in his solitary cell. He'd peed all over himself once again, this time as an adult. But really like a baby.

The words sounded far off, like someone was calling for him. He felt like he was underwater as he heard his name repeated in slow motion. Like one of the fish in the nearby tank, he felt himself swimming to the surface agonizingly slowly. Blinking a few times, Grant found himself staring into Hunter's concerned face.

"Grant? I want to you focus on your breathing. Look around the room and tell me what you see."

Frantically, Grant felt beneath him and breathed out with relief when he touched the dry sofa cushion. He followed Hunter's order and began haltingly scanning the room around him. When his gaze landed on his girlfriend's gorgeous face, he took in her splotchy cheeks, stained with tears. But when he saw her eyes, his heart stopped. She looked at him with an expression of such raw pity—he knew he'd explode if he stayed one second longer.

With wild eyes, Grant leaped off the sofa and flew to the door, exiting the office with lightning speed. He couldn't care less if he'd be in trouble with Officer Stone for leaving the session early. He had to get out of there. Now.

The door slammed behind him with a bang, and Sophie sat stunned. "What just happened?" she asked.

Hunter sat back in his chair. He was wondering the same thing himself. Grant had obviously experienced some sort of trauma reaction, but there was something else — something he couldn't put his finger on. Hunter had the distinct impression Grant was hiding something. He glanced at Sophie worriedly, praying another Mafia man wouldn't destroy her once again.

6. Conflict

A rash of goose bumps prickled her alabaster skin, and Sophie set aside her textbook and climbed out of bed, padding over to the thermostat on the apartment wall. Now that it was late August, the daytime humidity gave way to increasingly cool nights, and it was hard to keep the temperature just right.

After setting the thermostat two degrees higher, she turned back toward the bed, rubbing her palms over her arms. Wincing, she glanced down at her left arm and extended it straight out, taking stock of the ugly scar above the elbow. Despite the summer heat, she'd been wearing long sleeves to hide the circular wound, but she only owned a couple of nightgowns, and they were sleeveless.

She sniffed as she crawled back into bed, realizing her sudden chill had nothing to do with room temperature and everything to do with dread about seeing Grant for the first time since he'd fled Hunter's office that morning. She had no idea what she'd say to him. After leaving him desperate voice messages all morning long, she'd finally received a text from him this afternoon:

At work. C u tonight.

Though curt, the message had relieved her immensely. She'd been worried his intense distress would cause him to do something stupid, but at least he'd made it to the architectural cruise; at least he wouldn't return to prison for failing to show up at work. But her trepidation remained over what would happen when they did "c" each other tonight.

Sighing, she returned to her *Theories of Personality* textbook, trying to stay one step ahead of the students she'd begin teaching next week. This chapter covered one of her favorite theorists, Alfred Adler, a contemporary of Freud. Born in 1870 in Vienna, Adler was the second of six children and often had to compete for his parents' affection, leading him to focus his own work on key concepts like sibling rivalry, birth order, and the inferiority complex.

As an only child, Sophie was intrigued by the role of siblings in personality development. She'd never been forced to fight over toys or felt jealous of siblings receiving more attention than her. On the contrary, she'd often craved siblings for the very reason of *deflecting* her parents' attention.

Adler's theory was that people who felt inferior typically behaved in a superior manner to hide their inadequacies. Reading this material with a fresh eye, Sophie immediately thought of Carlo Barberi. Upon taking his last breaths, Carlo had admitted to killing Logan, and then bitterly complained that his father, Angelo, had always loved Logan more than him. Carlo had acted cocky and brash, yet Sophie somehow knew that was to cover up his self-hatred.

Adler further argued that some people responded to feelings of inferiority by simply giving up hope, whereas others compensated by searching for a way to succeed despite earlier setbacks. Now that they'd emerged from prison, she hoped she and Grant would be in the latter category.

Thoroughly engrossed in her reading, it took Sophie a moment to realize someone was unlocking the apartment door. Once she heard the telltale soft steps on the carpeted hallway, she scrambled out of bed and tiptoed to the doorway of the bedroom to find Grant coming toward her. They both stopped short, and despite her nerves, Sophie was captivated by the way his light blue, short-sleeved uniform shirt brought out the gemstone hue of his tired, troubled eyes.

At the same time, Grant's weary eyes took in the sight of his girlfriend, blocking the entrance to their bedroom and wearing only a sheer nightie, which did nothing to conceal her hard nipples pressing against the burgundy silk. Her hair, looking more strawberry than blond next to the deep shade of the short nightgown, tumbled across her shoulders, and his eyes trailed down the length of her graceful, slender limbs. God, she was beautiful. Warily meeting her forceful gaze, he swallowed, finding his mouth dry. He was at a loss for words.

"Thank you for your text," she nervously began.

He nodded, embarrassed he hadn't responded earlier to her pleading voicemails. "Ben told me to stop being a tool and at least let you know I was okay."

She smiled as she imagined the teenager saying those words. "Did you tell Ben about our therapy session?"

He shook his head vehemently.

"Roger?"

Another shake. "I don't want to talk about it."

Noticing Sophie's frown, he seemed to make a decision, and he confidently brushed past her, heading for the bathroom.

Anxiously Sophie called after him, "I could make you something to eat?"

"No," he said harshly, and then guiltily turned to face her. In a softer voice, he added, "I grabbed a bite with Rog before the evening cruise. I just want to take a shower and go to bed."

Once he actually looked at her, the tension in her shoulders dissolved. But when he turned and closed the bathroom door in her face, the shred of hope that he'd forgive her quickly vanished. Miserably she returned to the bed, clenching her hands together before picking up the textbook once again. The words explaining the concept of sibling rivalry swam before her eyes and were then replaced by memories of angry accusations from that morning. *How did it get to the point that you* fucked *my brother?*

Her throat tightened, remembering Grant's wounded glare. Then her own halting words, *Your dad…he b-b-beat you.* She held her head in her hands and told herself not to cry.

Inside the bathroom, Grant angrily jerked the spigot and water pounded onto the porcelain tub with a most satisfying sound. The energy it had taken to sustain his pissed-off mood all day long had exhausted him, yet he was scared to allow the rage to dissipate, unsure of what maelstrom of emotions lay underneath. He fumbled for the buckle of his belt and slid the black trousers down from his lean waist. As he peeled off and discarded his sweaty clothing, he wished he could do the same for the horrifying images filling his brain.

Unfortunately, the time alone in the shower only sparked more ruminative thoughts, seeming to intensify the disturbing pictures: flashes of his brother's muscular back hovering over Sophie, humping her on some fucking therapy couch. Grant had earlier pictured her dressed in a professional suit, but now that image was replaced by the wine-colored nightgown he'd just seen. Logan laughed in his deep rumble as his big hands slid up her naked thighs, lifting up the nightie and sliding lacy underwear down her long legs. Sophie smiled lustily beneath him, urging him on with her characteristic moans. Grant balled his hands into fists as the gushing water streamed over his heaving chest.

He quickly turned off the shower and stepped out to yank a towel off the rack. His jaw clenched as drops of water dripped onto the tile. Sophie was *his,* goddamn it! Logan had already taken so much from him — how could his brother also have stolen the one and only good, pure, devoted thing left in his life? How could Logan have betrayed him once again? How could *she* have betrayed him? Before he knew what he was doing, his fist came crashing into the wall with a resounding thump, sending shockwaves up his arm and into his torso.

Immediately Sophie was at the door, knocking frantically. "Is everything okay? Grant?"

Grant dumbly stared at the small crack in the drywall before looking down at his throbbing right hand, slowly turning and examining it for any sign of bruising. At the irritating sound of Sophie's continued knocking, he swiftly wrenched open the door and gave her a vicious glare.

Sophie gasped and took a step backward, her wide eyes trained on his, simultaneously fascinated and terrorized by a patina of green overtaking the typical palette of blues.

Her look of fear seemed to empower him, and he grasped her right elbow with his uninjured left hand, drawing her toward him. With a surprised cry, she felt herself pressed against his naked, dripping frame, scarcely daring to look up into his torrid gaze.

Once she did, without hesitation his full lips crashed onto hers, at once stealing her breath and her free will.

Attempting to steady her trembling, Sophie's hands slid up Grant's slick back, and she clung to him while he hungrily and breathlessly mauled her with kisses. Though she was kissing him back, it was impossible to match the intensity of his pulsating desire, and she found herself teetering between fear and excitement at his aggressive touch. Her mixed reaction was only compounded by the increasing force of his unclothed hardness pressing against her lower abdomen.

Somehow managing to pull away from the suctioning liplock, Sophie gulped for air and glanced down at his throbbing member. She sensed his rapid breathing and looked into his eyes — despite their continued intense green glare, she detected a hint of the cool, caring blue she knew and loved. Could she trust him? Would he hurt her? Feelings of fear and safety competed for her soul, her heart pounding and her body quivering.

Somehow his long fingers snaked under the elastic of her panties to knead and caress the tender flesh of her shapely rear end. Before she could speak he leaned into her and took her mouth into his once again, bruising her soft lips with insistent kisses while simultaneously tearing her lace panties down her legs until they puddled at her feet. His strong hands resumed cupping and clawing at her buttocks, now uncovered and exposed.

He had control over her entire being, and she felt herself guided backward toward the bedroom wall. Suddenly her feet lifted off the floor as he hoisted her up and back with a breathtaking thump, pinning her between his sinewy body and the wall.

Her heart raced as his relentless lips trailed down her neck, pulling and sucking, undoubtedly leaving bites and bruises on her that would be noticeable in the morning. He seemed to be supporting her only with his stalwart hold on her bottom, and she clung to his shoulders, panting and feeling a throbbing heat building in her core, despite his roughness. Not only did she feel his scorching hands digging into her butt, she also now felt the tip of his rock-hard penis brushing against her nightgown.

"Grant," she cried, beginning to feel unsure. He had her slammed up against the wall, unsteady and laboring to get air. He seemed not to hear her and continued thrusting his body into hers with each assault of his lips. Should she stop him? Was she safe with him at this moment? Was he so mad he was going to hurt her?

"Grant," she moaned, tightening her grip on his shoulders while tilting her head back, feeling his teeth cut into her collarbone. Should she listen to her fear and beg him to stop? Or should she listen to her desire and beg him to take her? Was he the compassionate man she'd fallen in love with or a green-eyed monster seeking revenge for her betrayal? "Grant—"

"What?" he barked, lifting his head and staring straight into her frightened brown eyes. His chest heaved, and his face was flushed.

Unable to look into those flaring green depths, Sophie closed her eyes, feeling perched on a high precipice. Whatever path she chose, she was going down. What did he want her to do? What did he need from her? How could she help him through his pain? Could she trust him?

"What?" he repeated, louder this time, still panting.

Meeting his powerful gaze, she made a split-second decision. She pressed up against him, creating grinding friction and feeling his body flinch in response. "Take me, Grant."

His eyes narrowed as he inclined his head forward, impatiently bashing her inflamed lips yet again. She felt her back peel off the wall, and then they were spinning together. Grant managed to support her weight while not letting go of her lips as he staggered toward the center of the room.

Once he felt his knees against the mattress he roughly released her, and she felt a terrorizing falling sensation before landing on the bed with a bounce. She barely had a second to orient herself before he'd crawled on top of her, brusquely hauling her body up so her head rested on the pillow.

His left hand held her right wrist over her head while his other reached down and forcibly breached her labia. She gasped when his long fingers entered her, deeply stroking and massaging her wetness. Despite being alarmed by his surprising brutality, she could not deny her arousal. Grant's probing fingers elicited an exquisite aching deep inside, and when she felt him poking at her abdomen she simultaneously felt desirous and apprehensive at the thought of him filling her.

Although Grant was blinded by a rushing, urgent need to consume her, regardless of any whimper or gasp she might offer in protest, his pulsing emotion did not totally void him of logic. Releasing her wrist, he reached for the nightstand, fumbling in the drawer for a condom.

Realizing what he was seeking, Sophie clasped his arm and pulled it away from the drawer. He looked toward her in surprise and was further bewildered to see her shaking her head. She could barely find the words to speak, but she gazed at him intently and simply said, "Now."

His body throbbing for release, he didn't argue. He'd barely said one word since emerging from the bathroom. Not only was he scared of what hostile, uncontrollable remarks might tumble out of his mouth, but he was also so tightly wound that he could only act with single-minded purpose: reclaiming her. Quickly he adjusted himself over her, sliding his fingers out a second before deftly sliding his penis in.

There was nothing gentle about this sexual encounter, and Sophie inhaled sharply at his swift entry and continued gasping with each hard thrust. The balance between pain and pleasure was tipping uncomfortably to one side, but she didn't allow herself to cry out. Instead, steeling herself to his aggressive plunges, she just took it. She hoped his assault on her defiled body would somehow help them both heal.

Clenching her teeth, she sensed his slowing pace and hoped he was almost done. He'd refused to look at her the entire time, but finally she caught a glimpse of his eyes, and the vacant sadness there made her well up with tears.

But Grant was so intent on discharging the screaming tension crowding his mind and body that he didn't notice her suffering as he limply rolled off of her. He didn't notice he was the only one coming down from a high, the shuddering climax of orgasm.

Sophie lay completely still. She stared at the white ceiling as tears silently leaked from the corners of her eyes. Numbly she smoothed her hands over the crumpled nightgown, covering herself, but she did not feel the return of her dignity. She'd thought if he took it out on her, they'd be done with it, but she'd been wrong. Evidently they were not done with Logan yet.

Feeling his breathing begin to slow, Grant noticed something felt off. Typically when he and Sophie made love they'd remain entangled for hours afterward, their enjoined sweaty bodies eventually cooling as they snuggled together. But tonight it was different. He was alone. He glanced over at her and was shocked at the sight of her tears.

She looked away, but he quickly grasped her slender hand in his.

"Did I hurt you?" he asked urgently, his eyes scanning her body, wincing when he noticed the angry circular scar on her left arm. "Your arm — is it hurt?"

She sniffed and shook her head. When she opened her mouth to respond, a sob escaped, piercing Grant's heart. "It's okay," she said, unconvincingly.

His eyes filled with sadness. "I hurt you."

"It's okay," she repeated, crying harder. In a quiet voice, she added, "I deserve it."

His mouth dropped open. "What? You deserve it?" He inched his body closer to her. "Talk to me. You deserve to get hurt?"

Wordlessly she rolled over, turning her back to Grant. She was silent for a few moments before whispering, "I'm a whore."

Grant looked horrified. "No!" He attempted to roll her to face him, but she resisted, pushing him away and curling into a ball.

"Don't touch me," she cried, beginning to sob again.

"Sophie," he pleaded, feeling sick. "Did I hurt you? Did I make you feel that way? You are *not* a w-w-who..." He couldn't say the word.

"Yes, I am," she choked. "I'm so sorry, Grant. I'm so sorry about Logan. I'd take it all back if I could."

He bristled, ignoring the truth. "This has nothing to do with Logan."

She sat up with a start, wiping her eyes. "Of course it does! What you just did to me has *everything* to do with Logan!"

Grant felt a weight in the pit of in his stomach as he pushed himself into a sitting position as well.

"Are you done now?" she hollered, tears coursing down her face. "Or are you going to ravage me again—just like you'd treat a whore!"

Once she erupted into sobs again, he didn't care if she pushed him away. Grant reached out and folded her into his strong chest. Mercifully she let herself be drawn into his embrace this time while her body heaved with weeping.

"Shh." He hushed her softly, rubbing her back. "You're my beautiful Bonnie, and I never meant to hurt you. God, I'm sorry." Remembering the scar tainting her perfect arm, he winced. "All I do is hurt you."

He was horrified. He'd brutally penetrated her, not worrying if it caused her pain, only caring about what *he* wanted. And he knew she was right—he'd done it to get back at her for Logan. He'd unfairly taken out his anger at his brother on her. He felt a sinking in his stomach as he realized he was no better than anyone else in his family. Just like them, he'd terrorized an innocent person to get what he wanted. He knew the pattern well—it was etched into his genetic code.

Utterly disgusted with himself, he experienced an overwhelming desire to flee. But as he tried to pull away, Sophie lifted her head and stared him down with glassy eyes.

She clutched onto him. "You're not leaving me this time. I'm not letting you run out of here."

He shook his head. "Please, I—I don't deserve you."

"I don't know what screwed-up messages from your family are floating around in your head right now, but you're staying right here."

A flash of unease shot through him. She'd read his mind.

Sophie waited until his eyes met hers. "You're Grant Macsen, not Grant Barberi, got it? We'll get through this Logan thing. We will. I didn't love him, and he was no good for me. But I love you, McSailor."

Grant exhaled loudly. "I love you too." His actions sure hadn't shown that tonight, but his words were true. He drew her close, resting his chin on her shoulder.

When she brushed her hand across his buzzed hair, she said wistfully, "Your hair's still damp from the shower."

They sat, twined together, as Grant continued to resist his urge to bolt from the apartment. Then another thought came to mind.

"Sophie?"

"Hmm?"

"The, um, the condom?"

"Oh." She pulled back to look him in the eye. "I started the pill."

His eyes filled with gratitude. "You did that? For us?"

Even after the emotional rollercoaster of the day, after the fear and uncertainty she'd experienced in his arms, Sophie knew the integrity that lay beneath the layers of abuse. She desperately hoped they could stay together while they peeled them away. Studying him intently, she whispered, "I trust you."

He gently sifted his fingers through her thick hair and drew her into a hug, cheek to cheek. "Thank you."

Sophie hesitated a moment, then added, "Especially after learning about your meager sexual history." She smirked, silently praying he would smile too.

To her relief, his eyes narrowed playfully.

Suddenly, a loud knock on the apartment door startled them both.

"Grant!" a muffled female voice called.

"Who's that?" Sophie asked.

"I have no idea."

He shimmied off the bed and reached for a pair of jeans.

"Grant, are you home?" the unknown visitor hollered, knocking again.

Sophie grabbed a tissue to blow her nose, then slid on her discarded panties before curiously following Grant into the family room. She didn't own a robe — that was one item of many still to purchase after getting out of prison — so she lingered by the bedroom doorway, cognizant of her flimsy silk nightgown. She was extremely curious about the late-night female visitor, wondering if perhaps Grant's sexual history wasn't so meager after all.

"Who is it?" Grant inquired, cautiously approaching the front door.

"Ashley!" came the response, spoken so vehemently that Sophie heard it plainly across the room.

Puzzled, Grant unlocked the door and came face to face with his sister-in-law and nephew. "Is it true?" Ashley asked shrilly, brushing past Grant with her son reluctantly in tow. She marched Ben to the center of the apartment and pointed authoritatively to the sofa.

"Mo-om," he whined.

She glared at Ben then at Grant, who appeared bewildered. At the sight of them, Sophie left her perch by the doorway and scampered into the bedroom to get dressed.

"Is it true?" Ashley hissed. "Is it true you caught him smoking pot and didn't tell me?"

Grant took a step backward.

"Is it true?" Ashley screeched.

"Yes," he confessed.

"Well, what a shock, Ben. You actually told the truth for once."

The sixteen-year-old's cheeks reddened, and he ducked his head, wisely following his mother's instruction to sit on the sofa. Ashley continued glaring at Grant, though her hostility had abated slightly. "Why didn't you tell me?"

"I'm sorry Ashley—I should've told you. Ben begged me not to since he'd have to go to rehab if he got caught smoking again."

"That *was* the plan," Ashley retorted. "I caught him smoking last night, and I tried to get him into a program today, but it turns out my crappy health insurance won't pay for drug rehab!" She sighed loudly.

"What kind of job do you have?" Sophie interjected, having emerged from the bedroom in a T-shirt and jeans.

Ashley looked startled, noticing the tall woman at the side of the room for the first time.

"You remember Sophie, Ashley?" Grant supplied.

Ashley looked from Grant's bare torso to Sophie's mussed hair before answering in a quieter tone. "I'm a waitress."

Sophie nodded. "Yeah, some professions have really awful behavioral health benefits. I had a lot of clients who only had like ten outpatient visits a year."

Ashley studied her curiously. "You're a counselor or something?"

Blushing, Sophie shook her head. "I was a psychologist. But not anymore."

"Well, maybe you can help Mr. Pothead over there." She gestured to her son. "*I* certainly don't know what to do with him."

Ben squirmed on the sofa, clearly uncomfortable about being the object of his mother's anger.

"I'd love to help," Sophie offered, "but—"

"Great," Ashley interrupted, "because Ben's going to be living here for a while."

Grant's jaw dropped. "Excuse me, Ashley?"

"You clearly think you know how to be his parent," she told Grant. "You made an executive decision not to tell me about his drug use. So you can be his parent. He obviously needs a strong father figure in his life — Lord knows Logan never fit the bill."

"Ashley, this is crazy!" Grant protested. "I can't have a teenager living in a one-bedroom apartment! Sophie and I both work long hours —"

"Figure it out," she snapped. "I'm sick of his outlaw behavior, which comes from your family, by the way. Ben's school is closer to your apartment than mine anyway, so that'll make it easier when school starts next week. Ben, go get your duffel bag from the car."

He bolted from the sofa, feeling immensely embarrassed, but he paused at the door. "Mom, don't make me stay here! I'll be good — I won't smoke ever again!"

"When have I heard that before?" she shrieked. "Go get your bag!"

Ben was close to tears. "Please, Mom!"

Sophie tentatively stepped forward, trying to infuse some calm into the situation. Ashley appeared to be at wit's end, and Sophie knew exactly how the teenager felt, being unceremoniously kicked out of his own home. "Ben," she said softly, "Grant and I would love to have you stay with us for a while. How about you get your bag, and we'll sort this all out?"

Everyone in the room stared at her incredulously.

Then, knowing he was about to cry, Ben decided to hightail it to his mom's car.

Still somewhat shocked, Grant looked at Sophie with pure gratitude. He definitely didn't deserve her.

With Ben gone, Ashley's whole demeanor changed. Her tough exterior melted, and she just looked tired. "It's not forever," she said, her eyes pleading. "I just need a break. Maybe you can help him."

Grant sighed. "I want to help him, Ashley — and help you — but *I* don't know how to be a dad. I can't make decisions about him."

"Well, I'm not asking you to do it alone," Ashley snapped, suddenly fierce again. "I'm not going anywhere. I'm still his mom. You can't figure it out? Give me a call."

Sophie returned to the bedroom to dig up some extra bedding for Ben, and Grant and Ashley exchanged phone numbers. Soon Ben knocked softly at the door and then shuffled in, his duffel in tow.

Not long after that, Ashley was on her way and Ben had settled in with sheets and a blanket on the sofa. By now all three inhabitants of the apartment were feeling the effects of a long day.

"We'll figure out the details of you staying here tomorrow, after we've all gotten some sleep," Grant said, fluffing a pillow for his nephew before tossing it on the couch. "Sophie and I have to meet with our PO at nine, and then I'll be back to pick you up for work. And this time you need to take a shower first, okay?"

Ben pouted but brightened when he heard his cell phone's blaring alternative-rock ringtone. Grant rolled his eyes. "And put that phone on vibrate. We don't want to be woken up all night by your friends calling."

Glancing at the phone, Ben decided to respond to his friend later. Eyeing Grant and Sophie suspiciously, he commented, "Looks like you two had some make-up sex. Am I right?"

Both adults narrowed their eyes at the teen, and Sophie told him, "That's none of your business, punk."

7. Contrition

Evidently they'd not heard him approach from down the hallway. Hunter stood still for a moment at the entrance to the waiting room, observing the curiously detached fit of Sophie's body against Grant's torso. Though his arm around her appeared to be a loving gesture, something was off. Perhaps it was the stiffness of Sophie's back, the whiteness of Grant's fingertips curled around her shoulder, or way their eyes avoided each other, but this display of affection definitely conveyed more tension than togetherness.

Filing away his observations, Hunter breezily announced, "Good to see you, Grant and Sophie."

They looked up at Hunter, who was instantly drawn to the icy blue of Grant's tired gaze. The man looked utterly exhausted, yet he didn't hesitate to spring to his feet and guide Sophie to a standing position as well. When Grant took her hand, Hunter caught an irritated tightness, which she quickly masked with a plastic smile.

"We're ready, Hunter," she said.

Hunter paused a second at her forced tone, then nodded, pointing toward his office.

Once the couple had seated themselves on the sofa, with a sizeable distance between, Hunter told Grant, "I'm glad you came back."

Did I have a choice? Grant wished he could say. But instead he replied, "Thank you for not telling Officer Stone I left early last time, sir."

Hunter appeared surprised — he'd not even considered reporting Grant's early departure to the parole officer. "It was only ten minutes or so. And I think I understand why you ran out of here — a bombshell had just been dropped on you."

Grant and Sophie both looked miserable at that comment.

Chewing on his lip, Hunter inquired, "So, um, how have you two been doing since last week's session?"

"We made up," Sophie offered.

Hunter scrunched his forehead. That was the last thing he'd expected her to say, given their aloof body language. "Really?" Neither spoke, so he added, "How?"

"Grant's nephew, Ben, came to live with us—" Sophie began.

"Sophie's been really great with him," Grant interjected.

She smiled. "—which was a good distraction, I guess."

Hunter looked perplexed. "Grant's nephew—that's Logan's son? He's living with you now?"

Grant nodded. "His mother's had it up to here with him. I think it's just for a little while."

Hunter took that in and said, "We'll get to that later." Turning to Sophie, he asked, "You mentioned that Ben was a distraction? A distraction from what, exactly?"

Sophie's smile faded. "Um, well, the night Ashley brought Ben over—it was kind of a tough night. But it's better now."

"How was it a tough night?"

Sophie paused and Grant squirmed.

"I made Sophie cry," he finally said.

"You were upset?" Hunter asked Sophie. "What made you cry?"

She seemed to have difficulty finding words. "I—I wasn't feeling very good about myself."

"How *were* you feeling?"

"It's over now, Hunter, no need to rehash—"

"Sophie, it's a simple question: How were you feeling?" He appeared irritated by her evasiveness.

Sophie took a deep breath, stealing a glance at Grant, who had turned away from her, seemingly lost in his own self-hatred. Meeting Hunter's compassionate eyes, she thought back to that night and confessed, "Used. I felt used. And scared."

She was surprised by the words coming out of her mouth.

Hunter tilted his head, wondering what had happened between them. "Used and scared? That sounds rather serious. Grant, do you have any idea why Sophie felt used and scared?"

Grant closed his eyes, feeling a wave of remorse crash over him. He'd desperately tried to forget that night. He finally rasped, "Because I hurt her."

"You hurt her?"

"I was rough with her." He shuddered.

"He didn't mean it, Hunter," Sophie rushed in.

"Wait a minute—you two were having sex?" They guiltily nodded. "Grant, you got, uh, *rough*, leading Sophie to feel used and scared?" More nods.

Hunter felt his voice rising as his body tensed. "*Were* you hurt?"

Sophie's eyes widened, and she opened her mouth to respond, but nothing came out. She felt her nose burning, a sign of imminent tears.

"Yes," she finally managed, "but like I said, he didn't mean to hurt me. He just needed to vent, and I, I was trying to help him—"

"You were trying to *help?*" Hunter asked incredulously. "Did you tell him he was hurting you?"

She shook her head as her face crumpled.

"Did you tell him you were feeling scared?" Hunter's voice took on a gruff edge, and he saw her warily shake her head again. He stole a glance at Grant before returning his attention to Sophie. "Were you too scared to speak?"

Feeling tears spring to her eyes, she kept shaking her head. "No. I thought I was h-h-helping him," she choked out. "He needed to take it out on me—for the Logan thing. I deserved it."

Hunter felt his chest tighten with anger. "You *never* deserve to be hurt!" His shout stunned them both, but his next question was even more shocking. "Did he rape you, Sophie?"

"No!" she cried immediately.

Grant started breathing again, close to tears himself.

"I told him to keep going," she added.

Hunter was incensed. "You were caretaking again, weren't you? You were putting his needs in front of your own! You thought you were helping him? So you're trying to play therapist with your boyfriend now? That's simply not going to work!"

Sophie sobbed.

Hunter stared at her, suspended in disbelief. He didn't know why he felt so angry, but he couldn't stop the chastising words. "When are you going to stop caretaking? This time you could've gotten really hurt — physically, not just emotionally. That's a dangerous game you're playing!"

Sophie could only sit there and sob, recognizing the true nature of her role in what happened that night.

"Please don't cry," Grant begged.

"And *you!*" Hunter nearly yelled, landing his livid gaze on Grant. "What the hell were you thinking?"

"I…I wasn't thinking, sir."

"Did you think you could get away with that?"

"No! I was so mad — "

"Did you think you had a right to hurt her?" Hunter seethed.

"No, sir! I feel awful for what happened. But all I could see was an image of her and L-L-Logan in my head, and I snapped." Grant's breath came in shaky gasps.

Hunter sat back in his chair, suddenly spent. Sophie's muted sobs continued to fill the room, and Hunter eyed her sardonically. "I guess you got yourself another bad boy, didn't you?"

Sophie glared at Hunter, surprised by his cruel comment. Ignoring her indignant stare, Hunter added, "Maybe these sessions aren't helping you. You just keep repeating old patterns."

"Stop being mean to her!" Grant countered, his nostrils flaring.

"Oh, *you're* the one to save her?" Hunter retorted. "The son of Enzo Barberi? Are you sure you're not out to hurt her? I think you're hiding something."

"Fuck you!" Grant was on his feet instantaneously, his hands balled into fists.

Sophie and Hunter stared up at him, wide-eyed.

Sophie reached up and frantically took his hand. "Grant, it's okay. You can't leave — we can't go back to prison. Please stay. Hunter's going to stop being mean. Right, Hunter?"

Hunter felt the heat of her pointed stare and suddenly felt embarrassed. He looked down. He was supposed to be the professional, and here he was yelling at his clients? What did *he* think he was doing? He wondered why he felt so incensed.

Hunter cleared his throat. "Yes, I'll stop. I apologize for raising my voice. It won't happen again." He glanced up at Grant and nodded to the sofa. "If you can get control of yourself, I'd like you to stay. Please have a seat."

Grant jammed his fists under his crossed arms and settled back onto the sofa. Biting his lip, he asked, "Are you going to report me to Officer Stone?"

"Why would I do that?"

"You said you thought I raped Sophie."

"No," Hunter corrected, crossing his legs. "I asked Sophie *if* it was rape, but it seems it was consensual — consensually stupid and destructive."

Grant blushed, and he offered meekly, "And then I told you to fuck off, sir?"

Hunter suppressed a smile. "You think you're the first client to tell me to fuck off, Mc — " he glanced at Sophie for help " — McN-N-Navy boy?"

Sophie couldn't stop herself from chuckling. "It's McSailor."

"Right. McSailor." Hunter returned his gaze to Grant. "I won't report you to your PO, but I do think you have some anger issues you need to work out or you *will* wind up back in prison."

Grant hung his head. It was pretty obvious he had a boatload of issues.

"You seem sorry about what you did to Sophie."

"Yes, sir."

Hunter leaned in. "And now you have a sixteen-year-old boy staying with you? A teenager who uses marijuana, disregards rules, and knows how to push your every button? What do you think is going to happen once he starts acting up?"

"Are you saying I'm going to hit him?" Grant looked aghast. "I would *never* hit my nephew!"

"It's not outside the realm of possibility," Hunter argued, "especially if you haven't worked through your own past abuse. It's all you know."

Grant sighed. "This again. It all comes back to my father, doesn't it?" He rubbed the bridge of his nose.

Hunter studied him. "You look tired."

"He hasn't been sleeping well," Sophie interjected. "Whenever I wake up in the middle of the night, he's still awake."

"Has it been tough to fall asleep?" Hunter asked him.

Grant shrugged.

"Are you trying to avoid sleep?"

Grant looked startled, and when he tried to answer negatively, Hunter didn't buy it.

Ignoring Grant's shaking head, Hunter asked, "So the nightmares have returned?"

A forlorn expression crossed Grant's face, and he looked down. "I just can't have any more nightmares," he admitted. "At least not while I'm in the same bed with Sophie."

Sophie remembered shaking him awake from his nightmare after the first time they'd had sex, dragging him away from some torturous scene in his mind. Once he'd come to and stopped thrashing about, he'd smoothed his hands across the bedding as if he were looking for something, feeling for something. He'd done the same thing in their therapy session last week, she realized—he'd run his hands over the sofa cushion as he came out of his agitated state.

She'd hated having to tell him she knew about his past. It didn't seem right that she was aware of the painful story before he'd had the opportunity to choose to share it with her. It didn't seem right that she knew about him peeing his pants…

Her sharp intake of breath turned both men's heads toward her.

"What is it?" Hunter asked.

Sophie's cheeks reddened. "I think I know why Grant's trying so hard to avoid nightmares, especially when I'm there."

Grant turned to look at her with a hitch in his breath, and she slowly met his gaze. "You're worried about what might happen if you have a nightmare about your childhood. You're…" she gulped "…you're worried that you'll pee in your pants again."

His anguished expression and subsequent huddling up into a ball, gripping his head in his hands, told both Sophie and Hunter she was right on track.

"But Grant," she said in a soothing voice, leaning over to rub his back, "you were only four then. You're an adult now, and that's not going to happen."

He abruptly lifted his head, letting his hands fall free. "But it did happen!" he insisted. "Two years ago! I'm not an adult. I'm a fucking baby!"

Sophie halted the smooth circles she was tracing on his back, unsure what to say next.

"What happened, Grant?" Hunter prodded. "Two years ago—you were in prison, right?"

Grant moaned, "Oh, God! I can't tell her, I can't." *She'll leave me.*

Maybe they'd finally get to whatever he'd been hiding, Hunter hoped. Sophie certainly deserved to know the truth. "It's okay," he gently encouraged.

Looking up at the psychologist, Grant expected to find a hateful glare, but instead he only saw compassion in Hunter's eyes.

"Go on, Grant. Keeping it all in obviously isn't helping you, and you have to get some sleep. Telling your story's a way for the past to have less of a hold on you."

"I don't want to do this!" Grant protested, looking wildly around the room. "I just want to get the hell out of here—but I can't. I have to stay, damn it. I can't escape from my father no matter what I do."

"Sometimes the best way out…is *through*," Hunter said.

Grant gulped. Could he do this? What he'd done to Sophie in bed had really thrown him, and the idea that his unresolved anger could lead him to hurt his nephew further rattled him. After all they'd been through, he knew he could trust Sophie, but what about Dr. Hayes? He sighed. He really had no choice.

Feeling hopelessly embarrassed, Grant gritted his teeth and began. "It was my first day at Gurnee State Pen."

Sophie felt a rash of goose bumps cover her arms. She didn't know if she could stand to hear this story.

"My father and his men approached me in the yard," Grant continued.

"Wait a minute," Hunter interrupted. "Your father was in Gurnee too?"

"Yes, sir. He still is. He got a life sentence for killing a kid."

Hunter tapped his fingers on his knee. "I have a vague memory of your father's crime from the news accounts—could you remind me of the details?"

Sophie sat frozen on the sofa while Grant dutifully responded.

"When I was eight, my father was about to be indicted for murder," he said, his voice hollow. "Somehow he discovered the location of the informant, Richie Fanocelli, and he went there to try to kill the guy before he had a chance to testify. But there were two kids in the picture that made it all go to hell. My cousin Carlo apparently snuck into my dad's car and then went into the house after my dad, and Fanocelli had his young son with him in the house."

Sophie was fascinated, but still unable to move. "How old was Carlo then?"

"I don't know — ten?"

"This is the same Carlo who shot Sophie a few weeks ago?" Hunter asked.

Grant nodded. "Anyway, my father and Carlo were both in the house, and Fanocelli shot Carlo."

Sophie gasped. "Carlo got shot? Where?"

"In his left arm, right above the elbow." Grant turned to Sophie with a look of wonder. "Exactly where he shot you."

The three absorbed that bizarre coincidence before Grant resumed, "When my father shot back, he hit Fanocelli's son. My dad killed him — Tony Fanocelli. H-H-He was only seven."

"Tony was just one year younger than you then," Hunter said.

Grant nodded grimly.

"That must have been terrifying to hear that your own father killed a little boy."

Grant's knuckles had gone white, gripping the edge of the sofa cushions on either side of his legs.

"What were you told about the shooting back then?" Hunter inquired.

"I'm not sure," Grant responded. "I do remember that my mom took us to the hospital to visit Carlo after my dad was arrested."

"She took you and Logan to see Carlo? How did Carlo get to the hospital in the first place?"

"My dad rushed him there." Grant exhaled with disgust. "Big magnanimous gesture on his part — saving his nephew's life in exchange for getting arrested right outside the hospital. Uncle Angelo was furious."

"Your Uncle Angelo blamed Carlo for Enzo going to prison?" Hunter shook his head.

"I think so," Grant said. "He seemed ticked off at Carlo when we visited him."

Hunter asked, "Angelo was at the hospital?"

"Yeah. He and my mom had words, and the next thing I knew she packed us up and took us to live with Uncle Joe at Great Lakes."

"Logan lived with Joe too?"

"No. Logan and Joe were fighting a lot, so Logan ran away to the compound — Uncle Angelo's house. My mom was really sad."

Hunter sat back in his chair. "So you were eight years old, and you'd just lost your brother and your home. Not to mention losing your father—and you'd learned your father killed a child your age. It must have been devastating."

Grant's throat felt tight. "I missed Logan, and I missed my friends, but it wasn't so bad. At least Dad couldn't beat up Mom anymore."

"And he couldn't beat you up anymore, either."

There was silence.

Sophie had listened to the rapid-fire questions and answers in shock. No wonder Grant never wanted to discuss his past.

After a moment, Hunter questioned again. "Did you ever visit your father at Gurnee prior to your incarceration?"

"No, sir, and that didn't exactly help my cause. My dad was pretty pissed off about me never visiting."

Grant sighed. He still hadn't answered the original question, and it *felt* like a nightmare just thinking about telling them what had led to his adult nightmares. Yet he knew he had to. Hell, Sophie had practically figured out the story on her own already.

"As I was saying, my father approached me in the yard, and he told me he'd protect me if I joined him." Grant grimaced. "Meaning I could never speak to Joe the whole time I was inside."

Sophie looked horrified. "Your father made you renounce Joe?"

He nodded. "But I refused. Well, I *tried* to refuse, but my dad wasn't having it. I could either join him or he would let the prison…*wolves* teach me a lesson."

Sophie's jaw clenched even more tightly.

Grant sighed again. "And they did teach me a lesson. They came after me, and the next thing I knew I was sitting handcuffed in the warden's office, being told I would spend sixty days in solitary as punishment for fighting."

"But that wasn't fair!" Sophie protested.

"That took incredible strength to stand up to your father," Hunter said.

"More like stupidity," Grant scoffed. He hesitated, clearly worried about sharing the next part of the story.

"What was solitary like?" Sophie asked. "I would've been terrified to go in the hole."

Flashes of memories appeared in Grant's head. *I was terrified,* he thought. "It was awful. I, um, I couldn't see—it was pitch black—and the walls; they were closing in…" Grant's voice cracked, and he looked down, feeling the heat of a blush on his cheeks and tears prickling at the back of his eyes. *Don't cry, don't cry.*

A thought dawned on Hunter. "It was just like the closet your father had locked you in when you were four."

Stunned, Grant lifted his head, blinking away tears. "Y-Y-Yes, sir."

Sophie resisted the urge to scoop him into her arms as he looked down in shame.

"I reacted just like I was four too."

She could hear the tears in his voice and was not surprised when a few plopped onto his jeans. She was instantly reminded of Logan crying in her office.

"How did you react?" Hunter gently asked.

"I—I don't know what happened," Grant said. "But I woke up three days later in the psych ward." He snuck a glance at Sophie, dreading her response to discovering her boyfriend was crazy. "The doctor said I'd been catatonic. They, um, they had to remove me from the hole because I hadn't been eating, and I, and I…" He took his head in his hands and whispered, "I peed in my pants."

Once he began sobbing, Sophie couldn't contain herself and launched herself across the sofa to gather him into her arms, murmuring soothing words while stroking his back.

Hunter wondered about the therapeutic value of her hug, which interrupted his story, but he also realized there was no way he could separate them at this point. They clearly needed each other.

"I bet you didn't know you had a psycho boyfriend," Grant muttered through his tears.

"You're not psycho. Of course you dissociated in there, Grant," she said, still rubbing his back. "It triggered a childhood trauma reaction."

Noting Grant's puzzled expression over Sophie's shoulder, Hunter said, "Sophie, let's give him some space to understand all of this."

She nodded and let go, but stayed close on the sofa.

"I agree with Sophie," Hunter said. "To be locked up in a small, dark place like that must have been very frightening and reminded you of that happening when you were four. It makes total sense that you had an adverse reaction to that situation, and it doesn't make you crazy. Sophie used the words 'dissociation' and 'trauma,' and I want to review some of that with you in the next session, okay? You're not crazy. You're just suffering from post-traumatic stress disorder."

Grant swallowed hard and nodded, swiping at his cheeks.

"You did well today—both of you," Hunter added. "This was a tough session, but I think we made a lot of progress."

Looking again at her shell-shocked boyfriend, Sophie crawled onto his lap, folding her slim body into his. At first Grant seemed surprised, but once she draped her arms over his shoulders, he responded by wrapping his arms around her back. They held each other tightly for several moments.

Hunter noticed that much of their tension was gone. This time their hug was genuine.

Sophie drew back and wiped a fresh tear from Grant's cheek, gazing into his eyes. They held their stare for over a minute, both trying to steady themselves after what they'd endured.

Eventually Sophie's face lit up in an evil grin. "Now that I'm on your lap, McSailor, you *better* keep your pants dry."

Amidst their snickers, Hunter shook his head disdainfully. "Jesus, get a room, you two." They smiled, and he added, "Let's make it gentle, clean fun this time, all right?"

Their cheeks flushed pink, and Grant appeared most contrite.

"And," Hunter concluded, "make sure your live-in teenager doesn't hear you in action. I think Ben's had enough trauma, don't you?"

8. Congenital

Uncle and nephew ambled their way across city streets, taking in the dapples of morning sun filtering through the trees interspersed on the sidewalk. Swaying the still-green leaves was a cool breeze, a prelude to the end of summer.

Then Ben broke their comfortable silence. "So, should I tell Rog today or tomorrow?"

Grant was grateful his nephew was no longer grumbling about him insisting they leave early for work. "Tell Mr. Eaton what?"

Ben exhaled with exasperation. "That I'm done for the summer."

"What do you mean?"

The teenager looked at his uncle like he was incredibly obtuse. "I'm starting school next week! I can't work anymore."

Grant's return stare was equally incredulous. "You get out of school at three fifteen, that's plenty of time to make the five o'clock and seven o'clock cruises."

"I don't wanna work after school! When am I gonna have time to chill with my friends?"

Grant had a sneaking suspicion that these so-called friends were no strangers to marijuana. Besides, he'd really enjoyed having Ben with him at work, and despite the teen's protests, he knew Ben had liked it too. They'd become closer — talking about school, girls, music, cell phones, and even Logan upon occasion. A conversation about the man who linked them both usually ended abruptly when one of them cleared his throat and changed the subject, claiming the Chicago wind was making his eyes water.

"The cruises only run another month or so, Ben," Grant patiently explained. "You can hang out with your friends the rest of the school year, but for now I expect you to work after school."

"Nooo!" he whined, beginning to drag his feet. "This blows. I already told Nick we'd go to ESPN Zone next week."

Grant stopped walking and turned to look at Ben. "I'm sorry, but the video games will have to wait. Sophie and I are both working in the afternoons, and I don't want to leave you unsupervised."

"I'm not some *baby*," Ben scoffed. "I can take care of myself."

Grant felt his blood pressure rising, particularly after Ben punctuated his statement with a defiant jut of his jaw.

"I never said you were a baby. But now that you're living with me, I'm responsible for you—"

"You can't make me!" Ben blurted, his cool blue eyes flaring indignantly. "I don't wanna work anymore for that asshole Roger on his stupid, shitty boat!"

Appalled by his nephew's sudden temper tantrum, Grant felt a heated flush warm his face. How dare he talk about his boss like that? He should be grateful he even had a job, much less a *home,* after all the crap he'd pulled.

"End of discussion, Ben. You'll keep working."

"You can't make me."

Grant's straightened his back, pulling himself up to his full six-foot-one height. His voice was ominously soft. "Do you want to try me?"

With a look of betrayal, Ben countered, "Oh, what're you gonna do? It's not like you're my dad or anything."

"You're right. I'm not your dad, but as long as you're living with me, you're going to follow my rules."

Grant cringed the second the hackneyed parental warning escaped his lips. His heart pounded as he stared into insolent eyes whose sky blue matched his own. He had no idea what he'd do if Ben refused to obey him.

"This is bullshit," Ben spat. "I'm *not* going to work next week, and that's final."

"Yes, you are!" Grant bellowed. "You'll do what I say, damn it!"

His scalp tingled and his hands itched. He lunged forward to seize the boy and shake some sense into him, when suddenly Grant froze. Sensing impending violence, Ben's eyes had widened, and he too seemed paralyzed, gaping at his uncle whose outstretched hands hovered inches from his body.

Swallowing, Grant dropped his hands and turned, walking a few steps away to stare at the sidewalk. Hot fury coursed through him, and he found himself clenching his fists. The overwhelming urge to physically dominate or even harm his nephew horrified him. *This is what Dr. Hayes warned me about. This is my father's blood running through my veins*

After a few long moments, Grant shuffled back to his wary nephew. "I'm sorry," he began. "I should've discussed your plans for work with you first."

Ben stood still, chewing his lip.

"I'm new at this, okay?" Grant pleaded. "I'm not used to having a teenager live with me, and I'm probably screwing it all up."

Ben's eyes welled with tears. "You don't even *want* me to live with you!"

Grant was taken aback. "Yes, I do! Why on earth would you think that?"

"Because when my mom dropped me off, you said I couldn't live there!"

Grant frowned. "Look, Ben, Ashley dragged you in there without warning—I was just trying to adjust to the idea. And your mom interrupted a really bad night I was having with Sophie. I wasn't thinking straight."

Ben listened, standing quietly beside his uncle. At first he hadn't liked the idea of sharing his uncle with an unknown woman, but Sophie was growing on him. She always made sure he had something to eat, and she didn't complain about how much food he snarfed down, unlike the nonstop bitching of his mother.

"Are you and Sophie gonna split?" Ben asked.

"No! Why would you say that?"

"'Cause you were fighting the night Mom dumped me at your place."

Sighing, Grant confirmed, "That was a really bad night, yes."

"Why?"

Looking away, he pressed his lips together, feeling repulsed by what he'd done to Sophie. Eventually he said, "It was an awful night because I was acting like my father's son." Grant immediately began walking again.

That response silenced Ben, and he hustled to keep up with his uncle. Was it wrong to act like your father's son? Would it be a bad thing to be like Logan Barberi? All his life, Ben had desperately wanted to be like his tough, cool, unflappable father. Was that a mistake?

Ben's thoughts drifted back to his father's funeral, when his mother revealed that his dad had forced Uncle Grant to commit robbery. Although

Ben initially refused to believe it, he hadn't been able to stop thinking about it since then. Was his own father responsible for sending Grant to prison?

As the ship appeared just ahead, Ben quietly asked, "Uncle Grant? Um, did my dad, um, did he make you pull that robbery?"

Grant stopped in his tracks. "What?"

Ben tried to stop the trembling in his voice. "Did my dad threaten to kill Joe if you didn't rob the club?"

A look of dread was etched onto Grant's face. "Where'd you hear that?"

"Did it happen?" Ben pressed.

Grant exhaled, feeling trapped. He didn't want to lie, but he didn't know if his nephew could take any more. The boy was already a mess. Locked in a moment of faltering uncertainty, Grant reached for Ben and scooped him into a tight embrace.

Smothered by his uncle's muscular arms, Ben felt a rush of sadness. He knew what his uncle's silence meant. Maybe it wasn't so great to be his father's son.

Ben's words were muffled: "So it's true then."

Grant voice was thick with emotion. "Your dad was a good man — he, he just lost his way. I don't want you to end up like that, okay?"

Ben nodded, and they let go of each other.

Grant waited until their eyes met, then explained, "That's why I want you to keep working with me after school. I want you to stay out of trouble, and I want...I want to spend more time with you. Your dad missed out on a lot in your life, and I don't want to make the same mistake. Will you keep working? With me?"

Biting his lip, Ben considered the question for several moments before attempting a nonchalant "Yeah."

"Atta-boy."

Grant heard the familiar sounds of The Eagles, Roger's favorite band, coming from the ship. He thumped his nephew's shoulder. "C'mon, we got some cleaning to do."

"You're going to be fine, Kirsten."

Sophie's soothing voice did nothing to quell the butterflies in Kirsten's stomach. She was minutes away from her dissertation defense, and she was visibly shaking as she leaned one shoulder against the brick wall in the corridor. Kirsten was quite afraid the only "revelation" happening today would be her failing her defense — and likely taking *another* eight years to finally complete her damn doctoral degree.

"Remember," Sophie assured her as she rubbed gentle circles on her friend's back, "your committee might be tough, but in the end, they want you to succeed. Why don't you go in there and make sure your PowerPoint presentation is all ready to go, okay?"

Kirsten nodded. "I wish you could be in there with me."

"Me too, but you'll be fine." Sophie thought of the warm smile of the young faculty member she'd befriended, Tanya Highgate. "Tanya's on your committee, and then your advisor's always good for throwing a few softballs. I'm sure David will take good care of you in there."

"Oh, great. You really think I'm going to fail this, don't you?"

Sophie rolled her eyes. "What are you talking about?"

"You must be pretty desperate if you're saying nice things about David Alton."

Sophie smiled confidently. "Don't worry — I'm over him."

Kirsten arched her eyebrows. "Wow, Dr. Taylor. How did you arrive to such a Zen place? Are you doing therapy on yourself?"

"I've actually found a great technique for moving on after painful episodes of unrequited love." Knowing she had Kirsten's full attention, Sophie leaned in and explained, "It's called the McSailor Method. Find a drop-dead gorgeous boyfriend who makes every loser you've ever dated utterly *pale* in comparison."

Kirsten giggled. "The McSailor Method? Sounds quite promising, doctor!"

Nodding, Sophie said, "I'm gonna write a book about it."

They chuckled again before Kirsten's mood sobered. "I better get in there," she said, biting her lip.

"Knock 'em dead, Dr. Holland."

Hearing her potential new title, Kirsten grinned at Sophie before disappearing into the classroom.

Sighing, Sophie turned down the hallway and headed back to her office, lest she run into David again. She'd been truthful with Kirsten — she *was* over her former crush — but it was still awkward. A smile crossed her face as she considered her book idea. She'd launched into a daydream about Grant when a woman rushed out of an office, plowing right into her.

"Oh!" the woman squawked, grabbing Sophie's right arm as they tried to orient themselves.

Instinctively, Sophie pulled her still-sore left arm out of the fray.

"I'm so sorry, Sophie!"

Sophie laughed. "Don't worry about it, Tanya."

In her ginger-colored blouse, chocolate-brown knee-length skirt, and tall leather boots, Assistant Professor Tanya Highgate was one fashionable lady, managing to look glamorous even mid-collision. She'd joined the department right after Sophie graduated, and once Sophie had accepted the visiting instructor position, they'd clicked instantly.

"Wow, you just can't *wait* to get to Kirsten's defense, huh?"

Sophie caught a quick grimace on Tanya's face before the woman composed herself again.

"Are you okay, Tanya? Uh-oh — didn't you like Kirsten's manuscript?"

"Oh, no. Kirsten's study was great and she's going to pass, no problem."

"Phew."

"I know you two are friends." Tanya winked.

"So what's wrong?" Sophie prodded. "What has you running out of your office like there's a stack of journals on fire?"

Tanya gazed into Sophie's earnest eyes, trying to determine if she could trust her. Though they'd shared quite a bit, they'd only been acquainted a little more than three weeks.

As Tanya hesitated, Sophie began to worry about hanging out in the hallway so close to Kirsten's defense. David could materialize at any moment. Sophie backpedaled, "If you'd rather not explain, no worries —"

"Oh, hell." Tanya backed into her office and gestured for Sophie to follow. Then she closed the door. "I'll probably end up telling you this anyway, so I should just get it over with." She grinned ruefully. "That's what happens when you have a shrink for a friend — you end up spilling all your secrets."

Sophie smiled and sat in one of Tanya's chairs as Tanya sat behind her desk.

"I *am* discombobulated right now," Tanya admitted. "It's not the student I have a problem with in this upcoming defense. It's the committee."

"The committee?"

"Well, one person on the committee, to be precise." She sighed. "David."

Sophie felt her chest tighten. "David Alton?"

"Is there another David in this department, Sophie?"

Tanya was quite direct, and Sophie loved her for it.

"No, uh, *one* David's quite enough, thank you," Sophie said.

Tanya squinted at her curiously before resuming.

"Anyway, I've managed to avoid him for the most part, but when Kirsten asked me to be on her committee, I couldn't refuse. The poor woman is just dying to graduate, I know."

Sophie's interest was definitely piqued. "So why have you been avoiding David?"

Taking a deep breath, Tanya tossed her head back and proclaimed, "God, this is so embarrassing!"

Sophie waited in silence for a few moments before Tanya admitted, "My first year on the faculty, I was fresh out of grad school and I didn't know anybody, and David sort of took me under his wing. We often went to get coffee—we talked about department politics, he showed me the ropes. He was very charming, and I, I found myself falling for him."

Sophie's lips parted but Tanya didn't notice. She looked at her lap as she mumbled, "I should've known better."

"What happened, Tanya?"

When she raised her head, a soft blush colored her smooth brown cheeks. "You know how David adores Theodore Millon?"

Sophie nodded, recalling how he'd swooned over the 'brilliant" personality assessments created by Millon.

"Well," Tanya continued, "I was at a conference, and I got Millon to sign one of his books and write a little message to David on the inside cover. I gave the book to him, and he absolutely loved it—he did that Richard Gere thing, smiling at me with his squinty eyes, thanking me profusely, sidling up to me, making me feel like I was the love of his life. Stupidly I lost my head, and I went in to hug him, but he, um, backed away…"

Now Tanya couldn't help but notice that Sophie's jaw had become unhinged. "What?" she asked.

"Go on," Sophie managed to get out.

Sighing loudly, Tanya said in a disdainful tone, "Being psychologists, of course we had to *process* what happened, and that's when I confessed I thought he was coming on to me. I must've sounded so damn desperate! He quickly assured me he was simply trying to be my mentor—that he, of course, was happily *married*, and he was very sorry I'd misconstrued his intentions—"

"Oh my God!" Sophie interrupted, almost shrieking. "He did the same thing to me!"

"He *did?*"

"When I was a grad student! When I was meeting with him in his office, he hinted around that he and his wife were having problems, which only magnified the crush I had on him. Then when I tried to take it further he totally blew me off! I think he said the exact same thing to me—that I 'misconstrued his intentions.'"

Tanya's brown eyes widened. "Bastard! I thought it was all me."

"Me too!" Sophie nodded enthusiastically. "I've been so embarrassed for four years, thinking it was all my fault."

"Sounds like a pattern—the little prick," Tanya scoffed. "He thinks he's so suave. Well, Rico Suave has finally been busted."

Sophie laughed. "Speaking of Rico, his student is about to start her defense. You better get in there."

"Crap!" Tanya glanced at her watch and grabbed a thick manuscript off her desk. "I'll let you know when Kirsten passes. Please close the door on your way out!" she called over her shoulder, hustling out of the office.

Sophie sat completely still, bowled over by what Tanya had just shared. She wondered how many others David had lured into his web, only to bite them with venomous shame. Sophie pursed her lips. She definitely intended to find out.

❧

Grant suppressed a smile as he listened to his boss and his nephew sparring verbally on deck. They were between cruises, and he was taking an inventory of the bar supplies while Ben wiped down the benches in the passenger section with Rog. Technically, stocking the bar was Dan's duty, but the slacker bartender was nowhere to be seen, probably off smoking a cigarette somewhere.

Grant stood and began stacking plastic cups on the bar.

His elbow perched languidly on the other side of the bar, Roger pointed to the bench Ben had just finished wiping. "You missed a spot, Barberi."

Ben rolled his eyes and ignored the comment.

"Did you hear me, kid? I want every inch of those benches to shine!"

Ben muttered something unintelligible and Roger sharply retorted, "What'd you say?"

Standing up, Ben shouted, "Nothing shines as much as your bald head, you big fat elf!"

Roger strode toward the teenager. "You're calling me an *elf*, you little shit? Look who's talking, midget. You sure you're related to Madsen over there? He's double your size."

"At least I'm still growing," Ben countered. "*You* will always be short."

"Yeah you're growing—growing dumber by the second. C'mon, Cheech, you're cleaning the engine room." He not-so-gently pushed the boy toward the hatch. Ben grumbled the whole time but allowed himself to be propelled forward.

Shaking his head, Grant still couldn't believe how disrespectfully his nephew spoke to his boss. But Rog let Ben's comments roll right off him, seeming to enjoy the banter. Grant gathered his list and headed to the office to call the liquor store. As he passed by the ticket window, he felt the hairs on the back of his neck bristle. Slowing his pace, he gingerly rounded the corner and, sure enough, found the reason for his sudden alarm.

Standing in the shadows was Angelo Barberi.

Behind the Mafia boss was a tall, muscular man, his hooded eyes staring menacingly over Angelo's shoulder.

Grant gulped and took a step backward. Here was Carlo's father, and Grant had no doubt he'd be seeking revenge for his son's death.

"Grant," Angelo called. "I want to talk to you, *nipote*."

His heart was banging so loudly he barely heard his uncle, and Grant retreated another step.

"Please," Angelo said, walking out of the shadows and opening his hands. Grant's eyes darted all around, but he detected no bulge in his uncle's jacket or pockets. He was quite certain the behemoth was packing, though.

Watching Grant's eyes flicker to the bodyguard, Angelo turned his head and spoke over his shoulder. "Leave us, Tank. This is a family matter."

A coughing spasm overtook the Mafia don, and Anthony Tanketti nervously hesitated, wondering if he should try to help his boss. Once Angelo was breathing normally again, Tank slunk away as ordered, retreating farther into the shadows, leaving the uncle and nephew warily eyeing each other on the dock.

Apparently Grant looked terrified because Angelo said, "Relax, *nipote*—I won't hurt you. Your father forbade it."

Grant forced himself to unclench his fists, and he took in his uncle's pallid complexion beneath his black suit. Beads of sweat cropped up on Angelo's forehead, and Grant could feel drops of sweat sliding down his back as well.

"My father?" Grant asked.

"I told Enzo everything," Angelo responded. His jaw tightened. "I told him how you killed my son."

"And did you tell him how your son killed my brother?"

Angelo was surprised by Grant's seething tone. He'd thought the boy was a wimpy non-entity, but perhaps he'd been wrong.

Coughing a few times more made Angelo's black eyes water, and suddenly Grant didn't feel so scared.

"For what it's worth," Angelo began, "I didn't approve of what my son did. No matter what you think of me, I loved Logan. Like a son," he added quietly.

"I loved him too," Grant insisted. *Before you destroyed him.* Sadness competed with intense anger as he spat, "What do you want?"

Angelo gave a weary smile. "It's not what I want; it's what your father wants."

Grant held his breath.

"Enzo wants to see you."

His heart pounded furiously again, and he slowly shook his head.

"He needs to see you, Grant. Soon."

Still shaking his head, Grant smiled bitterly. "Does he think he *deserves*—"

"Hey, Ange!" Ben's boisterous voice interrupted them.

Grant looked up with horror to find his nephew approaching.

"Ben!" Angelo boomed, erupting into a genuine grin. "I heard you were working on a boat."

Grant nervously glanced around him, feeling quite unsafe and wondering what else Angelo had heard. Thank goodness Sophie no longer worked with him.

"Yeah." Ben blushed, now standing next to the two men.

"But why are you working, *ragazzo?* You ever need any money, you can always come to me. You know that, right?"

The color on Ben's cheeks deepened. "Yeah, but, um, my mom, um, she told me I wasn't supposed to go to your place anymore."

A wicked smile bloomed on the don's face. "Since when do you listen to your mom, Ben?"

They both chuckled while Grant felt sick. The chuckle must have irritated Angelo's throat because he started coughing again, and the hacking drew Tank from the shadows.

He nervously clasped Angelo's arm. "Boss? We better go."

Angelo, gasping for air, nodded. Weakly, he murmured, "Take care of yourselves, you two." A few coughs later, he choked out, "Think about what I said, Grant."

Once Angelo and Tank disappeared, Grant found himself shaking. He had no idea how to protect his nephew from their menace.

"What'd Angelo say to you?" Ben inquired.

"Nothing." Grant aimed a deadly serious look at his nephew. "I want you to stay away from them. You're *never* to go to that compound again, got it?"

Ben hesitated. His uncle had never spoken so harshly to him before. "Why?"

"Because they're dangerous. Any money Angelo might give to you, you'll pay for with your soul. You stay away from them, Ben. I better not find out you've been anywhere *near* the mansion."

Grant stormed off to the office, leaving Ben standing on the dock like a chastised schoolboy.

Ben's eyes narrowed into slits. *Nobody* was going to tell him what to do.

9. Constant

"You look well-rested today."

Grant glanced up at Hunter and swallowed uncomfortably. He was still getting used to being so closely watched in therapy—he couldn't get anything by the observant psychologist. "Yes, sir."

Settling into his chair across from the couple, ready to begin the session, Hunter smiled to himself. He was accustomed to receiving one-word responses from stubborn clients, but he supposed the tag-on "sir," which transformed the response to two words, made Grant seem slightly more forthcoming.

Smiling gently, Hunter asked, "Are you sleeping better?"

Gazing at the beautiful woman next to him, Grant took her hand in his and gave it a squeeze. "Some nights," he answered.

Sophie felt Grant's body tense as he prepared for further questions.

Hunter nodded. "I'm glad to hear it. So, the other nights…they're not so great?"

Grant looked down.

His heart pounded and he tried to push away the hands groping for him, but he couldn't escape their unyielding embrace. "No!" he heard a hoarse voice repetitively scream, but it wasn't until he opened his eyes that he realized the voice was his own.

Though it was dark in the bedroom, he could feel his face buried in her luxurious hair, and her breasts pressing into his chest. She'd drawn him into her, evidently to soothe his distress.

"Shh," she fussed.

He felt her fingers caress his shoulder blades, holding him tighter.

"It was just a dream," she said.

He fought for control. His panting breaths and racing heartbeat took several minutes to slow down while she lightly stroked his back.

"You're safe, Grant," she murmured.

Once he trusted himself to speak, he said, "I'm sorry."

"Why are you sorry?"

Because I'm totally fucked up. Because I'm crazy. Because I'll never deserve someone as perfect as you. "Because I woke you up."

"It's okay, McSailor. I'm just glad you're letting yourself close your eyes. I'm sure we'll both be back asleep soon."

"I'm guessing you've been experiencing more nightmares recently?"

Grant glared at Hunter. "How did you know that?"

"Sometimes when you discuss traumatic memories in counseling, it, uh, stirs the pot a bit. You might have more flashbacks or nightmares—"

"Wait a minute," Grant interrupted. "You're telling me therapy's going to make me feel *worse?*"

Before Hunter could answer, Sophie squeezed Grant's hand and said, "Sometimes things have to get worse before they get better."

Grant sighed heavily, suddenly weary. He was *so* tired of things getting worse.

"The increase in nightmares is why we need to shore up your coping skills before we delve into the traumatic memories," Hunter explained. "Let's work on developing some tools to manage the memories first, okay?"

Grant bit his lip and slowly nodded.

In a calming voice, Hunter began, "Traumatic stress reactions can occur after any kind of life-threatening event, such as a car accident, sudden death, violence, assault. The symptoms of PTSD are reliving the event—like nightmares or flashbacks, avoidance of anything associated with the trauma, and a feeling of constantly being 'on edge.'"

Grant didn't appreciate being labeled with some psycho diagnosis—PTSD, OCD, ADHD, or whatever jumble of letters this crackpot was throwing at him. "Okay, I'll admit I have nightmares, but I don't avoid the trauma, and I'm *not* on edge."

Hunter noticed Sophie trying to suppress a smirk. "Sophie, do you have something to add here?"

Glancing nervously at Grant before returning her gaze to Hunter, she said, "He's *totally* on edge. I've seen many signs of increased activation—like his exaggerated startle response. And he has trouble falling asleep. Oh, and hypervigilance too."

"Hyper-what?" Grant said skeptically.

Hunter jumped in. "Hypervigilance is a response to trauma where your mind and body remain on alert. It's an increased state of watchfulness that's an attempt to protect yourself. But persistently being on edge is exhausting, and eventually you shut down. You may feel completely numb from trying to be so alert."

Grant nodded, wondering how the psychologist knew sometimes he'd been so numb he felt almost dead, especially in prison. Sophie had been the one to finally spark some emotion in him.

"Outbursts of anger are also a sign of PTSD," Hunter said.

Grant grimaced. He wasn't going to blame his out-of-control anger on some stupid diagnosis. He alone was responsible for hurting Sophie.

"Would you like to hear some techniques for managing these symptoms?" Hunter asked. "It's up to you."

Sophie was pretty impressed. The psychologist was handing Grant the reins, a smart strategy for working with an abuse survivor. Grant had likely experienced a complete loss of control when his father beat him, so allowing him to dictate the session would help him feel more in charge.

"Yes, sir." Grant surprised himself by agreeing.

Hunter looked pleased. "I want to explain some grounding techniques, but first let's talk a bit about your brain. When a trauma happens, it can stimulate a flood of adrenaline and other chemicals, activating the lower parts of your brain and keeping them disconnected from the higher levels. One lower brain structure is the amygdala, the center for emotions like fear. When children experience intense, frightening events, their basest survival instincts click in, and the higher levels of their brain may go 'offline.' They react purely on instinct and emotion, without logic and reason, and this reaction can help them survive. Are you following me so far, Grant?"

"I think so, sir."

"The problem is that when these children become adults and their emotional memories are somehow triggered—say they experience a certain sight, sound, or smell that reminds them of the trauma—they react just like they did as children. They might freeze, with a pounding heart, shortness of breath, sweating. Their brains are living in the past and preventing them from realizing the threat's no longer viable. Their higher-order brain functioning is thrown offline, and they can't distinguish past from present. These grounding techniques help bring the pre-frontal cortex back 'online' to help these individuals figure out they don't have to engage in fight or flight at the moment."

"Wow, do you specialize in trauma?" Sophie cut in. "I'm learning a lot here."

"Really?" Hunter responded. "I thought you'd have learned this stuff on your internship at the VA Hospital."

"Well, yes, but that was a few years ago and—"

"You worked at a VA hospital?" Grant interrupted.

Sophie nodded. "My pre-doctoral internship was at the Hampton VA, in Virginia."

Grant looked impressed. His eyes locked on hers as he said, "Thank you."

"I should be the one thanking *you*," she countered, "for serving our country. In that hospital I saw firsthand the sacrifices made by soldiers and sailors." Sophie smiled warmly and gave Grant's hand another squeeze, then she turned to Hunter. "Sorry, I got us off track."

"Getting to know each other on a deeper level is one of our goals in here." Hunter shrugged amicably. "Seems like you two have yet one more thing in common. Anyway, I was talking about grounding techniques. One thing that happens during a nightmare is your breathing becomes shallow and rapid. So, the first technique is to take deep, diaphragmatic breaths."

Hunter showed Grant how to push his stomach out with each breath, and Sophie joined in too.

"Then you want to try to reorient yourself to the present," Hunter said. "Look around you. Tell me what you see."

It took Grant a second to realize Hunter had given him an instruction, and he jumped in his seat. "Oh, yes, sir. Um, I see…your desk, uh, your aquarium…"

"There's Nemo and Nema," Sophie prompted, and all three grinned.

"What do you hear?" asked Hunter.

After a beat, Grant responded, "The aquarium pump and the clock ticking."

"Do you feel the surface of the sofa beneath you?" When Grant nodded, Hunter suggested, "Stomp your foot. Feel the floor under you."

Feeling rather dorky, Grant complied and stomped his foot. The ground felt solid beneath the sole of his leather shoe.

"Another way to orient your brain to the present is to tell yourself out loud that you're right here, right now. It may sound weird, but Grant, I'd like you to say, 'It's September sixth.'"

Cynically raising one eyebrow, Grant dutifully replied, "It's September sixth."

"I am an adult."

His voice was a little more confident as he mimicked Hunter. "I am an adult."

"Good." Hunter nodded. "When you experience a flashback or nightmare, I want you to try some of these grounding strategies. Perhaps you have a recurring nightmare and you wake up consumed by terror — that's the time to take deep breaths and orient yourself to the present."

Sophie chewed the inside of her cheek. "Recently, Grant keeps saying the same thing during every nightmare," she offered.

"I do?" Grant looked shocked.

"Yes." She glanced with uncertainty at Hunter, who gave her an encouraging nod. "He says, 'Don't make me do it. Please, don't make me do it.'"

Hunter's forehead creased. "Don't make you do *what?*"

Pull the trigger. The words immediately popped into Grant's mind, and his lips parted with surprise as his heart began thrumming in his chest.

Hunter stared at him intently. "Did you just remember something, Grant?"

His face was pale. "I — I don't know."

Had he pulled the trigger? *Had* he killed somebody? He'd been forced to shoot Carlo in self defense, of course, but this memory seemed different — from long ago.

Noticing Sophie was also staring at him, Grant blurted the next thing that came to mind: "My father wants to see me."

Sophie's eyes widened. "Did he call you?"

Grant shook his head. "No, Uncle Angelo visited me on the docks."

Her eyes got bigger. "Are you okay?"

"Yeah, he didn't hurt me. But he did insist on inviting Ben to the compound."

"I'll have to talk to Ben about that," Sophie responded in an unsteady voice.

"Don't worry—I already warned him not to go near there. That's the *last* thing he needs right now."

Sophie appeared pensive. "Is that why you made Ben keep working on the cruise? To keep him out of trouble after school?"

"Yeah," Grant nodded. "But the cruises stop running in a few weeks, so I don't know what I'm going to do with him then. I guess I'll be calling his mom for a consult."

"You have to find another job too, right?"

Grant sighed, "Yeah."

Hunter re-entered the conversation. "Do you know why your father wants to see you, Grant?"

"No, sir, but it's probably a moot point. Since I'm on parole, I don't think I'm allowed to go to Gurnee as a visitor. Hopefully I won't be returning as an inmate," he added scornfully.

"You might want to ask your PO if you're allowed to visit," Hunter said.

"Why would I want to do that, sir?"

"Because it might be a good idea to visit your father."

Grant and Sophie gaped at the psychologist.

"What?" Sophie shrieked.

"You're not ready now, of course," Hunter said. "But, Grant, when you work through some of this trauma, it could be quite healing to confront your abuser."

Grant tried to hide it, but he trembled at Hunter's suggestion.

"You remember when you said you don't avoid anything reminding you of the trauma?" Hunter asked, receiving a nod of recognition from Grant. "Your reluctance to visit your father is precisely that symptom. You're avoiding seeing him because he triggers memories of the abuse. At some point you may need to face that fear to reduce its hold over you. Your father hurt you when you were a child, but now you're an adult, and he can't hurt you any more."

Grant quietly considered his words, and Sophie asked, 'Is this like exposure treatment?"

"Exactly," Hunter answered. "Research shows that an effective treatment for PTSD is to expose oneself to the trauma—either by retelling the story or by facing significant triggers—and responding differently this time using new skills and perceptions about it."

Hunter let that sink in before continuing. "For example, many abused children believe the abuse was their fault. This makes sense because children are egocentric, assuming the world revolves around them—if they're hurt, they *must* have been the ones to cause it somehow, they *must* be to blame. But when they're older and tell their stories, they learn they couldn't have stopped the abuse, and they did the best they could to survive the situation. They learn it wasn't their fault. When they subsequently flash back to the trauma, they react with less shame. They tolerate the memories better by using grounding strategies."

Haunting coal-black eyes flashed through Grant's mind, and he felt beads of sweat on his upper lip. "I still don't want to see him," he stated decisively.

"I can appreciate that," Hunter responded. "I don't want you to see your father either, unless you're ready. We'll go at your pace and only proceed if we both make the decision that it's a good idea."

Grant gulped. "I don't think I could take it."

Hunter looked at him kindly. "I know you're strong enough to handle it."

"I'm not strong."

"Yes, you are."

Grant quietly asked, his voice barely above a whisper, "How do you know?"

"I know you're strong because you're the only one left standing in your family. It's taken incredible fortitude to survive the challenges you've faced. You're the only Barberi left."

Grant dropped his gaze, wringing his hands in his lap. The throbbing ache in his heart from his mother's death eighteen years ago was only compounded by the loss of his brother. Was Dr. Hayes right? *Was* he strong? Or was it just pure luck that he wasn't locked away in a cell or a coffin?

Sensing that Grant needed a little respite, Hunter turned to Sophie. "We haven't had the chance to talk about you much today, Sophie. How are things in your world?"

It was difficult for her to turn her attention away from Grant, but she eventually responded. "Kirsten passed her dissertation defense."

"That's wonderful!" Hunter beamed. "Another soon-to-be psychologist cut loose on the world."

Sophie smiled. "By the time Kirsten sits for her licensing exam, it will have taken her nine years to become a psychologist."

"She was All But Dissertation for a while, huh?"

"Yeah," Sophie replied.

"I was just reading that becoming a psychologist requires the longest training for the lowest salary of any profession," Hunter said.

She chuckled. "Sounds about right." Then she sadly added, "I still miss it, though."

Hunter nodded, and Grant reached out to place a steady hand on her forearm. Evidently he'd rejoined the conversation.

"My friend Tanya said Kirsten really nailed the defense," Sophie said, attempting to brighten the mood. "Her advisor David — the jerk — asked her an impossibly difficult question, but it didn't throw her at all."

Now Grant was *very* involved in the conversation.

"David?" he repeated.

Feeling his inquisitive stare upon her, Sophie blushed slightly.

"Yes, David Alton."

"Ah, the professor you had a crush on in grad school," Hunter supplied, earning a glare from Sophie.

"Actually, I found out some interesting information about David," Sophie said. Her eyes narrowed. "Apparently I'm not the only hapless woman he's misled. He did it to Tanya too."

"He did?" Hunter asked.

"Yes. Just like me, Tanya was mortified when he told her she'd 'misconstrued his intentions.'"

"So this guy gets his rocks off seducing pretty women, and when they finally express an interest in him, he cuts them loose, telling them they made it all up in their heads?" Grant shook his head.

"I *think* that's what's going on," Sophie replied. "Wait a minute," she added, looking at her boyfriend suspiciously. "What makes you think Tanya's pretty?"

Shrugging, Grant quickly said, "If David targeted you, it's clear he only goes for gorgeous women."

Sophie beamed while Hunter appreciatively shook his head. "Wow," he said. "That's impressive, Grant. You turned potential jealousy into a beautiful compliment in five seconds flat. I could learn a thing or two from you."

Instead of cocky bravado, Grant's cheeks flushed with embarrassment. "But I meant it," he said shyly. "Sophie's stunning."

What *he* wouldn't give to be called *stunning* by this Adonis… Hunter sighed and glanced at Sophie, who looked a bit uncomfortable.

"I was going to ask you how you wanted to handle this situation with David, but I see that our time's up. Perhaps we can discuss that next session."

Sophie and Grant rose from the sofa, and Hunter also got to his feet.

"Good work, both of you," he said. His hazel eyes crinkled with warmth. "I'll be giving a positive progress report to your PO. See you next week."

The pair left the office feeling pretty good about themselves.

As they stood outside the office building, preparing to say their goodbyes, Grant couldn't help but notice Sophie gazing at him intently, her twinkling brown eyes sweeping down the length of his body.

He tilted his head. "What are you up to?"

"Oh!" She grinned. "I was just imagining you in a Navy uniform, like the men at the VA hospital. Damn, I bet you looked hot."

He gave her an embarrassed, lopsided grin. "You'll just have to use your imagination, I guess. See you tonight, my little minx."

"I'll be home late tonight, remember?"

Grant looked befuddled—like he always did after therapy.

"I'm going to dinner with my dad," Sophie reminded him.

"Oh, that's right. Where're you going?"

"Some Italian place my dad likes."

"Italian, huh?" He pulled her body into his, resting his long fingers on the curve of her hips. "Stay away from the mobsters, Bonnie."

She smiled up at him, and the warmth dancing in her eyes was irresistible. He planted a soft kiss on her lips and she closed her eyes, reveling in the ripples of pleasure surging through her body.

When Grant finally released her, Sophie was the befuddled one. Eyeing Grant's dark Italian features, she teased, "But I like the mobsters. Especially this one."

10. Confidential

"After you, madam," Grant said, making a sweeping gesture toward the restaurant with one hand while the other held the door open for his date.

Sophie gave a warm smile, admiring the length of his tall, lanky body. His graceful leanness was emphasized by the pale blue dress shirt tucked into crisp black pants. She smirked. "Thank you, sir."

As she passed in front of him, he paused to appreciate *her* appearance. Sophie always had a knack for elegance, even in gym clothes, and tonight was no exception. Her long hair hung in loose curls, cascading over her shoulders, and her mini-dress, complete with embroidered embellishments, showcased her shapely legs, which ended in funky brown gladiator sandals. Sensing a hint of autumn in the air, Sophie was sneaking in one last outing for her open-toed shoes.

As they made their way into the Brazilian steakhouse, they were greeted by samba music, and the smooth underlying beat gave Sophie an itch to dance. The restaurant was hopping — Grant had told her about its growing popularity — but fortunately they had reservations. The host led them past the salad bar, and as they strolled to their table, Sophie enjoyed the comforting presence of Grant's hand at the small of her back.

As soon as the host left them, Sophie leaned in and said, "That's the most amazing salad bar I've ever seen!"

Grant smiled and also leaned forward. "It *is* amazing, but promise me you'll try some meat too. They're known for their steak, according to Rog."

"I'm not one of those girls who only eats salad, Grant," Sophie quickly clarified. "Filet mignon's one of my favorites."

Amused by the indignant glow of her cheeks, he brushed his long fingers lovingly down her temple. "Ah yes, Will Taylor's daughter is certainly accustomed to fine dining. I bet that Italian place you went to was much nicer than this."

Sophie demurely declined to respond. Her father had indeed taken her to a very fancy restaurant inside his buddy Alex Remington's hotel — a gorgeously ornate setting where the two of them generated an almost-three-hundred-dollar bill, which Alex promptly waived when he came to visit them at the table. "Actually, my family wasn't always wealthy," Sophie said. "My father worked extremely hard in the construction business to get where he is now. He persevered through some difficult times."

"I'm sure he did," Grant agreed. "He has that, um, tenacious *bulldog* quality about him."

Sophie blushed. At dinner a few nights ago her father had once again attempted to dissuade her from dating Grant, and she'd once again refused to listen. She wasn't going to let go of Grant, no matter what her father said.

Redirecting the conversation, Sophie asked, "So, how was work today?"

"Pretty good. At least there weren't any arguments between Ben and Rog. I told Ben he almost lost the privilege of going out with his friends tonight because of his disrespect for our boss."

Sophie gently stroked Grant's hand. "He'll be okay, Grant. He's sixteen years old. You can't supervise him around the clock, and Ashley agreed with you that he could go out tonight, right?"

He nodded distractedly. "You're right — it's just that I know him. I know that look in his eyes. He wants to self-destruct." Grant sighed, then spoke more quietly, "He wants to follow in his father's footsteps."

"I guess Logan and Ben are alike that way — trying to rebel to get back at their fathers for leaving them too young," she said wistfully.

Grant stared at her intently and she continued, "Logan was thirteen when your dad was sent away?"

Grant nodded.

"And Ben was only sixteen when he lost his dad."

They were quiet as the waiter filled their water glasses and explained the steakhouse menu. When he departed, Sophie's eyes pierced Grant's.

"But Grant," she said, clasping his hand in hers once again, "there's one big difference between Logan and Ben."

"What's that?"

"You."

Sensing his confusion, she explained. "Once Logan ran away from Joe's, he lost you. He lost his one reason to fight against your dad's family—he lost the one reason to become a good man. He no longer had to protect you. He lost his sense of purpose, and we all know where that led him."

"But no one forced him to leave! He chose that himself!"

She was surprised by the sudden anger in Grant's voice and nodded sadly. "Logan made many mistakes, but leaving his eight-year-old brother was the one he regretted most." She remembered sitting on her office sofa, holding Logan as he was wracked with sobs. *I hurt him.* Sophie remembered the pain in his voice. *I left my little brother all alone. He'll never forgive me.*

Sophie gazed at the younger, less hardened man across from her. "He loved you," she insisted. "He hated himself for not being there for you. But you had your uncle, who taught you so much. And now Ben has *his* uncle. Ben has you in a way Logan never could."

Grant's jaw clenched against unexpressed emotion. His focus had been trained on Sophie's voice for several moments, but now the lively Brazilian music once again entered his consciousness, and he glanced around him at the brilliant red hues of the restaurant's décor.

Sophie sensed a new topic would be helpful. "Let's not talk about him any more tonight, okay?"

Nodding readily, Grant took a deep breath and attempted a smile. "How about trying out that incredible salad bar?"

They rose and headed toward the long granite slab, heaped with everything from colossal shrimp and hunks of mozzarella to artichoke hearts and jicama. The maître d' was heading their way, escorting another couple to their seats, and Sophie gasped.

Grant glanced up and found none other than Dr. Hunter Hayes walking in their direction, followed by a tall, brown-haired man with a high forehead and intelligent blue eyes.

Hunter was zoned in on their table, and he'd practically passed Grant and Sophie before he was even aware of their presence. He jumped upon catching a glimpse of the couple. His personal and professional lives had just intersected.

Behind him, Dr. Bradley Washington noticed his partner's startled reaction, and he too glanced at the couple gawking at them from the salad bar. The woman was quite attractive and the man was smoking hot, with intense blue eyes that met Bradley's with a sparkle of curiosity.

The man was just an inch or two shorter than Bradley, and for some reason the plastic surgeon felt the hairs on the back of his neck bristle. He didn't know if he wanted to fuck him or to fuck him up, but he was definitely intrigued.

This interaction lasted less than one second before Hunter regained his composure, averting his eyes from the couple and coolly resuming his stroll to the table. He felt Bradley's large hand on his back, guiding him firmly. Typically that gesture was reassuring, but in front of his clients his partner's touch seemed possessive, controlling, and embarrassing.

"Well, *that* was interesting," Grant whispered when they'd passed. "Dr. Hayes didn't even say hi to us."

"He's not supposed to," she whispered back, selecting a plate from the stack and using tongs for the arugula. "When therapists run into their clients in social settings, they try to protect their confidentiality. They only acknowledge them if the clients say hi first."

Grant grunted, suspicious of this secret world of shrink etiquette.

"I wonder if that's his partner," Sophie quietly mused.

Grant stole a glance behind them, finding the tall, brown-haired man staring intently back at him.

"Whoever he is, he looks pissed off," Grant replied, quickly returning his gaze to the salad bar.

Across the room, the two men settled in at their table. "Do you know that couple?" Bradley asked.

"Who?" Hunter played dumb.

"That buzz-cut guy with the blonde at the salad bar — you seemed to recognize them."

Hunter glanced over his shoulder. Thankfully Grant and Sophie had turned their backs to him. "Umm, nope. Never seen them before."

Bradley's blue eyes narrowed. Hunter had never been a good liar. Drumming his fingers on the tabletop, Bradley continued glancing back and forth between his partner and the couple, who were now taking their seats at a nearby table.

From the corner of his eye, Hunter noted where Grant and Sophie were sitting. "What's wrong, stud?" he asked Bradley. "You look uptight."

Bradley reluctantly peeled his eyes from Grant and rested them on Hunter, whose royal blue button-down brought out a cerulean hue in his warm hazel eyes. Bradley loved that color—the gem tone really played up Hunter's tanned face and cropped blond hair. Inhaling deeply and smelling roasting chicken, sausage, and beef, Bradley gave his partner a crooked, knowing smile.

"Nothing's wrong, Hayes. I just realized why you're acting so weird: They must be your therapy clients."

Hunter blinked rapidly and attempted to keep his facial expression neutral. He would've tried to deny it, but running into Grant while out on a date had thrown him. He chose nervous silence instead.

"Relax." Bradley chuckled. "I know you can't say anything." He stole another glance at the couple. "Though what *that* beautiful couple has to argue about, I'll never know."

You'd be surprised, Hunter silently replied.

"Her cheekbones are structurally flawless," Bradley marveled, his voice clinical and detached. "I don't know if I could ever get that result surgically."

"Oh, I'm sure you could," Hunter said, but Bradley was still absorbed.

"Even though the guy's nose isn't perfect, it suits his face. The shape of his head is exquisite, and those plump lips… I wonder if he does collagen injections—"

"Good evening," the waiter said, and Hunter exhaled with relief. He'd been clenching the draped tablecloth with both fists.

Meanwhile, over where the "beautiful couple" was sitting, Sophie was giggling between bites of her salad.

"What's so funny?" Grant asked.

"I'm thinking of this article about confidentiality we read in my *Professional Issues* class." She grinned. "It's about when therapists run into clients in public. The authors interviewed therapists and clients about the chance encounters, and they found that the therapists were much more freaked out than the clients."

"Really?"

"Yeah, the therapists were all worried about protecting confidentiality, so they went out of their way not to acknowledge the clients, but sometimes the clients felt really hurt that their therapists ignored them."

"I get that." Grant nodded. "It felt like he was giving us the cold shoulder or something, but I guess that makes sense. Did you ever run into your clients downtown?"

Sophie shrugged. "Sure, a few times, but it was never that big of a deal. We'd talk about it in session afterward, and I told my clients I'd take their lead — if they wanted to ignore me, that was fine, but if they said hi, I'd reciprocate. Most of the time I was out with Kirsten or another therapist, and we just learned not to ask each other questions if we ran into people on the street."

Sophie stopped short, thinking about one of her clients in particular. She wanted to reassure Grant that she'd never encountered Logan in public, but she didn't believe it would be wise to bring up his name.

She sighed. "Frankly, I wasn't practicing long enough to experience many awkward public encounters with my clients."

Grant gave her a wistful look, thinking about their lost careers.

"What about you?" Sophie asked. "What was it like when you ran into your Navy colleagues out in public?"

"Well, typically there was a salute involved." Grant smirked. "So ignoring each other was out of the question."

Eventually the waiter cleared their salad plates, and Grant picked up a round cardboard coaster from the table. One side was green, indicating that the diner was ready for waiters to approach the table with a succulent cut from the slab on their skewers. The other side was red, communicating that the diner was full for now — or at least completely occupied by a plate full of meat.

"Ready?" Grant asked, looking playfully at Sophie.

She nodded.

"Okay," he replied, cautiously flipping both of their coasters to green. "We're going in."

Immediately two waiters swooped over, one offering roasted chicken and one presenting *pincaha* sirloin. In just a few moments, their plates were full, and Grant mercifully flipped their coasters back to red.

About an hour later, Bradley offered Hunter a succulent bite of filet mignon. He protested while clutching his distended belly.

"Oh, but I'm too full."

"C'mon," Bradley coaxed with a coy smile. "You have to taste this. We'll work out extra tomorrow."

Groaning, Hunter reluctantly opened his mouth, allowing Bradley to slide in his fork. As he chewed on the tender bite of steak, Hunter smiled dreamily. "That *is* delicious, you're right." He sat back in his chair, pushing his half-filled plate away from him. "I'm in a food coma."

Suddenly a shadow covered the table, and Hunter looked up to find Sophie, with Grant hovering behind her.

"Hi, Hunter!" she beamed, glancing back at her blushing boyfriend who clearly seemed to disagree with their visit.

Hunter cleared his throat. "Um, hi, Sophie. Hi, Grant."

He got an uncomfortable "Hello, Dr. Hayes" in return as Grant reluctantly sidled up next to Sophie.

Bradley watched the interaction with a bemused look.

"I thought we'd come say hello," Sophie explained. "It seemed kind of silly to sit just a few tables away and not even acknowledge each other." Her curiosity overtook her, and she extended her hand to the man across from Hunter. "Hi, I'm Sophie." As Bradley shook her slender hand in his, she added, "I'm one of Hunter's clients. He's a great psychologist, you know."

Hunter warily examined Bradley's reaction. He still appeared amused and seemed to be studying Grant more than Sophie.

"Oh, I know," Bradley replied. "Hunter tries to analyze me all the time."

The four shared a tense chuckle, and Hunter realized he was being rude. "Uh, Sophie, Grant, this is Dr. Bradley Washington."

Having already greeted Sophie, Bradley offered a handshake to Grant. "Hunter's *partner*," Bradley added, pumping Grant's arm vigorously.

Hunter wanted to crawl under the table, and Grant continued blushing. Bradley seemed to revel in his partner's squirming.

"Are you a psychologist too?" Sophie asked.

"Lord, no!" Hunter answered for him, finally smiling. "He's a surgeon."

Never taking his eyes off Grant, Bradley inquired, "So, Grant, you're Hunter's client as well?"

"Yes, sir," Grant responded.

Bradley's eyebrows formed an inquisitive arch.

"They're, uh, they…" Hunter paused, trying not to compromise their confidentiality any further.

"We're one of the couples Hunter sees," Sophie supplied, now noticing the awkward situation she'd created by dragging Grant over here in the first place. "And we should stop interrupting your dinner. It's very nice to meet you, Bradley."

She attempted a smile and then bit her lip.

"I enjoyed meeting you as well, Sophie." Bradley nodded smoothly. "And you too, Grant. What a treat to catch a glimpse into Hunter's professional life. Everything is so hush-hush, you know."

An awkward silence descended, and Grant fought the urge to simply run from the table. He nodded respectfully at Bradley, "Dr. Washington," then turned his gaze to Hunter. "We'll see you next week, sir."

"Have a lovely evening," Hunter managed as Grant gently led his girlfriend away from the table.

As soon as they were out of earshot, Bradley began laughing heartily. "That was awesome!" he cackled. "I don't know if I've ever seen you more embarrassed—you're totally adorable."

Hunter was not amused.

Bradley's blue eyes continued twinkling. "Does he actually call you 'sir'? What the hell is that about?"

"He's, um, he's former military," Hunter disclosed, unsure if it was appropriate to share that information.

"Why do they see you?" Bradley inquired.

"You know I can't tell you that!"

"Oh, c'mon, Hunt. Give me something here. They freaking came over and *introduced* themselves to me." He slid into a mocking, falsetto tone, "He's a great psychologist, you know."

"Shut up." Hunter's lips pressed into a taut line.

Bradley didn't heed the warning and instead sat up rigidly in his chair. "See you next week, sir!" He executed a sharp salute before bursting into laughter.

Hunter felt his chest tighten with anger. "Stop making fun of Grant."

Bradley's grin vanished, and he scrutinized his partner. "You're rather protective of him, aren't you?"

Hunter looked down, recalling some of the awful stories Grant had shared. How could he not feel protective of that wounded little boy who was abused by his father?

Bradley continued to study his partner thoughtfully. "Damn, that Grant is quite a handsome man, isn't he?"

Hunter locked eyes with his now-suspicious partner. A hint of jealousy crept into Bradley's tone. "You never told me you had a client who's so fucking hot."

"He's somewhat handsome," Hunter replied, choosing his words carefully. "*And* he's heterosexual."

"Are you sure?"

"Hey, you have attractive male patients too."

"Maybe *after* I'm done with them," Bradley said. "But nobody as fine as that man." He drummed his fingertips on the table. "Why haven't you told me about Grant?"

Hunter's heart began pounding. "It's confidential!"

"Yes, but you've never seemed so freaked out by this kind of situation before. There's something not right here. I've had the sense you've been hiding something for the past month, and when I see a man like *that*—a man you know, a man you've never told me about… I'm getting a funny feeling here, Hunt. This isn't another Robert, is it?"

Hunter's heart continued thumping, and his cheeks flushed with anger. "*Nothing* happened with Robert, damn it! How many times do I have to tell you?"

Bradley cut to the chase. "Can you honestly tell me you're not attracted to Grant?"

Hunter's hesitation told him all he needed to know.

"Great, fucking great," Bradley roared. "You're having an affair with your client."

"I am not!" Hunter shouted before nervously glancing around him. A few diners at nearby tables shot him questioning glances, but the lively music absorbed most of his outburst. "I am not having an affair with him," he repeated more quietly. "Why do you always jump to conclusions?"

"I'm just examining the evidence," Bradley replied coldly.

Hunter sighed ruefully, running his hand through his short blond hair. "I should have listened to Michelle."

"Michelle?" Bradley's mouth tightened. "You're talking to your hag about this, but not to me?" He appeared wounded. "Spill it, Hunt. Now."

Biting his lip, Hunter finally said, "I consulted with Michelle about this couple. I admitted to her that I felt attracted to Grant." Observing Bradley's increased glower, he rushed in to add, "It's totally normal to feel attracted to clients. And I followed ethical guidelines by consulting with another psychologist about it."

"What did she say?" he growled.

"She said I should think about referring them to another psychologist."

"Why didn't you?"

"It's complicated." Hunter exhaled loudly. "I can't explain without getting into the details of the case, but I thought I might cause more harm by referring them than by keeping them. And I felt confident there was no danger I would act on my feelings. I love *you,* Bradley. I would never do anything to hurt you like that."

He quietly absorbed Hunter's words, wanting to believe him, but feeling the remnants of distrust still flowing through his veins.

"Michelle gave me one more piece of advice," Hunter confessed. "She encouraged me to tell you about my attraction to my client, to, um, sort of guarantee I wouldn't act on it."

"But you didn't tell me! Why?"

Hunter winced. "I don't know. I was embarrassed, I guess. I know I just said feeling attracted to clients is normal, but I felt kind of humiliated about it—like I was being unprofessional or something. Bradley, I promise you nothing will happen."

"Somehow I'm not entirely reassured," Bradley said with a frown.

"I'm not even that attracted to him anymore."

"And why is that?"

"For one thing, he and Sophie are all over each other. Total PDA. He's obviously heterosexual."

"Ugh—you have to watch those breeders in action, huh? Poor you."

Finally Hunter and Bradley shared a grin. The waiter cleared their plates and announced he'd bring papaya cream to finish their meal.

Once he left, Bradley said, "You said 'for one thing'? What else has decreased your attraction to Grant?"

Hunter's grin faded, and he began fidgeting with the coasters.

Bradley furrowed his brow. "What is it?"

Hunter was silent for several moments. "His behavior disgusted me," he finally explained. "He reminded me of a time I'd rather forget."

Bradley looked worried and reached out to hold one of Hunter's hands. "You can tell me, Hunt."

Lifting his eyes, Hunter swallowed. "He has an anger management problem. He was rough and aggressive, and he scared his partner."

Bradley immediately dropped Hunter's hand. "Th-That was ten years ago."

"I know."

But Hunter still felt the sharp sting of the powerful punch careening into his face, bruising his cheek, busting his lip, and shattering the perfect relationship he thought he had. Bradley had been livid when he accused Hunter of cheating on him with his friend Robert, but when the anger morphed into physical violence, Hunter had been shocked. He'd fled from Bradley that night, and stayed away for several months. Only after much pleading and fulfilled promises to attend counseling had Hunter returned. The violence had since been forgiven, but never forgotten.

"You know I would never do that again," Bradley said.

"And *you* know it'd be over if you tried."

A tense silence blanketed them until Bradley tentatively reached out and caressed the warm skin of Hunter's palm with the pad of his thumb.

"I'm sorry," Bradley murmured sincerely. "I'm sorry you still think about that time." He sighed. "I was an idiot."

Despite Bradley's cocky bravado, fierce jealousy, and irascible desire to dominate, tender moments like this one reminded Hunter it was all worthwhile. His friends, his therapist, his mother—all had warned him that one episode of domestic violence would inevitably lead to countless more, trapping Hunter in an abusive relationship. But he and Bradley had beaten the odds—so far, at least.

The foundation of Hunter's profession was a profound belief in the possibility of change, and Bradley had seemed to change. Undoubtedly Hunter, too, had changed in many ways over the years.

The waiter brought their creamy Brazilian desserts, and Hunter paused for just a moment, gazing at Bradley, before digging in. He took one bite and groaned, patting his full stomach again.

"You keep feeding me these huge servings and I'll be too fat to attract other men, anyway," he said, willing himself to smile.

Bradley grinned slyly. "That's the plan, Hunt. And if you get too far gone I'll give you a free tummy tuck—one of the many advantages of dating me."

11. *Con*munication

After their dinner at the Brazilian steakhouse, Sophie and Grant took a long, romantic walk along the lake.

They returned to the apartment to find Ben still out with his friends.

Grant snapped his phone shut after his call went unanswered. "What is it, eleven?" He frowned. "I told him to be home by ten since it's a school night."

Sophie wearily plopped down on the sofa, grabbing a set of papers that needed grading.

"Do you think we should call Ashley?" she asked.

Grant chewed his lip. "Let's wait another hour or so — I don't want to scare her. I'll keep trying his phone."

Ten minutes later they heard a key turn in the lock. The errant teenager entered the apartment to find his uncle waiting with an icy glare.

"You're over an hour late," Grant barked, approaching him.

"Must've lost track of time," Ben mumbled, his eyes shifting to Sophie on the sofa.

Grant surreptitiously sniffed the air around his nephew and was grateful not to detect the scent of alcohol or marijuana. However, he knew his nephew was no angel.

"I'd like to see what's in your pockets."

"What?" Ben retorted angrily. "Why?"

"I want to see if you have any pot on you."

"Well, I don't," Ben said.

"Fine, then it shouldn't be a big deal to show me your pockets."

"Don't I get *any* privacy?" the teenager whined.

"You have to earn privacy, Ben," Grant explained. "Just like you earned an evening out with your friends by performing well at school and work. Every time you behave like you should, you earn more of my trust. So show me your pockets, and let's move on!"

His cheeks furiously blushing, Ben stole a glance at Sophie "Not with her here."

"Oh!" Sophie jumped a bit, surprised to be included in the conversation. "I'm sorry. I'll go to the bedroom."

Grant glanced back and forth from his girlfriend to his nephew. "That was rude, Ben. Sophie can sit wherever she pleases—"

"No, Ben's right, Grant," Sophie cut in. "This is between you and him." She headed for the bedroom and closed the door behind her, though she could still hear their conversation through the flimsy apartment walls.

Apparently Ben's pockets were clean because after a few moments Grant declared, "Good job. I'm proud of you… But wait a minute. There's still the matter of your broken curfew."

"Curfew?"

Sophie could picture Ben rolling his eyes at the childish word.

"I asked you to be home by ten, and now it's eleven fifteen."

"So what? I made it home, didn't I?"

There was an edgy silence and Sophie worried, hoping Grant was keeping his cool. He must've been taking deep breaths, like Hunter had taught him, because his next words were calm.

"To remind you to come home on time, I want you to do fifty push-ups."

Ben chuckled, but his laughter started to fade when he realized his uncle wasn't even smiling. "You're *serious*?" he hollered. "I'm not doing stupid push-ups!"

"Yes, you are. That's what's going to happen around here when you break the rules."

Inside the bedroom Sophie grinned, guessing Uncle Joe had something to do with this punishment. Teenaged Grant had likely pumped out endless push-ups.

"This is bullshit!" Ben railed.

Grant kept his voice calm. "I'm waiting."

"I'm *not* doing them."

"Oh, you'll do the push-ups," Grant said. "Even if I have to stay here all night with you."

The tense standoff continued for several minutes. Sophie changed into a nightgown, leaving out one component of her ensemble and hoping very much that Grant would *not* be with Ben all night.

Despite herself, she continued eavesdropping, edging closer to the door. Finally she heard Grant's voice, so soft she strained to hear it.

"I know this is tough, Ben, but I will not let you self-destruct like your dad. I won't do it. I won't."

That got him. There was a shuffling sound, and she heard Grant instruct, "Count them out loud, please."

She followed the teenager's begrudging progress by his verbal count—the first twenty went relatively easily, but then the numbers became more labored and the pauses longer between them.

Around number thirty Grant chastised, "Get your butt down—that one doesn't count."

"I can't do any more!" Ben shakily pleaded, his voice muffled by its proximity to the carpet.

"Yes, you can. Stay with it. You're doing great."

Somehow Ben managed six more before Sophie heard the thump of his body on the floor.

"I can't!" he gasped.

Grant sighed. "Okay, get up."

A few moments later Grant asked, "Are you pleased with your physical fitness, Ben?"

Still breathing hard, he rasped, "Not really."

"I'm not either," Grant said. "I think a boy of your age should be able to do fifty push-ups."

"That's a lot of push-ups, Uncle Grant!"

"It is, but I know you're up to the challenge. In fact, I'm going to give you a little motivation. Besides school and work, you're grounded until you can show me fifty push-ups."

Sophie heard a gasp.

"You can't do that!"

Grant didn't bother responding. "I'll even help you get in shape," he continued. "You can join me for my six o'clock run tomorrow morning."

"I'm not going on some — some — some freaking boot-camp run in the middle of the night!"

"It's your choice," Grant countered, his tone softer. "But I hope you come with me. It's awesome to be on the lakefront while the weather's still kind of warm. It's a great way to wake up… C'mon, let's get your bed ready."

Sophie listened to the snap of the sheet as she crossed over to sit on the bed. In typical Ben fashion, the boy augmented his sulking by escaping into music, and Sophie heard the pulsating beat from his earphones all the way in the bedroom. She hoped he wasn't destroying his hearing.

She resumed her reading of a student's paper, but looked up when Grant finally entered the bedroom, looking exhausted.

As he closed the door behind him and lifted his shirt over his head, he dropped his tough fatherly persona, turning uncertain eyes in her direction. "Did I do okay?"

"You did great." She smiled, grabbing his hand and pulling him toward the bed. "The push-ups were a perfect punishment, McNavy-boy."

They chuckled.

"What do you think the chances are that Ben will join me for my run tomorrow?" Grant asked.

"Slim to none," she said with a shrug. "Well, maybe he'll cool down by then and take you up on your offer. I know he likes spending time with you."

"He does?"

"Don't you see how he worships the ground you walk on?"

"He certainly wasn't worshipping anything about me tonight."

"You did what you needed to do — you were authoritative with him just like Hunter wanted you to be. You provided warmth and limit-setting, exactly what he needs."

Grant grimaced. "I hope so." He rose from the bed and began unbuttoning his jeans while Sophie looked on, admiring the view. "I never thought this would be so difficult," he mused, sliding off his jeans and folding them in the closet. "I have even more respect for Joe now. Maybe I should call him and get some advice."

He hooked his thumbs inside the waistband of his boxer shorts and peeled them down, stepping out of them while reaching for a fresh pair.

Dressed only in her silky emerald-green nightgown, Sophie's breath caught upon seeing the curve of his muscular backside. Then her eyes drifted to the red scar above his right buttock and she felt sadness overtake her.

As he slid under the sheet next to her, Sophie pursed her lips. "It's a different situation. You'd lived with Joe since you were eight. It's a lot more difficult to try to parent a boy who's dumped on your doorstep at sixteen."

"That's true." Grant fluffed the pillow and placed it between his back and the headboard. "Though Joe had to deal with some things I don't have to—like losing Logan to Angelo, for one." He halted, as if he'd misspoken, then rushed ahead. "And although Ben hasn't exactly had great parents, at least he wasn't..."

Sophie silently finished the sentence for him. *At least he wasn't beaten by his father.* She dropped her head and tried to focus on the student's paper in her lap, although her concentration was shot.

A few minutes later, Grant asked, "How's the grading going?"

She looked up, and he seemed to have recovered from the mention of his past. She nodded. "Pretty good. This first-year grad student, Nora, is fortunately a good writer. It makes reading the seventh paper in a row about Harry Stack Sullivan's interpersonal theory of counseling slightly more tolerable."

"What's interpersonal theory?" he asked, draping his arm across her shoulders.

"Well," she began, snuggling next to him, "the theory says we learn about ourselves and about relationships through repetitive interactions in our family, and we keep repeating those interactions as adults—like how I keep trying to take care of everybody's emotional needs just like I did with my mom."

"Huh. So Dr. Hayes believes in this theory, then?"

Sophie yawned. "I think so."

Feeling the warmth of her smooth skin and smelling her alluring perfume, Grant gently nuzzled her hair with his nose as he took the paper and pen and set both items on the bedside table. Caressing her soft shoulder, he looked deeply into her eyes.

His own eyes shined with mischief. "Want to get interpersonal, Dr. Taylor?"

Mesmerized, she could only dumbly respond, "Uh-huh."

His left hand floated down to her knee. The light touch of his warm fingers slowly skimmed up the inside of one thigh, eliciting goose bumps.

His fingers took their sweet time drifting upward, and Sophie marveled at how turned-on she felt simply from the kiss of his fingertips nearing her groin. She felt herself already becoming wet when Grant hesitated, his hand resting near her hot core.

"You're not wearing any panties?"

She gave him an innocent grin. "I was hoping we might get enmeshed tonight."

"Great minds think alike." He gently placed both hands on her hips and scooted her toward the foot of the bed so she lay on her back. Lifting her head, he positioned the pillow under her cascading strawberry curls, and stretching out on his right side, tucked in close to her. Their colliding skin already generated heat. He propped up his head on his wrist, pleased with the view provided by her hiked-up nightgown.

Sophie felt her heart thumping as he gazed down at her with an expression of utter devotion. "So, my Bonnie," he whispered, "we have a naughty teenager in the next room. Do you think you can keep your moans on the down-low tonight?"

She giggled, and he shushed her by placing a feathery kiss on her lips, which she receptively deepened. His mouth hovering over hers, she whispered, "If I'm too loud, it'll be *your* fault."

He grinned and covered her mouth with his once more. She'd been waiting for him all day and sighed at the exquisite pressure of his full lips. Enraptured by his sweet kisses as his right hand glided through her hair, she hadn't noticed what his left hand was doing until she felt his fingers gently slide inside her, pushing pleasure up her spine as her breathing quickened. His tongue dipped and danced while his fingers massaged and swirled. She clutched the bed with a sense of desperation, feeling lightheaded as blood drained from her head to the center of her body.

His artful ministrations *(damn those long fucking fingers!)* continued to undo her, and she felt a rumbling build up inside, threatening to leak out. Though she tried to suppress any noise, suddenly she let out at sated moan.

"Shh," he chuckled into her mouth, still attacking her with kisses.

"Like I said, it's all your fault," she panted, devouring his plump lips.

Lifting his chin, there was laughter in his velvet voice as he whispered, "Do you want me to stop?"

"No!" she loudly cried. Realizing her volume, she quickly clamped her hand over her mouth, leading Grant to shake his head in amusement.

Somehow the illicit nature of making love within earshot of a young family member made their encounter even more exciting, and as Sophie glanced down at Grant swiftly removing his boxers, she felt a thrilling rush of anticipation.

Grant gently maneuvered over her, his long legs covering her lithe frame, his weight resting on his forearms. When she reached down to stroke his hard length, Grant swallowed his own moan and began massaging her breasts through the light fabric of her nightgown with his mouth and hands. Her nipples darkened with his skillful assistance. They had not fully united, yet they were already moving together in a sensuous up-and-down dance, rocking together and becoming increasingly aroused.

Unable to wait one second longer, she guided him into her, and the immediate sense of fullness made her gasp. He pulled out part-way and then thrust into her repetitively, each time plunging deeper, as her lips parted and her eyes threatened to roll back in their sockets. However, she kept her eyes open, unable to tear them away from his sculpted face—a face attached to a body that was lavishing her with all kinds of pleasure. Constrained from using their voices, their eyes locked onto each other, communicating what words could not.

"How long will you be stateside, sir?"

As they camped out in the waiting room of Hunter's office, Sophie eavesdropped on Grant's phone conversation with his Uncle Joe, who'd just returned to his home in Norfolk, Virginia, after a month at sea.

As usual, they'd arrived fifteen minutes early for their session. Sophie had run late most of her life, but Grant had quickly disabused her of that habit—his precise, military bearing brought them early to every destination. Their prompt arrival at Hunter's office was also motivated by a desire to avoid taking any more risks with their parole officer by arriving late for their weekly sessions.

This morning Grant had nudged her out of the apartment before she'd finished blow-drying her hair. It amazed her that in the same amount of time it took her to crawl out of bed incoherently and groom herself for the day, Grant was able to complete a five-mile run, followed by countless push-ups, and fix a full breakfast for Ben, as well as shower and shave.

Feeling her damp hair on her shirt collar, Sophie watched Grant sit a little taller as the conversation continued.

"Ben? I haven't had to keelhaul him yet, Joe." Grant grinned. "Though I've been tempted."

As she listened to his smooth voice, Sophie's was transported to their dreamy, if overly hushed, lovemaking session a few nights ago. She had gazed into Grant's eyes, feeling him inside her as they moved together. Clutching each other, a powerful pressure welled up, along with shuddering spasms. Holding each other tightly, staring deeply, tenderly, adoringly…they had both climaxed, wondrously, at precisely the same moment—

"Are you coming, Sophie?"

She flinched, turning in the direction of the voice to find Hunter with a smirk on his face. Immediately she looked at Grant, who was also on his feet, studying her curiously while holding his hand out. He must have ended his phone call with Joe at some point.

"Y-Y-Yes," she blushed furiously, taking the offered hand and feeling herself pulled to standing.

She tried to regain her focus as they moved down the hall. Having McSailor around was definitely dangerous to her concentration.

After they were seated, Hunter decided to address the confidentiality issue right away. "It was interesting running into you two at the steakhouse."

"I'm sorry, Hunter," Sophie said. "I shouldn't have interrupted your dinner like that."

"Nonsense," Hunter responded, glancing at Grant guiltily. "Bradley enjoyed meeting both of you. I was kind of curious about what led you to come over to our table, though."

Sophie's cheeks reddened. "I'm not sure—it just didn't feel right to leave without saying something to you. I appreciate what you've done for us, and I guess I wanted Bradley to know that. I realize Jerry mandated me to come here, but you…you mean a lot to me. You've really helped me."

Now Hunter was the one blushing. "Thank you, but you're the one doing all the work."

Grant wanted to speak as well, but he had no idea what to say. He was also grateful for Hunter's help, but therapy had been an emotional rollercoaster, and he wasn't exactly looking forward to the next descent.

"I've been thinking about our session a couple of weeks ago." Hunter continued nervously. Although the public encounter with the couple had been awkward, his subsequent conversation with Bradley had helped him to realize he'd been experiencing countertransference with Grant. "I, uh,

I wanted to apologize for my behavior. It was unprofessional of me to yell at you two about what happened in the bedroom that night."

Grant frowned. "You're apologizing for yelling at us?"

Hunter nodded.

"Why, sir? That's exactly what I needed to hear." Grant looked down. "I'll never forgive myself for what I did to Sophie."

"But *I* have forgiven you," Sophie said, taking his hand.

Slowly he looked up at her.

"As Hunter pointed out, I behaved badly that night too." Noticing the psychologist's wince, she added, "And I agree with Grant—there's no need to apologize. I probably would've yelled at my clients too in that situation. Whatever you did, it worked."

Turning back to her boyfriend, Sophie's eyes took on a naughty glint. "Judging by our past few nights together, I'd say we're back on track."

"So things are going better for you two?" Hunter asked, observing Grant's adorable blush.

"Yes, sir," Grant replied. "And we're trying to keep quiet since Ben's in the other room."

Hunter chuckled. "Ah, yes, how's Ben doing?"

"He's grounded right now, until he can show me fifty push-ups. And then he had the nerve to leave the apartment when he was supposed to be grounded, so I had to take his cell phone away. *That* got his attention."

"I bet," Hunter grinned. "A teenager without a cell phone? That's like a scuba diver without an oxygen tank. He must be dying a slow death right now."

Sophie giggled. "Oh, he was *so* mad when Grant took it away!"

"Well, Ben gets his phone back tonight," Grant said, *"if* his behavior warrants it. And he's up to forty-three push-ups now, so hopefully he won't have to be grounded much longer."

"If you two can survive a pissed-off teenager living with you in a one-bedroom apartment, I think you can survive anything." Hunter smirked. "Okay, so I want to work on communication with you today."

"All right," Sophie eagerly responded.

Grant looked skeptical.

"We're going to do a speaker-listener exercise. One of you will be speaker while the other is listener, and then we'll swap roles. The speaker is going to use the 'I' language we've been working on to discuss a current issue in his or her life. It's about honestly expressing thoughts, feelings, and opinions. For example, the speaker might say, 'I feel annoyed when you don't share the TV remote control.'"

Sophie elbowed Grant and laughed before Hunter continued.

"The listener's task is to use empathy to reflect what the speaker's saying—to paraphrase the speaker's words. It's all about the speaker, and the listener isn't supposed to defend or argue—the listener will get a chance soon. An appropriate response might be, 'You feel annoyed when I hog the remote.'"

Grant looked confused. "But that's just repeating what she said. What good will come out of simply repeating how annoyed she is?"

Hunter nodded. "I see. So you're the one who monopolizes the remote, then?"

"Yes," Sophie said, rolling her eyes.

"But, but—" Grant sputtered. "She only wants to watch chick shows!"

His eyes full of mirth, Hunter looked at Sophie and scoffed, "*Men.*"

Returning his gaze to Grant, he explained, "It may feel like you're doing nothing when you're using empathic listening. But, Grant, it's a very powerful technique. Women crave the emotional connection that comes from being heard. They *don't* want their men to give advice or solve their problems for them. I've seen it many times—when the man listens and accepts what the woman is feeling without trying to change her or give her advice, he finds the woman much more receptive to him. And that receptivity extends to the bedroom, by the way."

As expected, Grant's skepticism suddenly disappeared. He nodded. "Let's get started!"

"Okay," Hunter instructed, "I want Sophie to be the speaker first, and Grant to be the listener."

"Does this have to be about Grant and me?" Sophie asked.

"No, you can talk about whatever."

"Good, because there's something going on at work that's bothering me." She turned her body to face Grant. "I feel…bothered, uh, disrespected when my colleague David refers to male professors as Dr. So-and-so and female professors by their first names."

"He *does* that?" Grant responded incredulously.

"The listener can ask open-ended questions, but first I want you to start with a paraphrase, Grant," Hunter said. "Start with a 'You feel' response, okay?"

Grant nodded. "I understand that you feel, um, you feel mad because that jerk is a sexist pig."

"Is that how you feel, Sophie?" Hunter prompted.

"Well, I guess I feel mad too, but he's so condescending. It's more like, I feel *belittled*—yeah, that's it."

Grant appeared anxious. "Did I screw it up, sir?"

"No, Grant, you're doing great. If your empathic reflection's slightly off, the speaker will correct you. You helped Sophie get to her true feeling: belittled. Do you want to try to paraphrase again?"

Chewing on his lip, Grant looked tentatively at Sophie. "You feel belittled when David doesn't refer to you as doctor even though you've earned it."

"Yes." She nodded vehemently. "And when he refers to male professors as 'doctor,' I think he's doing it intentionally."

"And how do you feel about that?" Hunter asked.

"Furious."

"Excellent. Let's switch roles. Grant, you be the speaker, and Sophie, the listener."

"Whoa," Grant said. "What about David? What's Sophie going to do about him?"

"I'm sure she'll figure it out, Grant. It's not your problem to solve, but you did help her by clarifying how she feels about the situation. Now, what would you like to discuss from the speaker's perspective?"

Grant sat back on the sofa, clearly uncomfortable, but also unwilling to disobey Dr. Hayes. He sighed. "I don't know, sir."

"Is there anything you have strong feelings about that you want to tell Sophie?"

Grant thought for several moments.

"You look kind of worried," Hunter prompted. "Is there something in particular you're worried about?"

Grant swallowed hard and slowly faced Sophie. "I feel…uh, I feel like I don't want you to get hurt any more by my family."

He looked so pained that Sophie wanted to reach out and hold him, but before she could respond, Hunter gently broke in.

"Grant? That's a great start, but how do you *feel* about Sophie possibly getting hurt by your family again? Nervous? Angry?"

"Terrified," he responded, surprising himself. He was further dismayed by the threat of tears pulsing at the back of his eyes. "I can't handle it if anything happens to you," he said in a warbling voice. "But I don't know if I can protect you. Angelo just showing up at the docks, my father wanting to see me—"

"Hold there," Hunter said. "Sophie?"

She sniffed, unable to turn away from Grant. "You feel terrified that I…that I'll get hurt by your family again."

Grant nodded grimly, and Sophie asked Hunter, "Can I say something?"

When Hunter agreed, Sophie took both of Grant's hands in hers. "I feel scared too. I know the danger of your family—hell, my father reminds me about it every day. But, Grant, no matter what your family does, I want to stay with you. I want to be with you…I love you," she added shyly.

He gulped. "I love you so much, Sophie. And I'll do everything in my power to keep you safe from them."

Hunter sat back in his chair, observing their interaction with satisfaction. The couple was communicating beautifully.

12. Conjunct

"Should we do our homework now?" Sophie asked.

They were sitting outside Jerry's office, waiting for their nine o'clock appointment, and Grant turned to her with an amused expression. "The communication exercise?"

"Yes. We're supposed to practice it twice before our next appointment with Hunter."

"Okay. I'll be speaker first." He leaned in and whispered suggestively, "I feel quite, um, *aroused* by that sexy outfit you've got on, Bonnie."

She smiled brightly with a coquettish batting of her eyelashes, but then frowned. "Somehow I don't think that's what Hunter had in mind."

"It's not?" Grant asked innocently, brushing his lips against the creamy skin of her neck.

"Mmm, and I feel…I feel—"

Her murmur was cut off by a scruffy man rushing past them to knock loudly on their parole officer's door. The man positively reeked of alcohol, and he swayed on his feet as he hung onto the doorframe for support.

Both parolees watched as Jerry opened his office door a crack. Upon seeing who was waiting for him, he wrenched the door open and grabbed the man by the collar. "You were supposed to report here yesterday!" Jerry hollered, roughly manhandling the con into his office.

"Sorry, bossss," the inebriated man slurred.

"You *will* be sorry!" Jerry slammed the door behind him.

Grant and Sophie exchanged frightened looks. They strained to hear what was happening, but all they could make out were Jerry's relentless shouts.

Quickly the scene progressed, with two uniformed officers arriving at the door, barging into the office, and yanking the hapless con to his feet. Through the open door, Sophie and Grant were riveted by their view of one officer forcibly handcuffing the man before shoving him out of the office. The con's plaintive wails of "I don't wanna go back!" floated down the hallway as the officers took him away.

Stunned, Grant and Sophie glanced back at the office and found Jerry standing by the door, beckoning them inside. They quietly entered. As they slunk into the hard metal chairs, they remembered that just like the man who'd been dragged away, they could return to prison at any time.

After Jerry took his seat across the desk from them, Sophie ventured, "That parolee—he was in the sixty percent?"

"Yeah," Jerry responded gruffly. Grant gave Sophie a questioning glance and Jerry continued, "Do me a favor, huh? If you know you're going to be arrested, don't take an all-night bender. It makes my office *stink*."

With that, Jerry stood up and rifled through the papers stacked haphazardly on top of his filing cabinet. He extracted a can of air freshener and sprayed a few puffs toward the ceiling.

Sophie reached into her purse and dug around for a moment.

Expecting a horrible antiseptic odor to waft in her direction, she was pleasantly surprised by a light vanilla scent floating over them. "That air freshener smells good, Jerry," she said.

"Marilyn gave it to me." The words were out of Jerry's mouth before he realized it, and he instantly began blushing. Grant worked hard not to laugh out loud.

"How are things going with Marilyn?" Sophie asked boldly.

Following his girlfriend's lead, Grant jumped in too. "Yes, how is Detective Fox?"

"None of your business, *parolees*," Jerry growled.

Grant felt his pocket vibrate, and he clandestinely read the text message from Sophie:

Jer says 60 percent of parolees return to prison

Grant winced. He *had* to keep himself and Sophie in the other forty percent. He had to find a new job—the cruises stopped running in less than two weeks.

Jerry interrupted his worries. "Now, what do you two have to report to me today?"

"Things are going well, sir," Grant responded.

"Taylor?" Jerry asked.

"I'm fine, sir."

The parole officer leaned back in his chair with their files open in his lap. "I'm inclined to believe you. Both of your recent drug tests were negative."

Grant bit his lip, wondering what would happen if his nephew had to get tested.

"And your progress reports from Dr. Hayes are excellent. You two must've really conned him, huh?"

Sophie chuckled. "Hunter is great—he's truly helping us, Jerry."

Jerry studied Grant. "You don't seem to share your girlfriend's enthusiasm for therapy, Madsen."

"Oh, um, well, I like Dr. Hayes all right, but therapy has been, uh, it's been tough, sir."

"I can imagine," Jerry said, thinking of Grant's less-than-fun family history.

Hearing the gruffness all but disappear from the wizened man's voice, Grant hesitantly said, "Dr. Hayes wanted me to ask you a question, sir."

"What's that?"

"I'm supposed to ask…" He sighed heavily and ran one hand through his closely cropped black hair. "I'm supposed to ask if I'd be allowed to visit my father." Grant swallowed hard. "In Gurnee."

Jerry studied them both and saw Sophie's face contort with fear. "What's wrong, Taylor?"

When Grant turned to stare at her, she paused. "Ah, maybe I should talk about this with Grant in private."

"What is it?" Grant asked.

Sophie wrung her hands in her lap. "It's just—I don't want you visiting your father, Grant. I know Hunter thinks it might be a good idea, but I'm, I'm scared for you. I don't want you near Angelo or his men either. Please promise me you'll stay away from them?"

Her frightened eyes made Grant's chest swell with love. Grasping one of her hands, he stroked her skin softly and replied, "Don't worry—I don't want *anything* to do with Uncle Angelo. And I don't want to visit my dad, either, but I, uh, I have to know if it's an option, at least. If making peace with him is the only way to get my life back, I at least have to try."

Jerry watched the parolees gaze intently into each other's eyes, feeling drawn in like he was watching one of those ridiculous movies Marilyn forced him to see with her.

Shaking himself out of his trance, he said, "Typically you wouldn't be permitted to visit a prison while you're on parole." He had both parolees' attention now. "Unless you were returning as a resident there," he added humorlessly. "But because you're family, the rules might be more fluid. I'll have to check with the DOC and get back to you."

Grant nodded gravely. "Thank you, sir."

Glancing at his watch, Jerry asked, "Any other questions today?"

Receiving simultaneous "No, sir" responses, Jerry stood up and bid them farewell.

As Grant guided Sophie down the courthouse steps, he could feel her tension and continued distress.

She was surprised when he stayed with her as they crossed the street; typically he peeled off toward the river while she began the trek to DePaul.

"I'm taking you to work today," Grant explained, noticing her inquisitive glance. "Roger cancelled the one o'clock cruise since hardly anybody takes it this late in the season, so I have more time." His hand remained firmly at the small of her back.

"Okay." She sighed with relief and felt the trembling throughout her body begin to abate. At least her McSailor would be safe from his family for the next hour or so.

❧

"Meat! Get in here!"

Angelo's bellow was softer and weaker than he intended, and he gasped for air as he fought off the urge to cough. His damn lungs were getting worse every day. Mustering all his strength, he cried out again, "Meat!"

Tank stuck his head in the door of the ornate study. "Need something, boss?"

Pulling his squinting black eyes away from the computer screen, Angelo frowned. "I need Mario, not you."

Tank cleared his throat as he stepped fully into the room. "Sorry, boss, Meat's at the range." Tank wished he was there too, practicing his aim, but they'd agreed somebody had to stay behind to keep an eye on their don. He wasn't looking so great these days. "Something I can help you with?"

Angelo felt a coughing spasm overtake him.

"Boss," Tank gently cajoled. "Let me take you back to the doc."

"No," Angelo rasped, fighting for air. "It's pointless." In a far-off voice, he added, "It's inoperable."

"Still," Tank argued, "maybe you can get some better drugs, you know?"

"I've got all the fucking painkillers I need," Angelo angrily retorted. "They make me too fuzzy. I gotta keep an eye on things, especially when I find shit like this." He gestured to the computer screen.

"What's wrong, boss?"

"I found an error in the books, and I'm going to turn Meat into a fucking vegetarian for his careless mistake."

Tank looked confused. "That don't sound like Meat. What's the mistake?"

Angelo indignantly pointed at the screen. "It says here one of our suppliers paid extra last month," he wheezed. "That can't be right. In thirty years, I've never seen that."

Tank leaned over his boss's shoulder to peer at the screen. "Supplier" was their code word for a business they extorted money from—a backbone of their income. Either the business paid the protection fee, or it wouldn't be in business for long.

"Who's the supplier that overpaid?" he asked.

Angelo frowned. "Taylor Construction."

"You're using Dr. Green's office while she's overseas?" Grant asked, looking around at the piles of journals, books, and papers in the cluttered space.

"Yes, Anita told me to use it until she returns in late December—"

"—when your position will end, and you'll have to find another job," Grant finished ominously. The threat of returning to prison because they were unemployed continued to hang over them.

Sophie sighed. "Don't remind me. You've got even less time. Any news on the job front?"

"Rog is trying to get me in with the company he works for, doing architectural bus tours, but they're laying off more people than they're hiring at this point."

She rested her hand on his wiry forearm. "You'll find something."

He nodded grimly, and she slid her hand down to clasp his.

"C'mon, I'll show you around," she said.

Sophie first introduced Grant to the department secretary, Judy, a short brown-haired woman in her fifties who smiled warmly. They chatted for a few minutes until the secretary received a phone call.

As they walked out of the front office and into the hallway, Sophie smiled. "Judy's a sweetheart. She was always so helpful to me as a grad student—with all the forms I had to complete for my thesis, dissertation, stipends, stuff like that. And she was tremendously welcoming when I started teaching this fall."

"She seems friendly," Grant said.

Sophie bit her lip and lowered her voice as they continued down the hallway. "Judy was actually my alibi."

Grant gave her a sharp look.

"I came here to try to do some work after we, uh…"

Her voice trailed off and Grant silently continued her thought. *After we yelled at each other, and you told me to stay the hell away from you.*

"Anyway," Sophie continued, "Marilyn interviewed Judy to make sure I was here that day…" *the day Logan was murdered* "…and Judy hasn't said one word about it since."

Grant *had* felt like the secretary seemed a little too curious about him. "Does she know, uh, everything that happened?"

"No," Sophie assured him. "The only people who know everything are Anita and my friend Tanya. Here's Tanya's office—I want you to meet her. Let me see if she's in."

She knocked on the door and heard an inviting response in return.

"Oh!" Sophie cried as she opened the door. "I didn't know you had company."

Tanya stood, followed by the blond woman across from her.

"No worries," she responded, eyeing the handsome man behind Sophie. "Please come in. Is this the famous Grant Madsen?"

Sophie grinned broadly, and Grant blushed as he trailed his girlfriend into the office.

"Tanya Highgate," Sophie said, "I'd like to introduce you to Grant Madsen." Grant gallantly reached out to shake Tanya's hand, and the five-foot-ten woman nearly swooned as she gazed directly into his sparkling gemstone eyes. Sophie then gestured to the other woman. "And this is Nora Rodriguez, Tanya's advisee."

The lean, five-foot-five woman with short, spiky blond hair also shook Grant's hand and nervously asked Tanya, "Should I leave and maybe we can finish this meeting later?"

"Please don't go," Sophie said. "We'll only be here a couple of minutes. Grant has to get to work soon. And I've told Grant what a great writer you are, Nora, so he kind of already knows you."

A delighted look lit up the grad student's face, accompanied by a reddening of her tan skin.

Grant felt proud that Sophie was praising students to encourage them, just like Anita had done for her. He turned to Sophie and asked, "Nora's the one who wrote the paper on interpersonal theory?"

Both Tanya and Nora were impressed.

Sophie beamed, touched that Grant remembered a detail about an important person in her life. She was also consumed by desire as she revisited what happened in their bed shortly after she read Nora's paper.

"And Tanya is your best friend in the department, as I recall," Grant added.

Sophie nodded, exchanging a smile with Tanya.

"Grant, you work on an architectural cruise, right?" asked Tanya. "I've always been meaning to take one of those."

Grant chuckled. "Most Chicago natives say that. You're welcome to come, but you'd better hurry because time's running out."

"Oh, I want to take one of those cruises!" Nora cut in. "What a great way to learn about a new city."

"Nora is from Texas, right on the border," Tanya said. "We were just talking about her research on counseling Mexican immigrants. We share an interest in cross-cultural research."

"Tanya will be a great advisor," Sophie assured Nora. In contrast, she instantly thought of Kirsten's advisor, David Alton, who she believed was at least partially to blame for Kirsten taking so long to finish her degree. Some advisors helpfully nudged their students through all the research requirements, whereas others became critical and inaccessible, thereby delaying the graduation of their students. David belonged in the latter category.

"I think Nora will have access to a large Mexican immigrant population here in Chicago," Tanya said.

"Yes," Nora agreed. "I was just running through Pilsen the other day, and it seemed like a huge Mexican community."

"Oh, right, that's something you two have in common," Sophie said, taking Grant's hand. "Nora runs half-marathons." She looked at Nora. "Grant runs every morning. He's even got his sixteen-year-old nephew out there with him sometimes."

"Begrudgingly," Grant added with a grin.

Nora laughed. "Sounds like my son. He's fourteen and thinks he's super-fit until he tries to keep up with me on a run."

"I didn't know you had a son, Nora," Sophie said.

"I have a son *and* a daughter. After my divorce I decided to leave nursing, and I figured I'd start training for a new career in psychology."

"Wow, I'm learning all kinds of things about you today." Sophie smiled. "Why did you want to leave nursing?"

Nora suddenly looked uncomfortable, and Sophie backpedaled. "I'm sorry for prying. Just ask Grant. I get into interrogation mode a little too easily — remnants of my counseling career."

"You were in practice?" Nora asked.

Now Sophie seemed the hesitant one. "Y-Y-Yes," she stammered, glancing anxiously at Grant. "But not anymore. I'm, uh, trying out the teaching thing now."

"Oh." Nora sensed the tension in Sophie's voice. "Well, to answer your question, my ex-husband's a physician, and I didn't want to continue working in the same hospital as him. I figured a fresh start was in order — new career, new place to live. Though how I'll keep up with the jogging once the weather gets cold is beyond me. I think I'll be missing the Texas weather this winter," Nora said. "Sophie, you should go running with Grant. It's a great stress reliever."

Sophie's eyes widened and she shot Grant an amused glance, snuggling against him. "I don't think I could keep up with this guy. He used to be in the Navy — you should see him in action on the ship."

Tanya grinned as she watched Grant blush and clear his throat. "Speaking of ships, I better get going."

Sophie nodded. "Okay, I'll walk you out. Now you guys can get back to your meeting—sorry for the interruption."

She followed Grant out of the office, and they paused in the hallway.

"Thank you," Sophie told him, looking up into his cool eyes.

"For what?"

"For just being you. It's nice to have a boyfriend I'm proud to introduce to my friends. You were great with them."

"I can see why you like working here. Your colleagues are a little more civilized than Roger."

They chuckled, and then trepidation crossed Sophie's face as her eyes darted to something behind Grant.

"Hello, David," she said tersely.

Grant spun around to find a gray-haired man of medium height moving their direction.

"Morning, Sophie," David replied, his brown eyes crinkling as he smiled. He wore a gray T-shirt under a navy blue sport jacket with faded jeans, appearing casual yet professional at the same time.

To her horror, Sophie watched David stop in front of them, inquiringly observing the tall, dark man at her side. She silently hoped the McSailor Method would work its magic. A tense silence descended upon them until Sophie remembered her manners.

"Um, David Alton," she forced out in a tight voice, gesturing to her boyfriend, "this is Grant Madsen."

Grant immediately draped his left arm over her shoulders and reached out to pump David's hand vigorously. "Sophie's boyfriend," Grant added smugly.

Feeling a possessive squeeze of his long fingers on her shoulder, it dawned on Sophie that Grant's visit was perhaps not only to soothe her concerns about his family. He seemed to relish meeting David. Had he somehow planned on them running into each other?

There was a glint in David's eyes—what was it? Anger? Jealousy? Whatever his reaction, he hid it well. "Nice to meet you, Grant," he said smoothly. "So *this* is the boyfriend Sophie's been hiding from us. I'm glad she finally decided to let you come for a visit."

Grant's smile was stiff. "I have a feeling I'll be visiting much more frequently."

Sophie gave a nervous chuckle.

"So what do you do for a living, Grant? Don't tell me you're a psychologist too?"

"Uh, no, sir," Grant responded, letting the respectful address slip out before he could stop it. "I work in a top Chicago industry." Seeing David's questioning look, he added, "Tourism."

David still appeared confused, but before he could ask a follow-up question Grant squeezed Sophie's shoulder reassuringly and said, "I gotta run, honey. See you at home tonight?"

With that question hanging in the air, he leaned in, dipped her, and planted an intense smooch right on her lips. He held the breathtaking kiss for several seconds, even throwing some tongue in there for good measure, before finally drawing her back up and releasing her to try to maintain her balance on wobbly, boneless legs.

She felt her cheeks on fire as Grant sauntered down the hall, appearing quite satisfied with himself. Looking back to David, she tried to resume normal breathing as they stared at each other dumbly, both with no idea what to say. Their awkward silence was broken when Nora came out of Tanya's office with her advisor in tow, still chatting excitedly about a research idea.

The women stopped short at Sophie and David rooted to their spots in the hallway. A slight step backward was David's only sign of discomfort; otherwise, he was suave as ever.

"Ah, ladies, I can see I'm outnumbered here, so I'll leave you to discuss female issues like men, or, uh, I don't know, fashion." He glanced down at his own ensemble. "Just don't make fun of me for wearing my Garanimal professor uniform, okay?" He winked and continued down the hallway.

Shaking their heads and exchanging an exasperated look, Sophie and Tanya were surprised by Nora's girlish giggle once David was gone.

"Garanimals?" Nora chuckled. "My kids used to wear those. *I* think his outfit looks pretty sexy, myself."

She looked to the other women, both too taken aback to speak, and wondered if she'd said something wrong. "I have to get to class," Nora announced more somberly, "Bye, Tanya. Bye, Sophie."

The women murmured goodbyes, and Sophie stared at Tanya incredulously. "What the hell was *that?*"

The blackness enveloped him and all he could hear were his desperate gasps for air. Then his eyes popped open and gradually adjusted to the dim light of the cell. He felt his racing heart begin to slowly settle down, one beat at a time.

The familiar noises of the cellblock began entering his consciousness—a random cough here and there, grunts from cellmates getting a little too friendly in the middle of the night, the measured cadence of a CO's footsteps patrolling the tier above. Fortunately, the only sound inside his cell was the steady breathing of the inmate on the bunk below. His man had slept through any disturbance created by the nightmare. It would be damn near impossible to lead men—to *own* men—if they knew of their leader's penchant for crying out like a baby as he slept.

Enzo Barberi exhaled loudly and turned over on his side, thumping his thin pillow in a futile attempt to make it more comfortable. Feeling fatigue press down on his eyelids, he dared to close his eyes again and was immediately rewarded with the image he'd been trying to avoid all his life: terrified brown eyes staring back at him, pleading and begging with their intensity. The gag prevented the owner of those eyes from speaking, other than muffled moans and screams, but his eyes did all the talking anyway.

Enzo snapped his own eyes back open, gritting his teeth with frustration. Why wouldn't the fucking image go away? Why did he have to relive it almost every fucking night? And why couldn't he get any fucking booze to erase the image? If only he could have one drink. God, he missed alcohol more than life itself. Sighing again, he shifted his body, feeling the metal bunk-bed frame vibrate with his movement. He was going to have to stay awake all night again—not that there was any need to be well-rested tomorrow. All that awaited him was another shitty day in Gurnee.

Grant was really getting into his rendition of Frank Sinatra this time. He knew he wouldn't have the pleasure of crooning tunes much longer. Even Roger, who was typically grumpy by the last cruise of the day, was dancing in place at the controls as Grant's smooth voice caressed each syllable, guiding the half-filled cruise home to the docks. Grant had come to find singing a release not unlike running. He was lost in the song, stringing notes together in a smooth melody, just like he strung his strides together into a five-mile run.

"What have you done to Ben?" Roger asked unexpectedly after docking the boat.

Grant gave him a confused look. "What do you mean?"

"When I asked him to wipe down the benches after the five o'clock, he didn't give me any lip — for the first time ever. Now he's down there seeing the passengers off, and he actually looks like he gives a shit. He sick or something?"

Grant suppressed a chuckle. "He hasn't quite earned his halo yet, sir, but he's coming around, I hope. He's trying to get out of being grounded."

Roger raised one eyebrow. "Well, whatever you're doing, keep it up. It's much nicer around here without his sassy trap mouthing off every second."

The owner of the "sassy trap" walked into the bridge. "Uh. Uncle Grant? This guy wants to talk to you down there."

Feeling immediate alarm, Grant rushed to the window of the bridge and stared down at the deck, but he didn't recognize any of Angelo's goons waiting for him. Instead, there was a gray-haired man in an expensive business suit, talking on a cell phone. "Did he say who he was, Ben?"

"Nope. He just said he wanted to talk to the docent. That's you, right?"

Grant rolled his eyes. "You've been working here now long, Ben? And you still don't know the terminology? Stay up here and help Rog clean while I go talk to him."

As Grant headed down the white steps, he heard his nephew say, "You get on *me* for my station being messy? It's a pigsty up here, Rog." He was relieved to be out of earshot before Roger gave his salty retort.

The businessman was just putting away his phone when Grant warily approached. The man squinted in the setting sun. "You're the docent? The one who was singing?"

"Yes, sir."

The man extended his hand, and Grant could detect warmth in his blue eyes. "Alex Remington."

"Grant Madsen, Mr. Remington. How can I help you?"

"How long have you been singing professionally, Grant?"

His eyes widened and he stammered, "Uh, never. I mean, um, I've only been singing for a few months on this cruise."

The man looked surprised. "But you've been trained, right?"

"No, sir."

"Huh, I thought she said…" His voice trailed off, but then he decisively resumed. "Never mind — obviously you don't need training with a voice like that."

Grant appeared confused. "Sir?"

"Grant, I want to make you an offer. I'm opening a new bar in my hotel in a couple of weeks—a really classy, old-Chicago feel to it—and I want you to be the musical entertainment during cocktail hour. I've already got a piano player, but his voice is awful, so you can sing some of those Sinatra tunes, maybe some Tony Bennett, Tom Jones—the works, you know. You'd be great."

"Mr. Remington, are you offering me a job?" Grant asked.

"You catch on real quick, don't you, son? Listen, it's only on a trial basis until I make sure you'll work out, but I think this arrangement will likely benefit us both." He extracted his business card. "Stop by the hotel tomorrow night when you're done here, and we'll iron out the details. How's that sound?"

Grant felt totally awed that a job offer had dropped out of the sky right when he needed it. He'd be *singing?* For money? He was floored. Then his giddiness came crashing down as he realized this stroke of good fortune was hardly locked in.

"It sounds great, Mr. Remington, but there's one thing you should know before we take this any further."

"What's that?"

"I'm, uh…" Grant bit his lip. "I'm on parole." His voice dropped and he looked down. "I've been convicted of a felony."

"Well, I can't see how that would affect your singing voice," said Mr. Remington, unfazed. "And that's all I need from you—that and your handsome face. The ladies will love you. See you tomorrow night, Grant."

Still in a daze, Grant could barely get out a "Thank you, sir" before the man was totally gone. Blinking, Grant let the reality of what had just happened sink in.

He had a new job!

13. Concern

Sophie emerged from the bedroom, suppressing a yawn. It had been a rough night. Grant had not one but two nightmares, waking them both each time with his cries: *Don't make me do it! Please!* Then he'd come to—panting, shaking, his eyes wild, and on the verge of tears.

He'd reluctantly allowed her to stroke his hair as she murmured soothing, grounding words: "You're an adult. It was just a dream. You're safe now here with me."

Eventually he'd fallen back to sleep with her comforting presence next to him. Having experienced this routine with Grant several times, Sophie had taken longer to drift off again—the ache in her heart had not been so quick to subside. She longed to go to that prison and slap the living hell out of Grant's father for all the problems he'd caused. Her vengeful thoughts surprised her.

"We got a blender?" Ben asked as Sophie entered the kitchen. He'd paused his rifling through the lower cabinets.

Sophie ran her hands through her wet hair as she approached the kitchen counter. "I don't think so. Why do you need one?"

Ben stood up and sighed with exasperation as he placed his hands on his hips. The indignant body stance reminded Sophie of Grant, and she smiled wistfully.

"'Cause I need to make a protein shake. My buddy Dylan gave me some of this powder stuff, and it's really supposed to do the trick. I'll be *ooge*."

Sophie grinned. "Why do you want to be huge?"

"When Uncle Grant gets back from his run, I'm gonna do fifty push-ups. I'm gonna do it this time. I, like, *have* to get out of here, Sophie."

She nodded, remembering clearly the misery of being grounded. "Let me make you some breakfast," she offered. Yanking a banana off the bunch, she handed it to him. "You can start with this. Potassium is good for your muscles."

"It is?" Ben begrudgingly accepted the fruit. "Bananas are kinda gross, though. All squishy and bruised and nasty." He played with the banana, twirling it around in his hand, while Sophie dug through the contents of the refrigerator.

"Well, we don't have any steak, Arnold Schwarzenegger," she teased. "And we're out of eggs, but I do have some turkey bacon here. You'll be pumping out fifty with no trouble at all when your uncle returns."

As she extracted a frying pan from the cabinet, she eyed Ben, who seemed absorbed in the unpeeled banana in his hand. He was uncharacteristically quiet, and he'd already showered and dressed, which was unusual for the sleepy teenager.

She was about to put the bacon strips into the pan when Ben quietly asked, "Does Uncle Grant have nightmares?"

So he'd heard the screams too. Sophie had naively hoped Ben slept through the noise, but that would've been difficult in the small apartment.

"Sometimes," she said. "Maybe you should talk to *him* about it, though."

"He doesn't like to talk about it," Ben countered, frowning. "He gets really embarrassed and, like, sad. Like how he gets when we talk about my, um, my dad."

Sophie tried to continue preparing breakfast, despite the stabbing sensation in her heart. Grant's vulnerability could absolutely slay her, and talking about his pain with Logan's son only overwhelmed her further.

"It's hard to talk about the past, I guess," she said eventually. Placing the last strip of bacon into the pan, she added, "We all have regrets."

Sophie took out a loaf of bread and placed two pieces in the toaster. "Uh, Ben, your friend Dylan," she began. "Does he drink protein shakes?"

"Yeah. He says it helps him with the ladies."

"Ah." Sophie hid her grin. "You guys worry about being muscular enough?"

Ben shrugged, continuing to play with the banana.

"Because you know, you don't have to be super-muscular to be a ladies' man." Sophie tried to remember what she'd read in an eating disorders book about helping men with their body image. She could tell it hurt Ben that he hadn't hit his growth spurt yet. "Your body's great the way it is."

Blushing, the teen looked down, not responding.

"In fact," she resumed, taking some butter out of the refrigerator, "research shows that women are attracted to more normal body types, not super-muscular guys. Women don't want 'roid-rage, beefcake boyfriends."

Ben couldn't help but chuckle.

"So…" Sophie smiled conspiratorially. "Is there anybody special in your life? Anyone you have your eye on?"

Startled, Ben's eyes enlarged and his cheeks reddened. "No!" he practically shouted.

"Okay, okay." She smirked as she turned the bacon over with a fork.

After a few moments, Ben said, "Hey, Sophie, look." She raised her head and found him grinning.

He'd peeled the banana halfway, but then carefully replaced the peel. Ben held the banana with one hand while the other suddenly whipped away the yellow flaps of the peel, exposing the cream-colored fruit.

"It's flashing you, Sophie!" he cried with delight.

She arched her sculpted eyebrows. "What?"

"It's flasher fruit," he explained, folding the peel back over the banana before unfurling the flaps once again, this time thrusting the banana toward her face and imitating a scream. "Aaaahhhh! Watch out, Sophie, the banana's flashing you!" He then pretended to be a passerby. "My eyes, my eyes!" he cried in horror.

Sophie took an immediate step away from the offending fruit. "That's, uh, great, Ben."

He appeared slightly wounded that she wasn't amused, but he was soon distracted by the ring of his cell phone. As he hopped off the stool and jogged to his backpack, Sophie cautiously stared at the banana, left exposed on the counter. She shook her head, putting together that they'd been discussing dating, girls, and masculine prowess before the "flasher fruit" display. She rolled her eyes as she transferred the cooked bacon onto paper towels.

Once she turned down the burner, ceasing the sounds of popping bacon grease, she could hear snippets of Ben's phone conversation. His humorous tone had long since faded.

"Why should I believe you *this* time?" he asked tersely. "Okay, okay, I'll think about it!"

When he returned to the stool at the kitchen counter, he somberly watched Sophie pour orange juice into three glasses.

She said nothing.

After a big sigh, he confessed, "That was my mom."

"Really? How's she doing?"

Another heavy sigh. "She wants me to come back home."

"That's great, right?"

He slumped on the stool. "I guess."

Sophie plopped another two pieces of bread into the toaster.

"Unless she kicks me out again when she gets mad at me," Ben continued. "Maybe I should just stay here and save her the trouble."

Her brown eyes found his, and the deep hurt there reminded her so much of Grant. "Maybe you should," she softly agreed.

She cast a glance at the bacon and toast and had a flash of inspiration. "How about we make BLTs?"

"For *breakfast?*"

"Yes, for breakfast," she said. "Get over here and help me slice some tomatoes."

They worked quietly together—Sophie washing the lettuce and Ben slicing the tomatoes—before he asked her, "Do you fight with your mom too?"

Sophie blinked, feeling a tightening in her throat. "Um, not anymore. She's...dead."

Ben looked horrified and began stammering, "I, uh, sorry, I didn't know—"

"It's okay, how would you know? I don't talk about my parents much. My father..." She grimaced. "He doesn't like Grant at all."

"Why the hell not? Uncle Grant's, like, Mr. Perfect."

Sophie chuckled. "Mr. Perfect-Who-Served-Prison-Time, you mean?" Without thinking, she added, "And then there's Logan—" She abruptly stopped, glancing nervously at Logan's son.

Ben looked at her sharply. "Dad? You knew my dad?"

"I...just forget about it, I..."

Seeing her frightened look, Ben felt his stomach drop. "How did you know him?"

Sophie's cheeks burned, and she didn't dare say a word.

Ben couldn't let it go. "Rog told me you met Uncle Grant outside your PO's office? That—that you were in prison too. Did—did you do something to my dad? Did you have him killed?"

Hearing him close to crying, Sophie instantly answered, "No! I would never hurt Logan. Sure, I was angry with him, but—"

"Why were you angry with him?" he demanded, his eyes glistening with tears. "I deserve to know! Uncle Grant won't tell me anything, and I can't live here if I don't know what's going on!"

"Ben, some things are better left unsaid."

"I deserve to know!" he railed. "Please, Sophie. How did you know my dad?"

She gripped the counter with both hands, staring at the floor. Would her crimes ever leave her? Would she ever stop paying for the past? Could Ben handle the truth? Did he deserve to know?

Lifting her head, she bit her lip, surrendering. "Your father—he was my client."

"Your client?"

"I was Logan's psychologist. The judge made him get therapy, after the, um, robbery."

Ben still looked confused. "So you were his shrink. Why would your dad care about that? Why would that make him hate Uncle Grant?"

"Because my father knows what Logan did to me, and he doesn't want Logan's brother to hurt me too."

"My dad hurt you?" Ben rasped.

"It wasn't that bad—it's not like you think."

"What did he do to you?"

There was no going back now. "Logan stored dirty money in my office. I discovered the money—there was a lot of it—and the police came. They found some guns hidden there too, and one was a murder weapon."

Ben's mouth dropped open, and he looked sick. "But my dad took the blame for it, right? He told them they were his guns?"

Sophie paused. She hated telling him this, but she didn't think lying would help him either. She quietly admitted, "Logan skipped town."

Ben's eyes were huge. "He left you all alone to deal with it? Y-Y-You went to prison because of my dad?" He was almost sobbing. "Uncle Grant too. My dad ruined your lives."

"Ben—no, I messed up too. And your dad's actions brought me and Grant together—"

Before she could finish, Ben had rushed out of the apartment. He slowed only for a second at the front door where he almost crashed into Grant, who was just returning from his run.

Grant took one look at his nephew's wild eyes and called after him, "Ben, wait!" But he was too late. Grant walked toward the kitchen and found Sophie completely shell-shocked at the counter. As the smell of frying bacon wafted toward him, Grant glanced at the sandwich fixings and suddenly froze.

Still dazed from her conversation with Ben, Sophie tried to make sense of Grant's silent stance. "What's wrong?"

Pale and trembling, Grant stood rigidly still, seeming not to hear her.

"Grant?" She took two steps toward him.

He flinched and stared at her with unbridled fear.

"Grant?" Her voice rose with concern, but she stayed put.

He clutched one of the kitchen table chairs, lips parted and chest heaving. He wasn't even blinking.

"Did something happen on your run?"

There was a small shake of his head.

She searched for the right words to draw him out of his trance. "Um, we have to be at Hunter's in forty minutes, okay?"

He finally spoke in a shaky voice. "Shower…I—I'm going to shower."

He slowly backed away, eventually disappearing into the bathroom.

Wringing her hands, Sophie wondered what the hell had just happened. She'd somehow managed to hurt Ben so thoroughly he'd probably never trust her again, and she had no idea what was upsetting Grant.

Glancing at the clock on the microwave, her jaw tensed. She sensed she was about to find out.

❧

As soon as Hunter entered the waiting room, he knew something was wrong. Sophie's face, riveted on Grant's vacant expression, was etched with concern. In addition to his empty, troubled eyes, Grant's body was like a tightly wound spring, held coiled only by Sophie's firm grip on his hands, which were clasped in his lap.

"What's going on?" the psychologist inquired. Fortunately there weren't any other clients in the waiting room.

"Oh, Hunter!" Sophie cried. "I'm so glad you're here. It's been an awful morning."

Grant grimaced but otherwise didn't move, continuing to avoid Hunter's probing gaze.

"Let's go to my office, and we'll talk about it, okay?"

Sophie rose from the sofa and was grateful that Grant joined her. She clutched his arm. "Are you okay?" she asked.

"I'm fine!" he snapped.

Hunter had begun to walk toward his office, and he widened his eyes at Grant's sharp retort behind him. *Today's session should be interesting.*

After they were seated, Sophie began speaking immediately. "I don't know what I've done, but first Ben was upset, and now Grant won't talk to me."

"Ben's upset?" Grant asked worriedly, seeming to return to the present.

"Didn't you see him fly out of there this morning? You were coming in from your run when he dashed out the door — right before you stopped talking to me, when you froze in the kitchen."

Grant massaged his temples, wishing his headache would go away. He also noticed a burning, stinging sensation in his lower back that bothered and perplexed him. He didn't remember Ben leaving — all he remembered was one scene, which now played over and over in his head.

"Why won't you talk to me?" Sophie pleaded. "What did I do wrong?"

"It's not you," Grant replied softly, looking down. He snuck a glance at Hunter and quickly averted his eyes when the psychologist met his gaze. "I can't talk about it. Please."

"I'm lost," Hunter said, his brows furrowed. "How about you start from the top, Sophie?"

Glancing nervously at Grant, who still wouldn't meet her eyes, she took a deep breath.

"Grant was out on a run. I was getting dressed after my shower when I heard Ben making some noise in the kitchen. I went in to help him with breakfast, and we got to talking…"

When she didn't continue, Hunter prompted, "What were you discussing?"

"His mom called."

She glanced at Grant, who seemed to be paying better attention now, then back at Hunter.

"I guess Ashley wants Ben to come home. Anyway, Ben started asking me about *my* parents, and somehow Logan's name came up."

Grant was definitely paying attention now, and he appeared increasingly distressed.

"Ben kept asking me how I knew Logan, and I didn't want to tell him, but he…he found out Logan was involved in my arrest."

"You *told* him?" Grant glared at her. "That was incredibly stupid. What were you thinking?"

"I—I didn't know what else to do! I couldn't lie to him!"

"Now wait a minute, Grant," Hunter said. "Did you ask Sophie not to tell Ben about Logan?"

He looked incredulous. "I thought it would be *obvious!* Here's my nephew, grieving the death of his father, and you go and tarnish Logan's name even more? Why the hell did you do that?"

"I'm sorry," Sophie said, beginning to cry. It was too much for Ben *and* Grant to be angry with her in the same day. "I didn't know what to tell him," she sobbed.

"Ben was going to find out the truth some day," Hunter pointed out.

Grant turned his glare toward the psychologist. "Why are you taking *her* side?"

Hunter was taken aback by Grant's fury. "Because I think you're being unfair to Sophie. She's not responsible for what Logan did to her. Ben's not responsible for his father's actions either. He's sixteen—he can handle the truth. He'll get through this."

Grant continued to breathe heavily, his mouth set in a tight line.

Hunter studied him carefully, wondering what had brought about this sudden, intense anger. "Grant, Sophie said you froze when you came into the kitchen. Why did you freeze?"

Abruptly Grant's body language shifted from fury to fear.

"Why wouldn't you talk to Sophie this morning?" Hunter asked.

Through her tears Sophie watched Grant's face crumple as he scooted his body away from her, into the corner of the sofa. She could hear his breathing speed up, reminding her of his choking gulps for air as he emerged from his nightmares.

"I can't," Grant mumbled, feeling overwhelmed by flashes in his brain—Ben's devastated blue eyes, sliced tomatoes on a plate, a shiny brass buckle, the smell of bacon grease…

"What do you see, Grant?" Hunter leaned forward and peered into Grant's engulfed aquamarine eyes. "You're having flashbacks? Was a memory triggered this morning?"

Sophie and Hunter watched with bated breath as Grant curled into himself.

"No," he moaned, "I can't." His body shuddered, and he felt adrenaline course through his veins, freezing him in a state of utter agitation. The stinging sensation had returned to his backside.

"You're safe here," Hunter encouraged. "He can't hurt you anymore. You can talk to us when you're ready."

For several moments the only sound in the office was Grant's labored breathing, and thick tension reverberated through the room. Sophie's throat burned with tears, watching him suffer.

Finally he broke.

"I was seven…"

Grant ran into the house, breathing hard. Logan had sent him to fetch the football, and Grant bit his lip as he fearfully studied the foyer's closet door. He was still scared as hell of that closet, but Logan and their neighbor were waiting for him, and he couldn't return empty-handed. Nervously he opened the door, kneeling and groping for the ball among the boots and other objects on the closet floor. He froze in place when he heard a commanding voice booming from the kitchen.

"Grant, is that you? *Vieni qui!*"

Oh God. A sick feeling of dread coated his stomach. When his father spoke in Italian, he was typically drunk — drunk and full of rage. What was he doing home in the middle of the afternoon? Obediently following the order, Grant gulped and stood, walking on shaky legs into the kitchen.

Enzo lounged against the stove, cradling a tumbler in one hand. His glassy black eyes bored into his seven-year-old son as the boy gingerly came to stand near the kitchen table. Gesturing toward the counter, Enzo slurred, "Who the *fuck* left this messss?"

Glancing at the counter covered by an open bag of bread, sliced tomatoes on a plate, half a head of lettuce, and greasy bacon strips congealing on a paper towel,

Grant's eyes widened. Had Logan forgotten to put away their lunch? Their mother had asked him to do it before she went out to run errands.

"I—I don't know," Grant answered in a trembling voice.

With an exasperated sigh, Enzo set his drink down and began unbuckling his belt. "Can't this goddamn family function when I'm not here?"

The whooshing sound of the belt sliding out of the loops sliced through the air, sending Grant's heart rate soaring.

The father's words were menacing: "Clean it up."

Without hesitating, Grant scrambled to the counter and had begun scooping up the lettuce when the belt striped his bottom. He almost dropped the lettuce from the force of the blow—and the searing pain burning his backside—but he managed to hold on, frantically taking the plate of tomatoes in his other hand.

"Wait!" his father commanded, causing Grant to halt once again. "I changed my mind. I want you to make me a sssandwich."

Grant looked over his shoulder, momentarily confused by the change in orders, which earned him another lick of the belt.

"O-O-Okay!" the boy cried, unsteadily reaching to the cabinet above to extract a plate. His trembling hands reached into the bag of bread, drawing out two pieces and setting them on the plate.

His stomach dropped as he realized he was missing one ingredient. "Do you want m-m-mayonnaise?"

"*Certamente*," Enzo replied.

Grant bit his lower lip as he reluctantly turned and walked toward the refrigerator, a path that unfortunately drew him closer to the belt-wielding drunk by the stove. Enzo managed to whip the leather at least five times before Grant returned to the counter, tightly gripping the jar of mayonnaise and attempting to prevent gathering tears from sliding down his cheeks. The belt stung so badly! His father's drunken aim was off, and Grant already felt bruises forming on his stomach and thighs from the wayward tip of the belt.

As Grant unscrewed the lid, panting with fear, Enzo un-looped the belt from around his hand. Enzo was quiet for a few moments, and Grant could hear the clank of the gleaming brass buckle against the metal oven as it hung in his father's hand.

"I made sandwiches for my father once too," Enzo wistfully recalled. "I was about your age then."

Grant tried not to make a sound as he began assembling the sandwich, and he waited for the next crack of the belt. Enzo's voice seemed different now: not as deep, less confident, and the slur all but gone.

"I brought the sandwiches down to my father," he said. "He and his men were in the basement. But they didn't want the sandwiches right away. They wanted me to do something else first."

Arranging the bacon strips on the bread, Grant had trouble breathing. His father had never spoken so many words to him at once.

"There was a man down there…tied up, tied to a chair, and, uh, gagged. His eyes—brown eyes—they locked on me. His eyes were terrified, and I couldn't look away after I set down the sandwiches. But my dad and his buddies didn't even notice the guy as he writhed in the chair, scraping it on the basement floor."

The belt continued to dance in Enzo's hands, turning and twisting. The buckle clanged a couple more times.

"Then my dad told me he had a job for me. And that's when he brought out the gun."

Grant held his breath and disobediently halted his sandwich production, but Enzo didn't seem to notice. His story continued to spill out of him.

"He said, 'Time for you to become a man. Shoot him three times.' Then he put the gun in my hands." Enzo laughed derisively. "I was such a fucking pussy back then. I begged my dad, 'Don't make me do it. Please, don't make me do it. Please, don't make me pull the trigger.'"

Utterly horrified, Grant shook so badly he could barely tear a lettuce leaf, but thankfully he'd stopped crying.

"My dad wasn't having any of it—there was no way he'd let me defy him in front of his friends. He started unbuckling his belt, and I knew what waited for me if I didn't do what he said. I shouted, 'I'll do it! I'll shoot him!' The guy in the chair looked even more terrified, and he started moaning, straining against the ropes. I held that cold metal in my hand, and I cocked the trigger…"

Grant turned to face his father.

Suddenly Enzo seemed to break out of his trance, and his cold black eyes narrowed at his younger son. "Did I say you could stop?" he growled.

His eyes as round as the plate he'd retrieved from the cupboard, Grant attempted to back up but the counter held him fast. Fear choked him, and he couldn't get out one word.

Enzo swiftly interrupted the horrible silence by lunging forward, grasping Grant's skinny elbow and spinning him around, wielding the long belt high above his head before whipping it down with vicious lashes.

Grant screamed; he'd never felt such intense pain before. Through his terror he realized the thumping clang he heard was the wasp-like sting of the belt buckle, which was normally held in his father's hand during thrashings but this time was free at the working end of the belt. The pain took his breath away, and Grant squeezed his eyes shut, beyond the point of begging or sobbing.

Finally Enzo stumbled out of the kitchen, following a path blurred by his own tears.

Grant stood alone in the kitchen, rooted in place, feeling warm, sticky blood flow down the inside of his trousers. This day would scar him for the rest of his life.

"Lo came to find me there in the kitchen later," Grant said in the same robotic voice he'd used to tell the entire story, still looking down at his feet. "I hadn't moved an inch. He kept asking me what had happened, until he saw blood on my shoe. I fought him when he tried to take my pants down, but he was stronger than me, and when he saw what my dad had done, he started crying. He never cried. I hated to hear him cry, all because of me."

Finally daring to look up, Grant was seized by guilt when he saw tears streaming down Sophie's face. Though his cheeks were dry, Hunter appeared equally distressed.

Clearing his throat, Hunter quietly asked, "How are you feeling, Grant?"

He gave a weary sigh. "Tired."

Hunter gestured to Grant's curled-up body position, his knees near his chin with his arms wrapped around his legs. "How about you put your feet on the floor?" he suggested.

Giving the psychologist a strange look, Grant complied. "Yes, sir."

Sophie finally found her voice, which was throaty from crying.

"Is that what you've been having nightmares about, Grant? You wake up saying 'Don't make me do it.' Is that what you're remembering?"

He nodded.

"That was an awful story your father told you," Hunter said. "Did he, um, did your father ever make *you* pull the trigger, Grant?"

"I don't think so," he immediately replied.

Sophie let out a breath.

"Still," Hunter resumed, "that story was very instructive, wasn't it? His threat of making you kill somebody, just like his father had done to him, was quite effective for keeping you in line. That threat..." he frowned angrily "...along with his belt. You had no choice but to obey him."

Grant felt a warm hand on his arm, and he looked down to find Sophie's tender hold on his elbow. He gazed into her glassy eyes, which poured their love into him.

"I'm so sorry," she said. "I'm so sorry you had to go through that. I'd be having nightmares too if that happened to me as a child."

Her eyes held his gaze as she slowly drifted her hand down his arm, toward the back pocket of his jeans.

His heart pounded and his breath faltered. "Don't," he said in a strangled cry, but she didn't stop until her hand rested on the scar, hidden beneath his jeans. As he felt her comforting touch on his throbbing skin, he knew he was about to weep.

"Don't," he whimpered again, while she softly crawled into his space, snaking her arm up his back and wrapping her body around his. He couldn't fight anymore, so he responded by clasping his arms around her, shifting his weight so she was almost in his lap.

They clung onto each other in a suffocating embrace, both sobbing quietly, until he finally relaxed into her body with a deep, shuddering release.

Hunter said nothing.

Eventually they let go of each other and shyly resumed a sitting position, with Sophie closer to Grant's side than before. She snatched a few tissues from the box and handed him one.

"I guess we need to go," Sophie announced after looking at her watch.

"Yes, our time is up," Hunter said. "But I don't like ending so abruptly. I'm concerned about you both. I'd like to schedule another session this week, to check in on how things are going after today's intensity. Are you available tomorrow?"

"Great," Grant replied flatly. "Two sessions in one week—aren't we lucky?"

Hunter shared a smirk with Sophie, pleased to hear Grant denigrating therapy. He was returning to his old self.

The journey would be a long and painful one, but he could make it. Hunter hoped *both* Grant and Sophie would make it back.

14. Confluence

"Madsen, you got that anti-corrosion spray I told you to buy?"

"Yes, sir." Grant peeked inside his shopping bag to double-check his purchase as he adeptly crossed over the gunwale onto the deck of the ship. Since he'd come directly to work from that grueling therapy session, he was rather surprised he'd remembered to make the shopping trip at all. However, for some reason, he felt lighter and more focused than he had in years.

"And how 'bout the fuel stabilizer?" Roger added, glaring suspiciously.

"Got that too."

Disappointed by the missed opportunity to chew out an incompetent employee, Roger grunted, "Good, then." He could hardly describe Grant Madsen as incompetent.

They worked together seamlessly, preparing the ship for winter storage.

"It's weird that we only have a few cruises left,' Grant mused.

"Yeah." Roger sighed. "The end of summer always makes me kind of bummed." He thought about the architectural bus tours that would employ him again soon. "Come every winter, I gotta start working for the man again. But in the summer, *I* get to be the man."

Grant chuckled. "God help the poor sap who has to be your boss."

"At least I don't have some pussy singing job," Roger jabbed.

Grant blushed. "Hey, I'll be working for the man too."

"Yeah, a *rich* man. Alex Remington's loaded, I hear."

"I wonder what a big spender like him was doing taking your crappy cruise?"

Roger's eyes narrowed. "We may have only one more day, but it's never too late to fire your ass!"

Grant nodded, suppressing a smile.

Resuming their cleaning, Grant's tone became more serious. "I wanted to, uh, thank you, Rog. Thanks for hiring Sophie and me right out of prison. Most people wouldn't have given us a chance."

Roger shrugged, uncomfortable. "Well, your uncle vouched for you." He paused. "And Joe was right—you *have* been my best employee." Doling out such a compliment seemed to nearly kill him, and Roger was quick to recover. "Jesus, Madsen! Watch the anti-mildew stuff—you're spilling it!"

Grant righted the bottle. "Sorry, sir." He felt the vibration of his phone in his pocket and nervously eyed his boss. "Is it okay if I take this call?"

"Go ahead, Frank Sinatra. It's probably your agent wanting to book you for Vegas."

Grinning, Grant answered the phone, but his smile abruptly vanished.

"Please tell me Ben is with you!" Ashley said frantically.

"No, he's at school."

"No, he's not!" she shrieked. "His school called me—he's not there! He's missing! How could you let this happen?"

Grant's heart pounded as he recalled Ben's hasty departure that morning. Why hadn't he realized something was wrong? Grant grimaced. He'd been too wrapped up in his own problems to worry about his nephew. Some uncle he'd turned out to be.

"I'm sorry, Ashley. Don't worry. I'll find him. I will."

He closed the phone with a sense of dread, knowing exactly where Ben was hiding. The one place Grant had expressly forbidden him to go. The one place Sophie had begged him not to visit. A place a man on parole was prohibited from visiting. He took a deep breath and met Roger's worried eyes.

        ☙

"You sure Grant's uncle is out of town?" Angelo rasped. He certainly didn't want Joe Madsen anywhere near the compound on this glorious day: the day his great-nephew had finally returned to him.

Ben carefully studied his great-uncle, whose pallid complexion and wheezing breaths worried him. "Pretty sure," he responded, nervously darting his eyes around the guest bedroom—his bedroom. He hoped his great-uncle couldn't detect that he'd been crying all morning. That would be entirely uncool.

"Okay, *ragazzo*, then I guess it's all right if you get your stuff back." He cocked his head toward the dresser. "It's in the top drawer."

Exhaling with relief, Ben crossed the room and yanked the drawer open, pushing aside rolled-up socks and lifting the false bottom of the drawer to reveal a fat bag of weed next to a stack of rolling papers.

Angelo smiled warmly at the delight on the boy's face as he took the contraband to his bed, laying out the marijuana in front of him.

As Ben scooted onto the bed, he was suddenly torn. Part of him sought the high and part of him dreaded the low. Part of him couldn't wait to smoke away all the painful memories of his no-good father, and part of him was seized by guilt for even being here, knowing Uncle Grant had clearly warned him not to come. *I won't let you self-destruct like your dad. I won't do it. I won't...*

"Tell me about my dad," Ben implored, gazing up at his great-uncle.

Angelo frowned, suddenly feeling weak. He backed into a chair and gratefully sat, coughing a few times. "Your dad?" he wheezed, glancing at the unopened bag of marijuana. "What do you want to hear?"

"Anything—I don't know. Something good about him?"

The tremble in the boy's voice was unmistakable, and Angelo felt a stab of tenderness. He eyed Benjamin intently. Though Logan had been physically more imposing at this age, he and his son shared particular quirks, like a palpable intensity and their brooding furrow of the brow.

A memory instantly came to mind, and Angelo was surprised by the wave of sadness that accompanied it. "Your dad," he said with a faint smile, "was the best prankster around."

"He was?" Ben's typically jaded tone was now full of wonder.

Angelo chuckled. "This one time, when he was about...hmm, how old was he? Let's see, Carlo was eight, so Logan must have been ten—yeah, that's right. And Grant was still small, maybe five or so. The boys were down in the basement, and me and Anna Maria were playing poker with Enzo and Karita. When Enzo got a phone call from one of our guys, I went to get a refill, and I noticed how damn quiet it was in the basement."

He looked at Ben sternly. "You don't have brothers, but let me tell you, when a group of boys gets together to hang out, they are *never* quiet. I knew something was up. So I snuck downstairs. I couldn't find the boys anywhere, but then I saw them in the bathroom." Angelo shook his head disdainfully, a hint of mirth in his gravelly voice. "Logan had wrapped Carlo's head in a towel. It looked like a fucking turban or something, and he was dabbing some sort of lotion on Carlo's forehead. Grant was watching them both with his mouth hung open."

"What was my dad doing?"

Angelo chuckled. "They'd found Anna Maria's hair removal cream, and somehow Logan had convinced Carlo to try it on his eyebrows. How he persuaded him to do that, I'll never know. When I discovered what they were doing, I yelled at them — those idiots — sometimes eyebrows don't grow back. I shoved Carlo's head under the sink to rinse off that crap, but we were too late. Those damn brows were history. Carlo was bawling his head off, and when I got a good look at him, he was the freakiest thing you've ever seen. Without eyebrows he looked like a fucking alien."

Angelo shook his head some more, laughing disdainfully.

"His eyebrows grew back though, right?"

"Yeah, lucky for him, the dipshit."

"Were you mad?" Ben asked.

"Nah, I'm sure Carlo had done something to provoke Logan. Those two fought constantly, unless Enzo intervened."

"Was Grandpa mad?"

This quickly wiped the smile off Angelo's face.

"We didn't tell Enzo."

"Why not?"

Angelo sighed. He knew what his brother had done to those boys. He'd even witnessed Enzo whipping Logan once, and it was not a memory he cherished.

"He was really strict with his sons," he said. Angelo looked zoned out, trapped in the past.

A knock on the door interrupted his memories.

"What?" he called weakly.

Tank stuck his head in the door. "Uh, boss? Taylor is here for you."

Angelo's eyes widened in alarm, and he quickly searched Ben's face for any signs of recognition, but Ben simply dipped his head, now focused on rolling a joint.

"In the hallway, Tank!" Angelo roared, managing to push himself up and off the chair without the bodyguard's offered assistance. Once Ben's door shut securely behind them, he turned to Tank with an icy glare. "I told you not to use that name around Ben! The boy lives with Taylor's daughter, for fuck's sake!"

"Sorry, boss. I forgot. But your man Taylor completely freaked out when we grabbed him, and he hasn't settled down since. He looks like he's about to cry, the pussy. I don't want him to rabbit on us—you gotta get down there."

"Fuck," Angelo muttered, walking as quickly as he could toward the stairwell.

Inside the bedroom, Ben stood with his ear flush to the door. *Sophie's father is here? Why?*

Silently Ben turned the knob and slunk down the hallway, stealthily following the sound of the men's footfalls.

Angelo slowly entered the tension-filled study, his wizened black eyes taking in everything at once. A man with graying brown hair and a classy business suit sat slumped in the easy chair, with Mario's controlling paw resting on his shoulder. Angelo noticed another of his men in the corner, and the thug nodded as he caught his boss's eye. Angelo returned his attention to Taylor, whose frightened blue eyes stared back at him.

After a few painful coughs, Angelo attempted a smile. "Welcome, Mr. Taylor. I assume my men weren't too rough bringing you in?"

Barely hearing the question over the pounding of his heart, Will tremulously asked, "Why am I here?"

Perched outside the study in the foyer, Ben cautiously leaned forward, straining to hear the conversation.

Tank guided Angelo to a chair across from their captive, and the don collapsed into it. "We have a matter to discuss," Angelo rasped. "A while back you refused to pay your friendly neighborhood watch contribution. And now you're overpaying. I want to know why."

Will met his steely glare but said nothing, fully cognizant of the three burly goons surrounding him.

❧

"You made it, sir." The relief in Grant's voice was palpable.

"You're lucky I was able to leave the office," Jerry Stone growled. "So, where're we going?"

Grant pointed down the tree-lined Gold Coast street, strewn with fallen leaves. "The Barberi compound's a couple of blocks from here." They began walking at a brisk pace.

"You sure your nephew is in there?"

Clenching his teeth, Grant nodded. "Yes, sir. It's where Ben went the last time he got disturbing news about his dad."

"What happened this time?"

"He found out Logan was responsible for Sophie going to prison."

They forged ahead, and Jerry noticed Grant wasn't loping along with his usual cat-like grace. Instead, he seemed tense, almost ferocious.

"I don't care how upset Ben was—I told him not to go to Angelo's!" Grant suddenly snarled. "It's the one place I ordered him not to go to. He's purposely defying me."

As Grant's hands balled into fists, Jerry more clearly understood Dr. Hayes' progress reports, which noted that Grant had been working on significant anger-management issues. Jerry had once seen Grant explode in anger—when Marilyn had informed him he was the prime suspect for his brother's murder (quite an understandable reaction)—but other than that, he'd seen only a docile respectfulness from the young man. Grant's atypical aggressiveness alerted Jerry's instincts, and he put out an arm to stop him.

"Maybe you need to calm down before we get there," Jerry suggested.

"We don't have time to waste!" Grant protested.

"What are you so worried about? Your nephew has been to the Barberi compound before and come out of it okay."

"*Okay?*" Grant fumed. "He's becoming an addict, just like his dad! Every time Ben gets under their influence, I lose him a little more. He's probably in there right now, lighting up a joint, just like I warned him not to do—I'm...I'm gonna kill him!"

Jerry took a step closer and grabbed Grant's arm with a firm grip.

"You will not *touch* that boy," he said in a low voice. "He's a minor, and you will not lay one hand on him, got it?"

Grant's lips parted, and he stood stock-still, suddenly aware of his own behavior as well as the officer's implied threat—cross Jerry and suddenly he could be violating his parole. He took a deep breath and willfully unfurled his fists.

Studying him intently, Jerry added, "*If* that kid is in there, I'll take care of it, okay?"

"Yes, sir."

Satisfied that Grant was back under control, Jerry dropped his arm and they turned the corner, immediately dwarfed by the massive homes lining the streets.

"Ben is not his father," Jerry said. "There's still time to save him."

Grant's throat tightened, and all he could manage was a nod and a soft "Yes, sir."

❧

"Please, I'll—I'll do whatever you want," Will Taylor promised, warily looking back and forth from Angelo to Tank.

Out in the hallway, Ben frowned. Why was Sophie's dad so scared?

"What I want," Angelo slowly enunciated, "is an answer. Why are you fucking around with your payments? Do you want your business to go under?"

"No!" Will shouted before more carefully adding, "Please. I was foolish back then. I—I thought I didn't need to pay for protection. But I learned my lesson. I paid extra as a sign of my goodwill and respect. I'll do anything you want—just please don't hurt Sophie any more."

Sophie? How was she part of this? Ben's forehead creased.

Angelo also felt quite perplexed, but he showed nothing. After Grant had shot and killed Carlo in a north-side apartment, Angelo naturally had ordered his men to investigate. They'd discovered that the apartment was leased by Kirsten Holland, a friend of Sophie Taylor. They'd also then discovered the romantic relationship between Grant and Sophie, and they now knew the two lived together—along with Ben currently, since the teenager was dumped there by his mother. But how any of that related to Will Taylor's protection payments was still a puzzle to Angelo.

"I assure you Carlo acted on his own that night in August," Angelo said. "I did not order him to threaten your daughter."

The fear momentarily left Will's eyes, replaced by skepticism. "Right," he scoffed.

"You don't believe me?"

The businessman leaned forward on his seat, seeming more incensed than afraid now. "You've been targeting my daughter for some time now, Mr. Barberi."

Again, Angelo was at a loss.

"And now you're siccing your nephew Grant on her, despite all my efforts to keep her away from him," Will continued. "I have to stand by and watch another Mafia man seduce her—just waiting for him to hurt her!" Will's voice had grown louder. As he glanced around, he seemed to grasp the danger of the situation. Looking down, he grimly resumed. "Anyway, I get the message loud and clear. There's no need to drag me down here and threaten me. I'll never miss another payment."

Angelo paused. Taylor thought Grant worked for him? And that mistaken belief had led him to overpay? For a split second the Mafia don saw Grant's innocent eyes swimming before his face, and he considered telling the truth. But then the reality of his impending death hit him, along with the familiar burden of responsibility for securing his family's future. Taylor was a wealthy man, and the Barberi family could definitely benefit from a potential windfall, even if it stemmed from making false threats.

"Look at me, Mr. Taylor," Angelo commanded.

Will slowly raised his head.

"I haven't had a reason to order Grant to harm your daughter—*yet*. You'll double your regular payment, and as long as we get that on time every month, Sophie will be safe."

"But that's impossible in this economy—"

Angelo held out a hand. "Surely your daughter's life is worth it, Mr. Taylor. And any plans to go to the police will result in the complete collapse of your business. I can guarantee it."

That threat quelled any further protest, and Will slumped in his chair, feeling a mixture of fear, resignation, and disgust. Angelo looked pointedly at the bodyguard in the corner. "Take Mr. Taylor to get a drink. He looks like he needs one."

The hulking man crossed the room and waited expectantly by the chair until Will stood up and allowed himself to be led out of the room. Ben quickly hid behind some hideous Roman statue, escaping detection by the two men leaving the study.

As soon as they were gone, Angelo shook his head uneasily, glaring at Tank and Mario. "Something's not right here—something's missing. What the fuck was Taylor talking about? He said we've been targeting his daughter for some time now? Something about 'another Mafia man' seducing her?"

Ben overheard every word, and his heart began thumping in his chest.

"The daughter was at Logan's funeral," Tank said.

Angelo looked shocked. "She was? Why didn't you tell me that?"

"Sorry, boss. Didn't think it was important." Tank's throat constricted as he told the lie. He'd been with *Carlo* at the funeral, and Carlo had ordered him to investigate Sophie's background. He hardly wished to mention that at the moment, though.

Peering at his bodyguards suspiciously, Angelo's mouth tightened. "Cut the shit, you two. I know you were the ones who held Logan down while Carlo shoved a knife in his gut."

Ben stopped breathing.

"Tell me what you know *now*," Angelo hissed.

Tank shot a desperate glance at Mario before looking back at his boss.

"C-C-Carlo had me call one of our police contacts after the funeral, and I found out Logan had history with Sophie Taylor. She was his shrink, you know, when that judge made him go to counseling, and he, uh, used her office to hide guns and money."

Silent tears slid down Ben's face as he hunched in the corner, his thin arms wrapped around his torso, hugging himself. Somehow he was grateful he'd heard this story from Sophie first.

"I guess the cops raided Taylor's daughter's office and found the cash, and they found guns too," Tank continued. His voice dropped lower. "One of the weapons was traced to the Salazar murder."

"Shit," Angelo muttered.

"The girl served about half of her two-year sentence, and she's still on parole."

"Why haven't I heard about this before?"

"Her dad used his influence to keep it outta the papers. I guess Logan didn't tell you?"

Angelo shook his head. "All I knew was the family was out one hundred Gs and Logan was on the run from the fuzz."

Tank sighed. "Logan sure got himself into a clusterfuck. When I told the story to Carlo, he immediately wanted to track down Taylor's daughter to try to get the money back. I guess he got to her through Grant...and we know the rest."

Yeah, Carlo shot Sophie, Ben silently responded. *And then Uncle Grant had to kill Carlo to save Sophie's life.* He felt nauseated.

Angelo tried frantically to sort through all the pieces of information, undeterred by the pain coursing through his weak body.

"Holy shit," he cried, having an epiphany. "Logan just started going to see Taylor's daughter randomly, right? After the judge ordered him to get therapy?"

Mario nodded, wondering where his boss was going with this.

Angelo started to get excited. "But Taylor thinks Logan went there on purpose! He thinks we sent Logan to set up his daughter as retribution for not paying the extortion fee. He blames himself for his daughter going to prison."

Tank's jaw dropped. "You're right, boss. Think we should set Taylor straight?"

"Hell, no," Angelo retorted. "I only wish we could make all our suppliers this scared of us. Taylor looked like he was about to crap his pants."

Tank and Mario chuckled while Ben's blood boiled. He'd heard all he could stand. He slunk away from his hiding place and headed back to his room to retrieve his backpack. He had to get far away from this place and never come back.

In the study, Mario tensed as he glanced at the security camera feed for the entrance to the compound, instantly recognizing Logan's brother, accompanied by an older man with "cop" written all over him.

"We got company, boss."

"How can I help you, Grant?" Tank asked pleasantly through the locked gate at the entrance. His glare at the man next to Grant was not so pleasant.

"We're here for Ben," Grant responded, not mincing words.

Tank shrugged and did what came naturally—he lied. "He ain't here."

A small seed of doubt sprouted inside Grant—what if Ben *wasn't* here? Where else would he be? Noticing the smirk on the bodyguard's face, Grant squared his shoulders.

"I know he's in there… Anthony, is it? Please bring him out."

Anthony Tanketti clenched his jaw in irritation. Angelo had instructed him to get rid of Grant, but the damn Boy Scout wouldn't be easily put off. Less assuredly, Tank griped, "I don't know why you're not listening to me—"

"Listen to *me*," Jerry butted in, whipping out his badge and shoving it near the bars of the gate. "You got a minor in there without his parent's permission. You have exactly two minutes to bring him out or I'll get a warrant lickety-split. You'll have thirty officers crawling up your ass, tossing the joint, in no time. What will it be, *Anthony?*"

During Jerry's tirade Tank had unknowingly retreated a few steps, and he now looked at the officer, dumbfounded. "Uh, I'll go relay that info, um, to the boss."

Watching the bodyguard scurry away, Grant leaned in and whispered, "Can you do that, sir? Get a warrant?"

"No," Jerry confessed, looking pissed off. "I could arrest you but that's about it—that's where my jurisdiction ends." He nodded toward the compound. "But *they* don't know that."

Grant smirked, feeling an even greater appreciation for his parole officer. Thank God he'd called him for help. Sophie would be proud. He grimaced, thinking about his beautiful girlfriend. She'd begged him not to come near his family, yet here he was again, mere feet from their menace. He hoped she wouldn't find out about this visit.

Back at the house, Tank swung open the massive front door and almost collided with Ben, who was wearing his backpack and had the air of a young man on the move.

"Just the guy I was looking for," Tank said, clasping Ben's shoulders in his brawny clutches and guiding him to the study, despite the boy's wiggling protests. Shoving the teenager into the room, Tank announced, "Grant's here for Ben."

Ben's eyes widened. Uncle Grant was here, for him? *Oh, shit.* Grant wasn't going to be happy he'd come to the compound.

"Well, he's not getting him," Angelo countered, glancing fondly at Ben. "You're happy here, right?"

Feeling his stomach twist with revulsion, Ben knew he couldn't stay. Yet going outside to face the music with his uncle didn't sound appealing either. Caught between two sides of the family, he decided to go with the one he trusted. "Actually, I, uh, I gotta go. I just remembered I got a chemistry test in sixth period. I can't miss it or I'll fail the class.'

Angelo shrugged. "No worries—I'll talk to your teacher. I'm sure he'll give you an A after I'm through with him."

"You don't have to do that," Ben said, trying to hide the quiver in his voice. "Please—I...I'll come back later. My mom wants me to come live with her again, so it'll be easier for me to visit here."

Ben felt a pang of sadness. Grant wouldn't want him back now anyway, not after he'd caused so much trouble. "I gotta go to school now, Gruncle."

Angelo closed his eyes. He felt utterly exhausted and simply wished to go to sleep. Snapping his eyes open, he frowned.

"Fine, *ragazzo*. We miss you around here. Make sure you come back pronto."

"Okay." Ben nodded, managing a half-smile. He squirmed out of Tank's hold and walked swiftly out the door.

"That fucking cop threatened to get a search warrant," Tank informed Angelo once Ben had left.

"Jesus! Get Taylor out of here."

"Yes, boss."

Grant was flooded with relief once he saw his nephew come out of the mansion. With each step, however, his relief morphed into rage, and by the time Ben arrived at the gate—his eyes locked fearfully onto his uncle's—Grant was visibly shaking with fury.

"I told you never to come here again!" he shouted.

Swallowing hard, Ben punched in the pass code and opened the gate, bravely facing his incensed uncle.

Despite his rage, Grant grabbed the teen in a suffocating hug, smothering him for several moments before releasing him and hollering, "You think you can just miss school whenever you want?"

"Madsen," Jerry growled, cocking his head to the corner of the fenced area. "Let me talk to the boy."

Fighting for self-control, Grant took a deep breath. "This is Officer Stone—my parole officer—and he wants to have a few words with you. Don't you dare mouth off to him." With that, Grant walked over to wait impatiently by the corner of the compound.

Ben stared at the officer with huge eyes, and Jerry immediately noticed the family resemblance.

Narrowing his gaze, Jerry authoritatively ordered, "Turn around."

Not daring to resist, Ben did as he was told. Jerry peeled the backpack straps down his arms and set the bag to the side. "Hands on the fence," he barked.

"Am I—am I under arrest?" Ben stuttered, raising his arms and curling his fingers around the solid wrought-iron bars as the man roughly frisked him.

"Shut up, kid," Jerry commanded. He wanted to put the fear of God in the boy. There were already far too many parolees in the system, and he didn't want to add this kid to the mix. After the pat-down failed to reveal anything of interest, Jerry yanked each arm down and locked Ben's trembling wrists into handcuffs behind his back.

"Please," Ben moaned, close to tears. "Please don't arrest me. I wasn't doing anything in there. I'm not like them."

Jerry paused. Coming from this family, the odds were certainly stacked against the kid; it'd be unlikely he could survive without turning into a two-bit criminal. Yet his uncle was trying his best to escape the Barberis, and maybe Ben could make it too.

"We'll see about that," Jerry gruffly replied, seizing the backpack in one hand and unzipping it with the other. Ben closed his eyes, swept over with relief that he'd decided not to take any of the pot with him. Standing helplessly handcuffed while a police officer rifled through his stuff, he promised himself he'd never *look* at marijuana again.

"It looks like you're clean," Jerry said. "That's too bad. I was hoping I'd be shipping you off to juvie today."

Ben looked down. "That's where Uncle Grant wants me, isn't it?"

"Of course not," Jerry said quickly.

"Then why did he bring you here with him?"

Jerry spun the boy around to face him. "I'm here because it's a violation of Madsen's parole to be anywhere near this place. He almost returned to prison in July because he attended your birthday party here."

Ben's eyes widened. "Did—did I make him get in trouble for coming here today?"

"Let's hope not. Your uncle loves you like crazy, and he would take all kinds of risks for you. But stop putting him in jeopardy, kid. Never visit this place again, you got it?"

Biting his trembling lip, Ben nodded. A tear escaped and rolled down his cheek.

Grant couldn't hear the exchange, but it did seem like Officer Stone was getting through to his nephew. Handcuffing Ben had been a nice touch. Startled by a noise behind him, Grant swiveled and noticed a side door to the compound sweeping open. He tensed as he prepared to face whoever emerged, and when Grant identified the man exiting the building, his jaw dropped.

Staring back at him, equally shocked, was Will Taylor.

15. Condemnation

Hunter was surprised to find an empty waiting room. Since Grant had begun joining Sophie for their appointments, they'd always been on time—early even. He glanced at his watch and frowned. They'd had barely twenty-four hours to forget their additional appointment this week.

Just then a tall, lanky figure came jogging through the door, and Hunter turned to find a very shaken Grant, cheeks flushed and chest heaving.

"Is Sophie here?"

Hunter shook his head. "Isn't she with you?"

Grant exhaled. "No, sir. She didn't come home last night, and she won't answer my calls. I—I don't know what to do. I don't know if my family tried to hurt her…"

He held his head in his hands.

Hunter felt a pang of panic himself. "Is there any evidence your family is coming after Sophie? Did they threaten her again?"

"Not that I know of," Grant said. "But Angelo might be upset with me after I went to his house yesterday."

"You did?"

Hearing the consternation in his psychologist's voice, Grant looked down guiltily. "I ended up taking something he wanted—"

He was cut off by the sound of the door sweeping open, and in walked Sophie.

"Thank God!" Grant cried, rushing to his girlfriend. "Are you all right?"

Sophie flinched when he tried to touch her, and her eyes flashed with fear. Grant stopped short as a wave of hurt and confusion washed over him.

"Don't touch me!" was her strangled cry. "Please don't make us do a couples' session today," she begged Hunter. "Can't I schedule to come back on my own?"

Hunter, like Grant, was dumbfounded. "Sophie, what's wrong? Why are you so upset?"

She stole a sideways glance at Grant and shuddered. "I can't talk about it around *him*. It's not safe."

"You're scared of Grant? Did he hurt you?"

"Not *yet*," she replied snidely, each word piercing her boyfriend. "But it's just a matter of time."

A hush fell over the three of them when a woman and her teenage son came in the door and halted to stare curiously at the tense scene unfolding before them.

"Let's take this up in my office, shall we?" Hunter suggested.

"No," Sophie pleaded. "Please don't make me go back there with *him*."

"You'll be safe," Hunter promised, looking pointedly at the man next to him. "Right, Grant?"

His expressive crystal eyes overflowed with conflicting emotions — bewilderment, betrayal, anger, and resignation — and flickered back and forth between his girlfriend and psychologist. Slowly realizing why Sophie was terrified of him yet again, Grant felt choked by fury aimed alternately at her, himself, and his family — but mostly at himself.

As Grant hesitated, Hunter glanced at the other clients, who'd taken a seat yet continued to gawk at the interaction a few feet away from them. The confidentiality of this conversation was severely compromised. Making an executive decision, Hunter commanded, "Let's go, you two. We'll get to the bottom of this."

Sophie glared at him but made no move to leave. Feeling hopeless, Grant quietly said, "Yes, sir."

Hunter latched onto Sophie's elbow and began ushering her down the hallway. Reluctantly she allowed herself to be led forward, though she couldn't help but snatch anxious glances behind her. Grant followed them with a shuffling gait, head down.

As they entered the office, Hunter asked Sophie, "Would you feel safer sitting in my chair?"

"Yes, thank you."

Hunter joined Grant on the sofa.

"So what the hell is going on?" Hunter asked.

Grant was the first to answer Hunter's question, staring darkly at Sophie. "Your father got to you, didn't he? He told you he saw me at Angelo's."

Her eyes narrowed into slits. "Oh, so you're admitting it? Are you also going to admit that you've been playing me from day one?"

His mouth dropped open. "*Playing* you? Are you sure you're not confusing me with your dad? What the hell was *he* doing there, huh?"

"He was dragged there!" she yelled, feeling the squeeze of tightness in her chest. "Your goons kidnapped him and dragged him to the compound to make sure he keeps paying his extortion money!"

Grant's mouth abruptly shut, and he looked stunned.

"He came and got me from work, right after he ran into you," Sophie continued. "He was sick with worry, and he finally confessed something that's been killing him for a long time. Apparently he refused to pay the protection fee two years ago — he refused to let your family just take his hard-earned money, like they've always done — and that's when your brother became my client. That's when your brother ruined my life. It was all a scheme to punish my dad for disobeying them!"

"Logan intentionally got you arrested?"

"Don't act dumb!" Sophie seethed. "You knew all about it too!"

"I did not! I was in prison then — how would I know anything?"

She scoffed derisively. "In prison with your *father*. I bet he masterminded the whole plan from his cell."

Ignoring Grant's incredulous denials, she forged ahead.

"My dad has been flooded with guilt ever since I got arrested. *That's* why he never visited me in prison — he couldn't look me in the eye, knowing his actions led to my arrest. He blamed himself for everything!"

Grant sat motionless. He couldn't believe his family had enacted such vengeance over a paltry extortion fee — sending Logan to set up a businessman's daughter? Was Logan even capable of such treachery? It had seemed like Logan really cared for Sophie. And even more shocking, how could she actually believe that Grant had been conning her the whole time? How could she *ever* think that?

His wounded eyes bore into her, but that didn't stop her hateful words.

"My dad's been through hell, and he was lucky to get out of there alive yesterday. But I'm glad he went through it, because he ran into you — now we *both* know you're still involved with your family. Now we know the truth."

"The *truth?*" Grant shouted, livid. "Do you care about the truth? Your dad explained why he was at the compound — did you ever think about giving *me* a chance to explain? Do you think I wanted to be there?"

"Oh, this should be good," Sophie retorted, folding her arms across her chest. "Let's hear your story. I'm sure it will be just as good as Logan's lies."

"I'm not my brother!" Grant exploded, earning a look of surprised satisfaction from Hunter. "You keep telling me how different Logan was from me, but then here you go, assuming I'm setting you up just like he did! You're not even giving me a chance. I—I…"

Hunter jumped in, guiding the tongue-tied, enraged man on the sofa next to him. "I feel angry…" he prompted, leading Grant and Sophie to pause their heated confrontation and stare at him like he was crazy.

Undeterred, Hunter continued. "You're doing great, Grant. Tell her how you feel using 'I' statements."

Squaring his shoulders, Grant said, "I feel angry that you, that, um, you still think I'm one of *them*. I'm mad as hell that you didn't even give me the chance to explain — after all we've been through!" His eyes flared. "I would do *anything* for you, Sophie. And yet you hear one accusation against me, from a man who's hated me from the second he met me, and you take his word over mine. You know what? Damn it, I deserve better than this!"

Hunter sported a half-smile in spite of himself. "Bravo, Grant."

Sophie's mouth dropped open. "Why are you taking *his* side?"

"Because that's the first time I've heard a shred of self-confidence from him! And because he needs somebody on his side. You have your father, but Grant has nobody — no father, no mother, no brother."

"He has his nephew!"

"My nephew is why I'm in all this mess," Grant interjected hotly.

Sophie looked puzzled, still breathing hard from her yelling. "What do you mean?"

"Sophie, I went to the compound to get Ben back."

"What?" She looked startled and met Grant's eyes for the first time. "He went there too? Oh God, is he okay?"

"I think so — he's with his mom now. Officer Stone took him home in handcuffs, so hopefully that taught him a thing or two."

"Jerry was there?" Sophie remained surprised.

"Yes, I called and asked him for help, just like you'd want me to."

Sophie felt her anger begin to dissipate, only to be replaced by a sinking sensation. Had she just falsely accused him?

"Wait," she gulped, struggling for air. "Can you explain what happened?"

"So you're giving me a chance to explain now? You're sure you wouldn't rather just leave because it's not 'safe' around me?"

Sophie looked at the floor. "I'm sorry. Please, Grant."

He studied her fine porcelain features, which reflected the same kaleidoscope of emotions he'd recently experienced on the receiving end of her anger. He took a deep breath. "I was at work when Ashley called, frantic that Ben wasn't at school."

"He didn't go to school?" Sophie clasped one hand over her mouth and shot a guilty glance toward Grant. "He was so upset after I told him about Logan."

Grant grimaced. "Yes."

Hunter sadly nodded. "That boy has been through hell."

"Yes, he has," Grant agreed.

"And when he got overloaded by stress, he returned to his old ways of coping," Hunter said. "Or should I say, he returned to his old stomping grounds?"

"Exactly, sir. I knew Ben had gone to the compound, and I had to get him away from there. But I also knew I'd return to prison if I got spotted associating with known criminals."

"So you called Jerry?" Sophie asked.

Grant nodded, and despite the tension, a grin spread across his face. "Officer Stone was so awesome, Sophie. He told one of Angelo's men he'd run and get a search warrant if he didn't bring Ben out *immediately*, and he didn't even have the authority to do that! Then when Ben finally walked out, I was totally yelling at him, but Officer Stone took over. He read Ben the riot act, and he searched him and cuffed him."

Sophie's eyes widened. "Ben must've been freaking out!"

"I think he got the message loud and clear," Grant replied. "He won't be going anywhere *near* Angelo's after that experience."

Hunter's eyes bounced back and forth between the pair as if he were watching a tennis match. From opposite sides of the net, the players had started the match snarling and hurling insults at each other, but now they were engaged in a reasonable discourse as they caught up on their time apart. Their caring for Ben was evident, and Hunter was pleased the conflict had seemed to resolve so quickly.

"I think Officer Stone took Ben straight to Ashley's then."

"You're not sure?" Sophie inquired.

"Well, I was standing near the side entrance to the compound, and that's when I, uh, when I saw your dad."

Sophie bit her lip, feeling immense guilt for her earlier accusations. "Did you guys say anything to each other?"

"No. I think we were both too shocked. We just kind of stood there, staring, until your dad took off and headed for the street. I watched him hail a cab, trying to figure out what the hell he was doing there." Grant looked nervously at Sophie. "I didn't know if I should tell you I saw him. I didn't want you to be hurt any more." He sighed. "It's awful what your dad went through, but I'm so glad he's not in cahoots with my family, Sophie."

She looked down. "Me too," she said softly.

"When I turned back, Officer Stone was leading Ben away, I assume to his car, which he'd parked a few blocks away," Grant added.

"Have you heard from Ben since then?" Sophie's voice was full of concern.

"Ashley called me once he got home, but according to her he's not saying much. Apparently he's been the perfect angel even in the short time he's been back." Grant and Sophie shared a smirk. Then Grant added wistfully, "I miss him already."

"Maybe he could come back and live with us?"

"Maybe, but he probably belongs with his mom."

A silence descended. Feeling rather superfluous, Hunter interjected, "So, Sophie, how do you feel about your father telling you he's responsible for you going to prison?"

She frowned. "He's not. I don't care if he refused to pay the money; he's not the one who acted inappropriately with a client. That's on me."

Grant felt a stirring of uneasiness at the mention of his brother, knowing exactly what her "inappropriate" behavior entailed. Feeling an itching sensation in his fingertips — the impulse to lash out aggressively — he sat on his hands and forced himself to take deep breaths.

"Shame's a tricky emotion," Hunter told Sophie. "It can sometimes make people hide or withdraw from those they love. It seems like your father feels horribly guilty for bringing the Mafia into your life, which explains why he never visited you in prison. He was too ashamed to see you."

She nodded her head thoughtfully.

"And it also makes sense why he's been so afraid of Grant being in your life—why he feels compelled try to avoid you getting hurt again."

Sophie considered Hunter's statement and sheepishly gazed at Grant.

"I'm sorry, Grant, but my father was convinced you were working for them. Angelo confirmed it."

Grant's eyes narrowed.

"And when my father told me he saw you there, what was I supposed to think?"

Leaning forward on the sofa, Grant said, "You were supposed to think about *us,* Sophie…about the promises I've made to you…about my love for you. I would never hurt you—don't you know that? Don't you feel that inside you?"

Gazing into his earnest, passionate eyes, she nodded, slowly at first, and then with increasing vehemence. The corners of her mouth turned down and her eyes began brimming with tears.

"I'm so sorry, Grant. It was stupid of me to doubt you. I should never do that—it's not fair to you."

"I feel…?" Hunter prompted.

Gulping, she returned her gaze to Grant. "I feel horrible for doubting you. I feel, um, remorseful for listening to my dad instead of you. He was just so upset, and I wasn't thinking straight."

"I don't blame your father," Grant said. "He was probably feeling lucky to get out of there alive, and then he ran into me right outside the compound? No wonder he was so upset. He's just trying to keep you safe, and I'd probably do the same thing, telling you to stay away from any potential threat. If I had a daughter as precious as you, I'd do everything in my power to try to protect you too."

A few tears had spilled over onto her cheeks, and Sophie's upper lip quivered. She sniffed. "You already have," she said. "You already have done everything in your power to protect me. And like an idiot I forgot it all for a second. I'm really sorry. I won't forget it again, Grant. I promise."

He listened to her apology with a keen sense of relief, his hope in their relationship returning. This misunderstanding had not been Sophie's fault or even her father's fault. Once again, the blame rested squarely on his family. The Barberi clan was yet again attempting to tear down all that was good in his life, but this time he wouldn't let them. He was fiercely determined to hold onto Sophie, no matter what his family tried.

"So what have we learned here today, people?" Hunter asked. "This isn't the first time one of you has been so upset that you've gone AWOL, leaving your partner feeling rejected and panicked. What did you learn?"

Sophie sniffled again. "We need to communicate," she said quietly.

"What was that?" Hunter mocked, dramatically drawing his cupped palm to his ear. "What did you say?"

"We need to *communicate!*" Sophie shouted, earning a chuckle from Grant.

"Precisely," Hunter replied. "Now, with our remaining time today I'd like to go over some communication exercises from the great marital researcher John Gottman. I know you two aren't married, but he has some wonderful recommendations for romantic relationships..."

Hunter began droning on about physiological responses to conflict, rules for fair fighting, and love maps, while Grant and Sophie listened halfheartedly. Their true attention was riveted only on each other as they sat on either side of their psychologist. Longing for their typical closeness on the sofa, Sophie's warm mahogany eyes smoldered with desire, and Grant's cool crystal eyes glittered with want. The curious transformation from livid to lustful was taking place, and if there ever was a time for make-up sex, this was it.

"Okay, so Gottman has found that successful marriages are built on successful friendships first. I want you two to take these love map questions," Hunter explained, holding out a photocopy for Grant to take, "and quiz each other before we meet again."

Hunter planned to hand a copy to Sophie once Grant grabbed his, but he hadn't reached to take it from his hand. Noting Grant's parted lips and glazed-over stare, Hunter followed his eyes over to Sophie's face, which looked equally dreamy.

"Has either of your heard a word I said?" he asked.

"Excuse me, sir, what did you say?" Grant stammered.

"I *said*, take these questions and ask them to each other!"

Grant took the paper and nodded. "Will do, sir."

Sophie let out a giggle of embarrassment as she took her photocopied paper. "Thanks, Hunter."

He rolled his eyes and wondered how long it would take the nymphomaniacs to get horizontal. "Okay, you two. Get outta here."

Grant popped off the sofa and headed toward the door, almost running into Sophie. "Oops." He blushed, holding his arm out for her to go ahead of him. She let out another shy giggle.

When his hand brushed up her side, landing on the small of her back, she felt the crackle of electricity on her skin. As they headed down the hallway toward the waiting room, their awkward excitement continued.

"I can't believe you ran into my father like that," Sophie mused, shaking her head.

"And *I* can't believe you instantly accepted what he said about me!" Grant countered, a twinge of anger still evident in his voice.

They arrived in the waiting room, whose sole occupant was the woman who'd earlier watched Hunter attempt to mediate their argument. Glancing at the flush of Grant's cheeks, Sophie felt a thrill of naughtiness course through her. Without another thought, she grabbed Grant's shirt and drew him into the unisex bathroom off the waiting room.

"What're you doing?" he hissed as she closed the door behind him and pushed him up against the bathroom wall.

"Making it up to you." She grinned, squinting her eyes mischievously before swooping in for a kiss. Grant's lips were instantly receptive, and their mouths collided as the temperature in the bathroom began to rise. Their hands snaked everywhere — caressing, groping, massaging, exploring, fumbling.

He loved that the daughter of a very wealthy man was making out with him in a *bathroom*. "Classy joint you've taken me to, Taylor," he teased between kisses.

She felt his lips rise in a grin, pressing against hers.

"Your dad would be appalled," he added.

"Maybe that's why I like it in here so much," she shot back, skating her hands inward from his muscled hips to the button of his jeans. As their mouths zigzagged across every inch of exposed skin, their bodies pushed against each other, creating a hot friction. With exquisite pleasure, Sophie let out one of her characteristic moans.

"While I'm going to miss Ben," she panted, "I do know *one* advantage of him going back to his mom's." She grinned devilishly. "Now we can be as loud as we want."

She heard the deep rumble of a chuckle springing up from his chest. "I see you're already testing that theory, and we're not even home yet."

Her laughter morphed into deep intakes of air as he worked his McSailor Method on her, swiftly and expertly.

About five minutes later, they emerged from the bathroom, utterly disheveled, with flushed cheeks, mussed hair, and a sated glow warming their skin. The woman gaped at the two lovebirds.

Despite her earlier demands for Grant's touch, Sophie felt her face on fire. Grant, however, looked the woman directly in the eye, pulling his unkempt girlfriend to his side. Winking at the woman, he announced, "This couples' therapy thing really works!"

16. Concert

"You ready, kid?"

Grant glanced up from the sheet music in his hand to the open doorway off the bar to find his gray-haired boss staring expectantly. He rose, trying to swallow his fear. "I think so, sir."

Alex Remington laughed. His performer looked anything but ready for opening night. He took a seat in the makeshift dressing room. "Relax, Grant. You sounded great in rehearsal."

"Thanks," Grant said, adding a giant exhale. "But I'm really worried I'll forget the lyrics."

"Nah, you'll be fine. Hell, I'm so confident my bar will be a hit that I invited a couple of old buddies to celebrate opening night. I really want to impress those two. Don't let me down, Grant."

A bartender walking past the doorway distracted Alex, and he abruptly got up to follow, calling after the employee with some question about champagne.

Standing alone now, Grant felt even more nervous. If that was supposed to be a pep talk, it had missed its mark.

He wished Sophie were here, but her department was interviewing a cognitive psychology candidate, and she had to go to dinner with the prospective assistant professor. A smile tugged at one corner of his mouth as he recalled how she'd attempted to calm his nerves the last time he'd been nervous about a public singing performance. One tequila shot had turned into quite a few more. He couldn't remember much about that night—except for kissing her in the cab on their way to Kirsten's apartment. It was one of their first experiences together, and even now it flushed his face with a warm glow.

Returning to earth, he realized he was on his own this time, and he'd better not blow it. He sighed heavily and sat back down, snatching the sheet music to *Mack the Knife* and closing his eyes while mentally reviewing lyrics about a man lying dead on a sidewalk.

He wished he could get through the song without thinking of Logan. Though Carlo was now six feet under as well, a heated desire for vengeance still rushed through Grant's veins. Feeling sickened by the lingering impulse, Grant realized no matter how hard he fought, he'd always be a Barberi.

Hearing light footsteps near the doorway, Grant opened his eyes to find the youngest Barberi tentatively entering the room. As soon as he and Ben saw each other, both broke out in big grins.

"I found you!" the teenager said buoyantly.

"Hey! What're you doing here?"

"Sophie texted me," Ben explained, holding up his phone as proof. "She said, uh…" He scrolled through his messages, locating the one he wanted. "She said 'Your uncle has his opening night at Capone's Spirits and needs your support.'" Ben looked up and added, "He's so nervous he's peeing in his pants."

Grant felt the blood drain from his face. "She didn't say *that*, did she?"

Ben grinned. "Nah, I may have embellished a little." Still peering at his phone, his face took on a wistful expression. "And she said, um, she missed me."

"That part I believe." Grant smiled. "We both miss you. How's it going at your mom's? What's it been, almost a week now?"

He sniffed. "It's okay." Blushing, he glanced nervously at his uncle. "I feel kinda bad that my mom's been all alone…so maybe I better stay with her—"

"Of course," Grant interrupted. "I totally understand. You're welcome to stay with us anytime, but I think it's great you're back with your mother."

Relieved, the teenager studied his surroundings. "This is a pretty tough hotel, huh? Super rich. When I asked where the bar was, the dude at the front desk called me 'sir.'" Ben grinned wickedly and glanced through the open door at the rapidly filling bar. "So, you're freaked out?"

Grant nodded solemnly. "I'm about to pee in my pants," he said with a completely straight face. They both chuckled.

"But you did okay on the cruise," Ben pointed out. "At least the passengers didn't try to launch themselves overboard or anything when you were singing."

"Thank you for that rousing praise. The difference is I only did *one* song on the cruise. Here I have at least six songs in the first set, and then maybe more if it goes okay."

"Hmm. Well, there *is* a bar out there—want me to get you a drink to chill you out?"

"Hell, no," Grant quickly responded. "I learned my lesson the first time."

As his nephew's eyes lit up with curiosity, Grant shook his head. "Forget it—there's no way I'm telling you that story."

Thinking for a minute, he narrowed his eyes. "Wait a second—you're *sixteen*. How on earth would you buy me a drink?"

The blush returned, coloring Ben's neck and cheeks. "Uh, um, I dunno—charm the bartender or something?"

Grant's eyes filled with suspicion. "Give me your wallet."

"C'mon, Uncle Grant, it's cool."

"Give it to me."

Ben frowned but reluctantly reached for his backpack, which he'd earlier slung over a chair. His uncle had some kind of hold over him, and he felt powerless to disobey. Slowly he unzipped the front pocket and handed over his thin wallet.

Grant opened it, instantly locating what he was looking for: a fake driver's license. Despite his disappointment, he couldn't help the laugh that escaped his lips as he read aloud. "Albert Fredo? Where the hell did that name come from?"

Despite himself, Ben chuckled too. "My boys came up with that name—Al is one saucy dude."

Grant shook his head. Scrutinizing the fake ID, his eyes bugged out. "You're supposed to be *twenty-five*? Has this ID actually *worked*?"

Appearing wounded, Ben started to answer but then thought better of it. "I'm taking the fifth on that one."

"You're taking the fifth?" Grant repeated, simultaneously dismayed and impressed. "Well, *I'm* taking this bogus ID."

"Hey, c'mon, Uncle Grant. Even you said the ID probably wouldn't work."

"And if it doesn't, you could get arrested! Do you *want* to go to juvie?"

"No," Ben conceded sullenly.

Pocketing the offending license before handing back the wallet, Grant nodded. "Good."

As Ben zipped up his backpack, he felt overwhelmed. He wished he didn't make his uncle so mad at him all the time.

Watching his nephew stare at the floor, Grant sighed. "Look, I didn't mean to yell at you. I'm probably taking out my nervousness on you, and that's not fair."

"'S okay. I probably shouldn't have a fake ID."

"No, you shouldn't, Mr. Fredo."

Ben looked up with one of his characteristic smirks. He was quiet for some time, then asked, "Are you mad at me for going to Angelo's?"

"I *was* mad," Grant admitted. "Now I'm just relieved you're okay. But if I ever find out you went there again, you'll be doing push-ups forever."

"I'm not going back," Ben told him.

Grant was surprised at the conviction in his voice. What had happened at the compound?

"Um, and the push-ups thing?" Ben said shyly. "Uh, I can do them now, I think." His face reddened as he confessed, "I've been training."

"You can do fifty now? That's great!"

"Want me to show you?"

Grant paused. This back room was hardly a convenient space to do calisthenics, yet he sensed his nephew's urgent need to make things right, to make him proud. Grant often felt the same way when it came to Joe.

"Um, sure. Why not? Here…" Grant scooted a small table against the wall and gestured to the floor. "You can do them here."

Ben nodded and bit his lip, totally focused on the task at hand. He bent down to rest his weight on his hands and toes, then pumped his body up and down while he counted off each rep. Watching the boy's determination and burgeoning physical strength, Grant experienced a swelling in his chest, an outpouring of love so deep it almost felt like an ache in his heart.

He remembered feeling the same sensation at age fourteen when he'd first held his infant nephew in his arms — when Joe had taken him to visit Ashley in the hospital's maternity ward. Nineteen-year-old Logan had been absent at the time, but Grant had been amazed that his ne'er-do-well older brother had created the tiny, beautiful bundle in his arms.

Before he knew it, Ben had returned to standing, fifty push-ups under his belt.

Grant gave him a bright smile. "That was awesome!" He reached out to ruffle Ben's hair, and his nephew looked embarrassed but didn't shy away from the touch. "I love how you persevered—that'll get you far in life. And now you're no longer grounded if you come back to live with us."

"Finally!" Ben cried victoriously, still panting a bit from exertion.

Grant glanced at his watch and his expression turned from affectionate to anxious. "Only twenty more minutes till show time," he croaked. "You've done a good job distracting me, though. Thanks."

"No prob."

Grant crossed to the door and peered out at the small stage area next to the piano, to the right of the bar. He gulped, letting his eyes float over the gathering crowd sprinkled at the semicircle of tables arranged around the bar and stage. His attention was immediately drawn to two stocky men standing behind one table. They reminded Grant of his father's goons. Casting his eyes down to the three men seated at the table, he caught the gray hair of his boss, who spoke animatedly to his guests. Scrunching his forehead, Grant wondered if Alex had his own bodyguards. Then he studied the profile of the man next to Alex and drew in a sharp breath.

"What is it?" Ben asked from behind him.

"That's the governor of Illinois!" Grant exclaimed. "Governor Tom Grogan. What's he doing here?"

"Holy shit—you'll be singing for the governor?"

Grant turned to look at his nephew with widening eyes. "Holy shit! I'll be singing for the governor. Oh, *no!*" He spun around and desperately stared at the table again, hoping his eyes had deceived him. However, when he looked back at the bodyguards, he detected an earpiece. They had the look of secret service types. One protection agent leaned in to whisper something in the governor's ear, at which time the third seated man, whose back faced Grant, turned away to give the politician some privacy. When Grant saw his face in profile, he stopped breathing.

"You okay, Uncle Grant?"

"Th-Th-That's Will Taylor."

"What?" Ben craned his neck around to get a look for himself. Sure enough, the man he'd seen in Angelo's study was sitting right there at the table.

"That's Sophie's dad," Grant numbly announced, beginning to feel nauseated.

"Maybe Sophie asked him to come and give you support too?"

Grant shot his nephew an incredulous glare. "He *hates* me! He's already tried to break us up several times, including last week after he ran into me at the compound. Sophie almost left me because he told her I was working for the family."

"But you're not!" Ben instantly recalled Angelo lying about Grant being on the payroll. He felt sickened that his uncle had almost lost Sophie as a result of having to retrieve him from the compound. He had to do something.

"I can't do this," Grant choked out, almost hyperventilating. He weaved his way over to a chair and collapsed into it, murmuring, "I can't sing, not with him out there. What the hell is he doing here? I—I can't sing. And if I don't sing, I get fired, I go back to prison, I lose Sophie…"

"It'll be okay, Uncle Grant."

Ben's promises barely registered with the man holding his head in his hands.

Patting his uncle's shoulder a few times, Ben instructed, "Just sit here, okay? I, um, I gotta run to the bathroom—I'll be right back."

Stepping out of the side room, Ben took a deep breath and headed straight for Alex Remington's table. As he quickly approached the three men sitting there, one of the agents stepped forward, ready to pounce if he made any sudden moves. The men ceased their chatter and curiously stared at the boy.

"You're a little young to be in a bar, aren't you?" Alex asked.

"That's okay, Alex. He's just looking for an autograph," Governor Grogan reassured him. "Do you have something for me to sign, son?"

Ben dismissively waved his hand. "No, actually I'm here to talk to *him*."

All interested parties followed Ben's pointed finger to the surprised face of Will Taylor. "Who the hell are you?" Will asked.

Ben swallowed against his tightening throat. "Ben Barberi."

Will flinched, and his blue eyes turned icy. "You're Logan's son? You've been staying with my daughter?"

"Yeah."

The governor watched the interaction with interest, already quite familiar with the Barberi crime family. He'd been furious when Angelo Barberi had weaseled out of extortion charges. The governor's advisors had warned him that failing to put the notorious crook behind bars might cost him the upcoming election.

When Ben said nothing further, Will tried again. "Well, what do you want?"

"I need to tell you something," Ben said, his voice quivering. "I was there."

"What?"

"I overheard the whole thing. I heard Angelo lie to you when he told you Grant's working for him. He's not. I promise. The only reason my uncle was there was to get me — he was worried about me."

"Will, what the hell's this kid talking about?" the governor asked.

Ignoring him, Will narrowed his eyes. "Sophie told me some story about Grant being there to retrieve you, but I didn't believe it. Now you're saying it's true? You were there?"

Ben nodded eagerly.

"Why do you care about this? Why does it matter what I think about Grant?"

"Because my uncle's about to sing in the bar tonight, and he freaked out when he saw you here. He, uh, he knows you hate him. I thought if you knew the truth, you might not hate him so much."

Will glared at Alex. "*Grant Madsen's* this new singer you were telling me about? The singer you dragged me here to see?"

When his friend nodded, Will's face reddened further, and his voice rose. "Did Sophie put you up to this?"

"Why are you so upset, Will?" Alex responded calmly. "Sophie asked me to keep it a secret when I hired Grant because she wanted to surprise you or something. I thought I'd invite you here tonight and save her an extra step."

"Did she tell you Grant comes from a Mafia family?"

Alex nodded. "She did. She *and* Grant told me how he's on parole, just like her."

"Then why the hell did you hire him? Are *all* your employees felons?"

Alex's jaw flexed, and he glanced over to see the governor's reaction to Will's accusations, but Tom looked placid as always. Turning back to Will, Alex insisted, "I hired Grant because Sophie loves him and trusts him. And I trust *her*. Maybe you should give it a try someday."

"How can I trust her when she dumped her career down the tubes, all for one man? For—for…" Will glared at Ben "…for your father! He purposely ruined my daughter's life. Did you know that?"

Seeing the devastated expression on Ben's face, Alex warned, "Will."

"I'm sorry," Ben broke in, trying not to cry. Perhaps this had been a bad idea. "I'm sorry for what my dad did. But if you could just give my uncle another chance—please, he needs this job."

Suddenly Ben felt a set of strong hands clasping his shoulders, and he looked behind him to find his uncle, looking pale and upset. The protection agent's hand snaked toward his holster.

"Ben, what're you doing?" Grant asked.

"He's trying to convince me you don't work for the Barbers," Will retorted snidely.

Grant nervously looked at Will. "I don't. I don't want anything to do with them. But I know you'll never believe me." He clenched his teeth and nodded at the governor. "Governor Grogan." Then he turned to his boss. "Mr. Remington, um, I think I have to quit, sir. I'm sorry for letting you down, but I can't do this. I should've known better than to try something like this."

Ben whipped around to face his uncle. "But you'll go back to prison if you don't have a job!"

"I'll find something."

"What if you can't?" Ben pleaded.

"I'll find something," Grant repeated, trying to feign confidence. To his horror, Ben burst into tears. Drawing his nephew into him, Grant asked, "What is it, buddy?"

"Don't leave," Ben whimpered, burying his face in his uncle's chest as Grant patted his back, not knowing what else to do.

"Don't you leave me too," Ben cried.

Stunned, Grant looked up at the three powerful men, all of whom wore helpless, uncomfortable expressions.

"You gotta sing. You can't lose this job," Ben begged.

Clearing his throat, Grant asked, "Would you excuse us for a moment, gentlemen?" When all three nodded, Grant led his nephew back to the side room.

After they were out of earshot, the governor looked at Will. "What was that kid saying? Are you mixed up with the Mafia, Will?"

"I don't want to talk about it."

"If they're threatening you, I can protect you," Tom promised.

"Really?" Will exploded. "Just like you protected Sophie from that scumbag Logan Barberi? That's Madsen's brother, by the way, in case you didn't catch that. My daughter's now dating the brother of the man who sent her to prison. And there's fucking nothing I can do about it. The only thing I can do is keep my mouth shut and pray that my baby stays safe from those monsters."

Inside the dressing room, Grant rubbed his hand over Ben's back. "I'm so sorry you lost your dad," he murmured soothingly. The boy seemed inconsolable. Months of pent-up grief came pouring out of him, and Grant had no idea what to do. "Listen, I'm sure I'll find another job, Ben."

"No, you w-w-won't," he sobbed. "And then your mean PO will throw you b-b-back inside."

Grant suppressed a grin. Jerry had sure made an impression on his nephew. He suddenly noticed he didn't feel nervous anymore, just concerned for Ben. Screw Will Taylor—he'd already come between him and Sophie too many times, and he didn't want the man to upset his nephew too.

"Would it help if I tried to keep my job?" he asked Ben.

Ben immediately looked up to stare at his uncle with glistening eyes. Sniffing, he nodded vehemently. "You'll sing?"

"I'll try, okay?" Grant forced a smile. "It's just like fifty push-ups. I'll take one at a time and do my best."

Just then the piano player, Andy, stuck his head in the room. "Boss told me we gotta get started. You ready?"

Grant took a deep breath, feeling butterflies dive-bombing his stomach. He glanced at Ben, then looked back at Andy. "Let's do it."

Patting Ben's shoulder, Grant asked, "Can you stay? It'd be nice to see at least one friendly face in the crowd."

Ben nodded and watched his uncle join the piano guy to approach the stage. He looked like he was walking to the gallows.

The bar was already loud and busy, and most patrons didn't notice the two men settling themselves onstage. But then Andy played a few riffs on the piano, and a hush fell over the room.

Leaning against the wall right outside the dressing room, Ben was surprised when a waiter approached him. "Mr. Remington would like you to join him at his table," he informed him, gesturing to a chair next to the hotelier. Ben bit his lip and nodded, walking over to sit next to his uncle's boss.

As Andy continued playing the piano, Grant plastered on a fake smile and grabbed hold of the microphone. The solid wooden stage beneath his feet made him long for the gentle rocking of Roger's ship, and the dark interior of the bar felt quite different from the sunshine of the river. *It's the same song to start,* he told himself, running his tongue over his suddenly dry lips. *You can do this.*

"Welcome, everyone!" he boomed into the microphone, feeling encouraged when his voice came out clear and strong. "Welcome to Capone's Spirits, the best of Old Chicago!" A wall of exhilarating noise bounced back to him with a smattering of applause, hoots, and cheers.

Grant swept his eyes across the room, watching people happily clink their glasses and continue chattering away. His gaze landed on a pair of light-blue eyes that stared at him excitedly. Refusing to look at the men next to Ben, Grant focused solely on his nephew as he gestured to the piano. "Andy Beecham on the piano, folks! And I'm Mick Saylor, here to take you back to a special time in our city's history. Have a great time tonight, and remember the wise words of Dean Martin: 'You're not drunk if you can lie on the floor without holding on.'"

Grant found the crowd's rousing laughter invigorating. Andy began pounding out the familiar intro to *My Kind of Town* and Grant closed his eyes for a second, envisioning his sexy Sophie serving drinks on the deck below while he brought home a cruise full of happy passengers.

As he began singing, his smile morphed from plastic to genuine. His velvety voice cradled and embraced each note, and the audience knew they were in good hands. Several of the women in attendance were absolutely riveted, believing the song was directed right at them. Who was this crooning, dark-haired hunk?

Feeling the energy of the evening, Grant cruised through *Mack the Knife* and several other songs before he suddenly realized he and Andy were starting their sixth song—the last in the set. Where the hell had the time gone? Grant was so absorbed in connecting with the song and the audience that time had become fluid and unimportant. He never wanted this fun to end, and he exchanged a goofy grin with his nephew, who basked in the glory of his uncle's success, oblivious to the high-powered men who surrounded him.

A curious transformation was also underway for Will Taylor. He couldn't believe he was actually *enjoying* the performance by his daughter's mobster boyfriend. Madsen was certainly a charmer. He performed each song with panache and skill, yet also possessed a sense of humility and vulnerability that made him instantly likeable. Will found himself inexplicably drawn to Grant, and he didn't like it one bit.

As Andy began the rolling melody of their sixth song, Grant announced, "This song is for Bonnie." Then he began *I've Got You Under My Skin*.

In his mind he pictured Sophie's big brown eyes, creamy-smooth complexion, tousled blond hair, and striking figure. He was surrounded by warmth as he considered her genuine caring for him and for others. He loved her keen intelligence, her clever sense of humor, her authentic hope in the world. She'd nestled her way under his skin, into his heart—deep inside him—and now he couldn't function without her. He could never lose her. Grant belted out the last stanza, thoroughly warmed by images of his Bonnie.

"We're taking a break now, folks!" Grant said as the last notes faded away. Did he actually hear groans of disappointment? He looked over at the piano, and Andy winked at him. It had been quite an auspicious beginning.

As background music started up again over the speakers, Grant heard his boss calling, gesturing him over to their table. Sneaking a glance at Sophie's father for the first time since he'd started singing, Grant was surprised to find Will's glare had faded. But it had been replaced by an unrecognizable expression. With uncertainty, Grant took a seat next to Ben.

"Looks like I got my entertainment locked down!" Alex grinned, reaching around Ben to thump Grant on the back.

Grant exhaled with relief. "Thank you, sir."

"Well done," the governor offered.

Blushing, Grant responded, "Thank you, sir. I wasn't quite expecting the governor of Illinois to be watching my first performance."

Tom chuckled. "Alex and I go way back, and I just had to be here." He elbowed Alex in his side. "He's all excited about his new bar." Just then one of the bodyguards nodded at him. "Well, time for me to head out. I can't let that campaign trail grow cold."

They all stood as the governor shook hands with Alex and Will, nodding to Grant and Ben across the table before being ushered out by his protection detail.

Slowly Grant's eyes widened. "Uh, Mr. Remington? You and the governor are friends? And you and Mr. Taylor are friends too?" Receiving a nod of confirmation, Grant then asked, "Did Sophie get me this job?"

Alex grinned. "I've always had a soft spot for Will's daughter."

"You didn't know?" Will inquired.

"No, sir." He felt quite touched by Sophie's behind-the-scenes help, just when he needed it most. Thank goodness he hadn't walked out of here earlier.

A waiter came by and set a highball in front of Grant.

"What's this?"

"From the lady at the bar," the waiter answered, nodding to a sultry black-haired woman staring from across the way.

Grant's lips parted and his cheeks reddened. "Oh, um, thank you," he stuttered, having no idea how to handle the situation. Ben started giggling.

A moment later a waitress sauntered over, placing a margarita in front of the singer. "From the woman at the table over there, three o'clock." Grant's blush deepened, and Ben's laughter increased.

"Looks like you have some admirers out there, Grant," Alex said, stifling his own chuckle.

When a third waiter arrived with yet another drink, Grant protested loudly, "Aw, come *on!* What am I supposed to do with all these?"

"You keep this up, you'll single-handedly keep my bar in business," Alex said warmly.

When Ben surreptitiously reached for one of the untouched drinks, Grant quickly slapped his hand away. "Back off, Al Fredo."

Ben rolled his eyes, but smiled.

Will found himself angry at the women buying all these drinks for Grant, wantonly making passes at him. Didn't they know Grant was dating his daughter? He'd dedicated a song to her! When that thought entered his mind, Will could scarcely believe it. He shook his head, try-ing to prevent Grant from worming his way into his good graces the way he'd done with Sophie.

"So, Ben," Will said suddenly, "why were you at Angelo's? Do you go there often?"

"He's not allowed," Grant answered for him. "It was a momentary lapse of judgment on his part, but he won't be returning. Or he'll be in even more trouble."

Will continued looking at Ben. "You got in trouble?"

Ben shrugged. "I almost got arrested by that parole officer dude."

"Jerry Stone was there? Why?"

Again, Grant answered. "I asked him to be there, sir. It's a violation of my parole to go there, but I had to get Ben out. Officer Stone was great."

Ben looked discomfited. "He, um, he told me you almost went back to prison for going to my birthday party there. Sorry."

"That wasn't your fault, Ben. That was my own stupidity. Sometimes I feel like a normal person. Sometimes I forget I'm on parole, that I'm not really free."

When Grant sighed, Will studied him curiously. That was exactly like a comment Sophie had made the other day. No wonder his daughter felt so understood by this man — only they knew the pressure and shame that came from being on parole. And he recalled Sophie explaining that Logan Barberi had also been responsible for Grant going to prison by forcing him to commit a crime. At the time, Will had refused to believe it, but now he was starting to wonder.

"What do you think, Grant?" Alex asked. "You want to start the next set in ten minutes or so?"

"Yes, sir."

"Okay, I'm going to make the rounds," Alex said, rising to leave.

Noting that Ben was still eyeing the drinks on the table, Grant said, "You should go home, Ben. Thanks for being here, but you're probably too young for a place like this."

Ben, who'd been sneaking glances at Will the whole night, finally blurted, "I have to say something before I go."

"Okay…" Grant said slowly, completely unsure what to expect.

Biting his lip, Ben said, "Um, Mr. Taylor? When I was at Angelo's, um, when they took you to get a drink…I heard them say some stuff. I thought you'd want to know."

Although embarrassed that the boy had likely heard him pleading with those damn criminals, Will's curiosity got the better of him, and he leaned in as Ben falteringly continued.

"Angelo said you thought he sent my dad to set up Sophie because you didn't pay them."

"That's right." Will nodded.

"But they didn't," Ben said. "I guess my dad just randomly went to see Sophie when he was ordered to get counseling. Angelo didn't know anything about it."

Will's mouth dropped open and Grant nodded. He *knew* Logan couldn't have done that to Sophie.

Ben forged ahead. "They wanted you to keep thinking that so that you'd pay them more money."

"Son of a bitch," Will muttered. "So Sophie isn't in danger?"

Ben shrugged. "I don't think they got many 'enforcers' left, from what I heard. They're losing money right and left—"

Grant interrupted, "They came after Sophie once, to get to me, and I think it'd be unwise to let our guard down, no matter what you heard, Ben."

"But Ange is getting really sick," Ben added. "He can't even go up the stairs unless Tank helps him…" His voice trailed off and he looked horrified, like he'd just remembered something awful.

"What is it?" Grant asked.

Ben was frustrated to feel his throat tighten once again, signaling imminent tears. Swallowing hard, he pressed his lips together, nervously glancing up at his uncle.

"I, uh, I overheard Angelo talking to Tank and Mario."

He shuddered, and Grant cupped his hand on his shoulder in support.

"He told them he knew. He knew what they did."

Feeling his nephew's body tremble beneath his touch, Grant prompted, "What did Tank and Mario do?"

Ben's eyes filled with tears. "They held down Dad while Carlo stabbed him."

Grant gasped and then helplessly watched the boy begin to sob once more. He scooted closer to his nephew and wrapped his arm around his shoulders, trying to console him.

"I hate that you had to hear that," Grant murmured. "I'm so sorry."

Will stared silently at the man and boy huddled together, both looking absolutely miserable, and he was struck by how they seemed to be every bit the victim he was. The Barberi family cut a wide swath of destruction, even hurting their own in the process.

"I'm going to walk him out, sir," Grant told Will as he helped the boy to his feet.

"All right." Will nodded, standing as well. He hesitated a second before blurting, "I better not find out you're cheating on my daughter with one of those hussies that bought you a drink tonight."

Startled, Grant paused. Then, grasping the hint of acceptance embedded in that threat, a slow smile spread across his face. "Yes, sir."

Once he and Ben made it outside the hotel, Grant reached into his pocket and extracted thirty dollars, handing the money to his nephew. "I'm getting you a cab."

"No," Ben protested, trying to give the money back. "I'll just take the el."

"Ben." Grant grasped both of his shoulders and stared down at him. "It was brave of you to tell Sophie's dad what you heard. But I don't want you doing something like that ever again. If they find out you're sharing their secrets, they're going to kill you. Do you understand?"

Ben gazed up at his uncle with confusion. "Angelo wouldn't kill me. He loves me."

"Angelo doesn't know how to love anyone but himself," Grant corrected. "And I agree with you — something's going on with his health. But a sick man makes a desperate man. You need to be careful, okay? Watch your back. Let's go."

Once he had Ben safely tucked into a cab, Grant hustled back, his head spinning like the revolving door he'd just come through. Sophie's father, the thrill and challenge of his new job, trying to stay out of prison — those stresses were nothing compared to the unease he felt constantly about his family. He just *had* to keep Sophie and Ben safe.

17. Confrontation, Part One

"And she got me a job!" Grant beamed and leaned in to place a grateful kiss on his girlfriend's blushing cheek.

"Really?" Hunter asked. "So you're returning the favor, Sophie? Didn't Grant help you get the teaching job at DePaul?"

Before Sophie could respond, Grant jumped in. "Yes, sir. But she's the one who's kept the job." He gazed at her fondly. "I wouldn't be surprised if they asked you to stay for spring semester too."

"I hope so," she sighed. "But what about you? You deserve the credit for landing your job. Alex only hired you after hearing you perform on the cruise. Even my dad said you were a wonderful singer."

"He *did?*"

Sophie chuckled at his shocked expression. "Yes, he said the women were falling all over you, buying you drinks."

Grant gave her an uneasy look. He wondered if Sophie's father had identified yet another means of trying to break them up.

But her glance was only playfully suspicious. "You better stay away from those women, McCrooner."

Apparently she hadn't taken her father's bait. "Not another nickname!" Grant protested, rolling his eyes.

"Hold on," Hunter interjected, looking curiously at Sophie. "Your father *complimented* Grant?"

"Hard to believe, isn't it?" Grant scoffed.

"But I thought your father didn't like or trust him."

"That's been true in the past," Sophie said. "And he's still rather wary of Grant. But my dad was invited to the opening of Alex Remington's hotel bar last night—Alex is a family friend—and he saw Grant perform." She glanced at Grant for confirmation. "I couldn't make it because of a work function, so I asked Ben to go for moral support. Grant gets kind of nervous."

"And that was *before* I saw both Governor Grogan and your dad in the audience," he added.

"Wow, Tom was there too?"

Both Hunter and Grant arched their eyebrows at Sophie.

"You're on a first-name basis with the governor of Illinois?" Grant asked.

Sophie appeared embarrassed. "Well, I knew him before he was governor," she explained. "My mom and dad would have Tom and his wife over for dinner, back when Tom was a state senator. Back then Tom was trying to quash a bill that would increase taxes on businesses, which made him my dad's new best friend. And then my dad contributed lots of money to his campaign back in 2004."

"So your dad's a staunch Republican, huh?" Hunter asked.

"He's about as far to the right as they come."

"I guess that's another thing you two fight about, then? Politics?"

Sophie eyed her psychologist with trepidation. "Actually, that's the one subject my dad and I agree on. I'm the only psychologist I know who's a Republican."

Hunter did his best to appear neutral, but Sophie thought she could detect a hint of disapproval. For her, "coming out" as a Republican to another psychologist felt almost like coming out as gay man to a drill sergeant.

"But I'm a Republican only because I'm economically conservative," she rushed to add. "On social issues I'm more in the middle—or even liberal. I strongly support the rights of minorities, women, and gay people."

"I see," Hunter responded. "You don't have to defend your beliefs to me, Sophie. It's okay if we have different political viewpoints."

"Is it?" she asked dubiously.

Hunter was taken aback by how well she could read him. His partner Bradley was one of the only gay men he knew who was totally right-wing, and Hunter was so tired of arguing about politics that he *had* felt dismayed at Sophie's revelation.

Sophie said, "I remember seeing a client who was a huge liberal. She would drone on and on about how the government should provide for everyone, and I have to admit I dreaded our sessions. It was hard for me to sit there and say nothing when I thought she was dead wrong."

Hunter leaned back in his chair. "We may see politics differently, but I enjoy meeting with you, Sophie," he said. "I guess it *is* true that we psychologists have certain values, and we can't be completely accepting or nonjudgmental all the time, especially when the client's values clash with our own."

"Thank you for that," she replied. "I enjoy meeting with you too. You definitely make me think, and I've been learning a lot."

Smiling at Sophie, Hunter attempted to draw in the other half of the couple. "So how 'bout you, Grant? Where are you on the political spectrum?"

He cleared his throat. "I don't think it would be possible to be raised by a Navy commander and not be a Republican."

Hunter nodded. He'd expected that response. "Did you two know that about each other? That you're both Republicans?"

"Yes, sir," Grant answered. "We discovered that early on when we were working on Rog's ship together. There was a fundraiser for Victor Ortiz at Navy Pier that got us talking." He recalled with a smirk how Roger, who shared their conservative philosophy, had wanted to slap a "Loser Ortiz" bumper sticker on the stern, hoping the Democratic presidential candidate would tank.

"We already knew we were both Republicans, but those questions you had us ask each other made us discuss politics even more."

"How did the love map questions go?" Hunter inquired.

"Pretty good," Sophie said.

"She got kind of mad when we started talking about women's rights," Grant interjected.

"I wasn't mad!"

"You sure seemed like it to me."

"Okay, I was a little mad when you said women shouldn't be in military combat. That's just archaic."

Grant kept his mouth shut, and Hunter watched their interaction with interest.

"I think I feel more confused than angry, though," Sophie said. "I've been a feminist since college, and typically I don't like it when a guy holds the door open for me or when he thinks I can't do things for myself. But with you…" She swallowed, looking at Grant. "I like it when you try to protect me. It feels loving. It feels good. It feels right."

"Then go with that," Hunter encouraged. "It sounds like your wise mind wants to accept Grant's chivalry."

"Oh, wise mind? Like in DBT?"

Hunter began to answer her question, and their shrink babble caused Grant's mind to drift away. As he thought about chivalry, he once again remembered his childhood.

"C'mon, boys!" Karita hollered from the bottom of the stairs. "We're going to be late!"

Six-year-old Grant thumped down the stairs, adjusting his scratchy light blue button-down along the way, followed by his eleven-year-old brother. Together they sounded like a thundering herd.

Their mother greeted them with a warm smile. "You boys look so handsome."

Grant studied his mother's red dress and cascading blond hair. "And you're so pretty, Mommy!"

Her smile widened, reaching her sparkling blue eyes.

In a rare show of affection, Logan leaned in and kissed his mother on the cheek.

She looked at her older son with wonder. "Well, thank you, Logan."

The three stood awkwardly in the foyer until she nodded at the door. "Let's go. Our dinner reservations are at seven."

Clutching his Han Solo action figure, Grant scampered out the front door and headed toward the idling car where his father sat in the driver's seat. He slid into the backseat, followed by Logan. Opening the driver's side car door, Enzo stepped out looking dapper in his black suit. He glided around the hood of the car, arriving just before his wife. Smiling, he opened the passenger-side door as his eyes swept appreciatively over her body.

"You look *bellissima*, honey," Enzo said, then nuzzled in to plant a kiss on Karita's neck.

Grant grinned. It was a good night.

"I'm sorry, Grant," Hunter said. "We must be totally boring you with all this talk about dialectical behavioral therapy."

Shaking his head, Grant blushed. "I sort of stopped listening, sir."

Hunter chuckled. "I like your honesty. Let's see, where were we? Talking about feminism and chivalry?"

Sophie perked up. "Oh! Speaking of women's rights, I helped score some points for our side yesterday at work." Turning to Grant, she added, "I haven't had a chance to tell you about this yet. You gotta hear this story." She giggled. "Tanya, Nora, and I cooked up a little plan to get back at David."

"Tanya's your colleague?" Hunter asked. When Sophie nodded, he asked, "Who's Nora?"

"She's a grad student in the counseling psych program—Tanya's advisee. Grant met her when he visited me at work. Anyway, it seems David had begun to play his game with Nora already—flirting with her, trying to get her to like him. Pretty soon he'd lower the boom and break her heart by telling her he's happily married and she naively misconstrued his intentions. But we wanted to lower the boom on *him* first."

Her grin was devilish.

"What happened?" Grant leaned forward expectantly.

"Well, we had Nora in Tanya's office, giving her a pep talk," Sophie began to explain.

"I'm not sure I can do this," Nora protested. "What if I laugh or something?"

Tanya frowned. "Nora, remember how angry you were when Sophie and I told you what happened to us? How David totally led us on and then pretended like we desperately made it all up?"

She narrowed her eyes. "The pompous prick."

Sophie laughed. "Keep up that attitude, and you'll be just fine."

Taking a deep breath, Nora nodded and patted her book bag for reassurance. Then she left, heading to David Alton's office.

"Do you think this'll work?" Tanya asked when she'd gone.

"Yeah, he's too self-absorbed to suspect anything," Sophie said. "Of course the prettiest grad student in the incoming class would be fawning all over him. He'll eat it right up."

Tanya rolled her eyes at Sophie. "We must take him down."

Receiving a nod of agreement, Tanya switched gears, knowing it would be a while before Nora returned. "Hey, could you help me with a manuscript? This abstract is just not sounding right."

"Sure," Sophie replied. They worked on the journal article for about twenty minutes before Nora burst back through the door, sporting a huge grin.

"Oh my God!" Nora laughed gleefully. "He was like putty in my hands!"

"Did the recorder work?" Tanya inquired.

"Let's see," Nora said, extracting a small digital voice recorder from her bag. "It's a good thing David required us to buy these for doing assessments." She pressed the play button, and her tentative voice came across quite clearly on the recording.

"Um, Dr. Alton? Do you have a minute?"

"Of course, Nora. Please come in. What can I do for you?"

There were muffled sounds of the student sitting down, making herself comfortable. "This is when I hiked up my skirt a little," Nora said with a chuckle. Her voice on the recording resumed.

"Well, I need some help with a research idea. I tried to ask Tanya about it, but she doesn't have experience in this area."

"Tanya's rather young," David answered in a knowing tone. *"It helps when you've been doing research for over twenty years. I'd offer to be your advisor, but I have a long waiting list of advisees already."*

"Oh, that's too bad, but I'll try to make it through with Tanya. Anyway, I know you've done some research on marriage, right?"

"Yes. I've administered personality assessments to thousands of married couples."

"Wow! Well, I want to study how acculturation affects marital satisfaction in Mexican-American couples."

"Sí, bueno," he said. *"Sounds interesting. One truth I've learned in all my years of academia is that we tend to conduct research on personally vexing subject matter."* He paused. *"So, Nora, is that true for you?"*

She cleared her throat uncomfortably. *"Um, is what true, Dr. Alton?"*

"I heard you're recently divorced, is that correct?"

"Yes."

"Your ex-husband must have been an idiot to let go of a girl as pretty as you."

"I had no idea what to say to that!" Nora interjected, hitting the pause button. "I was totally blushing."

She hit play and David's voice continued.

"But what I'm trying to ask is, are you researching marriage to make sense of what went wrong in your own?"

"Stop the tape!" Tanya demanded.

Nora quickly clicked the button.

"That is *highly* inappropriate of him to ask you that question," Tanya continued.

"I thought so," Nora said.

"Yeah, it's like he's your therapist, not your professor," Sophie added. "I hope you didn't feel pressured to answer that."

Nora grinned. "You'll hear how I handled the question." She rewound the recording a bit and pressed play again.

"Are you researching marriage to make sense of what went wrong in your own?"

"I could ask the same of you, David," Nora said. *"You study marriage—why is that?"*

"Touché," David responded. *"I've found that marriage can be quite complex and difficult—I guess I want to examine it and pick it apart in my research, to try to make sense of it all."* He chuckled. *"Though I'm twenty-five years into my own marriage and still as clueless as ever. Ah, one second."* The sound of David's chair squeaking came through clearly on the recording. *"Here's the old ball and chain now—sending me a text."* After a pause, David emitted a long-suffering sigh. *"She wants me drive to Wisconsin this weekend to visit her parents."*

"You don't want to go?"

"To visit those windbags? Hardly. Besides, I have some writing to do. My wife will never understand the demands of académe. I bet you'd understand, though, Nora. You wouldn't be incessantly nagging your man to spend every waking hour with you."

"That's enough," Sophie said. "I don't want to hear any more."

"Do you think that's good enough to confront him with?" Nora asked.

Tanya nodded. "Yes. Great job, Nora. And I know his office hours last a little longer, so let's do it now while we're sure he's available. But first I want to make a copy of this on my computer, just in case."

She attached a cable to the digital recorder and her hard drive and quickly downloaded the recording.

"So, are we ready?"

Sophie felt suddenly nervous. "Wait, don't we want to plan this out?"

"I've been rehearsing what I'd like to say to that slick bastard for over a year," Tanya replied. "Let us handle this, Nora. You have more to lose as a student than we do as faculty. C'mon, *chicas!*"

Sophie and Nora exchanged amused glances and dutifully followed Tanya down the hall. Once they reached the office, they were grateful to find David alone, typing on his computer.

"Oh, David," Tanya called in a sing-song lilt. "Could we have a word with you?"

He glanced up and seemed startled to find three self-possessed women standing in his doorway. He squinted his Richard Gere eyes and ran one hand through his Richard Gere hair. "Well, sure, lovely ladies. To what do I owe this pleasure?" He gestured toward the two empty chairs across from his desk and looked back at the three women. "Hmm." His eyes took on a naughty glint. "Nora, perhaps you could sit on Sophie's lap?"

Sophie looked stunned.

"Uh, no thanks," Nora stammered, blushing. She scooted behind the chairs and pointed to them for Sophie and Tanya. "I'll just stand."

Wasting no time, Tanya folded her arms across her chest and said, "We'll all stand." She glared at David. "We're here to discuss your wretched behavior with the women in this department."

He immediately dropped his smug grin. "My…what?"

Tanya had been correct; they didn't need any preparation. The words came spilling out of Sophie.

"Your behavior has been deplorable, David," Sophie said. "We're tired of the mind games you've been playing with me, with Tanya, and now with Nora."

"What the hell are you talking about?"

Sophie glared at him. "I'm talking about how you shamelessly flirt with young women — mostly students or new faculty — to get them to like you. You lead them on by inappropriately disclosing your own marital woes, trying to forge an intimacy with them. Then when the woman finally flirts back, you pretend like she's making up the whole thing. You act like she's some desperate floozy trying to break up your marriage."

"I do no such thing!" David protested. "Listen, Sophie, if you're still bitter about me turning you down, when I already told you I had a happy marriage…" His voice trailed off as his eyes locked on to the digital voice recorder Nora had extracted from her book bag.

Delighted in his shocked expression, Tanya snatched the recorder from Nora. "You do no such thing, huh? Let's see about that."

Nora and David's recorded voices filled the office space. As David listened to his compliment about Nora being pretty, he narrowed his eyes. "What girl doesn't want to hear that she's pretty?"

"First of all, David," Tanya said, clicking off the recording. "Nora is forty-one years old. She's not a girl—she's a woman. Secondly, it's *not* okay to comment on the physical appearance of a student like that. As a professor in this department, you have power over her, and that comment could create an intimidating or offensive environment. But that comment was not your worst, by any means. Let's proceed."

They played the rest of the recording, this time continuing past David's comment. *"I bet you'd understand, though, Nora. You wouldn't be incessantly nagging your man to spend every waking hour with you."*

"It does seem easier to get my graduate work done as a single woman," Nora agreed.

"Sometimes I wish I was single," David sighed. *"It would certainly make things more interesting around here."*

"This is ridiculous," David interrupted with blustery anger, and Tanya paused the recording. "You girls are way off base, and you've illegally recorded my private conversation. I should report you all to the chair."

Sophie had been studying his reaction intently. "Why do you look so nervous, David? What's next on that tape?"

"I'm not nervous. I'm furious! How dare you—"

"Play the tape, Tanya," Sophie ordered brusquely, and her friend obeyed.

David slumped in his desk chair as his recorded voice spoke again: *"Being married does have its advantages, though."*

There was a faint rustling sound, and suddenly his voice became louder, as if he'd leaned in closer to Nora—and closer to the recorder. *"Like sex any time I want it. It must be tough to be divorced, though you certainly don't look deprived. What's your secret, sexy Nora?"*

Sophie and Tanya both dropped their mouths open.

"This is totally taken out of context!" David blathered. "She was sitting there with her short skirt, coming on to me—"

"Don't you dare try to blame this on Nora," Tanya fumed. "You know you were inappropriate. You know better, David."

"Listen, I'm sorry if my comments were misconstrued."

"Misconstrued?" Sophie asked incredulously. "How is a woman *supposed* to take 'What's your secret, sexy Nora?' You know, David, you try to act so suave and subtle in this sick little game of yours. You've been playing it for years, and you probably would've gotten away with it for even longer, but I've dealt with men even more devious than you, so nobody's going to pull the wool over my eyes. We're not going to tolerate this from you."

"That's right, David," Tanya confirmed. "Let me see your cell phone."

David's mouth dropped open. "No!"

"I bet that text message from your wife never happened. I bet you made it all up as part of your little seduction act."

"That's ludicrous!" he spluttered.

Tanya simply shook her head. "If you *ever* try to lead on another woman like this, we're giving a copy of this recording to your wife."

He inhaled sharply, narrowing his eyes. "You'll do no such thing!"

"If you don't like our way of handling this situation, we can surely go to the university ombudsman and initiate sexual harassment charges," Sophie countered. "You *might* still be able to keep your job…"

That shut him up quickly, and Tanya added, "Nora's a student in this program, and we expect you to treat her fairly. If you try to use this against her in any way, the tape goes public—to your wife, to the chair, to anyone we deem appropriate. You will stop hurting women with your games."

David looked completely defeated. The gray hair and crinkles around the corners of his eyes, which usually added a dash of distinguished allure, now just made him appear aged and weary. "I didn't mean to hurt anybody."

"Well, you hurt me. I felt completely embarrassed after you led me on and turned me down," Sophie informed him, feeling stronger with each word. "I've met your wife, and she seems like a really nice woman. She deserves better. Get some help, David."

The three women rose to leave, and Nora, who'd been quiet up to this point, could not resist a parting comment. "Even though I'm divorced, David, I still have a very stimulating, satisfying sex life."

With that, the three swiftly departed, barely containing their excitement until they fell into Tanya's office, where they broke out laughing.

"That was so fun!" Nora exclaimed. "Can we do that again?"

"Hopefully we won't have to do that ever again," Sophie said. "Surely he's learned his lesson."

"Thank you both so much for saving me from that man," Nora said, smiling suggestively. "Now I can focus on the Mexican cutie I've met."

"Oh?" Tanya responded with a devilish grin. "Is he 'your secret'?"

"Careful, Tanya," Sophie advised. "David may cross the teacher-student boundary, but it doesn't mean we have to."

"Ah, I don't mind," Nora said. "After what we just went through, I know I can trust you both. His name is Esteban…"

"Do you realize what you just did?" Hunter asked as Sophie finished.

"What?"

"You set some boundaries," the psychologist responded. "Not only with David, but also with Nora. You insisted that you and Tanya avoid exploiting your power by protecting Nora's privacy."

Sophie shrugged, and Grant tilted his head to the side.

"Don't you see how much progress you're making?" Hunter prompted. "Crossing a boundary—exploiting your power—was the very reason you were sent to therapy. Violating a sexual boundary with your client was what got you into so much trouble. I think you've learned a lot, judging by how you handled the David situation."

As Sophie tried to process her psychologist's words, Grant narrowed his eyes. "Are you suggesting Sophie is the same as *David?*"

"There are differences," Hunter said quickly. "Given David's repeat offenses, his behavior seems a hell of a lot more premeditated. I think Sophie got in over her head and didn't realize the implications of her decisions. And the consequences of the boundary-crossing were much more severe for Sophie. She went to prison. David simply got a slap on the wrist and a threat of exposure if he ever does it again."

"I never would've thought to compare my behavior to David's," Sophie said, knitting her sculpted eyebrows together. She gave a sad smile. "But you're right. I exploited my power, and I crossed a sexual boundary with Logan."

"The difference is you're learning from your mistakes," Hunter added.

Feeling acutely uncomfortable, Grant jumped in. "And you shouldn't have gone to prison for that, Sophie. That's on Logan — not you."

She slowly raised her eyes to meet his, and he continued.

"I know how manipulative my brother could be. Maybe he learned that from my father, I don't know," Grant said. "But I'm sure Logan exploited you too." He gazed into the distance. "I remember one time he asked me for a lot of money — he was in deep with some bookie — and when I couldn't help him, he stormed off. I felt awful, and I wished I had the money to give him. I knew it'd be wrong to enable his gambling addiction, but there was nothing I wanted more than to help him out. I know him. I know how persuasive he could be. And I know it wasn't all your fault."

Sophie smiled through a mist of tears. Grant handed her a tissue, and she sniffed. "It seems like I always cry in here."

"Emotion precedes change," Hunter explained. "If you're crying, we're probably getting to the heart of the matter. You're doing some good work, Sophie. How're you feeling?"

"Kind of stupid and guilty."

"And how are you feeling about the David situation?"

"Vindicated," she replied immediately.

"You confronted a demon from your past," Hunter acknowledged appreciatively, "a man who led you to feel shame and unworthiness — a man who hurt you. You confronted him."

"I guess I did," Sophie replied, easing into a slow grin.

Hunter looked at Grant. "Is that something you want to feel as well? Vindicated?"

Grant appeared puzzled. "Yes, sir?"

"Then perhaps you need to confront your demon too."

A sudden understanding dawned on Grant, and his stomach clenched.

"Did you find out from your PO if the visit is permitted?"

Sophie caught on too and protested. "No, he shouldn't visit his father! Don't do it, Grant."

"Officer Stone said the DOC would allow me to visit him since I'm his son," Grant said grimly.

"What do you think, Grant? You've been making progress too, dealing with the trauma from your father. Your nightmares have decreased, and you can talk about him and your brother more freely now. Do you feel ready for that next step?"

Grant nervously glanced at Sophie and hesitated at her apprehensive gaze. "I've been thinking about visiting my father," he finally confessed. "But I seriously doubt that confrontation would go as well as Sophie's did."

"Well, what would be your goals be for visiting him?" Hunter asked. "Sophie reached her goal of stopping a colleague's inappropriate behavior, but you obviously have no control over your father's behavior. The one thing you have control over is speaking your mind, regardless of how your father responds."

"I do have some things I'd like to tell him," Grant said tentatively.

"I'm sure you do…Sophie, you look upset."

Her tears had started falling again, and she wiped them away with the balled-up tissue in her fist.

"I'm scared for you," she said to Grant. "I don't want you to go. But if you think that's what you need to do…"

"He'll be in a cage, Sophie. He can't hurt me."

"Physically," she said. "But what about emotionally?"

Grant bit his lip.

"Maybe we can check with Jerry to see if I could go with you," she suggested.

"No!" Grant snapped, startling her. "I don't want you anywhere near that place."

"Okay, okay, I'm sorry—it was just an idea," she said.

"Is this what you were talking about, Sophie?" Hunter asked. "The tension you're experiencing between wanting to be a strong, independent woman and wanting to be protected by Grant?"

"Yes." She slowly nodded. "I know how scared he is of his family hurting me — I know he just wants to protect me, but sometimes I want to protect him too."

"Well, what am I supposed to do?" Grant asked. "Just sit back and let them try to hurt you again?"

"Of course not, Grant," Hunter answered. "It's complicated. But we'll figure it out together." Glancing at his watch, he added, "Next time. Grant, I want you to write down what you'd like to say to your father, and we're going to review it in our next session."

"Yes, sir," Grant replied, nodding soberly.

Hunter rose, and the couple followed suit. As they began walking out, Grant once again placed his hand on the small of Sophie's back to guide her. Then he abruptly halted, removing his hand. "Uh, is that okay if I touch you here, um, Bonnie?"

Sophie grinned and guided his hand back to its resting place. "It's perfect, McSailor. Thanks for asking."

18. Confrontation, Part Two

If you don't like what you hear, just leave.

Dr. Hayes' words played over and over in Grant's head, running in a calming loop as he anxiously made his way to the visitor's entrance of Gurnee State Penitentiary.

You're in control now. You're an adult. He can't hurt you. Grant added a few of his own reminders to the litany of support. Swallowing hard, he joined the back of the rag-tag line of visitors waiting to enter the prison. As he surveyed the wait ahead of him, Grant was grateful it was only an autumn breeze flapping his jacket, not yet an icy winter wind.

Most of the visitors were shabbily dressed, haggard, and reeking of cigarette smoke. But whatever their scruffy appearance, Grant would've given anything to have a visitor like one of them when he'd been incarcerated here. Once his father had forced him to remove Joe Madsen from his list of approved visitors, there was nobody else. It had been a painfully lonely two years.

You have a shield around you. Nothing he says can get to you. You're an adult now.

Despite the soothing words repeating in his head, Grant's heartbeat continued to pound in his ears, thumping with a panicked cadence. He looked longingly over to the compact car sitting innocently in the visitor lot, rented for this visit. Drumming his long fingers against his thigh, Grant contemplated running back to that car and hightailing it away from this place that held so many shameful memories.

Then the youthful face of his nephew sprang to mind, and Grant's throat tightened. If he wanted Ben to escape the destructive forces of this family, he'd have to set the example. He'd have to stand up to them first. He'd have to face his own demons, before those demons sunk their claws into his nephew and dragged him down as well.

The line slowly shuffled forward, and when Grant finally approached the thick steel door held open by a corrections officer, he stole one last glance behind him at the parking lot before inhaling deeply and stepping into the dimly lit concrete structure. Greeting him was a familiar smell: the woven vapors of mildew, sweat, and fear—which instantly unsettled him.

When it was his turn to sign in, he reluctantly handed one CO his driver's license and submitted to a pat-down by another officer.

Peering at the ID, the CO told his partner, "Hold it, this one's not going in." He glared at Grant and pointed to the bright red letters stamped across his driver's license: REGISTERED OFFENDER. "Parolees can't visit prisoners, you idiot."

The other CO nodded, squinting at Grant. "Oh, yeah, I remember you. Back so soon?"

"Yes, officer," Grant said, keeping his head down. Thankfully neither CO had been involved when he experienced his psychotic break in solitary. He bit his lower lip, slowly pulling a folded letter from the inside pocket of his jacket. "This is a letter from the DOC attesting to the special permission I've been granted to visit my father."

The CO grabbed the letter and studied it carefully. "It looks legit."

But the other guard still looked suspicious. "We don't got no prisoners named Madsen here. Who's your dad?"

Grant took a deep breath. "Vicenzo Barberi."

Their eyes bugged out and one officer said, "No shit?"

"Yes, sir."

They stood gaping for a moment, then one officer grasped Grant's arm and cocked his head toward the visitation area. "Let's go, then, Mr. Barberi."

Grant winced.

As they walked toward the cages, the CO suddenly became chatty. "Why'd you keep your family ties secret, Madsen? Your dad could've provided protection in here."

Grant pursed his lips. "I've never wanted to be part of them. But I couldn't get away."

"They responsible for you doing time?"

Grant cast a sideways glance at the officer. "Something like that, yes, sir."

"That your brother who was murdered, then?"

Looking down as they arrived at the cage, Grant replied, "Yes, sir."

"My buddy Carl was the one your dad popped when he heard the news. Barberi broke his damn nose. As far as I'm concerned, he should *still* be in the hole for that stunt."

"Sorry about that," Grant offered, not knowing what to say.

Frowning, the officer said, "Have a seat, Madsen. Your old man will be along any second now." Leaning in once Grant sat down, he added, "And if he gives you any trouble, you come get me. I'd love to send the asshole back to the hole."

Grant looked up, surprised and bolstered by the CO's kindness. "Thank you, sir."

The CO turned to leave but then paused. "So why now? Why you visiting him now?"

Swallowing, Grant blushed. "Some stuff went down between me and my dad a long time ago, and my shrink—my PC ordered me to see one—he thought it'd be a good idea for me to get some things off my chest."

"Oh, Lord." The CO cracked a big grin and looked skyward. "You're taking advice from a shrink? Good luck with that."

The officer chuckled as he walked away, and Grant found himself smiling, which released some of his built-up tension—and also surprised him. He hadn't expected much to smile about today. This whole scenario was preposterous and likely ill-advised. Why the hell he was going through with it? But it was too late to back out now; he heard the jangling keys and the sliding cell door that announced another inmate's arrival for visitation. Feeling his stomach twist with fear, he instinctively stood. His smile vanished and his eyes became glued to the chained prisoner two COs guided into the cage reserved for the most violent offenders.

Though his father was sixty-one years old, there was nothing aged or feeble about him. He emanated ferocity, even chained and locked up in a cage. The gray had further invaded the black of his thick hair, and the hard lines of his face had etched deeper into his skin but the coal eyes looked exactly the same as they had five months ago when Grant had last seen him, just before he'd been released on parole. His father would never be released, thankfully.

As father and son sat down, separated by the metal cage between them, they stared at each other for several moments. Grant felt his heart racing, and beads of sweat dripped down his spine, but he also felt a sense of resolve, which kept his anxiety from blooming into panic. He nervously licked his bottom lip and clenched his hands into fists.

You're an adult now. He can't hurt you.

Slowly shaking his head, Enzo was the first to speak. "I can't *believe* you're wearing that White Sox jacket. You should burn that fucking thing."

Grant felt a sliver of relief at his father's attempt at humor. Enzo had been a die-hard Cubs fan all his life. In response, Grant had become an ardent supporter of the rival White Sox, Uncle Joe's beloved team.

"It's my favorite jacket." Grant held his breath, staring into those piercing eyes, but he exhaled after his father smirked.

"Figures." Enzo paused for a moment, eventually admitting, "I'm glad you came."

Grant's crystal eyes showed surprise and then determination. "I have some things to say to you."

Enzo arched one eyebrow. "I've got some things to tell you too. It's why I asked you here. Grant, I—"

He was interrupted by his son extracting a folded paper from his jacket. Knitting his bushy gray eyebrows together, Enzo asked suspiciously, "What's that?"

"I wrote down some things I wanted to tell you," Grant explained, smoothing the folds of the paper.

A hint of a smile tugged at the corner of Enzo's mouth. "We'll get to that. What I have to say is important—"

"This is important too!" Grant shook the paper for emphasis.

Enzo looked dismayed. He wasn't accustomed to men challenging him, and he intended to quash such rebellion immediately.

"You listen to me, Grant. We've got limited time here. I may be locked up in a cage, but you show some respect, damn it. You *will* respect me."

His father's icy tone sent a ripple of fear through Grant's chest, and he suddenly found it difficult to breathe. Flashes of his father's belt buckle gleaming in the kitchen light pushed at the corners of his mind, freezing him in place. His entire body tensed, and his eyes took on a far-off look.

"I want to talk about…Logan," Enzo continued, ignoring his younger son's lack of eye contact. "I know you two were never close. You boys couldn't have turned out more different — but what you did for him, well, it was simply…*sorprendente.*"

Grant stared at his hands as they twisted in his lap.

Enzo frowned. "Look at me when I talk to you."

Aquamarine eyes snapped upward, startled, and Enzo was bowled over by their crystalline beauty. He remembered those big blue eyes staring up at him with abject fear. But he'd only done what he had to do. His role as disciplinarian had come from necessity — just as his own father had done his duty to keep him in line. It was the natural order for fathers and sons.

Having difficulty speaking while looking into those vulnerable eyes, Enzo cleared his throat.

"I want to thank you for what you did." His expression morphed from sincerity to fury. "My son was taken from me," Enzo fumed, his mouth tightening, "and I craved vengeance. I had to have my vengeance. *You* got that for me, Grant. You avenged my son's death, and I want to express my gratitude. I'm deeply proud of you."

Completely overwhelmed, Grant focused on his neat handwriting, catching the one-word instruction at the top of the page: *Breathe.* He opened his mouth and gulped in some stale prison air.

"You're proud of me because I *killed* a man? Because I killed my own cousin?"

"Your cousin was a scum-of-the-earth piece of shit," Enzo raged. "You made the world a better place by taking him off it."

Grant kept breathing deeply. "Carlo was messed up, I'll give you that, but let's not forget he had some help getting there."

"What's that supposed to mean?"

"What that means is Carlo stood by and watched a seven-year-old boy, Tony Fanocelli, bleed out in front of him — a boy *you* killed. And now you're paying the consequences for that crime. You'll never leave this prison."

Enzo's eyes narrowed, and a hint of a smile crept onto his lips.

"Watching that boy bleed to death screwed Carlo up for the rest of his life," Grant finished.

Enzo's jaw dropped. "Are you trying to blame *me* for Carlo?'

"You and Uncle Angelo," Grant said. "Though it looks like Angelo won't be around much longer to shoulder the blame. You and Angelo destroyed Carlo — Logan too, for that matter — and I'm not going to sit by and let you destroy me as well."

"I *loved* Logan!"

"You loved him?" Disbelief coated Grant's voice. "No, you didn't. You hated him. You hated me and Mom too—you hated all of us."

"How on earth could you say that?" Enzo lifted his chained wrists to emphasize his point. "I sacrificed everything for my family!"

"This wasn't about us—this was *never* about us!" Grant sneered. "It's always been about you—what you wanted. You chose alcohol over us. You chose crime over us."

"I did what I had to do to provide for my family. Come back and talk to me when you have your own family! You'll see how hard it is. You'll see the tough choices you have to make."

Grant leaned closer to the cage. "I'll never become an alcoholic. I'll never beat my wife or children. I'll never steal or threaten or kill innocent people and then pretend I did it for my family." He clenched his jaw. "I'll never become you."

Enzo blinked his incensed black eyes several times, and then his voice came, low and menacing. "You ungrateful little shit. You'd be lucky to become *half* the man I am. I continue to be amazed by how far astray fucking Joe Madsen has led you."

He leaned forward as well, straining against the chains.

"This is what you've come to tell me today? This is why you're here? To bite the hand that feeds you? Here I wanted to express my gratitude, and you've come only to insult me with your *complete* lack of respect!"

That snarling, hateful voice sent Grant reeling once again, fighting for self-control. He glanced again at his paper, smoothing it out with a trembling hand.

"No," he forced out. "I didn't come here to insult you." *Breathe.* "I came here for some answers."

He tried to focus on the words swimming before his eyes, and keeping his head down, he began reading in a quivering voice.

"Dear Dad, I feel like I have so much to say to you, but I have no idea how to say it."

Shocked that his son was actually reading a letter to him, Enzo was speechless.

Unsteadily, Grant soldiered on. "I wish things could've been different between us. I wish you didn't leave us and go to prison when I was eight—now I feel like I don't even know you. I wish you would've made

Logan live with us instead of with Uncle Angelo, because I didn't get to know my brother either, and now he's—" Grant gulped "—gone.

"I wish I wanted to come visit you in prison, but I don't really want to be here. And when I got arrested and was forced to be here with you, I wish you would've taken care of me instead of threatening me and cutting me off from the only father I've ever known."

Grant's voice continued trembling, but he kept the tears at bay. "But wishing doesn't make it true. I wish I could stop wishing for things to be different and just accept the way things are."

He slowly lifted his eyes to sneak a peek at his father. Expecting him to be full of rage, Grant was astonished by Enzo's pained expression. The hard lines of his face had softened momentarily.

Sniffing, Grant wasn't sure if he should continue, but since his father remained quiet, he added, "I have so many questions for you—I know most won't get answered, but I have to ask them. I have to try." He took a deep breath. "Did you want to get married?"

Enzo stiffened. "Yes."

"Did you love Mom?"

"Of course," he said through clenched teeth.

"Then why, Dad?" The corners of Grant's eyes turned down mournfully. "Why did you hit Mom—"

"Don't!" The sharp word was out of Enzo's mouth before Grant could finish.

Grant ignored his father's pleading eyes. "What did she ever do to you? Why did you hit her?"

Looking away, Enzo begged, "Stop, please."

There was an extended silence between them. When Enzo turned back to face his son, Grant was shocked at the tears glistening in his father's eyes.

"There are things you don't understand. I—I never meant to hurt her. I never wanted to hurt any of you. It—it was the booze."

A look of disappointment crossed Grant's face. "Don't you dare blame this on alcohol. Nobody held a gun to your head and forced you to drink! You chose this—you chose to hurt us. Don't you know why Logan had an out-of-control gambling problem? Don't you know why he used drugs all the time? It's because he hated himself! He hated himself for not protecting Mom and me from *you*. You did that."

"Logan was a grown man; he made his choice. You're not pinning that on me."

Grant shook his head with disgust. "I don't know why I came here. I should've known what to expect from you."

You can't change your father. Hunter's words filled his head. *He likely won't apologize or validate you, but it's still important to tell him what you have to say.*

Grant looked at the paper, which was almost ripped apart from his grip. Perhaps his father could deny all responsibility for hurting his mother and brother because both were dead, but Grant was right here. Enzo couldn't deny the effects of his abuse on the man sitting across from him.

"I feel shame," Grant admitted quietly, so softly Enzo had to strain to hear. "I feel ashamed of myself. I—I question and doubt myself non-stop. Not so much because of the beatings…" He sniffed. "Though they're part of it. But mostly because of the way you talked to me. You called me weak, pathetic."

An image of a dark closet flooded his consciousness, taking away his oxygen. The burn of his backside, the wetness of his pants.

"You called me a baby." Grant hunched over and wrapped his arms around his torso, suddenly appearing younger than his thirty years. "You told me I was a fucking baby."

Each word made Enzo flinch. Sickened, he watched as his son continued pulling inward, rocking, almost whimpering.

Grant's breaths were shallow, and his body was frozen as he looked off into the distance. From far away, he heard a woman's voice calling to him, coming closer, and suddenly he realized it was Sophie, just like she talked to him when he awoke from a nightmare. *It's okay. You're not a baby. You're an adult now. He can't hurt you. I love you. I love my McSailor.*

Grant slowly sat up, tried to steady his breathing, and looked into his father's dismayed stare.

"What's *wrong* with you?" Enzo asked, taken aback.

Looking away, Grant clenched his teeth before bravely meeting his father's gaze. "I have posttraumatic stress disorder."

Enzo narrowed his eyes. "Vets get that, right? I knew you shouldn't have joined the fucking military."

Shaking his head, Grant scoffed, "This isn't from the Navy! This is from you! From your abuse!"

"Abuse? That wasn't abuse—that was discipline. You needed that."

"Discipline? Is that what you call it? Is that what you call beating your son black and blue for spilling a glass of water? Is that what you call a father forcing his seven-year-old son to shoot a man dead?"

Enzo gasped, slumping back in his chair. An anguished expression crossed his face as his cold, black eyes turned glassy. Images surfaced of a frightened man tied to a chair, his father's hand darting to unbuckle his belt, the feel of a cool metal gun in his hand…

"No," he cried numbly. "That didn't happen."

Watching his father recoil with fear, seeming to leave himself, Grant suddenly understood he wasn't the only one suffering from PTSD. Enzo's father had cruelly traumatized him just as he'd traumatized Grant and Logan in turn, all in the name of love, protection, and *toughening up*. It was a family legacy Grant was determined not to pass on.

"You're having flashbacks, Dad."

Enzo gave him a blank stare.

"Remember to breathe," Grant said softly. "Grandpa's dead. He can't hurt you anymore."

"What the fuck are you talking about?" Enzo's nostrils flared as he returned to the present and strained against the cuffs of his Y-chain.

"It's a flashback. My psychologist showed me some strategies to get through it."

"Your psychologist? The one who put you up to writing that ridiculous letter?"

Grant's face fell.

Enzo was seething. "I *knew* some shrink put you up to this—no normal person reads a fucking letter to someone sitting right across from him! Telling me Logan got in trouble because he *hated* himself—that's fucking bullshit. What the hell are you telling that shrink? You better hope you're not sharing family secrets in there."

"So what if I am, *Dad?*" Grant challenged. "You don't want him knowing you're an abusive, alcoholic, child-killer? Well, too late—he already knows. Everybody knows. I'm so *proud* you're my father."

"You son of a bitch!" Enzo yelled, jumping to his feet, clanging the chains. "You're lucky I'm in this cage or I'd beat the shit out of you!"

Grant's eyes widened as he looked to find his father almost frothing at the mouth.

"You better hope you don't get put back in here!" Enzo snarled. "Or what I did to you as a kid will seem like a fucking picnic!"

Grant caught motion behind the cage out of the corner of his eye.

Enzo thrashed in his restraints, causing the chains to clang loudly. "You said I'll never get out of here? We'll see about that." There was an evil glint to his eyes. "I may join you on the outside soon, son."

Grant stopped breathing. What the hell did he mean by that?

The back of the cage burst open and two COs grabbed the prisoner, yanking him back and half-dragging him out of the cage. "Either on the inside or the outside, I'll be seeing you soon!" Enzo hollered as he was dragged away. "And you'll wish you'd never been born!"

Left in silence, Grant's body shook as he carefully glanced around the visiting area, finding all eyes on him. He covered his face with his hands, feeling utterly miserable, his father's parting words running in his head.

"I already wish I'd never been born," he whispered.

19. Unconditional

A cold, swirling wind threatened to steal Sophie's stylish brown hat, and she clutched the crown with one hand while snuggling into Grant's warm, steady frame.

"I miss summer," she said, sighing.

"Me too. I can't believe it's almost November."

They'd just descended the stairs from the el and now passed storefronts littered with political signs, some for presidential candidates Gabe Kaufmann or Victor Ortiz and others hyping those vying to be governor of Illinois: Republican Tom Grogan or Democrat Darko Jovanovich.

"Well, I can't believe it's almost Election Day," Sophie said.

"Not that it matters much to us," Grant responded bitterly.

She snaked one arm around his back, and he draped his arm across her shoulders. Their simultaneous touches provided comfort. In addition to their weekly meetings with Officer Stone, there were countless reminders of their second-class status as convicted felons.

They arrived at Hunter's office ten minutes early — right on schedule — and spent their wait time catching up on their evenings. Sophie had fallen asleep by the time Grant got home from work.

"When did you get in?" she asked.

"Around one thirty."

"Isn't that kind of late for a weeknight?"

"Yeah." Grant suppressed a yawn.

There was a mischievous glint in her eye. "You missed curfew — maybe I should make you do some push-ups, Lieutenant Madsen."

"Hey, I have an excuse! I stuck around to help clean up the bar."

"Cleaning? Isn't that beneath you? You're a big star now! You have your own dressing room."

"I have my own broom closet." He sighed. "I can't believe I'm getting *paid* to sing for just a couple hours a night—I wish there was more to this job. At least with the cruise I could quiz myself on new facts about architecture every day."

She sat thoughtfully for a moment. "You still haven't told Uncle Joe about your new job, have you?"

A flush of his cheeks answered her question. "We spent most of our last phone call talking about my dad."

"Grant! Joe's going to visit you soon, right? What'll you tell him then?"

"The truth, I guess. I'll have to 'fess up about my job once he's here. I hope he won't think it's stupid. He takes his career more seriously than any man I know, and once he finds out I only work a few hours five nights a week *singing*, well, I don't know what he'll think."

"He'll be glad you're not in prison is what he'll think."

Abruptly deflecting attention away from himself, Grant asked, "How was your night?"

"Kind of boring, I guess. I was preparing a lecture for this afternoon."

"Theories of Personality?"

"Yep, we're on Carl Rogers."

"And how is my favorite couple today?" Hunter's voice rang out in the waiting room.

The pair looked up, surprised by his stealthy entrance.

As they stood, Sophie glanced at Grant and pointed to Hunter. "That's an example of Rogers' unconditional positive regard, right there," she said. "Hunter likes us even though we're on parole."

Hunter chuckled. "Ah, you're teaching Carl Rogers to your students?"

"And to me as well, it seems," Grant replied as they headed toward the office.

"Carl Rogers—what a great man," Hunter mused. "New theories may come and go, but his ideas about unconditional positive regard and empathy will always prevail."

They entered his office and took their seats while Hunter continued.

"Rogers modeled total acceptance of his clients, no matter where they were in their lives."

"He sounds like one of your favorites," Sophie remarked. "Do you have any teaching tips for me? We're reviewing Rogers in class today."

After a beat, Hunter asked, "Are you planning on covering how conditions of worth interfere with the organismic valuing process?"

Grant snapped to attention. "The orgasmic *what?*"

Hunter laughed. "The orga*nis*mic valuing process—each person's attempt to maximize themselves and their potential, the drive to do what feels valuable and worthy to the individual."

Sophie giggled. "Yes, I was planning on covering that."

"Well, when I was a teaching Rogers' theory to undergraduates, I came up with an idea for helping them remember the ovp," said Hunter. "You have to be willing to risk looking foolish in front of your students, though. Do you remember when Naughty by Nature did that song *OPP?*"

"I'm not sure—was that from the nineties?"

Hunter rolled his eyes. "You two are making me feel old. Yes, it's from *way back* in the nineteen nineties. I won't go into the meaning of opp because it's rather crude, but it was a hit song. So anyway, I started singing to my class." Hunter waved one arm over his head like a rapper, substituting ovp for opp as he sang the song's refrain. "The students loved it. They all got that test question correct."

Sophie snickered. "That's awesome!" Turning to Grant, she added, "See, *I* get to sing at work too."

"Can I watch?" he grinned. "This should be fun."

Sophie looked dubious. "Um, I'm not sure I want a professional singer critiquing my performance."

"I'm hardly a professional. And at least you won't have the governor of Illinois in your audience."

"Are you coming to work with me today, then?" Sophie asked.

"That'd be great—I don't have anything else to do."

"Have you been doing that often, Grant?" Hunter asked. "Visiting Sophie at work?"

"Yes, sir. I make sure that David Alton creep stays away from her."

Sophie smiled. "You don't have to worry. David has totally been avoiding me since our little confrontation. Tanya and I think it's hilarious."

"Speaking of confrontations," Hunter segued. "Grant, did you end up visiting your father?"

"Yes, sir."

"Excellent! That was very brave of you. How'd it go?"

Grant shared an uncomfortable glance with his girlfriend. "Um, my father wasn't exactly full of unconditional love for me, sir."

"No unconditional positive regard from the dadster, huh?" Hunter smirked.

"It's not funny, Hunter," Sophie replied. "Grant was really upset when he got home."

His expression turned more serious. "I'm sorry. I wasn't trying to make light of the situation. What exactly happened?"

Taking a deep breath, Grant answered, "Well, first of all it was bizarre to return to Gurnee, especially as a visitor. I definitely don't want to go back to that place."

Sophie patted his hand and then rested her hand on his.

"When they brought my dad out, I was really nervous. I tried to remind myself to breathe, but it was hard to see him again."

"How did it compare to when you first confronted him in the prison yard?"

"It was a lot different, sir. On my first day at Gurnee, I hadn't seen him in twenty years. I had this grand plan then that I wouldn't let him intimidate me, and I tried to stand up to him, but he knocked that plan down real quick. I was stupid to think I could outmaneuver him. When he allowed those guys to attack me, and I got thrown into solitary, I—I…"

"You can say it, Grant," Hunter encouraged, watching his client squirm.

"When I had um, a, um, psychotic break, well, I figured out I couldn't fight my dad."

"It was a smart survival strategy to accept his protection."

Grant shook his head. "It was weak. Once I got out of solitary, my father did let me kind of do my own thing, though, as long as I cut ties with Uncle Joe."

Sophie interjected, "It infuriates me that he'd try to interfere in your relationship with Joe. Why does your dad care about that? It's not like he ever took an interest in being a parent to you."

"My dad has always hated Joe. I think he's jealous of him or something. Dad thought Angelo should've raised me when Mom died. When Joe adopted me and gave me his name, I bet that killed my dad."

"That *would* upset a narcissist," Hunter agreed. "For another man to claim his son right out from under his nose—your father's pride must've been quite wounded, especially when he knew Joe was a much better father than he could ever be."

"I don't think my dad would ever admit that."

"Probably not," Hunter said. "So tell me about this confrontation—it sounds like you were trying to approach him more cautiously this time. Did you get to read your letter? How did Enzo react?"

Grant bit his lip, his father's mocking tone and menacing growl ringing in his ears.

Sophie gave his hand an encouraging squeeze. "I kind of want to hear this too." She glanced at Hunter. "He was too shaken when he got home to tell me much."

They both waited for a moment before Grant gave a faint smile. "He didn't like my White Sox jacket."

"I bet you felt like you were in Jerry's office." Sophie grinned.

"Your father's a Cubs fan, I gather," Hunter said. "What happened after he disparaged your jacket?"

"He said he was glad I came."

Hunter and Sophie were astonished.

"That was right before he screamed at me for disrespecting him."

"You? Disrespectful?" Hunter sported a look of disbelief. "You're one of the most respectful people I've ever met, Grant. And feel free to stop calling me 'sir,' by the way. It's really not necessary."

"But you're a doctor, sir."

Tilting his head to one side, Hunter said, "Sophie may not have her license anymore, but she's still has her PhD. She's still a doctor, but I don't hear you calling her ma'am."

Grant looked at his girlfriend, and both burst out laughing.

"Don't you dare start calling me ma'am, McSailor."

He winked back at her. "Yes, Bonnie."

Hunter got them back on track. "Why did your father think you were disrespectful?"

"Because he had things to say to me, but I had things to say to him first, and he didn't like that."

"What is he—twelve? Can't he wait his turn? What did he want to say to you?"

Pondering Hunter's question, Grant responded, "He wanted to thank me…for avenging Logan's death…for killing Carlo." He ducked his head. "He said he was proud of me."

Hunter pressed his lips together, and Sophie now nervously wrung her hands together.

"But you don't look too proud of yourself," Hunter said.

"No, sir, um, Dr. Hayes." Grant slowly raised his head, meeting the psychologist's eyes. "I had to do it—he was going to kill Sophie—but I'm not proud of pulling the trigger. I'm not proud at all."

Finding a resting place for her fidgeting hands, Sophie scooped up one of Grant's into both of hers.

"Thank you," she said softly. "Thank you for saving my life."

"Your life would've never been in danger if you hadn't met me."

She looked sad. "You're wrong, Grant. Carlo wanted his money back, and he would've found me eventually."

Grant looked away, sighing. "Earlier you said you miss summer… Well, I don't."

"Why's that?" Sophie gave his hand a squeeze.

"Because in the summer you sometimes wear sleeveless shirts." He swallowed hard. "And I can see your scar."

Her face flushed a rosy color. "You think it's ugly."

He inhaled sharply. "No! You're so beautiful—I'd never think that, Sophie. It's, it's just…I feel awful when I see that scar. I hate myself for not protecting you."

"But you did protect me." She shook her head, exhaling loudly. "Don't you know I feel the exact same way about *your* scar?"

His face tightened with dread, and she continued.

"You feel awful when you look at my arm. Well, I feel awful when I look at your back. I so wish somebody had been there to protect you when you were a little boy. I bet you were so adorable back then, and I…" She clenched her teeth. "I feel badly that nobody shielded you from your father."

Grant bowed his head again, unable to look at her. She felt his shame emanating, evident in the trembling tension of his grip, and she deeply wished she could take it away.

Hunter gently said, "Good work, you two. You're communicating very well. I also feel sad that Grant didn't have anybody to protect him as a child. But now that you're an adult, Grant, you have the resources to take care of yourself. You did a wonderful job standing up to your father."

"It wasn't so wonderful," he countered in a low voice. "I started yelling at him about how he ruined Carlo and Logan, which totally pissed him off, and then I told him I didn't want to be anything like him." He exhaled derisively. "What a joke. I was acting just like he was — raging on him like he used to do to me. I'm no better than him."

Sophie couldn't believe what she was hearing.

"Grant, you said you and your father cheer for different baseball teams, and you've obviously chosen very different careers," Hunter said. "How do your religious views compare to his?"

Grant shrugged. "My father's Catholic too."

"How about your mother?"

"She was Protestant — Lutheran, I think, but she converted to Catholicism when she married my dad."

Hunter turned to Sophie. "Didn't you say you were Methodist?"

"Yes, but I'm a bad Methodist — I haven't been to church in a while. My dad isn't very pleased with his heathen daughter."

"Let's get back to that," Hunter suggested, winking at Sophie. "Grant, do you consider yourself a Catholic?"

He tapped his long fingers on his thigh. "I guess, but I'm kind of like Sophie — I don't go to mass as much as I should."

"Hmm, you're both Christian, but it sounds like you have some religious differences. I don't want to veer off the discussion about Grant's father, so we'll have to get back to that topic too."

"Oh, boy," Sophie replied, feigning excitement.

"I'm not sure if I'm really a Catholic," Grant said. "I used to go to mass with Simkins on the aircraft carrier, but the last time I was inside the Basilica was for Logan's funeral." He exchanged a mournful glance with Sophie. "And the last time before that was for my mom's funeral."

Hunter looked thoughtful. "You certainly have some sad memories associated with the church. Perhaps you'll have to create some happier memories there."

Grant appeared confused. "Like what, sir?"

The psychologist shrugged. "I don't know, maybe, uh, get married there?"

Grant immediately looked at Sophie, finding her staring back at him. They both blushed, and shy smiles spread across their faces. Hunter also found himself grinning as he watched their coy exchange.

"I think maybe I'd like to get married in a Methodist church," Grant offered, causing Sophie's smile to widen further. His look turned more serious. "The Basilica reminds me too much of my father. He's the most amoral man I know, so I think I better avoid whatever religion he claims to follow."

Hunter continued his line of questioning. "What about politics? Do you and your father see eye to eye?"

Grant paused. "I'm not sure where he stands politically. I wonder if he'd support Grogan or Jovanovich for governor—probably Jovanovich because he gets the union vote. Not that it matters. My dad can't vote either."

"You have different sports teams, careers, religion, and maybe politics," Hunter listed, tapping each of the fingers on his right hand.

"And they like different food, too," Sophie added. "Grant's favorite is Middle Eastern. I bet his dad likes Italian."

"Do you see how different you are from your father?" Hunter asked, looking pointedly at Grant. "You may share some DNA, but that's where the similarity ends. You are definitely not your father."

Grant sat quietly, contemplating his words.

"Do you have *anything* in common with your father?" Hunter asked.

Yeah, we both have PTSD, Grant silently answered. Out loud, he said, "He claimed to love Logan and my mom, and I loved them too. But I don't really believe him."

"Did you get to read your letter?" Hunter asked.

"Most of it, yes, sir."

"How did he react?"

"When he wasn't making fun of me for reading a letter to him while I was sitting right there—" Grant noticed Hunter angrily shaking his head "—I guess he listened pretty well. But he wanted me to stop asking why he hit Mom."

"Did he take *any* responsibility for his actions?"

Grant exhaled derisively. "He told me he never meant to hurt her. He told me it was alcohol that made him do it."

Nodding resignedly, Hunter said, "I thought that might be his reaction. What about how he hurt you? Did you talk to him about that?"

His psychologist's tone couldn't have been gentler, but Grant still felt his heart begin to gallop and his chest tighten. "Yes, sir," he responded, his cheeks coloring. "I think I might've zoned out at that point."

He snuck a glance at Sophie, finding her watching him worriedly, and remembered how her soothing words just when he'd needed them most had brought him out of his trance while sitting across from his father. He cradled her hand in his.

"You lost some time?"

"Yes, sir. The next thing I knew my dad was staring at me like I was some sort of freak, asking me what was wrong with me."

"Of course you dissociated," Hunter said. "There's no shame in that. You're sitting right across from your abuser, opening yourself up to him, making yourself vulnerable to his cruelty. It took incredible strength to do that, Grant."

"My dad didn't seem to think so."

"He's too damaged to have the strength to allow himself to be vulnerable too. But I bet deep down inside he knows how much he hurt you. He knows he was abusive."

Grant exhaled loudly. "He said I needed it. He said it was discipline."

Shaking his head, Hunter scoffed, "He's concocted quite a story for himself, hasn't he? He's probably had to deny reality many times in his life just to survive. One memory he's likely tucked away is being forced to shoot a man dead as a child. I'm sure that one messed him up good."

"I actually brought that up."

"Wow, how did he take it?" Hunter asked.

"I'm not sure," Grant said tentatively. "But I think he zoned out too. He, uh, he looked like he was in pain, then like he wasn't really there for a second. He said something like 'That didn't happen.'"

Hunter nodded knowingly.

"I told Dad he was having flashbacks, and he should remember to breathe."

The psychologist stifled a laugh. Apparently Grant had really listened to his lecture on trauma. "It sounds like you were following your own advice. Did you remember to breathe?"

"Yes, sir—it helped a lot."

"So, you think your father might have PTSD too?"

Grant looked uncertain and Sophie volunteered, "It sounds like it."

Hunter nodded. "That would explain the drinking."

Grant shot an angry look at the psychologist.

"Sometimes trauma survivors get hooked on alcohol and other drugs as a way to stop the flood of intrusive images from the trauma," Hunter said. "They drink to numb out the intense distress."

"That doesn't give him an excuse!"

"I'm not saying it does," Hunter said. "You've suffered trauma yourself but you've made the choice not to touch alcohol." He grinned. "Well, except for that time Sophie got you plastered on tequila."

"Hey!" she protested, earning a rare smile from Grant in the therapy room.

"What I'm saying is we can *understand* your father's alcoholism but not condone it. He made choices as an adult that hurt you and your family immensely. You have every right to feel angry about that. I hope you told him that hiding behind alcohol instead of taking responsibility for his actions was complete bullshit."

"In so many words, yes I did."

"Good. What happened after your father dissociated?"

Grant felt the skin on the back of his neck prickle as he recalled the end of their meeting. "He went ballistic," he said numbly.

"He did?" Sophie asked, fear showing in her eyes.

"He stood up and started screaming at me, telling me I was lucky he was in a cage or he would b-b-beat the crap out of me."

Grant clenched his fists, angry with himself for stuttering.

"That must have been frightening," Hunter said.

"He was chained up an in a cage! Why the hell would I be scared of him?" *Baby…fucking baby.* His father's insults rattled around in his head.

"Grant, he's the head of a crime family! He's a ruthless killer who feels zero remorse for hurting others, and his threats are very real. Your father has, in fact, beaten you mercilessly — not only as a defenseless boy but also as an outmatched man when his goons came after you in prison. It is a perfectly sane, human response to be scared of him. Hell, we're *all* lucky that psychopath's behind bars where he belongs."

"That's just it," Grant resumed, looking guiltily at Sophie. "I didn't want to tell you this part because I didn't want to frighten you."

"What?" She looked alarmed.

"When they were dragging my dad away, he was yelling something—I don't know how he could pull this off, but he sounded very convincing."

"What did he say, Grant?" Hunter looked intrigued.

"He said he was getting out."

Sophie's jaw dropped. "Getting out? Of prison?"

Grant nodded and Hunter asked, "How? Isn't he serving a life sentence without parole?"

"He is. I—I—I don't know how he'd get out. I've been racking my brain trying to figure it out, but I've got nothing."

"You said he was threatening you, right?" Sophie said. "Maybe it was just an idle threat, trying to scare you."

"I may not know my dad all that well, Sophie, but one thing I do know about him: he doesn't make idle threats. It's real. He has some sort of plan cooked up—maybe he's going to escape or something."

The three sat quietly for several moments, sobered.

Finally Hunter offered, "What an intense confrontation. I know you doubt yourself, Grant—we've already discussed your tendency to question yourself as stemming from the abuse—but I think you did an admirable job of confronting your demons. That took balls to go in there and stand up to your abuser. I'm not sure I could've done the same."

"Me neither," Sophie jumped in. "My dad is about ten times less intimidating than your dad, and it took me *years* to get up the nerve to talk to him."

Hunter studied Grant, who seemed to have trouble taking in their praise. "I don't mean to sound condescending when I say this, but I—I'm proud of you."

Grant slowly met his psychologist's penetrating gaze, feeling warmth in his chest. His reaction to those words was much different than when his father had said them.

"Thank you, Dr. Hayes," he said.

"Well, I'm proud of you too," Sophie added, beginning to smirk. "And I *do* mean to be condescending."

Grant chuckled and swiftly locked his elbow around her neck, pinning her in place for a pretend noogie. "I'll show *you* how to be condescending!" he said over her shrieks.

They wrestled for a few moments, laughing the whole time, while Hunter watched in amusement.

"Okay, you two, take your roughhousing elsewhere, 'cause our time's up. This is a very serious place in here."

Sophie's laughter slowly faded as she smoothed her hands over her mussed ponytail, carefully replacing her fashionable hat. "Said by the man who performs rap songs for his students." She smirked at Hunter.

He snickered. "Hopefully your rendition of 'OVP' will be better than mine."

Rising to stand, Grant extended his hand. "Thank you, sir." He locked eyes with Hunter and solemnly shook his hand, the muscles of his forearm rippling.

Bradley, Bradley, Bradley, Hunter silently repeated. "Have a good week, Grant. You too, Sophie."

He watched them walk out, feeling deep satisfaction about their progress in counseling. Thinking about Carl Rogers as he sat down to write a case note in their chart, Hunter acknowledged that both Grant and Sophie were striving to achieve their bright potential. They had to fight and claw their way through, but there was no question they'd continue to prevail.

As the parolees strolled down the hallway, Sophie mused, "I wonder if I'll actually have the nerve to sing 'OVP' to my class this afternoon."

"You'll do great, Bonnie. You're an awesome teacher."

Grant stopped short, turning toward her and pulling her body flush to his, gazing down at her with a twinkle in his eyes. "You've sure taught *me* how to value the orgasmic process."

Sophie giggled and closed her eyes as he leaned in to brush his lips against hers. Between kisses she whispered, "I think I have some more lessons in store for you, McSailor."

His throaty baritone made her knees weak. "I can't wait."

20. Contender

The cab made its way north on the Stevenson, into the city from the airport.

"It's great you two came out to meet me, but I thought it'd be Roger," Commander Joe Madsen said. "I'm staying at his place, right?"

"Um, Roger's at work, Joe," explained a nervous Grant, wedged in the backseat between his uncle and girlfriend.

"Oh. Where should I put my bag until he gets home?"

"I have his key—we're headed to his apartment now."

Mollified, Joe nodded, but then thought of another question. "Rog is at work? Then why aren't you at work too, Grant?"

Feeling him squirm slightly, Sophie suppressed a smile. He'd unconsciously begun tapping his right thigh, and she scooped his hand in hers, soothing his jitters.

Grant finally said, "Well, sir, I don't work with Roger anymore."

"Really? I assumed you'd continue on with the bus tours in the winter."

"They weren't hiring."

"Oh—bad economy, huh?"

"Yes, sir." He squeezed Sophie's hand for courage. "I got another job, though. Sophie arranged it for me."

Joe leaned forward to catch Sophie's eye. "Thanks for keeping this one out of prison, Sophie," he said, tilting his head in Grant's direction.

"He did the same for me," she immediately responded. "Twice." She couldn't keep the smirk from spreading across her face. "Maybe you should hear what the job is before you thank me, though."

Joe looked at Grant, whose cheeks were turning crimson.

Grant cleared his throat. "Uh, you know how I'd end every cruise with a Frank Sinatra song?"

Joe nodded.

"I sort of turned that into a career. A friend of Sophie's dad owns a hotel, and I, um, I sing in the bar there a few nights a week."

Joe was silent for a few moments, and Sophie felt Grant tense next to her, awaiting his response. Then a strange sound came from the other side of the cab. It took Sophie a second to realize Joe was snickering. He tried to squelch his laughter at first, causing small snorting noises to leak from the back of his throat, but soon his body began shaking and a full laugh escaped.

Crystal eyes narrowed. "What's so funny?"

Once Joe settled down, a smile still brightening his tanned face, he managed, "You're a lounge singer?"

"It's a bar," Grant corrected defensively.

"I gotta tell Archie," Joe crowed, thinking of Grant's former boss at Naval Station Great Lakes. "He'll love this career change—lieutenant to lounge act."

Also grinning, Sophie added, "McSailor to McCrooner."

"Fine." Grant folded his arms across his chest. "Make fun of me."

"There's no shame in singing, Grant," Joe said. "A job's a job. Just please tell me I get to see you in action on the stage?"

Sophie leaned forward so she could see Joe. "We're hoping you'd like to join us tonight at the bar. After we watch Grant sing, we're going to have drinks, uh, with my dad."

Joe gave her a dubious look. When he'd first met Will Taylor at Logan's funeral, it wasn't such a pleasant encounter. He still felt a quick flash of anger, thinking of how Will had intimated that he worked for the Mafia before dragging his daughter away, yelling accusations. But Joe just nodded.

Grant's rendition of *Mack the Knife* mesmerized Sophie. This was the first time she'd experienced his singing as an audience member, and she thoroughly enjoyed the opportunity to watch him without the burden of filling drinks for cruise passengers. She was entranced by his charming smile as he held the microphone just close enough to capture the smooth intonations of his sexy baritone. The light in his aquamarine eyes danced with every note—he seemed to be having the time of his life.

Sophie glanced apprehensively at her father sitting next to her. Though he appeared absorbed in Grant's performance, he felt her gaze and turned, his stern expression melting once he caught a glimpse of her chestnut-brown eyes. She'd worried about the little foursome gathering this evening, but so far her father had behaved himself. And he'd actually been friendly to Grant's uncle.

Across the table sat Joe, dressed in civilian clothes for an evening out on the town—a dark blue suit jacket, white button-down shirt, and khaki pants. Sophie watched him smile warmly at his nephew as he listened with a combination of wonder and admiration. Apparently he hadn't realized the extent of Grant's talent.

Applause filled her ears, and she glanced around at the merry atmosphere in the bar. Even her father was clapping. She looked up to find Grant smiling shyly, taking in the adoration. Then he stepped down off the stage and headed to their table.

Once he arrived, he took Sophie's hand and pulled her out of her chair, unabashedly drawing her body into his and planting a definitive kiss on her startled lips. When he deepened the kiss her eyes widened, feeling the hot stares of both her father and Joe. "My dad," she protested, whispering against his lips.

Between kisses he murmured in return, "Trying to avoid…women buying me drinks."

Sophie giggled as they took their seats. Grant attempted to ignore Will's scowl.

"That was awesome." Joe beamed. "Look at this!" He surveyed the bar and then looked back at his nephew. "Grant, you're a hit!"

Grant bit his lip. "Thanks, Joe. I was a little more nervous tonight than usual. I wanted a good performance for my special guests."

"Who knew you could sing like that? That's definitely not from *our* side of the family." Joe shuddered. "Karita singing was like a yowling cougar."

Grant smiled, looking curious. Hesitating for a moment, he quietly asked, "My dad didn't sing, did he?"

Joe's grin faded. He stroked the weathered skin of his face, his light blue eyes gazing into the distance. Finally he said, "Your father used to have a brilliant voice. He…he sang to Karita at their wedding reception—a moving rendition of *Cara Mia*."

Sophie glanced at Grant, who seemed caught between wanting to end the conversation and yearning to hear more. Will also studied Grant.

"I—I never heard that before," Grant said. "He never sang for us at home."

"He probably ruined his voice with all those cigars he and Angelo would smoke," Joe said. "It was disgusting."

Grant suddenly remembered how Joe had gone ballistic when he'd caught Logan smoking as a thirteen-year-old. He hadn't wanted his nephews to turn out anything like Enzo.

"Well, Grant doesn't smoke," Sophie interjected, glancing at Joe and then her father. "He doesn't drink either."

As if to prove her wrong, a waiter swooped in with a vodka tonic, setting the drink squarely in front of Grant. Having performed this exchange countless times, the waiter appeared supremely bored as he reported to Grant, "The woman in the red shirt, twelve o'clock. She wanted me to tell you her name's Alicia."

Grant sighed, and Sophie squinted at the woman before shaking her head. "I guess your kiss didn't do the trick. That's okay, though, vodka tonics are my favorite." She leaned in conspiratorially, winking at him. "I *love* limes."

As the waiter took Will's and Joe's drink orders, Sophie stared straight at Red Shirt Twelve O'Clock and held the drink aloft. She smiled pleasantly while mouthing "thank you." The woman's lips tightened and her cheeks flushed almost the same red as her shirt.

Grant was utterly amused as he watched Sophie take a long sip from the glass. "I guess *Alicia* won't be buying me any more drinks," he said.

Sophie glanced up at a passing waiter. "Can you bring some hot tea for Grant?"

Grant looked taken aback. "What am I—seventy?"

She laughed. "You have to take care of your voice now, Mariah Carey."

Grant rolled his eyes, and Sophie added, "I want to get a drink for you that actually *helps* this time."

His eyes twinkled. "But the tequila *did* help me. Without it, I'd have never tried singing."

Sophie nodded thoughtfully. When she took another swig of her vodka tonic, Will gave her a harsh look.

"You shouldn't be drinking when you're on parole," he said.

"Why not?" she countered. "It's legal."

"I just don't think you should take any unnecessary risks,' Will said.

Sophie flipped her hair to the side with irritation. "Back off, Dad."

Grant was dismayed at their exchange, but he glanced at Joe to find him staring back with a look that said "stay out of it." Biting his lip, Grant asked Will, "Where's Mr. Remington tonight, sir?"

"He's at a political fundraiser for Tom Grogan in Springfield."

Sophie's irritation changed into curiosity. "Why aren't you there too, Dad?"

"I had some business in town to take care of. With the economy like it is, I try to supervise every job site to make sure the client's happy." He sighed heavily. "Besides, it looks like this race is a lost cause."

Joe interjected, "You support Tom Grogan, Will?"

Grant and Sophie exchanged glances, and Grant explained, "Mr. Taylor is a close personal friend of Governor Grogan."

Will grinned. "Yes, your nephew had quite a surprise for his debut. The governor of Illinois was here to see him sing."

Joe looked impressed. "Wow, I bet that was nerve-wracking, huh, Grant?"

"Yes, sir." He snuck a glance at Will, adding hesitantly, "But I was even more nervous to see Mr. Taylor in the audience."

Sophie's heart rate increased, and her eyes darted back and forth between the two significant men in her life. She'd drawn a begrudging promise from her father: as a condition of inviting him, he wouldn't be rude to Grant or Joe. So far he'd behaved, but she knew he could ruin the tentative détente with just one word.

"You did just fine, Grant," Will said, and Sophie breathed a sigh of relief.

A bashful smile crept over McCrooner's face.

"Sorry it's not looking so good for your friend Grogan," said Joe. "I was just reading the newspaper on the plane — there was an article saying Jovanovich is up by over ten points."

Will frowned, lamenting, "It's just not the Republicans' year."

"Ain't that the truth," Joe bemoaned. "Looks like I'm about to get a new commander in chief — a Democrat this time. But at least the other countries might like us more when Ortiz wins."

"Well, I'm only seeing negative effects on my construction business," Will grumbled.

"Maybe it won't be so bad," Sophie piped up. "I mean, I'm nervous about Ortiz winning too, but maybe he'll do a good job?"

Will shrugged. "I hope you're right. What concerns me is that we know so little about him. He's a charming speaker, but what does he really stand for? Is he as centrist as his campaign suggests?"

Chuckling, Joe shook his head. "That's exactly what the article questioned about Darko Jovanovich. Who is this future governor of Illinois? We know he's the son of Serbian immigrants, but beyond that he's a mystery."

"Exactly." Will nodded vigorously. "And Tom's campaign wants to find out where all his money's coming from. Jovanovich runs TV and radio commercials practically nonstop — Grogan can't keep up."

Grant felt warm relief wash over him as he saw Joe and Will getting along so well. "What's Governor Grogan going to do if he loses?" Grant asked.

Will looked sad. "I don't know. He's been in politics his whole life — he was even in student government at U of I."

"Is that where you met him, Will?"

Sophie's father nodded at Joe. "Yes. Tom, Alex Remington — the man who owns this hotel — and I were fraternity brothers, though I was two years behind them in school."

Sophie smirked. "And you remind them at every opportunity that you're younger than them."

"When did you graduate, Will?" Joe asked.

"Seventy-five."

Joe smiled. "I graduated from Illinois in sixty-eight."

"Wow, you're *really* old then." Will's teasing made Joe laugh. "What'd you major in?"

"Engineering. I was Navy ROTC."

"Ah." Will's eyes rested for a moment on Grant, sitting completely straight in his chair across the table. "Uh, Grant, Sophie tells me you were in the Navy ROTC as well?"

Surprised, Grant hesitated a moment before answering "Yes, sir."

"Grant went to *Notre Dame*," Joe cut in, mocking the school's name, "since he's smarter than me."

Grant chuckled, and his uncle winked at him.

Will added, "Yeah, I don't think I could've ever gotten in to Northwestern, but Sophie made it look like a breeze."

A rosy color flushed her cheeks.

"Northwestern — that's a great school," Joe said. "We're hoping Ben will go to Illinois, though."

"I don't know, Joe — Ben's grades *are* improving." Grant gave his uncle a wicked smile. "Maybe he won't have to go to a lowly state school."

"That's great!" Joe replied, ignoring the barb. "Are you keeping him in line, then?"

"I'm trying, sir. Out of the blue Ben joined the high school swim team, and that seems to bring some structure in his life. His first meet's next week."

"*Sophie* was a swimmer," Will proudly announced.

Grant looked at her with surprise, and she appeared embarrassed.

"Dad…"

"She was a great butterflier." He seemed nostalgic, remembering happier times.

"Does Ben know you were a swimmer?" Grant asked.

"Yes, we talked about it one night when he was practicing his push-ups. I told him I was never good at push-ups either, but my coach loved to make us do them."

Resting his arm across her shoulders, Grant nuzzled in to plant a kiss on her neck. "So Ben's decision to swim wasn't so out of the blue, then."

"Sophie once had a bright future in swimming," Will boasted, and then an angry look veiled his face. "Until she quit."

Grant felt Sophie's shoulders tense.

"How old were you when you stopped swimming?" Joe asked.

Her reply was terse. "Twelve."

Grant softly inquired, "Why did you stop?"

Sophie exchanged a knowing glance with her father, who said, "She couldn't handle the pressure."

Her eyes narrowed as she felt a familiar powerlessness — the same she'd felt as a child when she'd tried to argue with her father. "Well, you'd know all about that, Dad, since *you* were the one applying the pressure."

"Nonsense. I was only trying to help you, Sophie."

Her face felt hot. "Help me? By yelling at me and my coaches?"

Will stiffened. "You've got to be tough to survive in this world, kid."

Grant shared an uncomfortable glance with his uncle — both wished to be somewhere else.

"So you were trying to make me tough." Sophie exhaled derisively, taking another drink of the vodka tonic. She set the glass down and fixed a stare at Will. "Was that tough love when you didn't visit me in prison too?"

Will's face fell. "Now, I've already explained that to you, Soph—"

"Oh, right. You blamed yourself for me getting arrested. It's all about you, Dad, isn't it? It's always about *you!*"

"Sophie!"

Grant's sharp tone surprised her, and she was taken aback to catch a glint of anger in his eyes.

"You can't talk to your father that way!" he said.

At first she looked embarrassed, then betrayed. "Well, it's no different than how you talk to *your* father!"

He paused, feeling his heart thumping, and took a deep breath. He wanted to make an angry retort, but she was right. What she'd said to her father paled in comparison to the hostile words he'd shouted at his father in Gurnee. Grant recalled how Sophie's encouragement had helped him keep his cool, and he wanted to help her as well.

Leaning in, he whispered, "How're you feeling?"

Startled, she stared with questioning eyes.

"Are you feeling angry?" he prompted. "Why don't you tell him?"

Sophie slowly nodded, feeling her fury diminish with each deep breath. Clearing her throat she glanced anxiously at Will.

"Dad…I, um, I felt really hurt when you didn't visit me in prison."

Will's shoulders sagged. "I'm so sorry, Sophie. I regret that every day."

Her face softened.

"I just couldn't handle the idea that my decision not to pay the protection fee ruined your life," he said. "I couldn't live with myself."

Grant glanced guiltily at him. "You aren't to blame, Mr. Taylor — my family is."

"It wasn't anybody's fault but mine," Sophie amended testily. "Stop trying to take responsibility for my decisions, both of you."

Will and Grant openly stared at each other, slight smiles spreading on their faces. Eventually Will said, "Sophie told me Enzo threatened to get out of prison somehow?"

Grant's smile vanished. "Yes, sir."

Joe leaned forward, suddenly distressed. "There's no way, Grant. The State of Illinois would never let him out."

Grant's mouth tightened. "He's figured out a way, Joe. I know it. If only *I* could figure out what he's got up his sleeve, then maybe I could stop him. If he gets out—" he shot a nervous glance at Sophie "—none of us is safe."

A sudden chill blanketed the table.

❧

After they'd closed down the bar, Grant and Sophie sent Joe and Will off in their respective taxis before walking back inside the hotel.

"We had our moments, but that went surprisingly well," Grant said. "Who was that man, and what'd he do with your father?"

She chuckled, entering the door he held open for her. "You know, he seems to accept you more since he saw your debut here, after Ben talked to him."

"Well, bless Ben then," Grant replied. "Dealing with my father is quite enough. I certainly could do without your dad also hating me."

They strolled toward the bar, arm in arm.

"It's a good thing you reminded me of Hunter's advice in there, or my dad might hate me too."

"That was a wonderful 'I' statement you used, Sophie," Grant teased, imitating their psychologist. "Your assertive communication was quite effective. You really shared your innermost feelings, blah, blah, insert psychobabble here."

"Oh, thank you, Hunter!" she cried.

As they neared the closed doors of the bar, Sophie inquired, "Where're we going?"

Grant furtively unlocked the doors leading into the darkened bar. "How would you like your own private show?"

A look of keen anticipation crossed her face, and he smiled

His voice lowered. "I watched you down that vodka tonic, and I was completely turned on. I wanted you so badly. It's been torture sitting right next to you all night with your dad watching us."

Fumbling for the lights, Grant flipped the last switch in the row, igniting the soft glow of 1930s-style lighting fixtures around the stage. The seating area remained somewhat dark.

He took her hand and led her toward the piano, which was spotlighted on the cherry stage.

Sophie was intrigued when he slid onto the piano bench and drew her down to sit beside him. One of her eyebrows quirked. "You know how to play piano?"

"Not really. Andy's been trying to teach me a few songs in our down time, though."

"So you *are* challenging yourself with your new job."

"I have a long way to go, as you'll soon discover."

But when he placed his long fingers on the keys, it looked like they'd found a home. He began playing a vaguely familiar tune with a hip-hop rhythm. He swayed a bit, looking into her eyes and crooning soulfully, "It's goin' so right. Got my showty at my side…"

They both burst out in laughter.

"A little different from Frank Sinatra, huh?"

"Slightly. And I'm not really a showty."

"No," he agreed, sweeping his eyes down the length of her. "You're definitely not. Maybe I have a better song for you." He played a few notes of a recognizable rollicking melody, singing, "My Bonnie lies over the ocean. My Bonnie lies over the sea…"

He stopped playing and turned to her with a smoldering gaze. He stared straight into her eyes as he resumed: "My Bonnie lies over the ocean. Oh, bring back my Bonnie to me!"

He maneuvered her body around so she was straddling the bench, and his hands drifted to her hips, anchoring him as he leaned in and feathered a soft kiss on her lips. He continued singing, without the piano now.

"Bring back…bring back…oh, bring back…my Bonnie…to me, to me," he sang softly, all the while kissing her lips, neck, and shoulders between words.

He stood and swung one leg up and over to straddle the bench as well. Grant faced Sophie and scooted her closer. She lifted each foot over his thighs and wrapped her legs around him, their heaving chests flush to each other.

She hooked her hands over his shoulders, and he ran his fingers through her luxurious blond mane. Feeling his emergent hardness press into her belly, she whispered, "Your Bonnie's back, McSailor."

"Aren't I lucky?" He grinned, kissing her ear. "My Bonnie must never, ever leave."

His mouth trailed scorching kisses down the smooth curve of her jaw, up her chin, and onto her mouth, gently biting her lower lip as he gazed hungrily into her eyes.

"Bonnie's dad even likes McSailor," she added with a giggle, capturing his lips with her own as their roving hands explored the finer points of each other's physique.

"Can't say the same for McSailor's dad," Grant joked, stroking and kneading the back of her neck.

Her eyes fluttered shut at the glorious sensation.

Grant frowned. "He's a shark in the ocean, stealthily waiting for Bonnie to cross the sea."

Her hands cradled his head, smoothing his face and neck before coming to rest on his collarbone as she angled to kiss his upper chest.

"He can't get me, though."

Grant's breath hitched, feeling her tongue skate over his skin. "That's right—you're a swimmer," he said softly.

She glanced up, meeting his glittering gaze. "No. The shark can't get me because McSailor will protect me."

Twenty minutes later they stumbled, giggling, out of Capone's Spirits. Grant shushed her as he located the key in his pocket to lock up the bar.

"Grant?"

He looked up to find his boss coming down the hallway, staring at him curiously. He straightened his posture. "Uh, hi, Mr. Remington."

Once the woman with tousled hair spun around, Alex recognized her too. "Sophie!"

"Alex!" She rushed forward to give him a hug. "You look a little tired," she said, stepping away. "Did you just get back from Springfield?"

He nodded, suppressing a yawn. "Poor Tom. He's rather depressed, and all the empty tables at the fundraiser didn't help much."

"Isn't it kind of late for a fundraiser?" Sophie asked. "The election's next week."

Alex shrugged. "Desperate times call for desperate measures. But I fear it's a sinking ship — Jovanovich really has the momentum right now. Anyway, let's discuss happier topics. How did it go tonight, Grant?"

"Fine, sir, seemed like a good crowd." He looked nervous, gesturing behind him. "I was just showing Sophie around a little. Hope that's okay."

Sophie hoped it wasn't obvious what they'd been doing inside the bar.

"Of course!" Alex scoffed. "That's why you have keys." He glanced at his watch. "Well, this old man better get to bed. Goodnight, you two." He headed toward the elevator.

"Goodnight, sir."

"'Night, Alex."

Drawing Sophie to his side, they headed down the hallway. Suddenly, Grant froze, his lips parted with a look of awe.

"What is it?"

"Oh my God. I just figured it out! I know how my dad's planning to escape." He swiveled his gaze to her. "We've got to stop him."

21. Constellation

"Thank you for being here," Grant began in a shaky voice, making eye contact with each of the five guests gathered around the dining room table. His gaze traveled slowly from Sophie to Joe to Will to Jerry Stone, and finally to Marilyn Fox. "I know you're all busy people, so I'll try to keep this brief."

"What the hell's this about, Madsen?" Jerry grumbled. "Detective Fox needs to get back up to Lake County, and I've got a full slate of parolees on today's schedule."

"Just give him a chance to explain," Will said.

Grant and Sophie looked at each other in surprise. Grant supposed Sophie's father, acting as the host of this little soiree, felt obligated to speak on his behalf.

Grant smiled at his parole officer. "I'm grateful you took the time to be here, sir."

Joe was pleased by his nephew's respectful tone.

"I believe everyone here knows about my father's threat to get out of prison," Grant said.

"I know what you told me over the phone, Mr. Madsen," Marilyn said. "But I'm unclear on the details. Why were you visiting your father in the first place?"

Grant swallowed, exchanging a glance with Sophie, whose affectionate gaze heartened his resolve. "My psychologist, Dr. Hayes, encouraged me to meet with my father to, um, to try to heal from the past."

Sophie snuck her hand under the table and rested it on Grant's knee in silent support. His hands had been tightly laced together in his lap, but feeling her presence he unfolded them, bringing one hand forward to meet hers.

Drawing a deep breath, Grant continued, "I've been sort of struggling lately, with nightmares and other stuff, I guess." He sniffed. "You see, my father, well, when I was a kid, he…he physically abused me."

The last words came out in a rush, but everyone heard him clearly and looked stunned by the revelation. Joe and Sophie couldn't believe Grant had just shared this, and the others took in the news for the first time. Jerry looked down, not knowing what to say, and Marilyn appeared stricken. Will crumpled in his chair, feeling shocked then disgusted. He could never imagine hitting his child, no matter how angry she made him.

When Sophie squeezed his hand, Grant slowly looked up. Although she could detect some lingering shame in his bottomless blue eyes, she knew he'd come a long way from being that frightened little four-year-old locked in the closet. The fact that he'd openly admitted the abuse showed he was no longer shouldering the blame for his father's actions. He was no longer internalizing his father's cruel words.

"It must have been tough to confront your father, then," Marilyn said, breaking the silence.

Grant nodded. "Yes, ma'am. And then when he told me he was getting out—"

"What were his exact words?"

"He said, 'I'll join you on the outside,' um, 'I'll see you soon.'"

"And you think that's credible?"

"Yes, ma'am. He's been in there twenty-two years, and he's never even mentioned the idea of getting out before. I think he has a sure exit strategy all lined up. And his plan will begin next week unless we stop him."

"Next week?" Jerry asked.

Grant nodded, glancing at Sophie and then back at his PO. "After the election."

Will leaned forward. "Why the election?"

Clearing his throat, Grant said, "I've been racking my brain trying to figure out my dad's plan. Why now? Why does he seem so certain he's getting out now? I've also come to realize that after rolling in the dough for years, my family's having money problems. There's a reason Carlo came after Logan and Sophie so hard for that money. There's a reason they're pushing their extortion contracts so heavily. They're broke."

Grant looked around the table. Will, Joe, Marilyn, and Jerry all perched on the edge of their seats, staring back at him expectantly. Feeling Sophie's steadying presence next to him, he continued, "I think my father has bribed Darko Jovanovich. He funds Jovanovich's campaign, and Jovanovich pardons him once he wins office. My father will be released from prison by the new governor."

There was a moment of silence, then everyone started talking at once.

"How'd you figure this out?"

"That conniving bastard!"

"How'll we prove —"

"If Enzo Barberi gets free…"

Sophie gazed at Grant, both of them now feeling electrified by the energy in the room. It seemed Grant's theory had merit.

Over the cacophony of voices, one rang out, defeating the others with its intensity and gravitas. "Wait a minute, people!" Marilyn hollered, standing up.

Joe suppressed a chuckle as he watched her take charge — this little half-pint could command authority almost better than his captain.

"Mr. Madsen, I have a question," Marilyn said, meeting his gaze at almost eye-level from her standing position.

"Maybe if you stood up, Marilyn, we might actually notice you," Jerry teased.

She playfully punched his arm. "Shut up, Stone." She turned back to Grant. "Mr. Madsen, if I may continue, that's a very interesting theory. Do you have any evidence to back it up?"

Grant swallowed. "Not yet, ma'am. I was hoping we could work together to gather some." Sensing her skeptical glare, he rambled on. "Is there some sort of Chicago Police division focusing on the Mafia?"

Marilyn paused. "Not that I know of, but that's not what you want anyway. You think Jovanovich is making shady deals with a prisoner? You want a public corruption task force."

"A what?" Joe asked.

"The Illinois Public Corruption Task Force," Marilyn answered. "They go after corrupt public officials. The City of Chicago, Cook County, the State of Illinois and the FBI all participate, so this would be perfect. I worked with one of the FBI agents on the task force, Lucas Bourter, on a case in Lake County. We took down a corrupt county commissioner."

Grant asked, "Detective Fox, could you get in touch with Agent Bounter? Maybe get them involved and start an investigation?"

"Tom is going to want to hear about *this*," Will interjected hotly. "He'll get his staff on it right away."

"Be careful," Joe warned quietly. "If the Barberi family finds out you're investigating them, they'll come after you. They'll come after you hard. Tom Grogan's a politician, not a federal agent. Leave this to law enforcement."

"The problem is that law enforcement will need a warrant to do what you're asking, Mr. Madsen," Marilyn said. "We can't go sniffing around the Barberi family's financial records, or those of a high-profile gubernatorial candidate, without solid evidence that something's fishy."

Sophie's shoulders sagged, knowing what was coming next. Grant's reassuring hand-squeeze did little to squelch her dread.

"I thought you might say that," Grant replied, looking directly at Marilyn and Jerry. "But I said we'd be working *together* to gather the evidence. I haven't told you my part yet."

"Your part?" Joe asked warily.

Not looking at Sophie, Grant squared his shoulders. "I'm going to get you that evidence."

"How the hell will you do that?" Jerry asked.

"I'll go back inside Gurnee. Wired. I'll get my father to confess his plan."

This time the silence lasted much longer.

Finally, Joe said, "Are you *crazy*, Grant? Didn't Enzo threaten to kill you once he got his hands on you?"

"He's not going to kill his own son, Joe."

"The hell he's not. The man's unstable! He's probably been cultivating this exchange with Jovanovich for months! He's not going to let you step in and ruin it all."

"You knew about this?" Will stared at Sophie.

"Yes, Grant told me last night."

Will looked incredulous. "And you agreed to his plan?"

She sighed glumly. "He hasn't told you all of it yet."

"So there's more to this harebrained scheme?" Jerry scoffed, glowering at the plan's mastermind. "You know how bad it is in Gurnee, Madsen. Why the hell would you willingly go back inside?"

Chewing on his lip, Grant eventually replied, "Because if I go in there and get you the evidence — if it stops a corrupt politician from winning office…well, then I want Sophie's felony conviction reversed."

"Grant too!" Sophie rushed to add. "That's the only way I agreed to this: if Grant's conviction gets reversed too."

"Fat fucking chance!" Jerry exploded. "I should've known you two were up to something. The courts will *never* go for this."

Marilyn rested a hand on Jerry's forearm, trying to calm him. "Mr. Madsen, how exactly do you plan on getting your conviction vacated?"

Grant chewed on his lower lip. "I'm not sure, ma'am. I'm hoping if this works, someone will go to bat for us? There must be a way."

"Tom Grogan would certainly be on board," Will said. "If nothing else pans out, I'd think he'd be willing to issue pardons for both of you."

Marilyn nodded thoughtfully. "The task force has a local prosecutor and an assistant attorney general assigned to it, I believe. They'd have to figure it out. You both pleaded guilty, so that may make it easier — no jury trial convictions to be set aside."

Jerry looked nonplussed.

"They're conning us, Mar. This is all about them skating scot-free."

"Oh, come *on*, Jer, you and I both know they don't belong in the correctional system. The only reason they were arrested in the first place is they got caught up in the Barberi family web. And now that they finally have a chance to get free, you're going to stand in their way?" Her green eyes flared. "They're both good people, and if Grant's plan works, we'll be doing our jobs — protecting the people of Illinois from the likes of Enzo Barberi and from Darko Jovanovich too, assuming he's guilty of corruption."

Sophie and Grant gazed at Marilyn, their new hero.

His bushy grey eyebrows knitting together, Jerry squinted pensively at Grant. "If you succeed — and that's a big *if* — Enzo Barberi's going to be mighty pissed at you."

Grant swallowed. "That's why we need to be free, sir — in case we need to go into hiding."

"You honestly think you could elude the Mafia?" Marilyn asked, skepticism written all over her face.

"In its heyday, no," Grant said. "But I think my family's severely compromised right now. They've lost Logan and Carlo. Uncle Angelo's about to die, and I bet they've spent most of their money on my dad's freedom. My dad would've demanded it."

"I should inform my captain before I put feelers out to the task force," Marilyn said. "They'll have to move fast—the election's only six days away. Task forces typically work quickly, but this is fast even for them."

Grant nodded. "I propose we all meet back here tomorrow morning after we check out the feasibility of this plan."

Grant turned to Jerry with a hint of trepidation. "Officer Stone, would you check with the head of the DOC about me going back inside, sir? Maybe give him a head's up so he's ready if the task force decides to move forward?"

Grant held his breath while Jerry grumpily considered his request, drumming his fingertips on the opulent oak table. Finally he caved. "Fine. But don't expect miracles, Madsen. And since tomorrow's Wednesday, do you two plan on just blowing off your weekly meeting?"

"Would it be okay if we met here at my dad's house instead, Jerry?" Sophie asked. "It could sort of be like a home visit for you."

She received some muttering under his breath as a response.

"Thank you, sir," Grant replied, hoping for the best. Then he turned to look at Sophie's father. "Mr. Taylor, would you talk to Governor Grogan's people about this theory? See what they might've uncovered during the campaign?"

"Hell yes, I will. This'll be the first good news the Republicans have had in months."

"It might not work," Grant cautioned, dropping his voice. "I might be wrong."

"Could be," Will said. "But it just *feels* right. I haven't liked that Darko character from the second I met him. He's slick."

"You met him?" Marilyn looked curious.

"Yes, at the debate last winter. Tom introduced me to his opponent, and he just seemed off. He's got shifty eyes or something."

While the group pondered that characterization, Joe asked, "What do you need from me, Grant?"

His nephew guiltily returned his gaze. "I know you don't agree with this plan, Joe—Sophie hates it too. But I promise I'll keep myself safe. What I need is to learn all I can about my father before I go in there—his mannerisms, his likes, his dislikes. Even though I'm his son, I feel like I don't really know him. I tried to avoid him the last time I was inside, but obviously I can't do that now."

When Joe nodded, Grant added, "And for Ben — I need you to help me come up with a plan to keep Ben safe if this whole thing goes bad, okay?"

"Of course."

"But it's not going to go bad, right?" Sophie pleaded.

"Right," Grant confirmed, rising to standing and drawing her out of her chair as well. He wrapped his arm around her back and rested his hand reassuringly on her hip. "C'mon, let's walk Detective Fox and Officer Stone out. I'm sure they need to get going."

Will and Joe found themselves left staring uncomfortably at each other.

"Wow. That's some plan your boy's got there," Will said.

Joe nodded. "I guess he must have inherited Enzo's mastermind for strategy. There's no way the family would be crumbling like it is if Enzo was still at the helm." He exhaled derisively. "You know, I had a premonition that anyone named Darko had to be dirty."

Will cracked a grin. "According to Tom, Darko is a derivative of the Serbian word for 'gift.' Tom found that rather ironic, since his opponent thrashing him in the polls certainly hasn't felt like a gift."

Taking a worried breath, Joe grimaced in agreement. The idea of Grant returning to prison, and being in close proximity with his father, didn't feel like a gift either. Joe hoped the stars would align to keep his nephew safe.

22. Conflagration

"Now, Mr. Madsen," FBI Agent Lucas Bounter said as he fiddled with Grant's shirt, "make sure this microphone's kept in the 'on' position the entire time you're incarcerated, even if you're not talking to the suspect."

"Why's that?" Sophie asked, leaning in toward the digital audio-recording console, pressing her palms flat against her father's dining room table.

"It's procedure," Lucas gruffly replied. "We don't want to give Barberi's attorney any opportunity to question the investigation—alleging somebody threatened him while the mic was off or some such nonsense."

"As if I could threaten *him*," Grant scoffed, peering down at the button-sized digital voice recorder attached to his shirt collar. "This microphone seems sort of similar to the technology we used in the Navy."

"Oh, like an underwater pinger locator?" Joe asked.

"Yes, sir, 'cept those were a heck of a lot bigger than this little guy."

Joe glanced at the compact FBI agent. "And how does Grant get by with wearing the device in Gurnee?"

Lucas said, "It's a good thing the task force was already sniffing around Jovanovich's campaign funding, so we could mobilize right away when we heard Grant's evidence. Between his information and what we already knew, the US Attorney was able to secure a warrant for the wire and the task force got the DOC to approve the operation."

Jerry sighed, still not quite believing the DOC's cooperation. "The warden and one of the COs are going to be in on it," Jerry explained.

"The more people who know about this, the more likely the truth leaks out," Joe countered. "Can we trust these men?"

"Warden Arthur's a good man," Jerry said. "Right, Madsen?"

Grant licked his lips. "I can't honestly say, sir. The only interaction I had with him was when he threw me in the hole for standing up to my father."

"But the other guys also went in the hole for fighting, right?" Jerry asked.

"No, sir."

Joe inhaled sharply. "Enzo's obviously bought off most of the guards in there. I do *not* want one of the COs in on the sting. It's not safe."

As Jerry snapped back, defending the corrections officers, Grant glanced uneasily at Sophie, who appeared pale and frightened.

He reached out for her, smoothing one hand down the side of her head, feeling her silky strawberry hair under his touch. "It'll be okay," he promised.

"It just seems like too much of a risk. Even if it works…"

"We'll be all right. I won't let them hurt you again, okay? The best defense is offense."

She gave him a stern look. "That works with football, Grant, not with the Mafia."

He offered a slight smile. "Well, the cons typically play football out in the yard this time of year, so maybe that's a good sign. Maybe I'll get a chance to tackle my dad."

"Yes, tackle him, trip him, beat him up… I hope you grind his face in the mud."

"Hey, I thought psychologists didn't believe in violence," Grant said.

She shook her head. "I know. It's just that I hate that man. I hate him for what he did to you back then, and I hate him for what he's doing to you now—forcing you to go back inside."

"He's not forcing me to do anything, Sophie. I thought we agreed on this. We both agreed we'd get our lives back this way."

"But that was when I thought this wouldn't go through. I never thought they'd go for—"

"Cool!" Detective Marilyn Fox's voice cut into their conversation. Agent Bounter was showing her some of the finer points of the audio surveillance system. "You guys get all the fun toys," she said with a pout.

"They don't have this up in Lake County?" Lucas teased.

Her eyes narrowed, and she elbowed him in the ribs. "Thanks for talking to my captain and convincing him I needed to be here today. Not having any official role is frustrating, but at least I get to see the action up close."

Sophie allowed a faint smile to break through her worry as she watched Jerry, sensing competition, float over to Marilyn and Lucas.

"The mic looks kind of flimsy," Jerry observed.

"It's quite strong," Lucas countered, picking up the Gurnee-issue powder blue button-down shirt and rubbing the microphone, which was disguised as a button near the shirt's collar. "It's been field-tested and approved."

"How many live operations has the device been used for?" Joe asked.

Lucas paused.

"Agent Bounter?" Joe prompted.

"Well, this is a new technology, actually." Reading the dismay on the commander's face, Lucas rushed in to add, "But I can assure you it will work."

"I don't like this," Joe protested. "I don't like this one bit." He met his nephew's wary eyes across the table. "Don't do this, Grant. If they catch wind of your scheme, if they find that microphone planted on you…"

"It's too late to back out now," Grant responded, quiet determination in his voice. He crossed over to his uncle and stood before him. "I have to do this, Joe. I can't let my father win."

"He *won't* be winning. Who cares if he gets out—he'll still be the same miserable, morally depraved man he's always been. It's not your responsibility to stop him."

"Tell that to Richie Fanocelli," Grant said. "Tell him his son's killer is about to get out of prison before serving his full sentence. My dad's trying to cheat the system again. How can you just stand by and watch it happen? You taught me to stand up for what's right. You taught me to fight. You're a Navy commander! How can you be so passive about this?"

Joe exhaled loudly, gripping one of the dining room chairs. "Because he's destroyed so much already, and I don't want to give him the opportunity to do more damage. He took your mother—I know Karita died of cancer, but I blame Enzo. He hurt her, and he hurt you boys."

Grant's jaw clenched, and Joe continued. "And he took your brother. Logan's dead because of Enzo. Make no mistake about it." Joe's voice softened. "I don't want him taking you too."

"I won't let him, sir. I have to do this. I know I'm the only one who can get the information out of him. He wants to tell me how he's outsmarted the system. He *needs* to tell me. He needs to put me in my place for challenging him like I did. I can't stand by and just let him go free. Sophie and I will be in even more danger if he gets out."

Joe sighed grimly, running one hand through his graying blond hair. He looked weary, older than his sixty-two years. "You're right, of course. You have to fight. Don't make the same mistakes I did."

Grant looked bewildered. "Mistakes?"

"I should've fought Enzo back then, back when you were a child. I regret not getting your mom and you boys away from him."

Grant placed a hand on his shoulder. "You did get me away from him."

Their blue eyes met, and Grant felt relieved that his uncle had accepted the plan—although the relief was mixed with fear.

Joe gathered his nephew into a hug, quietly ordering, "You come back to me in one piece, ya hear me?"

"Yes, sir."

They thumped each other on the back a few times before releasing their embrace.

"And you're going to keep Ben with you for the next few days?" Grant asked.

"I'm heading over there once Officer Stone takes you away," Joe assured him.

Jerry and Marilyn had been uncomfortably watching the uncle-nephew exchange, and Jerry took Joe's statement as his cue.

"Let's get outside so I can arrest you publicly," Jerry said, looking pointedly at Grant.

"You don't have to look so happy about it, sir."

"It's always a pleasure to send a deserving con back inside," Jerry joked.

"You're an ass, Jerry," Marilyn retorted, causing Grant to chuckle. "But I do agree that it's wise to make the arrest as public as possible, to make it more legit. The story is that you violated parole by losing your job?"

"Yes, ma'am. Mr. Taylor's arranging things with Mr. Remington as we speak."

Jerry scooped up the wired Gurnee shirts and stuffed them in a bag. "Let's go, Madsen."

"Can we have a minute?" Sophie blurted. "Before you take him?"

Jerry frowned, but said, "Fine. Make it quick."

She'd grabbed Grant's hand and was already pulling him out of the room before Jerry finished responding. Sophie first guided him into her father's study, but finding a state police detective from the task force there, speaking on his cell phone, she abruptly spun around and headed in the other direction. Flustered, Sophie opened the front door and led Grant toward the gated entrance.

Watching her punch in the security code for the gate, Grant asked, "Where're you taking us?"

Sophie sighed with relief once they reached the sidewalk. "Just right here—I had to get out of there. All that talk about returning to prison was making me claustrophobic. I wanted to go somewhere to say goodbye."

He rested his long fingers on the curve of her hips, gazing at her fondly. "I'm only going to be gone a few days, Bonnie."

She nodded, shivering in the autumn chill.

He reached up to tuck a strand of hair behind her ear. "If this works, you won't have to worry about returning to prison. You won't have to feel claustrophobic ever again. You'll get your life back."

She tried to be tough but couldn't stop tears from pooling in her eyes.

When one tear rolled down her cheek, Grant murmured, "Oh, Sophie." He leaned down to kiss away the salty droplet with his soft lips. "We'll make it through this," he promised, pressing his mouth hard against hers, infusing her with strength.

Inside the house, the unmistakable sound of fervent kissing filled the dining room. Lucas cleared his throat, nodding at the recording mechanism on the console. "Looks like the device works."

Joe averted his eyes, stifling a grin.

"Jesus Christ," Jerry complained. "Do we really have to listen to Con and Conette going at it out there?"

"Let's give them some privacy, Lucas," Marilyn suggested, and the agent turned off the audio.

Back on the sidewalk, Sophie grudgingly peeled herself away. "I better let you go. Jerry's itching to get those cuffs back on you."

"More handcuffs." Grant frowned.

She reached into her pocket and extracted a small envelope. "I promise to write you letters when you're inside, but—"

"Sophie, really, I'm going to be out of there before the first letter will even arrive!"

"Don't try to stop me, McSailor. I can't visit you in there, and you said Joe shouldn't visit you either, so I want you to have at least some contact from the outside." She looked down. "I know what it's like not to have visitors."

"Yes, but *I* get to spend quality time with my dad."

She matched his sarcastic tone. "Lucky you. Anyway, what I was trying to say, before I was so rudely interrupted—" they both smiled "—was that I wanted you to have something to comfort you in there, until you get my first letter."

Handing him the envelope, she watched his face as he opened it. He extracted a wallet-sized photo and brought it closer to get a good look at the ravishing blonde staring back at him, her face slightly shaded by the bill of a baseball cap.

"Kirsten took that at a White Sox game a few years ago," she explained.

"You look so happy there," he mused. His eyes drifted from the cheerful image to her apprehensive frown. "This picture was taken before you came into contact with my family. Before they hurt you."

"I'm happy *now*," she insisted. "But I'll only stay that way if you come back to me."

He nodded guiltily, tucking the photo back in the envelope and sliding it into his pocket. His eyes glittered, though it was a cloudy morning.

"Thank you," he said. He planted a reassuring kiss on her trembling lips. She felt warmth emanating from his sure hands and soft lips, calming her with a sense of sanctuary.

They were so absorbed in their goodbye kiss that they barely heard the screeching tires, and only when several sets of pounding footsteps drew near did they realize something was happening. Once Grant glanced to the street, he froze.

Tank and Mario were jogging toward them, Mario's heft shifting with each hustled step, and Tank's menacing smile lending him an expression of triumph. Another set of large men loomed right behind them, and Grant stepped in front of Sophie, trying to shield her. It was too late to run—the men were on top of them in a second.

"We found you!" Mario huffed, breathing hard.

"Let's go, Grant," Tank ordered.

His blue eyes darted back and forth among the four men now encircling them. "Go where?"

"On a little trip," Mario responded, still panting.

Grant reached behind him to clasp Sophie's wrist, sensing her fear. He noticed the two cars waiting in the street, both with beefy drivers staring back at him.

"I'm not going anywhere," he declared, attempting to keep his voice steady.

Tank slid a handgun out of its holster, keeping it low by his hip but obviously aiming it at Grant. "We can do this hard or easy, *Madsen*. Move it."

Swallowing, Grant quickly countered, "I'll only go with you if you leave Sophie alone." He heard a small cry of protest behind him and squeezed her wrist comfortingly.

Tank chuckled. Madsen was outnumbered six to one and must have been incredibly stupid to think he could bargain with them. "Of course," he promised. "We only want you. She can stay."

Grant gave a slight nod and didn't fight when Mario and Tank grabbed his arms, forcing him toward the first waiting car. He snuck a glance over his shoulder, expecting to see the other two goons lock-stepping into place behind him, and he gasped when he saw them seize Sophie instead and begin to push her toward the other car.

"Hey!" Grant cried, struggling to escape the bodyguards' vice-like hold. He managed to free one arm, but Mario instantly punched a swift shot to his gut.

"Grant!" Sophie shrieked, unable to fight off the two men jostling her through the open car door.

Gasping for air and stumbling, Grant swiveled and jammed his foot into Tank's knee. "Son of a bitch!" the bodyguard hollered, raising his fist in fury and clouting his detainee on the side of the head.

Grant's vision blurred from the blow, and he barely heard Mario warn, "He said not to hurt him!" Before he knew it, he'd been shoved into the backseat of a black Lincoln town car, sandwiched between Tank and Mario.

"Go!" Tank shouted, and the driver obediently sped away.

Feeling woozy, his ears ringing, Grant was terrified to see the car carrying Sophie turn off onto a side street, widening the distance between them. *Where were they taking Sophie?*

He felt another blow to the side of his head and heard Tank bellow, "Eyes forward, damn it! Mario, get the plastic tie!"

"Got it," Mario huffed, and Grant felt himself hefted sideways to face the incensed Tank as Mario wrenched his arms behind his back. Despite his struggles, he felt his wrists instantly restrained, the hard plastic tie already cutting into his skin.

Tank manhandled him back in his seat so he faced forward. "Don't fucking move," he growled.

Grant's temple throbbed and his heart rate soared. His hands were already starting to feel numb. As the driver guided the car onto the Dan Ryan, Grant said nothing. Finally, once his breathing had slowed, he asked, "Where're you taking me?"

Mario eyed him carefully, watching for any sudden movement. "Enzo wants a chat."

Grant's heart skipped a beat. Had they already uncovered his attempt to thwart his father's plan? His mind whirred as a sickening dread overtook him. Eventually he asked, "And Sophie? Where're you taking her?"

Tank smiled smugly. "Well, that depends entirely on you, Madsen."

"What does that mean?"

"Shut up," Tank said. "No more questions. It'll all make sense when you talk to your dad. He's been *missing* you."

Mario joined Tank's low chuckle.

Grant slumped in the seat, ignoring the increasing ache radiating through his arms and hands. He was supposed to be handcuffed, but this scenario was all wrong. Jerry was supposed to be driving, not some Mafia goon. Sophie was supposed to be safe at her father's house, not kidnapped.

Grant's entire plan had been shot to hell, thanks to his family. White-hot anger coursed through him. It was a good thing he was restrained or he might have exploded, not caring one iota that the men guarding him had guns. They weren't going to take everything from him again, he resolved quietly. They weren't going to destroy everything he loved!

This time he was determined not to let his father win.

23. Confound

Damn, his arms hurt. He'd thought nothing could be worse than being handcuffed for the sixty-minute drive to Gurnee, but he'd been wrong — metal handcuffs would have been far superior to the plastic tie currently lacerating his wrists. Being sandwiched between two meatheads didn't make the backseat any more comfortable, either. And thanks to Ben's eavesdropping, Grant was acutely aware that Tank and Mario had been the men holding Logan when Carlo murdered him.

He looked down with despair. *Think.* Why were the bodyguards taking him to his father? Had they discovered his plan to thwart the early release? Would his father try to get him to confess the sting and then murder him and Sophie? Did they know he was wired?

He was wired! Grant tucked his chin to peek at the button-shaped device on his collar, wondering if Detective Fox and Agent Bounter had heard him and Sophie being kidnapped. Was the device on? Had it survived the bodyguards' assault as they shoved him into the vehicle? His scrambled worries overwhelmed him, and he drew in a panicked breath.

Leaning his bulk into the restrained passenger, Tank asked, "What's wrong?"

Grant's mind raced. "Where did you take Sophie?"

Silence greeted him. Undeterred, he asked, "Why are you taking me to Gurnee?"

Tank's lips were in a tight line as he spoke. "I already told you, numb nuts, you're talking to the boss."

"Why does he want to see me?"

"That's for you and him to sort out."

"I'm on parole—they won't allow me to visit him."

Tank's meaty hand seized the back of Grant's neck and drilled his head into his lap, doubling him over and knocking the air out of him. "Don't give me that shit," Tank seethed into his ear. "You just visited Enzo."

Grant strained to get oxygen into his compressed lungs, worried less about his own well-being than that of the recording device. Agent Bounter's promise about the durability of the digital recorder would be seriously tested this time around.

Grant's reply was muffled. "I had to get special permission from the DOC."

Tank released his neck, and Grant slowly sat up again, coughing.

"If they let you see him once, they'll let you see him again."

"Maybe not," Grant argued. "I had to give the guards a special letter. They might not let me in without one."

"I'm sure you'll find a way," Tank said, "*if* you want the Taylor girl to live."

Grant's stomach knotted.

"Yeah," Mario added, straining to seem relevant to the conversation. Somehow he didn't appear as menacing as his partner.

After another five miles, Tank began rubbing the side of his knee. Grant knew better than to say anything, but Mario didn't.

"This asshole kick you?" he asked, gesturing to Grant.

Tank grunted, and Grant stifled a smile over his small victory in the takedown.

Mario continued. "That the same knee that—"

"Shut the fuck up, idiot!" Tank roared, cutting him off. "Not with *him* here."

Admonished, Mario slumped back in the seat.

Grant tried to make sense of that exchange, and the rest of the journey went way too quickly. His mind swam with potential directions for the conversation with his father.

Once they neared the prison parking lot, Tank instructed, "Cut 'em."

Grant felt Mario's beefy paws swivel him toward Tank, who leered at him, threatening, "You make one wrong move, and we stick the Taylor chick."

Mercifully Grant heard a snap, and the pressure on his wrists instantly abated. Turning his body back to face the windshield, he drew his tingling arms forward, massaging his bloody wrists.

"Fuck," Tank spat. "You tied it too tight, Meat. The guards are gonna see the blood."

"It'll be fine," Mario replied defensively, yanking out Grant's shirttails. Grant held his breath, but began to breathe easier when the bodyguard simply patted the sore cuts on his wrists with the shirttails before instructing him to tuck them back into his jeans.

"Why ain't you wearing a coat?" Mario asked, as Grant shivered slightly. "It's almost November."

Because I only stepped out for a second to say goodbye to Sophie before I tried to take down the entire family. "I, um…I'm not cold."

Grant *had* to get out of this car soon.

As they rolled up to the guard station, Tank ordered, "Not one word."

A corrections officer peered into the vehicle. "State your business."

"We're visiting an inmate," the driver explained.

"Which one?"

"Vicenzo Barberi."

The CO quirked his eyebrow and radioed the inmate's name to the visitation area. He looked curiously to the backseat, poking his head partly into the vehicle. "Y'all cozy back there?"

Grant didn't move, feeling Tank's elbow jab into his ribcage. Mario gave a sweet smile, jiggling his double chin. "Yes, Officer."

After a moment of deliberation, the CO gruffly commanded, "Proceed to the parking lot."

Shortly, the black Lincoln town car came to a stop in the crowded parking area. Mario glanced at his watch. "We're cutting it close — there's only about thirty minutes left of visitation."

"Here's the deal, Madsen," Tank said.

Grant's military training took hold, and he looked straight ahead, sitting erect.

"You go in there and talk to your dad, and then you come straight back to the car."

Grant couldn't help but turn and look at Tank with surprise. "You're not coming with me?"

"Enzo don't want us in there for some strange reason. But you know what'll happen if you try to get cute?"

Grant swallowed hard. "You'll hurt Sophie."

Tank gave a tight smile. "I'm glad we have an understanding."

"What if I can't see my dad because of the parole thing?"

"What did I just say?" Tank countered, opening the car door and scooting out. "Make it work, Madsen, or your little cupcake gets squashed."

Mario chuckled. "I wouldn't mind licking *her* icing."

Disgusted, Grant hopped out of the car and took quick strides toward the prison, eager to put ground between him and his father's goons. If only he could also walk away from his father, instead of heading toward him... but there was no choice. Not when Sophie's life was in danger, which was once again his fault.

Stepping into the entrance, he glanced warily at the two COs checking in visitors.

"Hey, you're back! Your dad didn't scream at you enough the first time?"

Immediately recognizing the chatty CO from his last visit, Grant's chest collapsed with relief. He offered a wry smile. "I can never get enough of my dad's love and affection."

The CO grinned and peered at Grant's proffered driver's license. "Let me guess — your shrink wants you to gain closure on some unresolved childhood issues?"

Lifting his arms parallel to the ground to assist the officer's search, Grant held his breath as the CO examined his arms but didn't seem to notice the blood stains at the cuffs of his shirt. He heard himself respond, "How'd you know, sir?"

After administering a perfunctory pat-down, the CO guided Grant to the visitation area. As they stood by the cage, he leaned in to confess quietly, "My wife's a therapist."

Despite the tension of the situation, Grant actually smiled. "Really? I know what that's like — my girlfriend's a psychologist."

The CO looked shocked at the coincidence. "Run, Madsen. Get out while you can, before she shrinks your brain to the size of a walnut."

When the officer laughed and affectionately patted his shoulder, something about the gesture seemed familiar to Grant.

"Um, did we interact much when I was an inmate here, sir?"

The officer paused. "I guess you don't remember. I worked in the, um, psych ward."

Grant's face fell.

"But I work primarily in visitation now."

"W-W-What made you change?"

"I thought I'd like the whack shack, you know, with my wife being a therapist and all. I thought it'd give us something in common." He sighed. "But it was, um, too hard. It was too hard to see grown men…" His voice faded off, and his smile was one of embarrassment. "Well, I like visitation better—it's happier. People are mostly happy to see their loved ones." He took in Grant's look of dread. "Except for you. You don't seem too happy to be here."

The understatement of the year. "No, sir."

Noticing the prisoner being led into the room, the CO softly told him, "He's in chains—you'll be fine. It's good you're on *this* side of the cage now. I knew you could make it." Then he turned and headed back to the visitor check-in area.

Grant's wistful look abruptly faded as he faced Enzo Barberi in the cage. His father appeared somewhat triumphant this time around, and as the officers guided him to a seated position, chains jangling, a smug expression crossed his hardened face.

Grant sat down as well, watching his father with trepidation.

"What, no letter?" Enzo asked with a sneer, eyeing his son's empty hands.

Grant took several deep breaths before responding. "You're the one who dragged me here. What do you want from me?"

Enzo tilted his head to one side, studying his son—who didn't seem quite as terrified as the last time they'd met. Sighing dramatically, Enzo said, "My brother is dying."

Grant creased his eyebrows, puzzled. "Yes?"

"Nobody fucking told me my brother was dying!"

Grant leaned away from the cage. "You didn't know?"

"When you visited me, you said something about Angelo not being around much longer, and I didn't know what the hell you were talking about. Then I had Meat hauled in here, and he confessed Angelo ordered him not to tell me about his lung cancer."

"Why didn't he tell you?"

"Who the fuck knows? Meat told me some bullshit about Ange not wanting to burden me—about Ange not going to the doctor till it was way too late or something, the dumbass. It doesn't change the fact that Angelo was supposed to do something for me, and now he's too goddamned sick." Black eyes bore into Grant. "He's supposed to do an errand for me, but he's too fucking weak to walk five steps. That's why I need you."

Grant looked aghast—running an "errand" for the family was what had gotten him incarcerated in the first place. "But you have Tank and Mario."

"I can't trust *them*."

"Why not?"

Enzo paused. "They're not family."

With a slight upturn of the side of his mouth, Grant countered, "There's more to it than that, though, isn't there?"

"What do you mean?"

"You know what I mean. Tank and Mario helped kill Logan."

Enzo's expression didn't change, confirming that he already knew of the bodyguards' betrayal. "Well, well. How'd you find out?"

Refusing to implicate Ben, Grant forcefully challenged, "You *knew* they held Logan down, yet you let them live? What kind of mob boss are you?"

Enzo's jaw clenched. "They'll be dealt with when the time is right."

"What time is that? After you're out?"

Enzo sat back in his chair, again staring curiously at his son. "Who said I'm getting out?"

"*You* did!"

Obsidian eyes tapered into slits. "I'm in a maximum security prison, Grant. How the fuck would I get out? Clearly I was joking. I'd give anything to be free, but it's exactly like you said, 'Wishing doesn't make it so.'"

Grant ignored his father's mocking tone and leaned in closer. "No, you weren't joking. You wouldn't joke about that. Getting out of here's way too important to you."

Enzo remained quiet for a moment. "So what if I *was* getting out? Hypothetically. What business is that of yours?"

The icy look from his father sliced through him, and Grant found it difficult to breathe. "None," he managed. "It's none of my business."

"Good." Enzo lowered his voice. "Now, back to what you'll do for me. Tomorrow night you're going to deliver a package. Angelo will give you a briefcase, you'll personally hand it over to a guy, and then you'll leave. It's that simple."

Grant's mind whirred. "What's in the briefcase?"

"Only Angelo will know. It'll be locked, and you keep Meat and Tank's grimy paws off the merchandise. Make sure Fuckledee and Fuckledumb don't fuck up the drop."

"And they'll let Sophie go if I do it?"

Enzo leaned back in a placating gesture, smiling. "You'll both walk scot-free."

Grant pondered his circumstances. "Why the hell should I believe you, *Dad?*"

"Because you have no choice. Do what Tank and Meat tell you to do or your girlfriend dies."

At last his father was speaking the truth. There was indeed no choice. Yet despite the bleak circumstances, Grant felt a spark of hope within — the seed of a new plan forming and taking root. His family had destroyed his initial plan, but if he was correct about the nature of the errand his father was forcing him to undertake, this might be even better. Squaring his jaw, Grant pledged, "Okay, I'll do it."

He felt his father's emanating intensity as he leaned toward the bars. "And this time, don't fucking get caught. I don't want to see your sorry ass back in here."

Grant suppressed a smirk. That last comment confirmed his suspicions. The hardened criminal across from him was simply trying to protect his exit strategy. Grant was determined to blow that strategy to pieces.

Aiming earnest sky-blue eyes at his father, Grant held his gaze for several moments. It could have been different between them. Instead of mistrust, fear, and hate, there could have been love. But wishing didn't make it so. "Am I free to go, Dad?"

A surprising flash of tenderness crossed Enzo's face. "Be careful, son."

Grant stood up and backed away a few steps, his eyes never leaving the prisoner. His throat tightened with worry, wondering if Sophie would survive this drop or if he would soon be joining his father on the inside. Committing Enzo's face to memory, Grant prayed this would be the last time he'd ever see his father.

His perplexed mind went into overdrive as he stepped onto the sidewalk outside the visitation area, a brisk breeze scattering a few leaves across the concrete. The drop was supposed to happen tomorrow night, meaning Sophie would be held at least until then. A sliver of fear crept up his spine as he thought of his Bonnie tied up and hidden somewhere, her life depending on his actions.

He stared through the enclosed, fenced-in walkway leading to the parking lot, first noticing the black sedan still waiting for him. With his elbows propped on the hood of the car, Tank sent him a menacing glare. Then Grant looked to the left, his eyes sweeping over the parked cars and coming to rest on a nondescript gray vehicle. Agent Lucas Bounter popped his head out of the open driver's side window, catching Grant's attention. His presence here could mean only one thing: the mic was working! Squinting, Grant saw another man in the front seat but couldn't make out who it was.

Grant's stomach dropped. Were they going to try to steal him back? Abruptly he spun on his heel and swiftly made his way back inside the prison, ignoring the cry of protest from Tank behind him.

Breathing heavily, Grant burst back into the visitation check-in area, pleading, "Do you have a visitor's bathroom?"

The CO cocked his head to the right. "Sure, it's down there."

"Thank you, sir."

Grant jogged to the restroom, luckily finding it empty. Securing the lock, he leaned against the door, words frantically tumbling out of his mouth. "Don't take me. Please don't take me. Enzo wants me to make a money drop, and it's gotta be to Jovanovich's people. Please let me do this. Follow me and make the bust tomorrow night, just don't take me now—I'll be okay." His gut clenched, knowing he'd be in the custody of Logan's killers until then.

"Find Sophie," he continued, speaking aloud to the empty bathroom. "They took her somewhere, and they're holding her to make sure I do the drop. Please find her."

Reckless thoughts careened through his brain—what was he missing? He knew he had to get back out there before the bodyguards came looking for him. "And Ben—make sure Ben's okay, too. Please, sirs. Find Sophie."

Grant unlocked the door, trying to collect himself as he hustled to the exit. Noticing the CO watching him, Grant took the time to meet his gaze and assure him, "I won't be back, I promise. Thank you, sir."

Every muscle in his body tensed as he walked to the town car, silently pleading for no move from the FBI agent and the officer to his left. Fortunately Lucas and the man stayed put, but he could feel the heat of their distant stares.

"What the fuck was that?" Tank hollered, grasping Grant's elbows and shoving his back into the car door. "We told you to come right back here!"

"Sorry," Grant breathlessly explained. "I had to go so bad I thought I'd pee in my pants."

Abruptly releasing his arms, Tank took a step back and sneered at him, exchanging an evil grin with Mario. "And according to the boss, that's a genuine threat. I suppose we should thank you for not pissing all over yourself. That would've made for a long, smelly car ride."

Mario laughed heartily as color rose in Grant's cheeks. He allowed himself to be shoved inside the backseat, once again stuffed between the bodyguards. Grant hoped Agent Bounter would be discreet in tailing the vehicle, wherever they were headed.

Once they cleared the guard station and were barreling toward I-94, Tank instructed, "Do it."

Mario whipped out a fresh plastic tie, and Grant tensed. But the portly bodyguard secured the tie with his hands in front of him this time, and he allowed slightly more slack. The hard edges of the tie wouldn't sear into the existing cuts as long as Grant kept his hands still.

"Can't have you bleeding on the leather seats," Tank explained maliciously. "And we can't have you seeing where we're going, either."

Before Grant knew it, Mario wrapped a blindfold over his eyes, tying the dark material tightly against the back of his shorn head. As darkness descended, Grant's stomach dropped. He didn't like the dark very much. Fighting for oxygen, Sophie's soothing words came to him: *You're an adult now. They can't hurt you anymore.*

His yearning for Sophie was palpable. Clenching his jaw, he fought the hot tears burning his cool crystal eyes. All was black.

24. Confinement

Sophie awoke to sheer blackness.

Frantically tossing her head and struggling to escape the darkness, she tried to figure out where the hell she was. She strained to release her arms from an unknown binding, desperate to find something, anything recognizable. Her thrashing caused a sharp pain in her forehead and a throbbing ache to radiate up the length of her arms, and then it all came back.

They had her.

They had her blindfolded and tied down, probably on some hard wooden chair, by the feel of it. She moaned in despair.

"She's awake," a harsh, nasal voice announced, and Sophie froze.

She heard a faint, tinny reverberation, followed by a snapping sound.

"Boss is happy to hear that," Nasal Voice continued, sounding like he was looking in her direction. "He thought that blow to the head mighta killed you, and we didn't know how we were gonna get rid of your body."

This conversation was so astounding that Sophie had to suppress an inappropriate urge to laugh. "Where am I?" she feebly inquired, hearing the rasp in her voice. How long had she been unconscious?

"Somewhere safe," the man responded, stepping closer.

Sophie shivered and suddenly noticed the damp coolness of her surroundings.

"You cold?" the voice asked. "You didn't have a jacket on when we took you. I'll be right back." He hesitated, and a hint of amusement then entered his voice. "Now don't go anywhere, you hear?"

She focused on breathing steadily as footsteps faded into the sound of a door sliding closed, and then she shifted her thoughts to making sense of her predicament. Why had they taken her? What was happening to Grant? Had they found the recording device—had they figured out his plan? Oh, God…had they hurt him? She felt her eyes well up with tears.

Too quickly she heard the heavy footfalls return. As a soft material descended over her shoulders, she sensed the man pause in his efforts to blanket her body.

"Don't cry," he pleaded. "You'll be okay—we're just holding you for a while."

She felt a rough thumb skate across her cheek, wiping away the tears. However, more tears were forthcoming.

"Stop crying," he ordered.

"Sorry." Her voice was shaky and her throat too dry to swallow. "I, um, I'm scared."

His tone was softer. "You're perfectly safe here."

It dawned on her that it might be a good sign she was blindfolded—if she hadn't see his face, maybe he'd let her live. Taking a deep breath, she asked, "Why are you holding me here?"

"Co-ladder-all," he answered.

Did he mean 'collateral'?

"Boss wants to make sure somebody does a job right. Gotta provide the *proper motivation.*"

For a fleeting moment, Sophie wondered if they were forcing her father to do a job for them, but the "somebody" was more likely Grant. She'd seen them kidnap him too. What were they making him do? Undoubtedly another crime. Sophie said a silent prayer he wouldn't be caught this time. She couldn't bear for her McSailor to return to prison.

Suddenly she felt a cool glass pressing at her bottom lip.

"Drink this," the man commanded, but she shied away.

They're trying to drug me!

"Drink this!" he loudly repeated, corralling her weaving head with a heavy clamp on her neck. He forced her to take down the liquid. "It's just water!" he exclaimed.

She couldn't fight any more and swallowed the unknown fluid pressing at the back of her throat. Sophie noted with relief that it did indeed seem to be water—no poisonous aftertaste—but the struggle had sent tears cascading down her cheeks again. She felt helpless and terrified, and she panted for air after the tussle. *Grant,* she silently cried, her body shaking despite the blanket slung across her shoulders. *Please stay alive. Please save me.*

❧

It didn't look like he'd be able to save her this time.

Grant's mind kept flashing back to Kirsten's apartment, where he'd crept inside to find Carlo aiming a gun at Sophie. Miraculously he'd kept her safe then, but Mario and Tank weren't going to let him go anytime soon. His body seized up in terror as he thought about what could be happening to his Bonnie.

Grant glanced over at his captors to find them casually stretched out on crates, using the warehouse floor as their poker table.

At least they'd removed the damn blindfold after forcing him to hug a water pipe and securing his wrists with a new plastic tie. When his back throbbed from hunching over in his seated position, he could get to his feet and slowly glide his hands up the pipe to stand for a time. Then when his legs ached from standing, he'd slide back to the floor. He'd alternated between these two positions throughout the night, somehow managing to catch a few restless minutes of sleep in between. His long legs, straddling the pipe, now stretched out on the cold concrete floor.

He only hoped Sophie was faring better wherever they were holding her.

Tonight was the drop, and Grant couldn't wait to get out of here. Not only was he terribly uncomfortable, there was something ominous about the warehouse that he couldn't identify—an eerie unease that chilled him. He wished he could access the photo of Sophie, but he had no way to reach into his pocket.

The poker game must have ended, and it was obvious who the winner was. Flashing a sated grin, Tank stood up and stretched his arms over his head, growling as he yawned. "I'm gonna take a piss."

"Thanks for sharing," Mario irritably replied, watching his partner limp to a makeshift bathroom in the opposite corner of the warehouse.

Twenty feet away, Grant coolly observed the man called "Meat." Mario gathered the cards, scratched himself a few times, and glanced at his watch. "Shouldn't be too much longer now," he muttered.

"We, uh, we going somewhere far from here?" Grant questioned, trying to sound casual.

"Nah. We take you to Angelo first, then we make the drop. It's all close by." As soon as he finished speaking, his portly face reddened. He seemed to realize he'd said too much.

Trying to capitalize on his alone time with the less ruthless, more dimwitted bodyguard, Grant continued, "What's it like working for my family?"

This seemed like safer territory to Mario. "Eh, it's a job. Working for Angelo's not too bad."

"But Angelo's dying of lung cancer."

"Yeah," Mario confirmed, looking genuinely sad. "He told us we're getting a new boss soon, though. I wonder who he'll bring in."

So they didn't know about his father's plan. The bodyguards were in for quite a surprise once Enzo took the reins.

"Gotta be better than Carlo," Mario added.

"You didn't like Carlo?"

Mario looked embarrassed. "Well, God rest his soul, he, ah—"

"I told you not to talk to Madsen!" Tank yelled, returning quickly and pointing an accusatory finger in Grant's direction, glaring at his partner. "*He's* the one who killed Carlo in the first place!"

Grant locked eyes with Tank. "I didn't want to do it, I swear. He forced my hand—he...he shot Sophie."

"That's right, and she'll get shot again if you don't cooperate."

"I know that," Grant sullenly replied. "I won't do anything to jeopardize her safety. You don't have to keep me tied up. I'm not going anywhere."

"Yeah, right," Tank scoffed. "You're staying put, Madsen."

Mario bit his lip. "How did, um, how did Carlo die? I mean, did he take it like a man?"

Tank started to reprimand his partner again but stopped short. He wanted to hear Grant's response as well.

With a far-off gaze, Grant answered, "I suppose so. His last words were that Logan...that Logan died trying to protect me." Grant's eyes pierced into the bodyguards. "Was Carlo telling the truth? Did Logan die trying to protect me?"

Mario's jowls quivered like a cornered hamster, but Tank maintained his composure, saying nothing.

Grant continued prodding. "How did Logan die? Did *he* take it like a man?"

Tank exploded, "How the fuck should we know? We weren't there when Logan died!"

"Yes, you were." Playing this exchange carefully, Grant lied. "Carlo confessed it as he was dying. He told me you held Logan down while he killed him."

Mario turned white. "B-B-But we didn't know Carlo was going to *stab* him!"

Tank swallowed hard, and it was the first time Grant had seen him look shaken. "Does Enzo know about this?"

"Do you think you'd still be alive if Enzo knew?"

"Good point," Tank conceded. "You—you planning on telling him?"

Ben's devastated eyes flashed in Grant's mind. Pushing that memory aside for now, he answered grimly, "Logan already got his justice when Carlo died. I know Carlo forced you two to be there—you were only doing your jobs. You had no idea what Carlo was going to do."

Mario's big head bobbed up and down enthusiastically. "Exactly! Logan was a cool guy. I'd never try to kill him."

Sadly, Grant said, "Logan got what was coming to him."

He stole a glance at Tank, who still appeared unconvinced that the son of Enzo Barberi would let the past slide. Grant added, "Besides, I hate my father, so I'm not going to tell him anything. I never want to see him again."

"You'd better not speak that way about him," Tank warned.

"What's he going to do?" Grant challenged bitterly. "He's already taken everything from me."

"Not everything," Tank amended, towering over his seated detainee. "You still got your girlfriend, if you play this right."

Kneeling down by Grant, Tank whipped out a knife out of his boot, slowly unsheathing it. Grant studied the dull gleam of daylight reflected on the blade. Was Tank going to murder him now, just like he'd killed his brother? Was the FBI right outside, listening in? Could they save him in time if he was stabbed?

Hesitating, Tank glared at Grant, whose shoulders stiffened.

The bodyguard clutched the knife with one hand and ran the other through his short brown hair, considering what to do. "If I cut you free, you gonna do what we tell you?"

Grant exhaled. "You have Sophie. I'm not going to do anything stupid as long as she's in danger."

Evidently satisfied with his response, Tank quickly sliced his blade through the plastic tie.

Reveling in his freedom, Grant immediately began stretching his sore shoulders. He tentatively asked, "Is it okay if I use the head?"

Tank looked pensive as he replaced the knife. "Fine. Meat, go with him."

Mario waited for Grant to rise to standing and followed him to the bathroom. It felt good to use his legs, and Grant set a swift pace until something on the floor brought him to a halt. There on the concrete was a rust-colored stain, splotchy and smeared. Grant stared at the bloodstain in horror.

When Mario noticed where Grant's gaze had landed, he drew in a sharp breath. "You don't wanna see that. C'mon." He latched on to Grant's arms and shoved him forward.

"Logan was here," Grant mumbled, feeling a sickening dread sweep over him — a chilling sensation that made him want to vomit.

Mario said nothing as he pushed him, which confirmed Grant's suspicions. His mind whirling, he barely remembered making it to the bathroom and shutting the door, but now found himself enclosed in the small, dark space. Feeling his chest spasm with hyperventilated breaths, Grant fought for control, gripping the counter of a grimy sink.

"We've got their confessions," he whispered urgently, hoping his shaky voice could be deciphered by the ears listening to the recording device. "If anything happens to me, bring Tank and Mario to justice. Make them pay for killing my brother." He closed his eyes, feeling his nose burn as he fought back tears. "And I hope you've found Sophie by now." Swallowing hard, he begged, "You have to find her."

"You must be getting bored," Sophie called out into the darkness. "How long have we been here?"

Nasal Voice grunted and was quiet a few moments before offering, "Only a day or so."

A whole day? Her father must be insane with worry by now, and she knew Grant would be even more panicked — if he was still alive. *Concentrate,* she told herself. *How can I win this guy over?*

"Thank you for making sure I'm safe here."

There was silence. Eventually he asked, "Do you need some more water?"

"No, thank you."

"You sure? I can just run upstairs and get some."

Upstairs? Are we in some sort of basement?

"No, I'm fine. You're very kind to ask though."

"You're sure pretty," he offered. "No wonder Logan gave you all that money."

She licked her dry lips, trying to comprehend his comment. "He didn't give me the money. Logan stashed it in my office, and I'm sure he intended to retrieve it when he needed it. But then I found it, and I kind of freaked out. Then the police got involved."

He sounded wounded. "You gave the cops our money?"

"They took it," she corrected. "Right after they arrested me."

"You got popped?"

"Yes. I spent a year in prison, and I'm still on parole." Forcing a smile, she added, "So please let me go by next Wednesday 'cause I have to meet with my PO that day."

The man chuckled. "You'll be outta here for sure by then, sweetie."

"That's a relief."

"Why'd you get popped? Just for having our cash?"

Sophie gave a rueful smile. "Logan hid guns in my office too."

The man whistled between his teeth. "Carlo never told me that."

"I'm sure he didn't." She couldn't stop the anger seeping into her voice.

"You mad at Carlo? What'd he ever do to you?"

"He shot me!"

There was a stunned silence. Slowly he said, "I didn't know that either. They never tell the bodyguards nothing."

"Carlo shot me, and then Grant wrestled the gun away from him."

"Huh. And this whole time I was thinking that was a pure revenge kill—you know, Grant getting back at Carlo for offing his brother. But he did it to save you?"

"Yes."

She heard a faint chuckle. "No wonder Carlo used to call him Saint Grant."

The ring of a cell phone filled the air, and Sophie listened intently to one side of the conversation. "Yeah… Shit, now?… But… I thought you said it was soundproof… Yes, boss, right away."

Sophie heard a resigned sigh followed by the sound of his heavy footsteps approaching her. The hairs on the back of her neck bristled, and her heart rate soared. Was he going to kill her now?

"You look thirsty," he said ominously.

"No, please—" She struggled, feeling the rim of the glass forced to her lips again.

"Drink this!" he barked, spilling some of the liquid down her chin as she resisted.

Most of the drink went into her mouth, though. It was a sickeningly sweet orange juice, gagging her as it slid down her throat. The bitter aftertaste made her feel nauseated and light-headed, and she struggled to keep her head upright, feeling the walls close in on her, darkness fading to black.

He watched her body slump forward on the chair and couldn't resist placing his large hand on the crown of her head, petting her mussed blond hair fondly.

"Sorry 'bout that," he whispered. "But we got unexpected company raiding the compound, and nobody can know you're down here." He sighed. "You sure are pretty."

It was a good thing they weren't playing for money or Grant would've owed them a fortune by now. Not only did he lack experience playing poker, but his mind was far too preoccupied to focus on cards. A game of life-or-death was about to play out.

Tank shifted his body on the crate, wincing as he put pressure on his knee.

"Sorry about your knee," Grant offered.

Glaring at him, Tank replied, "Your brother kicked me in the same fucking knee as you did, asshole."

Mario smirked, and they resumed playing. Tank's phone rang, and he reached into his pocket. He answered, but listened to the caller for a moment before speaking.

"What put us behind schedule?" Tank frowned. "No shit… They gone now?" His response showed his agitation. "We can't go there! Are you fucking kidding me?… Of course I know about Ange… But surely Enzo didn't know this would happen… Fuck… Make sure you get me a good driver is all I have to say." He closed the phone.

Glancing at Mario and then glaring at Grant, Tank announced, "It's time."

25. Confiscate

An edge of desperation permeated the Gold Coast residence.

"Every room — the police searched every room, Jerry?" Will asked.

"Yes!" he snapped, collapsing into one of the luxuriant chairs surrounding Will Taylor's dining room table.

Marilyn let out a guilty sigh. If she hadn't suggested they turn off the audio in the first place, they'd never have allowed the Barberi family to kidnap Grant and Sophie right out from under their noses.

In a gentler tone, Jerry continued, "I've already told you, Mr. Taylor. The officers investigated every inch of that compound. They're not going to hold Sophie in such an obvious place anyway."

Standing beside the table, Will gripped the back of another chair and clenched his jaw. The ebullient hope he'd experienced prior to the raid had been replaced by a sick dread since discovering his daughter was missing.

FBI Agent Bounter watched the father's pained expression, and then he looked across the table at Jerry, who appeared equally frustrated. He then resumed listening to the happenings at the warehouse as transmitted through the device Grant was wearing.

The state police detective, John Vidri, was on his cell phone in the kitchen.

"And they bought your cover story for searching there?" Joe asked from the corner of the room where he leaned against the hutch.

Jerry looked up. "Yeah. The detective explained that Sophie wasn't there for my home visit, forcing me to put out an APB on her, and told them a cop thought he saw someone matching her description on the grounds of the Barberi house."

"I hope they swallowed it," Joe replied. "Did Angelo seem like he knew *anything* about Grant being wired?"

Jerry grimaced. "John didn't think so, but Angelo Barberi wasn't exactly up to saying much. He was in bed the whole time they were there, sounding like each breath he took could be his last. Apparently he doesn't look so good."

Joe shot a glance at Ben, who appeared to be the only one in the room slightly saddened by the news of the don's impending demise. Joe had wanted to keep eyes on Ben at all times while this situation was sorted out, but he was beginning to question the wisdom of having the boy in such immediate proximity to the action. Ben had been horrified to hear Grant and Sophie were kidnapped, and he seemed close to tears upon learning the raid of the Barberi compound had failed to locate Sophie.

But thanks to the transmitter, at least they knew Grant was still alive.

"Can they search there again?" Will begged. "Maybe she's hidden somewhere in the compound. It's a big place, right?"

Marilyn bit her lip. "I doubt they could get another warrant. No judge wants to take on the Barberi family twice."

Suddenly Ben bolted upright out of his chair. "The CC!"

The five adults stared at the teenager, and Joe asked, "The CC?"

"Carlo's Crypt," Ben responded quickly. "It's a secret room in the basement Carlo showed me—he said that's where they interrogated drug dealers who were trying to skim off the top." He turned to Marilyn and Jerry. "Did they search there?"

Marilyn's cheeks flushed with excitement. "I don't think they found anything like that, Jer?"

Shaking his head, Jerry also appeared keyed up.

"Can they get back in there, Mar?"

Her green eyes took on a fierce glint. "They have to try. Ben, let's get the detective so you can tell him everything you know about this room."

"They're on the move!" Lucas cut in, lunging for the audio console to turn on the speakers. John rushed in from the other room.

Everyone froze, listening intently to Grant's unsteady voice. "*You don't have to put me in the trunk. I told you I won't try to escape.*"

"*Get your ass in there now, Madsen,*" Tank's voice, slightly fainter in volume, transmitted.

"*It's unnecessary,*" Grant countered.

They heard a gasp, and Lucas tightened his lips. "The bodyguard probably just pulled a gun on him," he said.

There was a rustling sound on the audio, followed by panting breaths. Tank supplied a grim warning: "*You try anything cute, we hurt Sophie.*"

The rapid breathing continued.

"*Have a nice ride!*" Tank's and Mario's chuckles were cut off by the harsh slam of the trunk.

Now on a cell phone, Lucas instructed his men at the warehouse stakeout to keep a healthy distance when tailing the Mafia car. John also resumed his phone conversation.

With each of Grant's panicked breaths coming over the airwaves, Joe's expression became icier and more incensed. He wanted to rip Enzo's fucking heart out for involving Grant in his little games—as if he hadn't hurt his sons enough when he'd lived *outside* the prison walls.

Finally Grant's breathing began to slow, though his voice trembled as he whispered into the microphone. "*They're—they're taking me somewhere. I think we're getting the briefcase from Angelo first.*"

There were a few moments of silence before Grant resumed. "*I don't know why they put me in the trunk… Maybe they don't want me to see where they're keeping Angelo.*"

It sounded like he was forcing himself to calm down, gulping big breaths. "*The only thing that's keeping me going is the hope Sophie is safe. I know you've found her by now.*"

Grant's faithful plea sliced into all of them. Will swiftly left the room, and Joe worriedly watched him go. After a beat, he followed him to the kitchen.

Marilyn exchanged a culpable glance with Jerry before resting her eyes on the sixteen year old biting his nails next to her. "We're going to find her," she promised.

Attempting to focus on the hum of the tires and ambient city noise—horns honking, rap songs blaring, pedestrians shouting—Grant compelled himself to relax in the darkened interior of the trunk. With only the hellish red glow of the brake lights as company, he considered the irony of his abduction providing him with plentiful practice using the grounding skills Dr. Hayes had taught him.

The night was turning cold, and he could not stop shivering. As the city sounds faded, Grant wondered if they'd reached the sedate mansions of the Gold Coast. He could faintly make out the bodyguards' conversation from the backseat.

"This is horseshit," Tank railed. "We gotta go to the compound when we're certain the cops got their eagle eye on it? They're gonna tail us for sure."

"It's what Enzo wants," Mario suggested. "We gotta go to Ange, and Ange is too sick to relocate."

"It's still horseshit," Tank muttered.

"Ah, Salvatore will lose 'em for sure. Won'tcha, Tory?"

Grant couldn't hear the driver's answer, but it made both bodyguards laugh.

"Look alive, gentlemen," Tank warned as the car slowed and made a turn.

"I don't see them," Mario whined.

"There — that grey sedan at ten o'clock. Fucking unmarked. Fucking cops."

After Tank's identification of the stakeout vehicle, all was quiet. Then the car pulled to a stop. Grant heard the squeal of a garage door closing and suddenly he was blinded by light. Blinking furiously, he squinted up at the behemoth figure of Mario, who reached in and pulled him out by the plastic tie on his wrists, cutting him even deeper.

When Grant was standing and could open his eyes without pain, he looked down and was relieved to see that the wetness on his hands was only blood from his wrists. This would not be the time for another kind of wetness.

"Let's go. We're on a schedule," Tank ordered, shoving Grant forward.

As the bodyguards led him through a maze of hallways, Grant noticed that the house had been redecorated since his last real visit — over twenty years ago — yet it still managed to convey an aging, unkempt milieu. Tank shoved him into a murky bedroom, the only source of illumination a copper bedside lamp that cast an eerie glow over his uncle's pallid complexion. Angelo's head lolled back on the pillows. A stale, fetid odor pervaded the room.

He appeared to have shrunk since Grant last saw him on the docks of the Chicago River. The oxygen tubing ascending into each nostril didn't seem to assist his labored wheezing, and his intense black eyes were dulled and desperate. Grant looked slightly aghast at what his powerful uncle had become.

Tank dragged a chair over to the bed and roughly forced Grant onto the pale-yellow cushion. He nodded respectfully at Angelo and backed away, promising, "We'll be right outside."

"Free…his wrists," Angelo demanded weakly.

Tank paused before approaching Grant. "Of course, Godfather." The knife came out once again, and once again the plastic tie snapped off, providing a glorious range of movement for the captive.

Grant sat quietly once Tank and Mario had departed, entranced by his uncle's arduous respiratory rhythm. He had a fleeting thought of grabbing a pillow and attempting to end the Barberi family regime. But his father would still be alive, and he was the one Grant *really* wanted to end. Realizing he was contemplating murder, Grant felt flooded by remorse.

Finally Angelo spoke. "Your father loves you, Grant."

He couldn't have said anything more surprising, and Grant recoiled.

"He does," Angelo insisted. "He trusted…you…with this important… errand. That shows his love."

Grant had no idea how to respond to the preposterous statement.

"I'm dying." Angelo stated the obvious. "And when I'm…gone… your father will need you more than ever."

Grant couldn't stop the expression of disgust creeping onto his face.

"Why do you reject our family?" Angelo asked bluntly.

Grant hesitated before answering. "Because you hurt innocent people."

A gleam of light shone in Angelo's black eyes. "Like Sophie Taylor, hmm?"

Grant clenched his fists and averted his gaze, feeling murderous urges return. *You'll get your chance to take them down,* he assured himself.

"So you admit to abducting Sophie?" he asked.

Angelo smiled. "She'll be fine, as long as you—" he tried to cough and sounded like he was strangling for several seconds, eventually getting out "—continue cooperating."

Grant was alarmed when Angelo slumped back against the pillows. But after closing his eyes for a few moments, appearing to marshal his energy, he instructed, "Reach under my bed."

Grant got down on his knees and fumbled under the dust ruffle until his hands bumped into something solid. Carefully he extracted a heavy, locked briefcase and returned to his seat, setting it next to his chair.

"Take that to the car with Mario… Don't let go of it… Tell Tank to come back…in here."

When Grant rose, Angelo wheezed, "Wait. Give me…one dying wish, nephew."

He looked down on the decrepit man with pity. "What's that, uncle?"

"Make peace with your father."

Grant attempted a poker face. Feeling the cool leather handle of the briefcase and the warm anticipation of destroying his father, he simply replied, "Yes, Uncle Angelo."

He confidently exited the room and succumbed to Mario marching him back to the car, not even complaining when he was forced back into the trunk, clutching the briefcase.

Back in Angelo's room, Tank listened to his boss. "He's not ready to join…the family just yet," Angelo said. His nephew was a horrible liar. "He needs more motivation."

Tank nodded.

"After the drop," Angelo wheezed, "secure him in the crypt."

"What about the girl?"

"Put her in long-term storage."

Tank grinned. "*She's* the motivation, huh?"

"Grant's ours as long as…she is too."

"And when we let him out, he ain't going to the cops because he's on parole?"

Angelo feebly nodded. "Go…they're waiting for you."

"At the honeycomb, right? Apartment 1510?"

Angelo erupted in a coughing fit, his black eyes glazing over and his ashen complexion turning ruddy from the effort. All he could manage was a slight nod.

Tank was already at the door. "Take care, Ange."

He bowed his head respectfully, but as he turned to leave, his fake sympathy morphed to a delighted grin. *Maybe you'll die while I'm gone,* he thought as he headed toward the garage. *And whoops—maybe Maasen will die too before he makes it to the crypt. That'd be such a pity.*

 ❦

"Shit," Jerry muttered, closing his phone with one hand while the other tightened its grip on the steering wheel.

"What is it?" Joe asked from the passenger seat.

"What happened?" Ben's younger voice piped up from the back.

Jerry eased the car to a stop at the red light and sighed. "They lost them."

"The FBI? They lost Grant?" Joe's normally calm voice rose to a panic.

"Yeah, they lost the tail about five minutes after leaving the compound. Marilyn sounded devastated."

Ben slumped back in his seat.

Joe was incensed. "How did that happen, damn it?"

Jerry glanced at Joe, and then proceeded through the green light. "They're not sure—they were by the river, and suddenly the trail went cold. The car vanished."

"Does Grant know we lost him?"

"Yeah. He could hear the whoops and hollers of the bodyguards."

Ben leaned forward as Jerry parked the car on a tree-lined side street near the Barberi compound. "That means we gotta get Sophie out of there now!"

Turning to look at his great nephew, Joe warned, "No! It's too dangerous."

"C'mon, Gruncle! We gotta save her. I know the code!"

"There's no way in hell I'm letting you in there with those killers."

Joe turned back to Jerry, who'd been noticeably quiet during the argument. "We wait for them to get a new warrant, right?"

Jerry cleared his throat. "Marilyn doesn't think they'll get it, since they found no trace of Sophie the first time. And the team's all spread out now, looking for Grant. There's no manpower left to go in again."

"Sophie could be dying!" Ben wailed. "We gotta get her."

Joe ran one hand through his graying cropped hair, rubbing his head furiously. After a long sigh, he conceded, "Okay. We go in."

"All *right!*" Ben scooted toward the car door.

"Hold it!" Joe commanded. "*I'm* going in. *You're* staying in the car."

"What?" Ben shrieked.

"Hang on," Jerry held up his hand. "If you're going in, I'm going in. Ben will stay in the car by himself."

Joe shook his head. "Officer Stone, you don't need to do this. This isn't your battle."

"The hell it's not. If one of my parolees is in there, I'm not sitting out here twiddling my thumbs."

"I'm not either!" Ben hollered. "I'm the one who knows how to get to the crypt!"

"Then you're going to tell us everything," Joe countered. "There's no way you're going in there."

"This is bullshit!"

Joe looked nonplussed. "This isn't some cops-and-robbers TV show, Ben. The bodyguards have guns. And if they catch us in there, they're going to know right away this isn't a friendly family visit."

"But I can convince them I'm just jackin' my style, you know, all epic chill."

Jerry and Joe exchanged a puzzled glance.

"Jerry, don't let him do this to me," Ben pleaded.

"That's Officer Stone to you, punk. Shut your trap and listen to the commander or I'll slap the cuffs back on you."

Jerry's threat didn't seem to have much of an effect on Ben. Defiantly lacing his arms in front of him, Ben challenged, "You're never going to find the crypt without me."

"You're right. We won't as long as you keep stalling. Now start talking."

When Ben hesitated, the commander exploded. "Start talking *now*, mister, or you'll be doing push-ups all night long!"

Jerry found himself sitting up straighter at the booming, authoritative voice, and the whites of Ben's widened eyes became visible. Nervously he began spilling information.

After listening to a few minutes of detailed instructions from the rebuked sixteen-year-old, Joe reached out to rest a hand on his shoulder.

"Thanks, Ben. I know you want to get in there and save Sophie, but Grant specifically asked me to keep you safe. It'd destroy your uncle if anything happened to you."

Ben looked down, quiet.

"Stay here in the car, okay?"

He reluctantly nodded.

Jerry and Joe slunk out of the vehicle and stealthily made their way to the Barberi compound. Both wore faces of stone, belying their pounding hearts.

"I don't suppose parole officers carry guns?" Joe whispered as they neared the gate.

"Some do—not me, though. I don't suppose Naval officers do either?"

"No, sir. It's a good thing we're equally qualified then."

Jerry gave a smirk as he reached up to punch in the security code Ben provided. "Yeah…equally qualified to get shot."

As the gate creaked open, he looked at his partner in crime. "I should've handcuffed that kid to the car."

The elation he'd previously overheard had faded, and now the passengers in the car grew silent. Grant shifted in the darkness of the trunk and fought the urge to kick out a taillight and signal for help. He didn't feel so brave now that he knew the good guys were no longer with him.

Feeling the hard briefcase by his knee, he tried to listen intently to pick up any clues about where they were heading. His entire plan would be shot to hell if the FBI missed out on busting the illegal money exchange. He heard indistinguishable city sounds for several minutes, and then the hum of the road changed pitch, becoming higher, almost like the tires were singing. It sounded like they were crossing over metal grating…possibly a bridge…a drawbridge?

Grant's eyes darted around the blackness—were they crossing the Chicago River? The same river he'd traversed all summer long in Roger's ship?

C'mon, think! Chicago had the most moving bridges of any city in the world—how many moving bridges were there? He started mentally checking them off from west to east: Franklin, Wells, LaSalle, Clark, Dearborn… He felt the car slow and turn left, and a hush descended around them as honks and road noises were no longer detectable. Were they in a parking garage? His mind frantically searched for buildings near the river, trying to recall each architectural wonder he'd described to ship passengers.

Remembering he was still wired, Grant urgently whispered, "We just crossed a bridge, uh, and now w-we're in a parking garage, I think. It could be…Trump Tower, maybe?"

His weight shifted round and round before he realized the car must be ascending some sort of spiral parking ramp. A round building? What round structures were on the riverbank?

Grant sucked in a huge breath and excitedly whispered "Marina City!" He hoped he didn't say it too loudly. "I think we're in Marina City," he continued more somberly, visions of the funky, honeycomb towers filling his mind.

Foreigners loved the towers, a distinctive Chicago landmark. Would Serbian-born gubernatorial candidate Darko Jovanovich happen to have a residence at Marina City?

The illumination of red lights combined with the jerk of the brake, and Grant heard a male voice with some sort of Latino accent outside the car: "Welcome to the East Tower. We'll park your car for you."

"We're in the East Tower," Grant informed whoever was listening.

"We don't want valet," the Mafia driver gruffly replied, and the car inched forward.

"Sir!" the valet called out. "You must valet here. We don't want your car falling into the river now, do we?"

"Fuck you, Diego" came the snarling reply. "Move your asscheek-ohs or they're gonna have tread marks all over them."

Apparently the valet got out of the way because the car resumed its forward motion. Grant figured it might be hard to explain his presence to the valet. After parking, someone quickly popped the trunk to release him.

As he climbed out, Grant asked, "Are we in Marina City?"

Tank delivered a swift uppercut to the abdomen, nearly doubling him over, but Grant maintained his hold on the briefcase.

"No questions," Tank threatened.

Grant hid his smile. He had his answer.

Joe found it hard to believe they'd not been confronted by bodyguards yet. Maybe Grant was right about the Barberi family faltering. The commander's throat was dry, and each corner they crept past accelerated his heartbeat, but Jerry detected none of this apprehension. *Fake it till you make it,* Joe's superiors had always taught him, and that philosophy had gotten him through more than one treacherous situation during Vietnam.

He moved forward confidently yet quietly as he mentally rehearsed the directions Ben had provided.

He came upon the basement door and winced as it creaked open. Jerry defensively scanned around them, but all was silent.

"Let's do this," Joe whispered, taking the lead down the darkened, carpeted staircase.

They turned to the right and headed toward the wine cellar, carefully entering the cool, dark stacks. Expensive bottles of Chianti and cabernet stared back at them. They counted ten paces along the left interior wall, which left them standing before two stacked wine casks. The men worked together to slide the top cask to the right, heaving the heavy container, which made a grating noise against the lower cask.

Standing stock-still, ever-vigilant, both waited several moments before proceeding, feeling for a small keypad on the base of the cask. "You ready?" Joe asked, and Jerry nodded, stepping to the right and assuming a centered fighting stance. Turning back to the keypad, Joe told himself, "Carlo's birth date," and punched in 0-5-1-5-7-6.

There was a slight rumbling as the wall slid open, and brightness poured into the cavernous wine cellar. Jerry rushed forward into the now-accessible room with Joe hot on his tail, and they screeched to a halt upon seeing a large man resting his pock-marked face on blindfolded Sophie's shoulder as both slumped over in side-by-side chairs.

Sensing movement, the bodyguard lifted his head and appeared dumbfounded to find two men near the entrance of the soundproofed room. His beady eyes darted to a side table, and Jerry and Joe followed his gaze to a Glock 23 gleaming in the fluorescent lighting.

With a roar, the bodyguard leaped up and lunged for the gun at the exact moment Jerry careened toward the table. Unfortunately for the larger man, Jerry reached his destination first and snapped up to standing, pointing the weapon at the bodyguard.

"Stop right there!" Jerry ordered. "Police! Don't you fucking move."

Alarmed that Sophie hadn't stirred at all, Joe narrowed his blue eyes at the big man. The bodyguard's attention was so riveted to the muzzle of his own gun that he failed to detect a rush of movement to his left. Joe's body slammed into his, sending them both sprawling to the floor.

The attack stole all air from the bodyguard's lungs, and he was defenseless as Joe's steel fist smashed into his nose, immediately creating a bloody mess. He groaned as relentless punches peppered his face and chest.

Seeing scarlet, Joe felt like he was outside his body, and he observed himself whaling on a man who weakly raised his arms to deflect the repeated blows. Years of repressed rage against the Barberi family flowed from Joe's fists, and the only thing that stopped him was Jerry hollering "Commander!" while hauling him off of the bodyguard.

Joe somehow found himself back on his feet, panting from exertion, his hands covered in blood. Jerry had a firm grasp on his arm and they gazed down at the untidy, unmoving heap lying at their feet.

"Let's get Sophie out of here," Jerry urged, and Joe nodded, coming out of his haze and rushing over to take her pulse.

"She's just unconscious." He breathed out in relief after locating her faint but steady heartbeat.

"Taylor!" Jerry hissed in her ear while loosening her bindings, receiving only a woozy groan in return.

Once she was free, Joe bent down and hooked her arm around his neck, while Jerry pocketed the handgun and did the same with her other arm. They quickly carried her out of the room, the tips of her high-heeled boots dragging on the carpeted floor. Stepping into the wine cellar, Jerry held onto Sophie's slumping body while Joe swiftly entered the code and watched the door slide shut, becoming hidden in the wall once again.

"Give me the gun," Joe demanded, and Jerry handed him the weapon.

The commander crashed the butt of the Glock into the keypad console with a loud crack, which had both men scanning the basement for any movement. Joe's third try was the charm, leaving the keypad smashed and disabled — he hoped.

By the time Joe had risen again, Jerry had scooped Sophie into his arms, her head flopping limply.

"You sure you can carry her?" Joe asked.

"You take point with the gun, and I'll be right behind you," Jerry promised, squeezing her protectively.

They crept up the stairs, and Joe could hear Jerry grunting softly with exertion behind him. Once they reached the main floor, Joe tightened his hold on the weapon and peered out into the foyer, miraculously failing to detect any bodyguards. They kept moving speedily and soundlessly, and both felt sheer elation when they emerged into the compound courtyard. It had been almost too easy. If Enzo did indeed make it out of prison, he certainly wouldn't be pleased to learn how weak his empire had become.

Joe punched in the pass code, and the exterior gate swung open. Jerry stepped in front of the metal bars to hold the door open with his back.

"Hold on," Joe whispered, using his shirttails to grasp the gun with one hand and wipe away the fingerprints with the other. Tossing the gun into the bushes inside the gate, he glanced at Jerry's strained face and leaned forward to scoop up Sophie. "Let me take her. Go."

Ben had popped out of the vehicle and hopped all around Joe as he approached the car, almost impeding his progress. "Ohmigod!" he gasped. "You got her! Is she okay? Why are her eyes closed?"

Joe ignored the rapid-fire questions until he'd maneuvered Sophie into the backseat and scooted in next to her.

"Front seat!" Jerry shouted at Ben as he scrambled into the driver's seat.

Bewildered, Ben slid into the passenger seat but instantly turned around, his eyes glued to the beautiful woman slouched unnaturally in the back.

"Where's the nearest hospital?" Joe implored.

"I'm on it." Jerry sped away, flinging his cell phone into Ben's grasp and barking, "Call Marilyn! She's in my contacts."

As Ben located the number, a wave of fear swept over Joe. What if Tank and Mario found out Sophie had been freed before Grant completed the drop? His nephew would be a dead man. *Find Grant,* he silently implored the FBI. *Find my boy.*

✑

As Grant jostled along the circular interior hallway, he noticed his hand was throbbing as it gripped the briefcase handle. He'd seen Tank eye the briefcase covetously, and he wondered if he'd try to make a move for the money before it exchanged hands. Grant hoped Tank was too afraid of Enzo to pull such a stunt.

Attempting to figure out a way to notify the task force about their exact location, Grant feigned curiosity at each apartment door they passed. "Fifteen oh-five…fifteen oh-six—"

The muzzle of Tank's gun slammed into his ribs, and he inhaled sharply. Tank leaned in and hissed, "We already know college boy can count. Shut the fuck up."

They arrived at apartment 1510, and Tank knocked softly. Tension rippled through the three men while they waited for an answer. In a quiet, menacing tone, Tank instructed, "They need to think everything's copacetic with the family. Go along or the girl gets it." As if Grant needed a reminder.

A man with jet-black hair and Slavic features opened the door, peering at them suspiciously. "You're late," he said.

Tank shrugged. "Had some trouble losing a tail."

A storm cloud crossed his dark complexion. "You sure you lost them?"

"Of course," Tank scoffed. "You letting us in or what?"

Still appearing mistrustful, the man opened the door wider, stepping aside to allow the tall trio into the apartment. Grant knew every Marina City apartment had a balcony, but in this residence velvet curtains were pulled closed over the wall of sliding glass doors. If they were in the East Tower, he wondered what view hid behind the rich, dark-red curtains — perhaps the river? The Hancock Building?

"…assuring me your father sent you?"

Grant turned to the other dark-haired man in the room, who waited impatiently for a response to his question. Grant nodded. "Yes."

"I can't get a fucking straight answer from you people," the man continued as he stood and stepped toward Grant, invading his personal space. "Do you or don't you work for your father?"

"Yes, I do."

One bushy black eyebrow peaked. "Then why haven't we talked to you before?"

Grant's mouth felt dry. "My father puts me on his most important jobs…the ones requiring the most trust…the ones with people he greatly respects. These guys—" he gestured to the big bodyguards behind him "—handle the more menial tasks."

Watching Tank's face redden with rage, the Serbian bodyguard chuckled. "Indeed. This is quite an important meeting. You have something for us?"

"I do," Grant confirmed, relieved that the hand offering the briefcase was steady. "Please accept this delivery."

The man gave a tight smile and took the briefcase from Grant's grasp. He spoke in a foreign language to another bodyguard, who crossed the room while extracting a folded piece of paper from his suit jacket. Apparently the paper contained a written code, which the man used to unlock the briefcase on one of the end tables. A satisfied sigh filled the room, and the man grinned as he spun the briefcase around, revealing piles of cash inside.

"Beautiful," he murmured. "Your father keeps his word."

"He is a man of his word," Grant forced out.

Suddenly the apartment exploded with chaos and conflict.

"FBI!"

Shouts rang out around him, and abruptly the residence was teeming with men in shiny navy-blue jackets over their bulletproof vests who aimed weapons at Grant and the four bodyguards. Grant watched Tank being stripped of his gun, and it was only a second later that he felt his own body pushed down, his face shoved into the thick carpet.

"Got him!" a voice exclaimed. From his floor-level vantage point, Grant turned his head to see a recognizable man being led out from one of the bedrooms.

"Darko Jovanovich," Agent Bounter crowed, and Grant grinned as Jovanovich tried to quickly back away from the open briefcase.

The agent smiled brightly at the gubernatorial candidate. "Looks like we caught you being naughty, hmm? Perhaps it would've been smarter to let your men handle the money exchange without you."

Jovanovich wisely stayed silent, but he couldn't keep the scowl from his craggy face.

One FBI agent read the politician his rights while others did the same with the men on the ground. Grant felt warm hands gently tug his arms together behind him, carefully snapping cuffs onto his bloody wrists. With all the action around him, he almost missed Bounter's whisper as he knelt by his prone body. "We have Sophie. It's over."

Grant's body shook and relief coursed down his spine. He barely heard the agent's barked orders for taking the criminals into custody. It was over.

26. Conspirators

In the foreground was her bright smile and in the background jubilant White Sox fans on the upper deck of U.S. Cellular Field. Her freshly scrubbed cheeks lent her a warmhearted glow, only partially muted by the shadow of her black baseball cap. Grant sighed, stroking the pad of his thumb over the photo. His restrained wrists and less-than-friendly company had prevented him from looking at the picture in his pocket the entire thirty-two hours his family had detained him. But he'd known she was there the whole time.

All was quiet in the interrogation room. Here he was again: stuck in some law enforcement hole while Sophie was laid up in the hospital, fighting for her life. All because of his family…all because of *him*.

Studying her carefree expression in the photo, Grant silently wished, *I want you to smile like this again someday — a big, genuine smile. I want to make you happy. I love you, Sophie. I'll do everything I can to keep you safe from my family.*

"Uncle Grant!"

He looked up to find an FBI agent letting Ben and Joe into the room, and he popped out of his chair to envelop his nephew in his arms, quickly moving on to do the same with his uncle. At times he'd not been sure he'd ever see them again, and he closed his eyes with relief as he pressed each family member tightly to his chest.

The three blue-eyed men stood staring at each other for a few seconds, flooded by so many questions they had no idea where to start.

Noticing the darkened blood on Grant's hands, Joe frowned. "What'd they do to you?"

"I'm fine." Grant changed the subject. "Detective Fox told me you and Officer Stone rescued Sophie?"

Joe grinned and ruffled Ben's hair. "Only because *this* one made it happen."

"What?" Grant gaped at his nephew. "You helped rescue Sophie?"

Ben blushed. "I could've helped more but *he* didn't let me go in."

Joe suppressed a smile. "Ben knew about a hidden room in the basement of the mansion, off the wine cellar. Carlo had showed it to him."

"That's where they held Sophie?" Grant's voice began to rise. "What'd they do to her? Why's she in the hospital?"

"I think they drugged her," Joe solemnly answered.

Grant grabbed his head in both hands. His nephew tentatively approached him, tapping his elbow. "It's okay, Uncle Grant. She was coming to when we left the ER."

"She's there alone?"

"Her father's with her," Joe assured him. "She's going to be okay."

"I…" Grant dropped his arms and shook his head. "I don't know how to thank you for saving her, sir."

"You just did, Grant. I'm so relieved we found her," said Joe.

"And Ben," Grant continued as their eyes met. "I can't believe what you did—you took something bad and made it good. You used our family's awful secrets to save Sophie's life." He fondly gazed at his nephew. "Do you know how proud you've made me?"

Ben unflinchingly met Grant's gaze. "Yes, sir."

Both Grant and Joe were startled by the teenager's respectful response. Perhaps there was hope for him yet.

Thinking now might be the right time to share the news, Joe told Grant, "There's a reason Jerry and I got into the compound without interference from the bodyguards." He shot a sideways glance at the teenager and cleared his throat. "Apparently the men were upstairs in Angelo's room, trying to revive him. He was coding."

Grant's eyes widened. "Uncle Angelo died?"

"Yes."

Swallowing hard, Grant realized he'd been one of the last people to see Angelo alive. "I'm sorry, Ben," he offered softly as he gathered his nephew into a hug once again.

"'S okay," Ben mumbled softly, and then his voice became fierce. "He let them kill my dad."

Stepping out of the hug, Grant nodded. "Yes, he did." He glanced at Joe. "Did you get their confessions on tape?"

"The FBI is interrogating Tank and Mario as we speak. Apparently you were right—they started with Mario, and he's proving to be very loose-lipped. He's confessing to all sorts of crimes."

Grant gave a wry half-smile. "He's just not ruthless enough to work for my family. He was in the wrong job."

"Just like you were, Mr. Madsen." Agent Bounter swept into the room, followed by a paramedic. "I think your singing days are over."

Confused, Grant stared at the FBI agent as the paramedic reached for his hands to check his injuries. "I'm fine." He shook his shoulders, trying to slough off the pesky EMT. "What do you mean my singing days are over? Am I returning to prison?"

"Hell, no!" Lucas replied, gesturing to a chair. "Grant, would you please sit down so the EMT can attend to your wrists? I'll explain if you take a seat."

"I really don't need medical attention, Agent Bounter."

Joe pointed to the chair. "Grant, park it."

"Yes, sir," he replied with a sigh, and Ben smirked.

As the paramedic opened his bag, Lucas took a seat across from him, leaning in eagerly.

"We've got Jovanovich right where we want him."

Grant couldn't help but wince when the paramedic began flushing his cuts with saline. "Did he confess?"

"No, he lawyer'd up just as I expected, but we'll secure his financial records soon, and then he's toast."

Joe cut in. "Grant's not going to be implicated, is he?"

Lucas shook his head, grinning. "Your nephew's very clever, Commander. We used his idea to blame the sting on Marina City's valet, who supposedly called the police after being threatened by a Mafia driver. The valet 'saw' Tank hold a gun on Grant in the parking garage and followed them up to the fifteenth floor."

"You better get that valet into witness protection," Joe said, shaking his head.

"We're taking care of him. He's here legally and has been sending money to his wife in Costa Rica, hoping she'd join him in the States one day, so he was thrilled when we told him we'd place them both in California."

Shivering at the cold snap that had overtaken Chicago, Ben asked, "California? Can I be in witness protection too?"

Grant smiled. "I'm afraid you're stuck here with me in cold Chicago, kid."

"There's no need for any of you to enter witness protection, actually," Lucas added. "Angelo's dead, and just about every Barberi employee is going to be locked up with their boss in Gurnee soon. Given that Jovanovich's people think the Barberi family screwed up and ruined their plan by letting the feds tail them, Enzo and his ilk will be too busy looking over their shoulders to come after you."

Grant watched a smile erupt on his uncle's face.

Joe sat back in his chair, awed by all that had transpired. "This worked out far better than I ever imagined — even better than Grant's initial plan."

"It's all because you kept your cool, Grant," Lucas told him. "You showed grace under pressure out there in the field. You brought down a corrupt politician — hell, you brought down an entire crime organization."

Grant blushed, looking down.

"Which brings me back to the end of your singing days." When Grant looked up, Lucas resumed. "We'd like you to think about working for the FBI, Grant. We need your skills to go after organized crime."

Stunned, Grant said, "But *I'm* a criminal. I'm still on parole."

The FBI agent nodded. "That *is* a major stumbling block. If the task force's attorneys go to bat for you like they say they will, you'll have a good chance of getting your conviction set aside. When that happens, talk to me. I've got a project just for you, with your insider's perspective on the Mafia and the Navy. And you've obviously proven your mettle by the way you've handled yourself the past few days."

When no response was forthcoming, Lucas stood. "Think about it. I gotta get back to Donnie Darko."

Once the agent left, the paramedic finished bandaging Grant's wrists and provided some advice for tending to the wounds. Grant barely heard any of the instructions — his mind swam with possibilities for the future.

Shrugging at his semi-responsive patient, the EMT packed up and departed as well.

Glancing at his nephew, Grant suddenly remembered something. "You had a swim meet tonight! Are you missing it?"

Ben nodded. "It's okay. Coach was going to make me swim the one-hundred 'fly anyway." His shudder let Grant and Joe know exactly how he felt about that prospect.

Just then a female voice countered, "Hey, don't knock butterfly — it's the best stroke there is."

Grant bolted out of his chair and rushed to engulf Sophie in an overpowering embrace, almost lifting her off her feet and nearly knocking over her father in the process.

"You're okay?" he asked, setting her down and scanning the length of her body to detect any injuries.

Nodding quickly, she replied, "It was just a sedative the guard put in my orange juice." With an ironic grin, she added, "Mom always warned me to make sure nobody put anything in my drink."

Grant's mouth dropped open. She was joking at a time like this?

Will quietly added, "Your mother was a wise woman."

Sophie exchanged a wistful glance with her father and turned her attention to Grant's bandaged wrists. "What happened?" she asked.

"I found out Officer Stone's handcuffs aren't all that bad," he said. "I'll be okay."

She cradled his bandaged wrists in her hands, staring into the depths of his eyes. His hold over her lasted several seconds, until she remembered others were in the room.

Sophie looked up to find Joe and Ben watching her fondly. Without hesitation, she crossed over to them, timidly stepping forward to wrap her arms around Joe. "Thank you," she whispered.

At first surprised by her tender gesture, Joe quickly recovered, drawing her to his chest and smoothing his hands reassuringly across her back.

Next she turned to Ben, smiling warmly. "My dad tells me you're the one who figured out where they took me."

He shuffled his feet, embarrassed. "Yeah…"

She felt tears spring to her eyes, though she continued smiling. "You saved my life, Ben." After pausing for a moment, she told him, her voice quivering, "Your father would've been so proud of you."

Ben's upper lip began to tremble, and he seemed grateful when she folded him into her arms for a tight hug. When she let him go, he bowed his head, sniffling. Their collective tears made Grant's throat tighten, and he clasped Sophie's hand when she returned to his side.

Sensing that the two might want to be alone, Will told Joe and Ben, "I'm very grateful to you both as well. Can I buy you a cup of coffee?"

Ben grimaced, and Will amended, "Coke?"

Ben shook his head. "No thanks."

Standing rooted to his spot, Ben didn't get the hint until Joe roughly guided him toward the door, following Will into the hallway.

"But I'm not thirsty!" Ben protested as he went.

Once they were gone, Grant reached up to tuck a wayward strand of strawberry-blond hair behind Sophie's ear, gazing down at her with wonder and relief.

"So they drugged you?" His voice was laced with guilt.

"I guess the FBI was raiding the compound, and they didn't want me screaming for help. The guard made me drink some juice that tasted awful."

Grant's long fingers continued tenderly stroking her hair. "Were you scared?"

She nodded. "I was so afraid they'd found the wire on you. I was terrified they…that they'd killed you."

"But I'm okay," Grant said quickly. "We're okay."

He slowly leaned forward, nudging her nose with his and resting his soft lips tantalizingly close to hers, breathing her faint floral scent. Her arms had wrapped around him, and his hands caressed her silky hair as they held each other, completely still. Finally they joined their lips in a deep, slow-burning kiss.

"We're okay, Bonnie," he repeated, pressing his lips into hers again and lowering his arms to guide her body closer, flush to his hardness.

Sophie closed her eyes, sensing her body melting into his strong, steady hold. She felt the warmth radiating off his skin and the scratchy stubbles on his chin and upper lip. They'd navigated through stormy seas, threatening to capsize more than once, but McSailor had plotted a magnificent course. He would not steer them astray.

"The man guarding you," Grant hesitatingly asked. "What was he like?"

"Well, I was blindfolded, but he seemed huge. Big and stupid… and creepy."

Grant's face clouded. "He didn't do anything to you, did he?"

"No. They checked me out at the hospital."

Grant exhaled and she added, "I tried to align with him, to make him look at me as a person and not as an object."

"Did he speak to you?"

"He said they wouldn't hurt me, but they had to hold me there to motivate somebody to do a job."

His jaw clenched. "It worked."

"What happened when they took you away?" Sophie asked.

"Well, first they brought me to see my father."

"Oh, no! You had to go back there? You must have been devastated when they screwed up your plan."

"At first I was. But then I remembered I was wired, and I figured out my dad was going to have *me* make the drop with Jovanovich's people, so I decided it might be an even better way to prove what he was up to."

"How'd you figure that out?"

Grant looked distressed. "I guess I know my dad better than I thought I did."

"Remember what Hunter showed you? You're nothing like your father."

Taking a deep breath, Grant nodded. He averted his eyes and seemed distracted.

"Tank and Mario — they held me in a warehouse. It was…the same warehouse where they killed Logan."

"Oh," she said softly, rubbing her hand over his shoulder.

Grant looked down, picking at the bandages on his wrists. "I miss him. I miss my brother."

Sophie halted her rubbing motion, trying to find the right words. "In a weird way, Logan brought us together," she finally said.

Grant raised his eyes to meet hers. "I guess you're right." Her fingers grazed his cheekbone, and he reached up to capture her hand in his. "I'm so grateful to Logan for bringing you into my life."

Her eyes shone with affection, and she leaned in to kiss him once again.

"All right, cons." Jerry breezed into the interrogation room. "Break it up already."

Grant and Sophie looked up to find Jerry and Marilyn just inside the doorway. Jerry's expression was stern as usual, but Marilyn sported a huge grin.

"I'm having a total blast watching them interrogate Barberi goons," she said.

Jerry smirked. "I think she likes the perks of her job just a tad too much."

Her green eyes sparkled. "Grant, your recommendation to lean on Mario was spot on. When the FBI explained that his cooperation would prevent him from serving time in Gurnee, he sang like bird."

"A big, fat, meaty bird," Jerry added.

"Tank won't be so lucky," Marilyn continued. "They got all they needed from Mario, so he wasn't given a deal. Tank's quaking in his boots."

"They're really scared of being inside with my father, huh?" Grant asked.

"I don't think Tank is long for this world," Marilyn said. "Not now that Enzo knows he had a hand in killing his son."

"But Tank doesn't know Enzo knows," Grant said.

Jerry gave a grim look. "He will soon." Changing the subject, he added, "So, I hear they asked you to join the FBI?"

"What?" Sophie stared at Grant, startled.

"Yes, sir. I said I'd think about it."

"You won't be the first con working for the other side," Jerry said.

Sophie absorbed this information, nodding slowly. "You might get along quite well with FBI agents, Grant," she said. "The MMPI personality profiles of criminals and police officers aren't all that different, actually."

Jerry shook his head, disgusted. "Jesus, Taylor, enough with the psychobabble! Now that I might be done with you, I'm praying I don't get another shrink parolee before I retire."

"Excuse me, sir, did you just say Sophie might be done with her parole?"

Jerry narrowed his eyes. "Apparently the state attorney's talking to the prosecutor, exploring ways to get your convictions vacated in exchange for your help. And if that doesn't work, I doubt the governor will have a problem pardoning you both. How you managed to con the legal system, I'll never know."

Sophie grabbed Grant in a gleeful hug.

"We'll be free," he murmured, squeezing her tight.

Jerry coughed uncomfortably. "For now you're still on parole, though. And if this works, you should still stop by and visit me sometime, uh, you know—to make it look legit."

Sophie grinned knowingly, snuggling into the nook of her boyfriend's shoulder. "Oh, yes. We'll definitely visit you, Jerry—to keep up the ruse and everything."

"Does this mean we won't have to go to therapy anymore?" Grant asked hopefully.

Sophie looked up at him warily.

"It wouldn't be mandated any longer if your convictions are set aside," Jerry replied, "but I think you two nut jobs still need it."

Tapping a finger to her chin, Sophie mused, "Maybe you should go to therapy too, Jerry, to work on your excessive irritability."

Grant grinned, and Sophie continued, "Or how about you and Marilyn get some couples counseling? I'm sure she could use some help, dating *you*."

Marilyn giggled and Jerry scowled.

Turning to Grant, Sophie suggested, "We should at least say goodbye to Hunter before we terminate counseling. It's wise to go through that process, reviewing what did and didn't work, what we learned, what's left to work on… You know, to gain some closure."

Jerry shook his head slowly, sending an exasperated look at Grant. "She's killing me." He squeezed Marilyn's shoulder. "Let's go, Mar. My head hurts from listening to all this shrink-speak."

Marilyn beamed at the couple. "I'm so glad you're both okay. We'll be in touch."

As they departed, Jerry tossed over his shoulder: "Come see me Wednesday morning, you two. And don't be late!"

Left alone, Grant drew Sophie nearer. "Don't worry about his teasing—I find it interesting to learn about all the therapy stuff. We'll talk more about whether or not to keep seeing Dr. Hayes, okay?"

She nodded gratefully, and he planted a tender kiss on her lips.

"One thing I know for sure, Sophie…I definitely don't want to terminate with *you*."

He felt her lips curl into a grin as they pressed against his mouth for another kiss.

Freedom awaited them. McSailor and Bonnie would be free!

27. Congratulations

Hunter couldn't stop staring at Grant's bandaged wrists. The three had just sat down in his office, and Grant appeared predictably nervous. Sophie, on the other hand, was brimming with excitement.

"We have so much to tell you, Hunter," she gushed.

"Really?" His wary eyes swept over the couple. "Did something bad happen to Grant?"

Sophie looked puzzled by his cautious tone. "Well, yes. Something bad happened to both of us."

"Both of you?" He swallowed, his mind racing. "Are you hurt too?"

She shrugged. "It was just some sort of sedative overdose. The doctors cleared me pretty quickly at the hospital."

Grant added, "And I'm fine too."

Hunter sternly sat back in his chair, folding his hands in a little tent in front of his chin. "You're both being rather cavalier about this, aren't you?"

Sophie and Grant exchanged bewildered glances. "What do you mean, sir?"

"What do I mean?" Hunter's voice rose. "You attempt suicide, and then you dare to tell me you're *fine?*"

Sophie just looked confused, but Hunter stared straight at her and continued his onslaught. "I don't think *you* overdosing on drugs" —he turned and glared at Grant— "or *you* slicing your wrists open, is not fine at all. You two better start explaining what the hell's going on."

Hunter finished his lecture, and Sophie and Grant suddenly burst out laughing, wildly shaking their heads.

Sophie pointed to Grant's wrists. "You thought his wounds were self-inflicted?" She chortled gaily. "They're not. Hunter, I assure you, Grant's quite mentally stable." Giving her boyfriend a coy sideways glance, she added, "Well, stable for *him,* anyway."

"Watch it, Bonnie," Grant warned.

"And I didn't try to off myself either, I promise," Sophie resumed. "I'm in such a great mood right now, I'd never even *think* about that."

Now it was Hunter's turn to be confused. "I'm sorry for the misunderstanding," he said, his face a little flushed. "It's just that I know how much trauma you've both endured. What was I supposed to think?"

"Yeah," Sophie mused. "I guess when you see wrist bandages on a psychotherapy client, it's easy to assume the worst."

"How *did* you hurt yourself, Grant?"

"It's kind of a long story, sir."

"You heard about Darko Jovanovich withdrawing from the race, right?" Sophie offered.

Hunter scoffed. "How could I miss it? It's been plastered all over the news for days! I can't believe he just dropped out of the race at the last minute—there's absolutely no ethics left in politics these days…" His voice trailed off, and he gave the couple a wide-eyed stare. "Oh my God, you were involved in that?"

Sophie nodded vigorously.

Grant explained. "My father tried to buy his way out of prison by financing Jovanovich's election campaign. He was expecting a pardon in return."

Hunter looked incredulous, scooting to the edge of his seat. "Why didn't the media name your family in this mess?"

"Several reasons," Grant answered. "They couldn't prove Jovanovich knew about the money exchange since he wasn't in the room, but they had enough on him to make him withdraw from the race. And that worked out for us since a public trial would expose our involvement in busting up his plan, putting us and Ben at risk."

"*You* broke up his plan?"

Sophie cut in, "Hunter, this is confidential, right?"

"Of course, Sophie. You know that."

Receiving Sophie's nod of approval to go on, Grant continued, "When we figured out how my dad would get out of prison, Detective

Fox connected us with a corruption task force. The plan was for me to go back inside Gurnee, wired, to get my dad to confess what he was up to."

Hunter looked appalled.

Sophie shrugged guiltily. "Grant was the one who figured it out. I just stood around and did nothing."

"That's not true!" Grant insisted. "Where do you think I got the idea of wearing a wire in the first place?"

She stared at him blankly.

"From *you!*" Grant exclaimed. "I got that idea from your revenge against David Alton. When you and Tanya cooked up that plan for Nora to secretly record her conversation with him, I thought it was brilliant."

A bright smile dawned on her face. "So I did help you?"

He squeezed her hand warmly. "You have no idea how much, Sophie."

Grant turned his attention back to Hunter and slowly explained the rest of the story.

Hunter blinked several times, trying to take it all in. "Wow, you won't get the opportunity to confront your father about this, though, since your involvement is secret."

Sophie took on a fierce look. "I wish Grant could shove it in his face."

Grant bit his lip. "I'd rather keep us safe. Besides, gloating about the victory is something my father would do, and I don't want to be like my father." His jaw clenched. "I'm *not* like him."

"No, you're not," Hunter agreed and looked at Sophie. "I'm so grateful Ben knew where to find you."

"Dr. Hayes?" Grant hesitantly glanced up. "Do you, um, see teenagers? I think Ben needs therapy too—he's been through a lot."

"How old is he again?" Hunter asked.

"Sixteen."

"I could see him. I'm not trained in child therapy, but I've worked with a number of adolescents." He smiled. "They can be quite a challenge."

Grant grinned. "You'll be earning your fee when you see him, that's for sure. Thank you, sir."

Hunter nodded.

"Ben did great, but he wasn't the only one," Sophie added proudly. "The FBI said Grant was *extremely* cool under pressure."

"It's because of you, Dr. Hayes," Grant added.

"Me?"

"Yes, sir." Color rose to his cheeks. "I never could've made it through all that if I hadn't been in therapy. They blindfolded me, they held a gun on me, they threw me in the trunk of the car—"

"They did?" Sophie asked, alarmed.

Grant placed a calming hand on her forearm and continued gazing appreciatively at his psychologist. "But I used the grounding strategies you taught me, and I didn't dissociate once. I want to thank you, Dr. Hayes."

Hunter looked into those expressive blue eyes, earnest and yearning, and noticed his feelings toward Grant were undergoing a change. While nobody could deny that Grant continued to exude pure sexiness, Hunter no longer felt the hot spark of physical attraction. It was a warm fondness that filled Hunter now. Witnessing all the pain Grant carried, experiencing the honor of trying to help him through that pain, observing the fathomless love he shared with Sophie—Hunter found himself feeling more paternal toward Grant than anything else. Though he was only about ten years older than his client, he was immensely proud of Grant and wanted good things for the young man, just as a father would.

"You're very welcome, Grant," Hunter responded with a faint smile. "You've worked quite hard to arrive at this spot."

"And he hasn't told you about his potential new job yet, either," Sophie announced. "He did *so* well that the FBI offered him a position."

"That's great! Special Agent Madsen, huh? I could totally picture you in that job."

"You could?" Grant asked, looking pleased.

"Absolutely. You know, though, it seemed like you were enjoying the singing gig too. You'll probably miss that."

"Actually," Grant said with a smile, "I'm going to keep singing at Mr. Remington's bar. 'Lounge singer' will be a nice cover for my day job." He glanced at Sophie. "We don't want my family knowing I'm on the other side now—it might be dangerous."

Hunter nodded. "That makes sense. So you'll still have women buying you drinks every night then, huh?"

Noticing her psychologist's wink, Sophie countered, "They better not."

"Don't worry, Sophie. If you survived my family, surely you can take on a few middle-aged women," Grant joked. "Though you're going to be busy too," he glanced at Hunter, "since she'll likely be offered an assistant professor position at DePaul."

"Congratulations!" Hunter looked quite pleased. "You two will be busy indeed between working full-time jobs, keeping tabs on Ben, attending your parole appointments—"

"That's the best part of all of this, Hunter," Sophie said. "Because Grant helped the government so much, and after learning more about the circumstances of the crimes we were charged with, they agreed to move to set aside our convictions. They're working on the final details now, so we won't be on parole anymore."

"Wow, that must've killed Officer Stone, huh?"

Sophie laughed. "You know him well. We promised we'd still visit him, though."

"Does that mean you're finished with couples counseling too?"

Having expected this question, Sophie glanced uneasily at Grant. "We're not really sure. You've helped us a lot, Hunter, and we're doing great right now. Do you think we should continue?"

He sat back in his chair, studying them. "Hmm. There's probably more to work on in here, but if you wanted to take a break, that'd be okay with me. But I don't think it's my decision to make. How do *you* feel about it?"

Sophie appeared pensive. "Well, I know counseling's been painful at times for Grant, but I don't think I'm ready to end it. This is my first romantic relationship that's really surviving—thriving even—and I don't want to mess it up. So I guess I'd prefer to keep coming." She looked at her boyfriend. "What do you want to do, Grant?"

"Hold it," Hunter interrupted, marveling at Sophie. "That was beautiful!"

She appeared startled. "What?"

"Do you realize how far you've come, Sophie? What you just said? You weren't engaging in caretaking at all. You weren't enmeshing yourself with Grant's needs. You directly and respectfully shared your feelings, not apologizing for them or making assumptions about what your partner wanted. You were behaving interdependently, bringing the man you love closer by sharing your inner thoughts and feelings, but also making it okay for there to be disagreements, because you know you can communicate effectively to resolve conflict."

"I did?" Sophie looked surprised.

"Well done," Hunter murmured approvingly. "So, Grant, what do you think? How do you feel about continuing couples counseling?"

Instantly Grant's anxiety seemed to amp up, and Hunter curiously watched him take a shaky breath. "Well, um, I've been giving this a lot of thought, Dr. Hayes. And, I…I have a question to ask first that might clear this up."

"Okay." Hunter nodded.

To the bewilderment of both Hunter and Sophie, Grant slid off the sofa and sank to one knee, gazing up nervously at his girlfriend as he clasped both her slender hands in his long, capable fingers.

For a split second she looked alarmed, but then her lips parted in a wondrous, joyful smile, and her eyes began glistening with tears before he got out even one word.

"Sophie," Grant began in a wobbly voice, uncertain whose hands were trembling more. "I've been alone all my life. Joe did everything he could to be there for me, but most of the time he was out at sea, and Logan… Well, I never got close to my brother. I thought that's how life had to be because of my family: lonely. And I'd grown to accept that. But I didn't know how much I was missing. I didn't know how miserable I'd been until I met you."

He smiled warmly, pausing to wipe away a wayward tear on its path down her cheek. "You were such a breath of life, standing there outside our PO's office. God, I was so stunned by you at first, and then when I got to know you—when I really got to know the amazing person you are—well, I loved you even more. You gave me hope, Sophie. I hadn't felt hope in a long time. It's good to feel some hope."

Speechless, Sophie cried silently as he let go of her hands to extract a square velvet box from the pocket of his White Sox jacket.

Gulping, he gently cracked open the box, revealing a sparkling diamond ring nestled in the satiny black cushion. "Mr. Remington gave me an advance on my pay," he shyly explained, and Sophie smiled through her tears.

Seeming to emerge from her state of shock, Sophie finally asked, "You're proposing to me in our psychologist's office?"

For the first time since getting down on one knee, Grant unlocked his gaze from hers and snuck a peek at Hunter, who was watching with rapt amusement.

"There's a first time for everything," Hunter said.

Grant looked up at Sophie, shrugging boyishly. "I considered proposing over a meal of hot dogs and sexy vegetables." He grinned. "But I thought it might be *slightly* more romantic to propose during our therapy session. I figured it'd be a unique story to tell our kids."

She gasped, drawing her hand to cover her mouth. "Yes," she softly told him, yet he remained still, poised, waiting. "Yes!" she cried more firmly. "Yes, I'll marry you!"

"But I haven't asked the question yet," he pouted.

"Do you want to get married or not, McSailor?"

Smiling, he leaned in closer, plucking the ring out of its casing as he cast his dazzling blue eyes up to meet hers. "I do, Bonnie. And do you want to marry me?"

The hand perched indignantly on her hip dropped into her lap, and her tears began falling again. Simultaneously crying and laughing, she rasped, "I do." With one graceful motion, he slid the diamond onto her finger, where it would remain for quite a long time. For as long as they both would live.

Their kiss was soft yet passionate, weaving them tightly together. Hands caressed, lips compressed, and faces flushed. Two did not become one, but rather two came together—each one strong, healthy, and resilient, making the whole steadfast and true. They didn't lose themselves in each other, but found themselves in each other instead.

Slightly embarrassed to witness such a tender kiss, Hunter stood up and playfully made the sign of the cross over the couple, blessing their merger. Grant caught the motion from the corner of his eye and began chuckling, grasping Sophie's ring-laden hand while he pulled himself back onto the sofa next to her.

"That seals the deal," Hunter proclaimed. "Now that you're getting married, you *definitely* need more counseling. Over fifty percent of marriages end in divorce, and we're going to make sure you're not one of them."

"What a buzzkill, Hunter," Sophie protested, making a face.

He laughed. "Sorry. Just being realistic."

"I think we've had enough realism to last us a lifetime," she replied.

"We *have* been through a lot," Grant agreed. "But it's going to be smooth sailing from here."

"Right." Hunter's sarcasm was evident, and he smiled wryly. From the moment he'd met them, he'd sensed he'd be in for quite a ride with this couple, and he hadn't been wrong. But it had been a gratifying journey, and he was glad he wouldn't have to say goodbye to them just yet. Now that the cuffs were off, Hunter knew there'd be much more to come from the engaged parolees.

Excerpt from *On Best Behavior*, Book Three in the *Conduct* series by Jennifer Lane:

Walking briskly toward his job at Alex Remington's hotel, Grant weaved around slowly moving pedestrians on Michigan Avenue. Even though it was a balmy twenty-one degrees, shoppers were teeming on the Magnificent Mile, toting bags from American Girl Place and Niketown. He huddled inside his long, navy blue wool coat — a Christmas gift from Uncle Joe. His White Sox jacket just wasn't cutting it in these temperatures.

Some passengers disembarked a tour bus, and as he crossed in front of them, a voice calling out made him stop short.

"Madsen!"

Grant knew that voice anywhere, and he searched the area for his irascible former boss but failed to locate him.

"Madsen, I'm right here, dammit!"

Grant looked again at the man getting off the bus — a shorter man of average weight with carefully combed black hair and wearing a crisp business suit jacket — and did a triple take.

"*Rog?*"

Then came that familiar hearty laugh. "Of course! Who the hell else you know leads architectural bus tours, dumbshit?"

This was *definitely* Roger Eaton. Grant tried to retract his slacked jaw. "You look, uh, great, Rog. I barely recognized you, you look so good! I mean, uh, that didn't come out right..."

"Real nice, little fucker. Way to treat your elders."

"Sorry, I—you must be following your diet, huh? You're back on good terms with Ms. Broccoli?"

Roger gave a proud grin. "I got me a real life Ms. Broccoli now. A real sweetie."

"You—you have a girlfriend now?" Grant squinted.

"Ana," Roger confirmed. "She lives in my building."

"That's great! Did you meet her in the mail room or something?"

"Nah." Roger shook his head. "She was at the gym on the sixth floor."

"*You* were in the gym?"

Roger scowled. "Don't look so surprised, Madsen! I used to be real fit, back in the Navy. I know my way around a gym."

"Yes, sir."

"I met her doing free weights. This hard-body señorita was putting me to shame on squats, and I asked her how she got such a tight ass—"

"And then she decked you."

"Nah, she loved it! She's real proud of that butt—she should be. She took me to one of her classes, and I got hooked. She's a Zumba instructor."

Grant absorbed that information for a moment. "You do…Zumba?"

"It's great! Much more fun than PT. You just get going…" He did a little two-step maneuver on the city street, dancing to an unknown Latin beat. "Cha cha cha. Heeuh? Ana does this a little better than me…"

Grant tried to hold it in. He really did. But his body started quivering, his shoulders shaking, and soon a whooping laugh erupted—which lasted quite a few seconds.

Roger abruptly stopped his dance, all enthusiasm vanished. "You judge, Madsen. Not cool."

"You're right," Grant said, finding it difficult to compose a straight face. "That wasn't cool of me. Zumba's obviously working for you."

"Lost thirty-five pounds since September."

"Wow! And your hair…piece…looks real good too."

"Ana helped pick this one out."

Grant hadn't realized there was such a selection of toupees. *Don't laugh, don't laugh.* "So, uh, when do Sophie and I get to meet Ana?"

"I was thinking of bringing her by Capone's one night, make her suffer through your singing."

"I'd be honored," Grant said. "But it might be too dangerous," he added quickly. "I was going to call you, Rog. Um, I'm going by an alias now—some things have changed…"

Roger looked at him with a newfound respect, and his voice lowered conspiratorially. "Last time I talked to Joe, he said you were in conversations with the FBI, thinking of working for them."

"I'm giving it a shot. Nothing's happened yet, though."

"What's it like working for those tight-ass feds?"

Grant smirked. "Probably the same as working for *your* tight-ass boss."

"True that. So what's your alias then?"

"Mick Saylor."

Roger eyed him suspiciously. "What the fuck kind of name is that?"

"Sophie helped me come up with it. It's sort of a private joke."

Roger shook his head. "So it's Saylor and Taylor now. The fucking Bobbsey twins."

Grant looked surprised. "I never put our names together like that before."

"Way to think it through first, Mick Dick."

Grant tried to keep pace with the insults hurled his way.

"How's Taylor doing, by the way?" Rog continued.

"She's great. She's teaching full time at DePaul now."

"You two still shacking up?"

Grant grinned. "Yep, but not for much longer. We're engaged now."

Roger's eyes widened. "Finally! About time you both realized nobody *else* would want you. You might as well stick together."

Grant sighed fondly. "I've missed this."

"Then come back and work on my ship this summer."

"I'd actually like to ask you something about that, sir."

Roger took a step back. "You sneaking behind my back again, trying to hire someone else for my cruise like you did with Taylor?"

Grant looked offended. "As I recall, that worked out pretty well for your business. You should be so lucky."

Roger grunted.

"I wanted to ask if Sophie and I could have our wedding reception on your ship. Saturday, June eighteenth."

Roger tilted his head, considering.

"We'll pay you, of course," Grant added.

"With what? My ship's expensive to rent, you know."

"Mr. Taylor has agreed to foot the bill."

Roger's eyes bugged out. "I thought he hated you!"

"I charmed him with my singing."

Roger rolled his eyes. "Keep dreaming, Sinatra. Hey, I haven't met Ana's dad yet—maybe I should try singing for him too."

Grant looked dubious. "Don't you want him to like you? If so, I'd advise against it."

Roger's brown eyes danced. "I've missed this too, you pecker." He glanced at his watch. "Gotta get back to Willis Tower for the next bus tour or my tight-ass boss will be all over me. So, June eighteenth? Sure, that should work. I'll cancel the two evening cruises and expect a fat paycheck from Taylor's dad to cover the losses."

"You got it, Rog. Thanks."

"And Madsen?"

Grant halted.

"Be careful out there."

Grant nodded, taking a step toward his destination. "You too. Don't let those tourists hit on you. You've got a girlfriend now."

"A *hot* girlfriend!" Roger echoed, starting a little merengue dance. "She's one lucky woman!"

Grant just shook his head, grinning as he walked away. "Zumba," he muttered. He couldn't wait to tell Sophie.

ACKNOWLEDGMENTS

My sincere gratitude extends to:

Omnific Publishing Team BB, including Jessica Royer Ocken, Cindy Campbell, CJ Creel, Lynette McCann, Coreen Montagna, and Micha Stone.

Attorneys CJ Creel and Jennifer Sinclair for their diligent efforts to set me straight on the complicated legal aspects of the story.

Elizabeth Harper for giving me and my novels a fighting chance!

Janine and Gwynn for their amazing friendship.

Cècile, Jaquita Chiquita, Marilyn, Nora, Shannon, Riem, Ashley, Karina, Danni, Deb, and Lily for their constant support.

Lorne, Amy, and Ina for being there from the beginning of this crazy writing adventure.

Sherri Hayes for help with the David Alton storyline.

Book Club #1: Lisa, Colby, Jennifer, Sue, Janelle, Sally, Suki, Patty, Amy, Christy

Book Club #2: David, Joan, Jessica, Nan, Carolyn, Tom, Cindy, Michelle

My psychologist colleagues and swimming friends for being so encouraging.

Most of all, my family: Nancy, Roger, Jan, Laurie, Susan, Scott, John, Nicholas, Dylan, Henry.

Bless you all!

ABOUT THE AUTHOR

After surviving the rigors of writing a psychology dissertation, the author known as Jennifer Lane has happily turned to writing fiction. She still maintains her psychology practice in Ohio, but please rest assured that she's not psychoanalyzing you right now. The tales of healing and resilience from her career have inspired her to write her own stories: The *Conduct Series*. *With Good Behavior* began with two cons trying to make it on the outside: running from the Mafia, joking about sexy vegetables, and just maybe falling in love. *Bad Behavior*, the next in line, reveals that it's not so easy to escape the past, but the plucky parolees once again strive to persevere. Jen is currently at work on the third and final installment of the series: *On Best Behavior*. She's found that whether writing or reading, she loves stories that make her laugh *and* cry. In her spare time Jen enjoys competitive swimming, attending book club, and hanging out with her sisters and their families in Chicago.

Please check out her website http://jenniferlanebooks.com.